VIOLENT
MIND

THE ANIMAL IN MAN BOOK 1

VIOLENT MIND

JOSEPH ASPHAHANI

4 Horsemen
Publications, Inc.

4 Horsemen Publications, Inc.
1497 Main St. Suite 169
Dunedin, FL 34698
4horsemenpublications.com
info@4horsemenpublications.com

Cover & Typesetting by Niki Tantillo

Library of Congress Control Number: 2023945361

Paperback ISBN-13: 979-8-8232-0268-8
Hardcover ISBN-13: 979-8-8232-0270-1
Audiobook ISBN-13: 979-8-8232-0267-1
Ebook ISBN-13: 979-8-8232-0269-5

To Hanah and Ayame, for reminding me every day of life's limitless wonder.

TABLE OF CONTENTS

PROLOGUE XIII

I: THE CITY
CHAPTER ONE 1
CHAPTER TWO 30
CHAPTER THREE 51
CHAPTER FOUR 62
CHAPTER FIVE 85

II: THE TOWER
CHAPTER SIX 113
CHAPTER SEVEN............................. 133
CHAPTER EIGHT 145
CHAPTER NINE.............................. 171
CHAPTER TEN 202

III: THE DENLANDS
CHAPTER ELEVEN............................ 217
CHAPTER TWELVE 234
CHAPTER THIRTEEN 269
CHAPTER FOURTEEN 294
CHAPTER FIFTEEN 306
CHAPTER SIXTEEN 337
CHAPTER SEVENTEEN 361
EPILOGUE 371

PREVIEW TO FEROCIOUS HEART 377
BOOK DISCUSSION QUESTIONS 382
ACKNOWLEDGMENTS 384
ABOUT THE AUTHOR 386

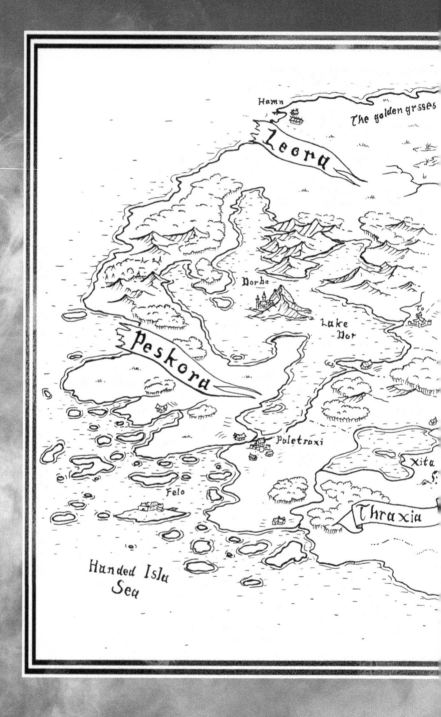

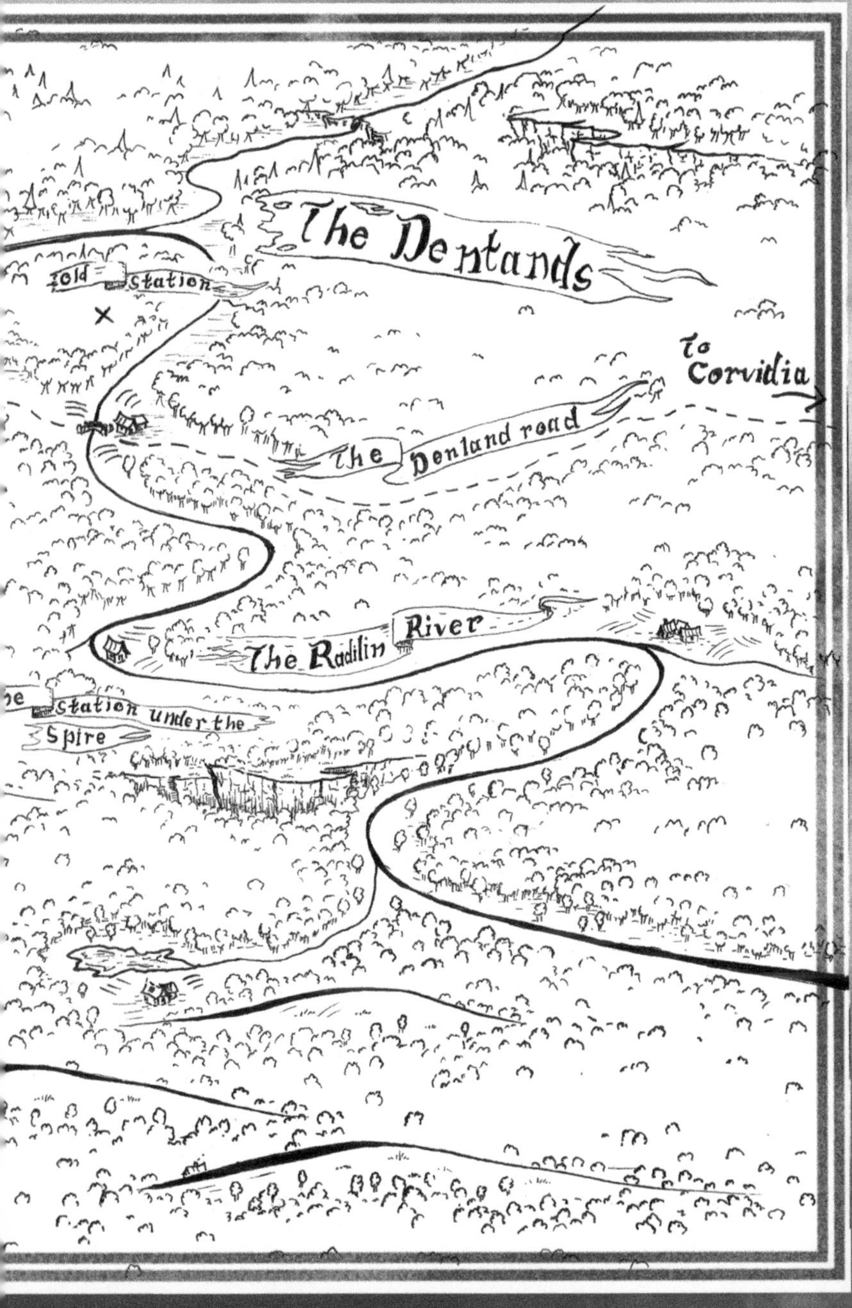
The Dentands
Old Station
to Corvidia
The Donland road
The Radilin River
The Station under the Spire

Prologue

THE FOX AWOKE AMID THE GLARING RED FIRES. He was numb, not from the cold but from the venom spreading throughout his body. The heat reflecting off the metal walls of this familiar place was enough to rouse him all the same. His fur was matted with sweat along his back. It had been singed nearly to the skin all along his right arm and tail.

Blood welled in a pool beneath his right shoulder where the snake had pierced him with a dagger. The red in his veins had blackened. It wouldn't be long now.

"I'd hoped we could have a few more words before parting."

The snake's red scales were a camouflage against the dancing flames. The hissing voice seemed to come from within the fox's own mind. These walls—so unnatural compared to the world above, so *advanced*—had a way of doing that, distorting reality. The sensation of this hidden place was something the fox's nerves had never grown accustomed to, despite all the lifetimes he'd spent here.

When he couldn't find the speaker among the flames, the fox shut his eyes and envisioned the wide-open prairies and hills of the Denlands. He wondered if he'd ever see that corner of his homeland again.

He slowly raised himself with both paws.

"Conserve your energy, old friend." The snake was closer now.

Smoke curled all around, spewing from the shattered glass containers on either side of the grated walkway, choking the corridors and chambers of the vast subterranean complex. Only one of the containers remained intact. A dark mass floated in a green fluid within. The snake at last materialized beside it from among the licking flames. His orange eyes glowed unnaturally bright, twin fires all their own.

The fox's labored breaths came in gasps. His mind formed the meaning, his mouth felt the words, but the only sound he made was a gargle. Black blood drained from between his bared fangs. He crumpled back to the floor, and he doubted he would ever rise again.

"All your plotting. Your clever tricks—just like they say, you know, about your species…" The snake let out a deep sigh, straightened himself to his full six-foot height, and looped his slender fingers through his sword belt. He was naked to the waist, his scaly red skin flecked with yellow and orange patterns, stretched tight over the muscles of his abdomen and up the curve of his long neck. His body did not simply *blend* with the fire—it was the fire. "It's all burning down, all around you, and there's nothing you can do."

The snake studied the spasms in the fox's body, the black blood seeping into the red. He watched it reach the edge of the walkway and drip over the edge. He leaned over the rail and saw the splatter it made on the nest of pipes and valves and conduits below.

The snake squatted close to the fox's head and whispered. "I … loved you, you know." His long black nail traced a swirl in the pool of blood. "The *real* me, I mean. And the real you. But you betrayed me. Your death won't be enough to pay for what you did."

It was true. The fox had played dead several times in his long life—to escape capture, to lie in ambush, to get away with theft and murder. But now, he wasn't playing. He was hoping death would hurry up. Anything to escape the droning of the snake's pitiful story about hurt feelings. The fox smiled through the agonizing pain, his lips curling wide along both sides of his face, and he released a wet, coughing laugh, spurting more black blood from his mouth with each burst.

The snake's nails dug into the scruffy fur at the back of the fox's head and dragged it up. His slit eyes blazed with fury.

"I don't know what you did to lock the gate, but I will find a way through. I have eternity on my side. For you? Only oblivion awaits. As it does for all the others."

The snake waved his second dagger around to indicate the fiery facility. By now, the flames had charred all the machinery, melted every device, warped every panel. The many globes set into the walls that had once filled the place with light were shattered. Smoke belched from their faces and collected in the air over the animals' heads.

The only thing that had survived the destruction was floating mindlessly in a glass tube. But its time was running out too.

The snake's dagger came down, the blade sliding between the sinews of the fox's left arm, pinning it to the metal grating of the floor. A fresh splash of blood gushed from the wound and dripped through to the lower level. The fox didn't even react.

"Fassscinating," the snake hissed, noting how the poison had turned the fox's blood inky black.

The snake rose over him. "Keep that," he said. "One of my finest." The rubies on the dagger's hilt glinted in the firelight. "You're dying now," the snake said over his shoulder. "Your body is anyway. But if your … soul survives, well, maybe we'll meet again, old friend. Sssoon."

The snake returned to the last remaining container and pressed his palm against the glass, wiping away a layer of soot concealing the thing within. The translucent brilles closed slowly over his reptilian eyes, welling with regret. He pressed the top of his broad head against the glass. "I can't bring myself to kill *everything* you ever loved. So I will let you choose."

Tears broke from the fox's eyes. They felt clean, pure. The only piece of him free of corruption. He flexed the claws of both his paws, sensing the vibrations of the approaching footsteps but feeling nothing else, not even the searing heat. He wasn't dead yet.

"Show me, old friend." The snake's whisper rose just above the roaring of the fires. His forked tongue flicked against the fox's fanned ear. "Show me which thing you love most, and I'll spare it."

Death had come, but the fox made it wait a few moments more. His green eyes opened for the last time, and the blinding firelight burst through the veil of darkness.

My legacy, he thought. He willed his body to use the strength it had left to raise his arm and choose.

I

THE CITY

THE SHADOW OVER CROSSWALL

SUNLIGHT ERUPTED FROM THE DAY-STAR Yinna, striking the world from behind a passing cloud, and the fox tried to escape it. He winced at it—the corners of his wide mouth lifting involuntarily, exposing two rows of sharp fangs—and pulled the hood of his dark cloak over his orange-furred ears and as far down his muzzle as it could go. Maxan had been leaning against this wall for nearly an hour, watching as the square slowly filled with crowds of all kinds of species, mostly the mammalian citizens of Crosswall, capital city of the Leoran kingdom. He had been waiting for his latest mark to show himself among them.

"Worst part of the job," he mumbled in annoyance.

He scanned the endless lines of the supposedly afflicted animal folk that had been quarantined here in the western district as they shuffled closer to the central wall of the cross-shaped city. A mob doing its best to be civil. If any of them truly were going astray, it wouldn't be long before snarling and raking claws tore the peace apart and the square filled with panic. Hardly a day went by that it didn't.

Maxan reached into his pocket and sank the tips of his claws into the apple he had brought with him from the store-room before setting out from the guardhouse barracks earlier that morning, well before Yinna's first rays chased the night away. He savored the first, crisp bite, then wiped a dribble of juice from his chin with the back of a furry paw.

Foxes were not the tallest of the Leoran species, so Maxan, being just a hair above five feet and in need of a better view, hopped just a little to his right where his hind paws planted themselves on a stack of empty crates. *Better,* he thought, sinking his fangs into the next chunk of his apple. Foxes were not renowned for their superior vision either, unlike a Corvidian eagle, so he had to narrow his mismatched eyes—the left forest green, the right a brilliant gold—to scan the throng gathered in the immense space before him.

He was in the busiest part of the western district of Crosswall. This part here, right up against the high stone wall dividing it from the center of the city, was where the con-demned animal folk—males and females, old and young, some alone, some with their entire family in tow—would gather every morning to receive their daily food rations.

The whole district had been cut off from the rest of the cross a year ago when the plague called the Stray began to claim more and more of its citizens. Anyone who showed signs of "going astray"—from the early stages of stooping shoul-ders or claws that seemed harder to retract, to the later stage of losing one's capacity for language and recognition of one's own family—was herded and packed between the four great walls surrounding the western district. And every morning they lined up, and the endless lines terminated at the equally end-less row of tables, across which the green-robed initiates of the

Mind handed over baskets or sacks filled with ripened fruits, dried strips of game meat, handfuls of berries and shelled nuts, baked roots, and boiled greens. At other places along the tables, the Mind's so-called designers, in white robes, provided the afflicted masses with basic sets of figurines and checkered game boards to play rounds of apotheosis, or apoth for short. Farther down, crowds of apoth players gathered to receive the latest list telling of the victories earned and defeats suffered by the city's heroes in the famed cross-shaped arena far across the city in the eastern district, where the real games were played, where real blood was spilled. Here, the only kind of participation the isolated, neglected, and downtrodden animals of the western district could hope for was a kind of simulation.

An escape, Maxan surmised, biting a third chunk from his apple. *Something to keep them busy. Occupied. Distracted.*

Right. His thoughts turned against him, as they so often did, voicing some other cynical, sarcastic self within him. *Look who's getting distracted, Max.*

Maxan shrugged, conceding the point, and swept his eyes back over the crowds nearer the middle of the square. Sometimes the extra voice in his head was helpful, an extra perspective to catch details he might have missed. Of course, most often, he found it simply repeating asinine observations he was already well aware of.

Still, he thought, *it's an improvement over talking to myself out loud.*

Since the quarantine began nearly a year ago, the Mind had taken charge of the afflicted animals' quality of life, ensuring as much as they could that these citizens were fed, cared for, and given a source of activity and entertainment.

They do what they can to ensure we don't...

He turned the apple over in his paw, frowning, feeling a sudden loss of appetite.

Eat each other.

Throughout the city, rumors spread that the Mind had found a cure for the Stray, some mental trick or alchemical mixture that soothed the inner beast that raged in the afflicted Herbridian's heart. Rumors were easier to hand out than game boards and, arguably, did more to keep everyone hopeful.

Hopeful, Maxan's cynical self thought. *And docile. All of this goodwill is just a con. Look at it! To win the Mind ever more influence over our hearts and minds, ever more quickly than they already have.*

It was likely that many of the very people who received these rations, the poor wretches whose lives were destroyed by showing symptoms of the Stray, had tended to the orchards, farms, and livestock pens just outside the city before being condemned to this district-sized cage. But this place was packed equally with a variety of species from arguably the most diverse kingdom in all of Herbridia, from the lowly wolves, weasels, raccoons, and rats to the high-born stags, panthers, and gorillas.

Hunger makes equals of us all.

Maxan glanced at the apple and turned it over in his right paw, which was covered in a black leather glove that extended from the tips of his claws to the top of his shoulder. He tossed the apple across to his left, covered only by his amber fur, and back again, juggling the single fruit, thinking about the injustice on full display before him. He had lost his appetite.

"Still no sign of them," he muttered to no one.

So, you are *talking to yourself again.*

Maxan shook his head, but the critic in him droned on.

Nothing quite like a game to distract yourself from the terrible pangs of hunger. Or dying with the name of your favorite arena hero on your lips. Why not take in a puppet show to forget those fangs sinking into your throat? What a farce!

He couldn't stop his eyes from wandering hundreds of yards beyond the crowd to the stage the Mind's initiates had set up for such entertainment.

We are *the puppet show.*

Maxan broke away from these dark thoughts and refocused on the business that had brought him here. He had been waiting all morning to spot a band of murderous hyenas. An informant had seen the infamous pack of raiders entering the city two days ago, then spotted them again coming and going through the avenues of the western district. The rumor was they had recovered some treasure of great value from the river lands and come to Crosswall hoping to catch the scent of a buyer. It was unlikely the hyenas would pass up the chance to earn a free meal or two, delivered right to their paws courtesy of the Mind's initiates, so waiting at this square for them to show up was the best lead Maxan had.

He already knew how they had entered the city. The Crosswall Guard did what it could to seal the gaps in the city's crumbling outer walls, but in a place this enormous, filled with hundreds of thousands of Herbridians encompassing a hundred or more different species of mammals, reptiles, birds, and ocean dwellers, it was impossible to keep all the unwanted elements away. Maxan knew of several spots along the quarantine zone's northern wall where smugglers brought in sacks and crates full of supplies from outside to feed the hungry. He thought it perhaps just as likely that the sacks and crates sent back out were packed with weapons to feed the growing rebellion in the Denland forests east of the city. He had done his duty—mostly—observing from the shadows and reporting all he had seen, but the overworked Crosswall Guard was often too late to arrive at the hidden entryways and seal the gaps before the hungry rebels were through with an operation. Whether the haul was food or weapons, it was only a matter of time before the smugglers found a new chink in the city's armor and brought in more.

And so the cycle of uselessness starts anew.

At first, Maxan felt ambivalent toward the rebel sympathizers and smugglers. After all, the folk they were supplying were poor, hungry, and desperate—animals quite literally backed into a corner. Many of them, although labeled as going astray, did not deserve to be here. From his vantage point atop the crumbling rooftops of this district, whenever he could confirm in the dead of night that the sacks they smuggled were full of food, he was most certainly not in any rush to report the affair. He was glad to think those who starved would eat a better fill the following day.

Weapons, however, called for immediate action. Anyone with a sharp object, Maxan reasoned, was likely to turn it on his fellow starving prisoner over a scrap of bread before the day came that the rebels called on him to raise it against the Leoran king. So Maxan would sprint back to his guardhouse station and tell his captain, the rhinoceros Chewgar, to rouse the soldiers and get moving, no matter the hour. *Wherever there are weapons*, Maxan thought, *there will also be death.* The bloody history of this world had already claimed the lives of enough Herbridians. Violence was the unspoken law of life.

The band of hyenas that Maxan searched for now ranked among the deadliest creatures that could possibly sneak into Crosswall. Hyenas were not so common outside of the Golden Grasses to the north, where their particularly vicious species originated. After Maxan told Chewgar what the informant had told him (but keeping the part about a treasure all to himself), the captain had enough time to put his guard contingent on full alert, ready for Maxan to spot his mark and report.

This should be easy, he had thought before.

Quite untrue at the moment, he thought now.

"Sir?" A thin voice broke Maxan's vigil over the square. It belonged to a young weasel kit, no more than half the fox's height. Maxan could see the boy's ribs beneath the shoddy vest he wore. There were spots on his chest where patches of fur had shed. The weasel was starving, weak. He blinked his large black eyes at Maxan, then at the half-eaten apple in the fox's paw.

"Did you wait for your rations today?" Maxan asked.

"They turned me away. Said they'd seen I had tried to come through already."

"Had you?"

"It wasn't true."

He's lying, Max.

Oh, shut up.

Maxan was no stranger to a con, having employed probably over a thousand of his own design during the decade he spent in his former career, years before joining the Crosswall Guard. *Maybe he is lying. But this is no con. This is hunger.*

"Here," he said, tossing the weasel boy his apple.

The weasel snatched it from the air and set to hungrily gnawing what was left.

"Where are your parents?"

"Just me and Mom left. My pop, he … turned. And he ran off."

"Ran off…"

Maxan understood. The farther west one ventured in this district, the farther away from this square at the center, the more dangerous and wild the streets became, and the more likely it was one would meet with death at the claws and fangs of the Stray. The boy's father, apparently, had answered the call of his inner beast and joined in.

Maxan thought it best not to dwell on the emotion he saw welling up in the emaciated weasel's eyes. "Have you seen any hyenas?"

"Hyenas? What's a hyena?"

"You're from the Denlands," Maxan reasoned. Weasels, foxes, wolves, bears, and other forest-dwelling creatures who had never set foot in the capital city would have little to no familiarity with their tribal neighbors to the far north of Leora, where clusters of jackals, hyenas, rhinos, lions, and other species prevailed.

The boy nodded as if it had been a question. He ripped a large bite from the apple. The fruit was too big for his mouth, but he forced his little jaws upon it all the same.

"Hyenas are grasslanders from the north. They're spotted, and their fur sticks out like spikes on their backs. They hunch, like this. See?"

"Oh! Do they smell bad?"

"Ah, I suppose."

"They tramped by me and Mom last night. Farther in from the wall. Their stink woke me up. And they were laughing."

That's them. They're here.

"They weren't laughing," said Maxan. "That's just how hyenas breathe."

The boy took another bite, at this point from nothing but the apple core, and he clambered up a second stack of crates beside Maxan's, although much less gracefully than the fox had.

This kit would make a fine shadow someday. Maxan smiled as he watched the weasel boy scanning the crowd. He smiled and followed his example.

Five more minutes. If they don't show, ask the boy exactly where he saw them. Exactly where he and his mother sleep. Then ten minutes, another twenty to sweep the alleys and arteries, then—

"Listen, sir! I hear them. Somewhere."

The weasel's high-pitched excitement broke Maxan from his calculations. He pulled his hood back and fanned out his black-tipped ears.

"Hear that?"

Maxan's ears twitched, changing their angles, scooping up waves of sound from different locations, scraps of conversations, arguments, the smacking of hungry tongues against teeth, rolls of the dice, consultations of lists, the scraping of apoth figures across the boards, accusations of cheating. Maxan heard everything. But he picked up a peculiar sound. "Huu-huu-huu-huukk. Huu-huu…"

There! Maxan saw five hyenas standing perhaps fifty yards away, near the middle of the bustling square. They stood near a dusty, decrepit fountain, their shoulders the highest parts of their gangly bodies, their scarred and spotted heads swiveling about to see who among the crowds they could menace. Maxan caught the glint of sunlight on the curved daggers they flashed at families' ration baskets, paid as a kind of toll just to move past unharmed.

"Bastards," Maxan muttered.

Their leader, clad in tattered leather plates bound by twisted metal rings and thick cord, sat on the fountain's rim gnawing on a stick of cured meat with his grimy, crooked fangs—Yacub, the border raider, chief of this jolly, chuckling company of murderers and thieves.

Maxan rarely wore his official guard's uniform anymore. Too many buckles, too much bright white, too much weight to effectively carry out his unique duty. But he always carried his badge, a strip of soft leather branded with a cross to resemble the sprawling city's shape. He briefly considered how simple it would be to flash it at the guardsmen keeping watch near the Mind's tables, to point a single claw tip at the fountain, to apprehend Yacub and his crew, to put an end to their abuse of the already too abused. But then he would lose the chance to see the *real* business that brought the hyenas to the city.

Raider groups like Yacub's had sprung up in great numbers as the Extermination War drew to a close two decades ago and soldiers whose entire lives were based on armed conflict found it hard to put their weapons down, find mates, and live peaceful lives in the city among other species. So instead they wandered, and they pillaged and cheated and stole from villages and settlements all across Leora, and they did no one any good but themselves.

Yacub had been caught before, but he had evaded his long-overdue punishment. Maxan did not know for certain, but he suspected that Leoran coins had changed paws somehow, jail keys had fallen off their key rings, and jailers' eyes had conveniently changed the direction of their watch.

"Not this time," Maxan told himself. He hopped down from his crate, thanked the weasel boy once again—who seemed in finer spirits after the apple and the assist—and moved into the crowd, closing in on the hyena pack at the fountain, glimpsing them through the gaps in the throng that he wove through.

Yacub sucked down the rest of the meat and used the pointed stick to pick leftover gristle from his fangs. It didn't work so well. He spat at the fountain, stood up, stretched, chuckled loudly, and said, "Sun's up full, boys. We're off."

"We should all go with you, boss."

"Not all you. Head back to the inn. We're not there by night, we're dead."

A shrieking frenzy of laughter overcame Yacub, widening the space around the hyenas. "But don't you worry," he added, patting the naked blade of the scratched and serrated sword belted at his side. "I got my ripper."

Maxan followed in the wake of wild chuckles as three of the hyenas joined their boss and moved toward the far western side of the square.

Maxan was a shadow, a special kind of city guard. While his uniformed counterparts carried a variety of instruments that could bludgeon offenders and criminals into submission, Maxan's most effective weapons were his sharp eyes and sharper ears. *And perhaps my legs.* He observed, he listened, and he ran swiftly back to report on his findings. Shadowing required stealth and anonymity and speed, so the fox wore clothes of the common people overlaid with a dark hood that concealed his eyes and the amber fur on his face.

He felt the edges of his cloak swish about his legs as he kept pace with the hyenas, who strutted casually several yards ahead through the busy walkways beyond the square.

The weasel kit was right, he realized, cupping a paw over his snout to block out the distinct odor left in Yacub's wake. *I could follow them with my eyes closed.*

They meandered their way ever westward through thinning crowds of animals until the hyenas and their unseen shadow were soon passing by only a vagrant or two. The afflicted huddled in doorways, shifting, twitching, reaching through the layers of rags to scratch at their furry necks and chests incessantly, perhaps trying to contain the feral urges that identified them as later-stage Stray.

As Maxan shadowed Yacub into the sprawling maze of abandoned and dilapidated structures, he knew that without crowds to conceal him from his mark and without the ferocity of the bigger species to defend himself if the Stray found him, his mission—*Not to mention your life!*—was at risk.

Time for some elevation, Max.

He sidled into a doorway and watched Yacub and his crew disappear around the next corner. He pulled back his hood, craned his neck skyward, and swept his eyes over the closest wall, noting its damaged pits and protruding bricks.

Ten seconds up, ten seconds over.

Maxan leapt, gaining twice his height in a split second, and grasped an exposed brick. He hauled himself up and caught another, counting the seconds—*Five, six, seven*—expending every muscle, buying himself speed. He pulled himself over the edge of the slate-shingled roof, then sprang into motion toward the point where he calculated Yacub would be, concluding his second count—*Eight, nine, ten*—as he ran.

At the edge of the roof, he grabbed the upward-jutting post of an unfinished balcony and scanned the avenue below. Sure enough, the hyenas continued their march onward.

Onward toward... Well, I have no idea.

The rooftops of Crosswall suited a shadow's work perfectly. Most of the high-steepled tops of the buildings, designed to carry rainwater away in channels along their edges, were crowned with long wooden beams that were at least two feet wide—ample space for a fox, even one at full sprint. There were arches and beams that linked the ancient wooden and brick structures to others across the street, and nearly all of the buildings in the western district had fallen into disrepair, exposing masonry and slanted railings everywhere Maxan needed them to be. Anyone else who might try hind-legging their way along the rooftops of Crosswall would be in great danger of breaking their neck. But Maxan had years of practice. *In a life before this one, running away from the law, not bringing it in my pocket.* One might think he would envy the Corvidian bird species' natural gift of flight, but an elongated wingspan soaring low over the city would draw too much attention, rendering the whole point of his mission moot. Moving quickly while staying out of sight was what made Maxan one of Crosswall's best shadows.

Maxan had been following his targets for what felt like hours. The cackle of hyenas wound its way farther west, enhancing its chances of encountering a pack of feral Stray with every step. But the streets were thankfully deserted. *So far so good. I'd say it's luck, but you know well enough.*

Of all the animals of all the kingdoms in all the world of Herbridia, Maxan had observed the afflicted perhaps the longest and lived to report what he had seen: whole packs of animals that were no longer anything more than beasts. Their howling and wailing sent all the fur along his spine standing on end. He shook his head violently, defending against the horrific images that tried to slither into his mind.

Yacub's cackle turned another corner. Maxan wheeled back onto the slope of the roof, then dashed forward and sprang across the ten-foot gap to the next one, landing atop the crumbling building on the other side of the street. Within a few swift strides, he was once again over Yacub's position.

Maxan scanned the city's skyline to the west. He knew this area well. *Too well. Too many bad memories here.* No more than half a mile farther on, near the outer wall of the cross, was the granary where Maxan had spent over a decade of his youth.

This better not be a homecoming.

Why? What are you afraid of?

Besides fire?

I know—seeing the old granary, seeing it happen all over again.

Maxan regarded the tight leather glove encasing his right arm and paw. He turned his arm over slowly, then balled his paw into a fist, extinguishing the memory before it could reignite in his mind.

The hyenas rounded a corner in the other direction, away from the granary. *No more open avenues where that way leads. Dead end. Wherever we're going, we're here.*

It had taken the hyena and the shadow the entire morning and part of the afternoon to reach this place. Yinna had already risen to her apex and now began her descent.

Maxan slowed his sprint to a quickened creep, ducking from cover to cover, from crumbling chimney to unfinished wall to wide wooden plank, approaching what he knew would be Yacub's final destination. The hyenas had passed through the only entrance to what was once an open-air corral, a former home for burden-beasts used to tend the fields years ago.

Maxan couldn't help himself from scanning the jagged line that Crosswall cast across the horizons all around. This close to the wall, if he were a little higher, he would see those fields just to the north.

From the granary's top we could—
Forget it!

He bit down hard, exposing his fangs in a pained grimace. *Just forget it.*

Just then, a darkness crept in from the east, plunging the whole city into shadow, an eerie event that drew Maxan's attention now as it always did, day after night after day. It was the Aigaion. The colossal triangular leviathan that floated aimlessly miles above all the world of Herbridia drifted into view. No one living could tell by sight what the thing was made of. Metal? Stone? Wood? Not even the Corvidians, who flew above all others, had ever been able to agree on the details of its construction. No one had ever risen high enough to see its top. And no one dead had ever recorded where it came from, if it had even been *built* at all. The Aigaion was simply a part of this world, coming and going at random for hundreds of years or more.

Yet the Mind regarded the mystery of the shrouded wanderer with the greatest reverence, choosing to model its sigil after its triangular shape. The organization thought of itself as an institution of discovery and goodwill, charged with spreading knowledge to all Herbridians. But it believed the Aigaion represented the ultimate knowledge just out of reach, as though it held secrets animalkind was never meant to grasp.

The Aigaion's size was literally overwhelming. No matter where a creature stood on this planet, if he kept his eyes skyward all day, he would glimpse the city-sized object overhead at least once. Whether one saw a black mass that slowly crawled across the horizon's rim or an overhead shadow that completely snuffed out the light of Yinna for an hour or more depended on random chance. Just now, it seemed to Maxan that its shadow would be upon him, Yacub, and the entire population of Crosswall within ten minutes, bringing an early twilight to the city and shrouding them all in darkness.

Twenty feet below Maxan's perch, Yacub and his cackle had finally worked their way through the inner pens and stalls of the old corral. The claws at the ends of their hind paws made distinct prints in the dirt floor as they moved to the center of the circular ruins.

Six figures emerged from doorways opposite where Yacub had entered. All of them were wrapped in layers of thick, drab robes that brushed the dirt floor of the beast pen. Four remained behind, pulling back their hoods to expose their species—a raccoon, a bearded ram, a long-horned ibex, a black-spotted leopard—and Maxan saw them shifting their arms beneath their hoods, perhaps readying concealed weapons.

Bodyguards, Maxan surmised.

The two others—one a Corvidian with great gray-feathered wings folded at its back, the other still disguised—met Yacub in the very center. The robed Corvidian made no move as the other threw back its hood, exposing the face of a male wolf. His fur was pure snow white speckled with gray, like meteoric ash raining within a blizzard. Most wolves wore their manes shaggy and wild, but this one's had been slicked down to the nape of his neck. The white wolf clearly took pride in his grooming, but nothing could distract an onlooker from the hideous pink scar that began at the corner of the wolf's mouth and ended at his left ear, permanently displaying his fangs and freezing his face in a constant, grotesque snarl.

"Did you bring it?" The wolf's voice came from that maw with a rush of air escaping his open scar, a rasp that seemed hardly above a whisper, yet it carried a power that resounded around the circular place like a sudden wind.

The hyenas' arched backs began heaving upward and downward, letting a faint, collective chuckle escape from them. The matted, spiky hairs along Yacub's spine quivered, perhaps with fear, maybe excitement. "Plan's changed," Yacub said. "Feyn, sir. Something happened."

The white wolf Feyn said nothing, merely glancing back at the unmoving hooded Corvidian. Feyn's winged counterpart had no reaction either, and by their silence, the tough demeanor Yacub tried to put forth was broken in seconds.

"Something happened, I says," Yacub pleaded. "I told my boys not to handle it. Just leave it be, like you sent word of. But curiosity killed the rat, they says, and some red light washes over us, and Ulbur lost his eye before any of us knowed what's happened. And Baynay... he takes Ulbur's blade in the shoulder, and he... And thanks be, I jumped in and grabbed it—the, the light, I grabbed it—and I dashed it against the floor."

"You what?" Feyn snarled, his icy blue eyes narrowing.

"I mean I dropped it. And it's fine. No scratches. Ulbur's not so fine. Swears he'll gut whoever stole his eye. Wasn't me... I think. I can't remember."

"Nice story. But you have not answered me." Feyn's already low voice fell lower, becoming a rumbling growl. "Do so. Now."

"It's not here. I failed you, I know. Just we were sc—I mean, fright—I mean, I'm not scared of no one, you know. But I… We lost ourselves in that light, Feyn." Yacub spun about to his cackle, who nodded their spiky, chuckling heads to corroborate their boss's account. "And we thought it best to leave it where it lie. Well, no. Baynay grabbed for it—I don't know how he could, with all the—and he held it … before he…" Yacub's dry throat made a cracking sound as he tried to swallow. He let out a desperate, dry chuckle at the growing impatience in Feyn's eyes. "We left it there. Tucked in his vest. We voted on it, then we left it. With him."

Feyn kept his withering gaze fixed on the hyena, and within a few breaths, the hyena withered sure enough. Tears welled in Yacub's eyes and ran down his speckled fur. The spiky hairs on his back shivered with every guilty, sorrowful spasm. The sudden, hysterical sobbing mingled with the hyena's chuckling gasps for breath was unlike any sound Maxan had ever heard. Yacub fell to his knees, and his cackle followed him to the dirt.

"I'm sorry. Please don't shut us out."

Peeking through a hole in a wooden railing, Maxan saw everything happening at the beast pen's center. The white wolf's claws hovered in the air shakily over the hyena's exposed neck, as though he were about to rip the raider's spine from his back. But Feyn kept control, closing his paw into a fist at his side. Although Feyn carried no weapons that Maxan could see, the way in which the wolf carried himself as he paced about the dirt floor of the pen carried an invisible danger. The gray-winged Corvidian might as well have been a statue. Feyn stepped around it and shook his head at the three others farther back, against the wall. The fox knew the only reason the hyenas weren't dead was because they knew the location of whatever it was that Feyn wanted. Their ignorance, or their fear, is what saved their lives.

Red light. An inn. Maxan's thoughts ran through all the places he knew in the western district. *Not enough of a lead.*

Some motion drew Maxan's attention to the opposite side of the pen. A creeping silhouette flitted from cover to cover across the rooftops, inching closer to the walkway that ran around the place. "Another shadow?" Maxan whispered to himself, squinting, waiting for the figure to emerge from the last spot where he'd seen it.

No. Can't be. Chewgar would've told me.

A shadow of a different sort then swallowed the entire world, and he lost track of this newcomer as the gigantic Aigaion loomed overhead. The absence of Yinna's light crept westward over Crosswall.

Below, Feyn had halted in his tracks. He closed his eyes and sucked air deeply into his nostrils as the shadow enveloped him. He let out a great exhalation through his mouth, with a slight whistle where the scarred lips could not close over his fangs. "Aaaah," he breathed. "My child. My poor, poor lost child. I know your pain. Your confusion. Tell me, Yacub, do you feel inadequate as you are?"

As gifted a speaker as this Feyn was, he could not swallow the distaste that saying this lowly hyena's name left on his tongue. Maxan heard it. Yacub apparently did not. The hyena looked up sincerely and stifled a sudden burst of laughter as he spoke.

"Yes. I do."

"Every Herbridian has a destiny. Even you. Yours was not death on the field, fighting against the insects. Neither was mine. Tell me, did you know many who the Thraxians claimed?"

"Yes, sir. My brothers. Sisters. My mates. My mother. Fa—"

"All right. Yes. Enough!" Feyn barked. Maxan heard the growing agitation, but the hyenas all seemed entranced by the snowy wolf's gravelly voice. Yacub bowed his head again. "You survived," Feyn went on, "as did I, for a greater reason. You lived this long because fate chose you to find the artifact you did. Fate placed it in *your* paws, Yacub. And told you to bring it here, to us."

The wolf again glanced back to his Corvidian counterpart. At last, the robed figure moved. A slight nod of its hood was all Maxan could make out amid the darkness under the Aigaion.

Who are they? Maxan couldn't help but feel that what was happening here was bigger than a simple transaction over treasure. He looked again across the expanse for the silhouette of whomever he'd thought had been following him, but the world itself was one thick shadow. If anything had been there, it was gone now. *Are they Denlanders? Rebels? There's a wolf, a ram, a raccoon, but also tribals from the north.*

"Tell me," Feyn said, turning back to Yacub. "Do you seek a greater purpose?" He rested his snow-white paw upon the hyena's shoulder.

"Yes."

"And acceptance?"

"Yes. More than anything."

"Do you renounce your dependence on ignorance? Your lust for cruelty?"

"All we want is to be your soldiers."

"We've no need of soldiers, wretch. We are *students*. We are *scholars*."

"Yes. I'll be one of those." The sobbing had subsided a little, but the hyena's feverish chuckling still rattled in his neck.

"Then tell me. Where is the artifact?"

Maxan tensed his muscles, ready to sprint, to run back to Chewgar and the Guard, to descend in great numbers upon whatever inn Yacub was about to reveal. *After, of course, I've had a chance to see about this treasure.*

The city skyline in the distance and the edge of every misty cloud glowed in the smoldering orange light, weak as it was far beneath the Aigaion's belly. Maxan and the rest were gathered here under the giant's dark center. The great thing in the sky seemed to lurch slower above them as if grinding to a halt.

Yacub was hysterical, wildly sobbing, laughing, drawing deeper and deeper breaths that could not calm him.

"Tell me where it is, my son," Feyn urged, grasping the hyena's shoulder tighter, the patience in his voice straining to its breaking point. "Transcend from this loathsome animal inside, and you shall find your home among us."

His words broke Yacub. The hyena chief sputtered another few words between fitful sobs and chuckles. Maxan drew back his hood, fanned out both his ears, gripped the railing, and leaned closer—anything to catch Yacub's mumbling.

"What?" said Feyn.

"The Aurochs' Haunch, Principal. It's at the Aurochs' Haunch."

The inn! I know it!

Before Maxan could turn to bolt away, his world was frozen by a shrill scream that echoed from every wall and shook every grain of dirt on the beast pen's floor.

A Corvidian knight in plates of polished armor plunged from the skies. Her legs and lower talons led her way, the tips of her brown-feathered hawk wings trailing high behind her. She gripped a long spear tightly, angled at the clustered hyenas. She fell like a meteor, inches from where Maxan crouched on the walkway, then flapped her wings outward at the last possible instant to break her fall. The blast of air sent Yacub, Feyn, and immense clouds of dirt rolling several yards away, but aside from the whipping of its drab cloak, the gray-winged figure beside them was unmoved, as if it had barely noticed the new arrival. The knight's spear sank through a hyena's back and plunged deep into the ground; an explosion of blood changed the dirt to mud.

At the same time, just as the four figures along the opposite side of the pen were scrambling to draw their weapons from beneath their cloaks, a streak of silver light cut across their necks from the shadows behind, catching the ram and leopard but sparing the shorter raccoon next in line. The two stricken creatures fell to their knees, their weapons forgotten, and their heads rolled easily off their shoulders.

A crossbow bolt whistled through the air just in front of Maxan's nose, embedding itself in the plank railing. If he hadn't been blown a few inches back by the hawk's blast, the bolt would have speared his skull through his ear.

He snapped his head sideways, losing sight of the chaos below, and saw the thin silhouette toss the spent crossbow aside, then the flash of diminished orange daylight on the figure's two blades, then its swift and silent charge straight at him.

The stranger glided so fast, a shadow flowing in shadow, as though its low paws never touched the woodwork.

Don't panic!

Maxan was fast, but not that fast. He fumbled with the snap that kept his guard's short sword secure.

What do I—

Before the thought was complete, his weapon was out of its scabbard, leaping up in his paw just in time to lock with both of the stranger's descending blades, just an inch in front of his muzzle.

The force of the charge rocked Maxan back on his hind legs, and he nearly toppled over. He pushed hard against the stranger's blades, broke free of the attack, and hopped back. The stranger swiped across the air where his belly had been only a second before. The idea of just how close he'd come to being gutted ran circles in his mind, tipping him off balance, and Maxan tripped and crashed to the walkway.

Without losing a beat, the stranger pounced directly onto Maxan's chest, knocking the wind from his lungs. It straddled him, both blades pressed to his neck.

That's it. He felt the other side of his mind let go. *It's done.*

"Not like this," Maxan answered himself. He let go of his short sword, unsure of what else to do with his paws.

From within the dark hood of the figure bearing down on him, Maxan could just make out two rows of fangs glinting in the sliver of artificial twilight. The fur of the silhouette's mouth was rimmed with orange-and-white fur.

Oh, c'mon. Are you crying, Max? Is this how you want to go?

"It's just…"

Maxan closed his eyes. All the clamor from below—the din of ringing steel and wild, chuckling laughter—was drowned by the rushing in his temples. He swallowed, feeling the razor-sharp blades' edges scrape against the amber fur on both sides of his neck.

"I never … did anything."

He waited.

Nothing happened.

"You're a fox?" The voice above him was female, startled.

Maxan blinked through his tears but could not make out her face, only two large orbs of blue, clearer and calmer than the Peskoran seas.

"Yes?" was all he could muster.

The silhouette hovered, seemed about to speak again, but the piercing scream of a hawk overpowered everything, even the wailing laughter below.

"RINNIA!"

The blue eyes held Maxan's gaze a second longer, and then she was off him at once, leaping over the walkway railing to the dirt floor below.

I'm alive? Must be a dream. A dream.

No time to dream, fool! Get up!

Maxan rolled over. He saw through a crack in the floorboards that the hawk knight was down on her knees, her left talon hand oozing bright red blood, as was Yacub's vicious ripper, which had bitten deeply into her side, its teeth punching through her bright armor. Unsure of who their enemies were yet more than happy to tear anything living apart, the two other hyenas of Yacub's cackle had drawn their similarly vicious swords and charged the white wolf and cloaked Corvidian at the center of the pen, where they were met by the two remaining bodyguards.

From the shadowed doorway at the far end of the corral, a slender figure in form-fitting dark red leather armor stepped delicately over the headless corpses of the ram and leopard and made its way slowly to the center, swishing its thin sword and spattering the dirt with flecks of blood. Even in the darkness beneath the Aigaion, Maxan could see its long green-scaled neck and knew it was a Drakoran snake.

The hawk held her spear up, trying to drive its point at Yacub's snarling face, but the hyena held its shaft tightly in his left paw. They were locked. But it was clear that the hawk's strength would give out far earlier than the hyena's.

It seemed to Maxan there were too many sides—or no sides at all—in this battle. Yacub's raiders had offset whatever balance there might have been, dashing in and reveling in the violence just for violence's sake.

Feyn disengaged as his raccoo,n and ibex bodyguards met the hyenas' charge and stood calmly a few feet away, both his snow-white claws outstretched toward the knight, his knuckles rolling up and down. His brow was furrowed in concentration. He growled something, the rhythm of the sound matching the movement of his claws, and the hawk's head jerked side to side involuntarily. She struggled to keep her focus on the hyena about to end her life.

The silhouette who had attacked Maxan appeared, landing in the dirt, and tumbled forward beyond the combatants, then lashed out at the wolf with both swords. But Feyn was fast. He dropped his claws and skirted backward in the dust. The two short blades caught the ends of his cloak, slicing two razor-perfect lines in the fabric.

Feyn's attacker did not rest. She darted forward immediately to cover the distance and strike again, but the wolf's claws came up. He lunged forward, then swung apart with all his strength as though tearing an invisible paper. The silhouettes' short swords were torn from her paws and flung like arrows in opposite directions across the pen.

Maxan's mouth hung agape.

How did... He didn't even touch...

Get up! Go! Get the guard! Get Chewgar!

Maxan was up on his hind paws. In his mind, he was racing, leaping, sprinting, bounding over rooftops all the way back to the guardhouse. But his body lagged behind this vision of himself. Without thinking, he stooped and retrieved his short sword. While the vision of what a shadow ought to do leapt farther away across the city, he stood rooted to the spot, staring at the untarnished steel in his hand.

I've never used this...

Who cares?

Maxan found himself turning back to the walkway's edge and leaning over.

Had the hyenas not been set loose, the battle might have made sense. Yacub was still locked in combat with the hawk, only now his sword's serrated edge sawed through her armor rip by rip. The snake had been intercepted by the raccoon and ibex, though the latter was twisting his tall-horned head back and forth to deal with the wild, cackling hyena stabbing at his flank. The other hyena stooped low, nearly on all fours, circling the battle's sole spectator, the hooded gray-winged Corvidian, who by contrast still stood with its arms calmly at its sides. The hyena flinched and wetted his lolling tongue, his muscles tensed for a pounce. But then he shook his head angrily and seemed to reconsider, as though forgetting his intention altogether.

Meanwhile, Feyn's unexpected disarmament of his attacker had caught her by surprise. She had tried to reverse herself midstep, but the momentum of her lunge had already carried her too far forward. Feyn's snow-white paw shot forward and enclosed around her neck, squeezing tightly. Maxan saw her bushy tail swish in the air as she tried in vain to take them both over onto their side, while her thin arms beat uselessly against the wolf's forearm. She was fast, but not strong. Not as strong as Feyn.

"Monitor," the wolf snarled at her. "You were so close. Witness now your own death."

With his other paw, Feyn drew some shape in the air, and the silhouetted figure's own dagger rose from the dirt several yards away, floated in midair, and shot impossibly fast once more, straight at the head of its owner.

But it never arrived.

The white wolf howled in agony as the edge of a short sword cut deeply into his forearm, with all the weight and gravity of a falling fox behind it. Feyn let go of his victim's neck, and her sword flew by, sticking and wobbling in a wooden beam many feet behind her.

Blood splattered the wolf's snow-white fur. It dripped upon the dirt floor.

Yacub was inexplicably shaken by the wolf's howl. He ceased his laughter and the motion of his sword at the sight of Feyn's blood, and the Corvidian knight seized the moment, her strength resurging. She stood at her full height, wrenched Yacub's ripper sword free from her side, and from the hyena's grasp, and tossed it aside. She clenched her spear in both hands and advanced a step into the hyena's stance, bowling him over onto his back. A desperate, shuddering, pleading chuckle escaped from Yacub's crooked mouth.

The ibex had fallen, the cruel edge of the hyena's weapon having torn his throat open. But the mad, laughing creature reveled in his victory a little too long, allowing the snake's thin blade to slice through his shoddy armor and open his guts. He clutched at the wet red mess, said "Boss?" to Yacub, then slumped over and did not move again. The raccoon, horrified, broke away from the snake and dashed through the shadowed doorway without looking back.

Feyn backed away from the combat in the center of the pen, leaving behind a trail of his blood. His howl of anguish shifted to a roar of anger.

Maxan clutched the short sword stained with the wolf's blood. He pointed its tip at Feyn, then swept it shakily back and forth at everyone else. "Stay away!" He brandished the badge of the Crosswall Guard. His muzzle felt like it was stuffed with cotton, and he slurred his words, but he somehow made up for it with the volume of his voice. "All of you, stop this right now! You will know the city's justice!"

Am I really doing this?!

He glanced over his shoulder. The hawk stared at him in some kind of awe, cocking her head, blinking her piercing yellow eyes at him. Even the hyena beneath her looked at the fox from where he lay sprawled on the ground, uncharacteristically silent.

The cloaked figure pulled back her hood, revealing the beautiful face within. A fox, like Maxan. She cast the gaze of her twin blue eyes at him.

"Who are *you*?" was all he could say. Struck dumb as he was by the commotion, by the serenity of those twin blue seas, he realized a moment later he'd emphasized the wrong syllable.

Who are you*? Idiot. You mean who* are *you.*

"Shut up. I mean, all of you, silence!"

"No one is talking," said a calm voice from Maxan's side. He whirled about, pointing his sword at the cloaked Corvidian, who pulled back her hood at last. The gray-horned owl with impossibly huge, abyssal black eyes clasped her taloned fingers in front of her waist. Behind her, the corpse of a hyena lay sprawled in the dirt, his eyes rolled to the back of his head, his tongue lolling from his mouth, the teeth of his own weapon sunk deep into his own throat. "No one but you," the owl finished, blinking once very deliberately.

"I mean, ah, I am Crosswall Guard. You will lay down your arms and come with me to—"

"Please," the owl said suddenly, the sharpness of her voice cutting him to silence. She thrust her arm in Maxan's direction, and as she stepped closer to him, there could no longer be any denying it: the Aigaion no longer moved in the sky overhead. It seemed the very center of the black triangle was directly over the abandoned beast pen. The hawk and hyena, the snake and the wolf, the two foxes—all were struck silent by the gray owl's overpowering presence.

"Stop talking," the owl finished. The tips of her talons rolled in similar motions to those Feyn had made at the hawk.

And nothing happened.

Maxan felt nothing.

The owl blinked again. She dropped her arm to her side. Her head swiveled about to Feyn, who still clutched his wounded arm. "There is no connection," she told him.

"Then kill them," Feyn answered.

The female fox had seen enough. She did not wait for their next tricks. She rushed for her short blade that had buried itself in the wooden beam.

"Wait!" Maxan called after her.

The green snake burst into action, flinging a small metallic sphere in the wolf's direction. Feyn threw up a paw just as it struck the sand, cracked open, and burst into a spiral of flame that engulfed much of the facade ringing the pen. But the wall of destruction stopped flat against an invisible force just inches from Feyn's paw.

"Enough!" shouted Feyn, sweeping his arm toward the wall, carrying the explosive energy with it. "Harmony, *kill them all*."

As the snake's thin sword led his charge on the wolf, as the wild hyena wrested the hawk's spear free, as the fox took up her blades, as all of this happened, the gray owl raised her talons high, and a pulse of white light flashed on the Aigaion's black underside. Then a blast of force struck the world like a hammer, throwing the very dust they stood upon into the air. Maxan felt his body bend against it, crunched, folded over. He experienced the pain in slow motion, then came the rumbling quake, catching up with the drift of time and sound that popped his eardrums, and then he was dragged aside, spinning in a vortex, swirling around the gray-horned owl standing calmly at its center.

Everything—wood and stone, beam and brick, foxes and hawks, shadows and snakes and silhouettes—everything crumbled. Whatever glass remained in the broken windows shattered. The slate roofs of the structures surrounding the pen split and sank inward, bringing the buildings they covered down with them.

Everything was a raging, violent storm, and somewhere inside it, Maxan's head slammed hard against something. And although the Aigaion had already passed him that day, the whole world turned dark for Maxan once more.

CHAPTER TWO
THE STRAY WANDERERS

WINDOWS. IN WOODEN FRAMES. IN PACKED dirt walls.

It's my den. My ... mother's den.

And light too. Yinna's light. Through the window. Fading light. Golden.

Gold, like the iris of your eye.

A door. A slit beneath, where light shines through.

Now I can dream. Has to be a dream.

Because you know all this is gone.

A fox sits at the table in the center of the den, her back turned, her tail gliding over the floor, back and forth, in time with the melody she hums.

Maxan sees all this. He is behind her. Himself just a ghost. Disembodied. Weightless. Just watching.

Mother always looked worried.

And look at you. You didn't care.

Maxan sees a kit, no older than five, playing with string, some game half-remembered, on the floor not far away.

I should've cared.

But you were so small.

Doesn't matter.

The golden light shining through the window and under the door darkens, then diffuses as though the world outside were suddenly drowned in water. The light writhes.

It writhed like… like…

Snakes. Black, orange, yellow, red snakes, all the colors of fire. They slither in through the slit beneath the door. They poke through the windowpane, melt the glass, make holes that spew dark, suffocating smoke. Trails of fire erupt on the floors, the walls, the table, everywhere the snakes' bodies touch. Within seconds, flames fill the den.

No. NO! Not this!

The mother fox sees them, leaps into action, turns before the ghost of her son can see her face. She races to a bed, unlatches a chest, clutches something, then screams, stamps her hind paws, slams herself upon the snakes. But they slither up her legs, across her chest, flexing and squeezing and strangling her. And burning. The whole den is ablaze, and still the boy plays with his string.

You idiot! You'll burn!

Mother's dead. I…

Run! She died so you could run!

I did. I ran.

And that's why you're still here.

"I'm … still here." The words rattled in his throat, and the feeling roused him. Maxan stirred, his eyes closed, both his paws pressed flat against something solid. He sensed he was not pushing against it, though. It was pushing against him.

The orange firelight in his dream faded, and his eyes fluttered open, taking in the early-evening darkness of the collapsed beast pen. Yinna had passed while he lay unconscious, and she had taken her daylight with her.

In her place, Yerda—the bright day-star's dark sister, Herbridia's moon—dominated the sky overhead. Her entire distant sphere glowed. One could easily discern the dried-blood brown of Yerda's surface rock, laced with white and gray that could be snow, and wrinkles that could be mountains. But Maxan found his gaze drawn to the colossal, gaping hole at her center. "Yerda's Wound" it was called, an enormous dark crater that marred the moon's perfection, with a pinpoint of yellow light at its center, like a candle seen through a keyhole. Her ring of asteroids, "Yerda's Belt," was also illuminated by her sister's rays as she traveled away. On this cloudless night, the broken moon could be seen clearly despite the immeasurable leagues of empty space that separated it from Herbridia.

Maxan never tired of gazing at Yerda's celestial beauty. He never bothered to wonder about what had wounded her. To him, there was no value in looking to the past to find where things went wrong, no matter how horrible. One might miss the perfection of the present.

For an instant, Maxan believed that his shadowing of Yacub and his cackle, his encounter with all the strangers, the fox who attacked him, all of it, had just been a part of his dream—*a very bad dream*—and that he was, in fact, just staring at the night sky, perched on his favorite spot atop the guardhouse tower, entranced by the turning of the celestial sisters, one light, one dark.

But no. It had all been real.

As real as this damn heavy thing crushing me!

He shifted his limbs by whatever inches he could, but it didn't take much before the heavy wooden plank that pinned him slid off to his side, down the mountain of debris where he lay, bringing an avalanche of crushed brick, pulverized wood, twisted nails, and swirling dust down with it.

Maxan breathed heavily as he propped himself up on his elbows, then sucked in a sharp breath as pain spiked through his leg. In the storm, something had cut across his right thigh, and blood now dribbled down his trouser leg and stained his amber fur red. He was lucky.

Always lucky.

He ripped a shred from his cloak and did what he could to bandage the wound, then clambered down the slope of what had once been a building.

Just a building? Correction: Buildings. Plural. Looks like half the district is in ruin!

He came to rest on the dirt floor of the pen, right where the owl had raised her arms, at the epicenter of the—what was it? *A blast? Like a wind, stronger than anything. Straight down from above.* Maxan snapped his eyes skyward. *It's gone. Did she … stop it somehow? It doesn't just … stop.*

But she did. It all happened. Look around you, Max!

He stood at the bottom of the long trough of devastation that cut through several buildings in all directions. The buildings still intact beyond the devastation rose like bones on either side of a rib cage that had been torn wide open, the organs inside shredded and rearranged. All signs of the battle and bloodshed were gone. *Well, ah, besides the acre of toppled buildings, all of the blood the hawk lost, the hyenas, Yacub, and the heads of the ram and the leopard, all of it's gone. Swept away with the dirt.*

The two cloaked strangers—the white wolf and the gray owl—out of all the combatants had clearly been in the least amount of danger. *They were in control*, Maxan thought. *No weapons. No armor. Just … tricks.* Maxan recalled how the wolf had bent the fiery explosion away from himself. He'd felt a phantom quake under his feet as the air above hammered

down at the owl's call. These two had ripped apart every structure surrounding them and scattered it all into unrecognizable
mounds of dusty, disjointed materials. The only other thing
Maxan knew to be capable of such pinpointed and instanta-
neous destruction was a meteorite flung from Yerda's Belt, and
those were an extreme rarity.

There was no meteorite. This was the owl. You know it.

How could she...?

"I don't know," he mumbled as his thoughts trailed off, his
voice the only sound in the stillness.

Why are you talking to yourself again?

I don't know.

*Yes, you do. Same reason as always. You're lonely. And feeling
lonelier since you saw her. Right, aren't I?*

"And what was it I said? 'I never did anything,'" Maxan
chided himself, recalling how he'd reacted when the silhouette
had him at her mercy, both blades pressed to his throat. "Rinnia,"
he traced the sound of her name on his breath, remembering
how the hawk had screamed it and how the fox had leapt away
after it.

The rest of the moments played again through his mind's
eye, up until the moment he had found himself facing a choice,
and he had not hesitated to make it. Choice was a closed door
in an unfamiliar house; he could never know where it would
lead until he was through. No one could. The only certainty
was that the door was unlocked, and once he stepped through,
there would be no turning back. Ever. In a way, every moment
was a choice, and every moment had led him to that door. And
he chose to step through.

Maxan stooped to retrieve his short sword. Like him, the
thing was lucky. It had come out of the storm hardly damaged.
The wolf's blood stained the blade under a thin layer of dust

and scratches. He remembered how before today he had never really used it.

I saved her.

Did you?

He flung her own sword at her head!

You could've run. No. In fact, Max, you could've followed orders! Observe. Report. Never engage. Remember? But you threw those orders away. You leapt in there after her. You sliced the damn wolf's arm wide open!

He was going to kill her!

He lowered his eyes and shook his head, refusing to carry on this pointless argument with himself any further. But the voice persisted, ridiculing him for another reason.

"I'm Crosswall Guard!" He heard the echo of his proclamation, feeling the embarrassment wriggle under his skin. It rankled his fur all over. *"Lay down your arms!" Quite the valiant warrior you were.*

Wait!

Maxan patted himself down, felt in his pockets, and realized that his guard's badge was gone, carried off by the vortex.

A wailing howl sounded in the distance, freezing his blood, rooting him to where he stood. Maxan suddenly remembered exactly where he was. This far west, he should have realized why what must have been an incredibly loud crash hadn't attracted crowds of onlookers. He remembered who this place really belonged to.

One by one, more feral throats added their howls to the first. Maxan did not wait for them to die down. He sprang into action.

And fell immediately onto his left knee. He clutched at his bandaged thigh and saw the red on his palm in Yerda's moonlight.

"They can smell the blood."

He heard a skittering commotion to his left, nearby what had once been the pen's entrance, where Yacub and his cackle had first emerged for the meeting. He knew exactly who made such a noise. They were coming for him.

The rooftops!

Dulling the searing pain in his leg, adrenaline was already pushing his body ahead of his mind. He ground his fangs together, cinched the makeshift bandage tighter in one balled fist, and limped as fast as he could up the slope of debris toward the nearest building with a roof he hoped was still intact.

The skittering of claws against cobblestones grew closer.

He'd made it about halfway up the precarious mountain of jagged nails and splintered wood when the first Stray crested the slope on the opposite side of the pen. For the briefest of moments, the beastly black-furred wolf perched on all fours upon its mountaintop of ruin, what once were clothes hanging in tatters about its shoulders, its hot breath puffing in the chill night air. Its eyes, fixated on the fox—its prey, only twenty yards away—reflected the white moonlight.

Used up all your luck, Max.

Just have to rely on my speed, then!

The Stray black wolf charged, and the rest of its pack followed, crashing down the slope. Maxan didn't bother to take a head count as he burst back into action, scrambling up the twisted heap of fallen building materials toward the edge of the closest roof.

It's high enough! Has to be!

Or else you're dead.

Five feet. Four, three, one more lunge!

The slathering, guttural groans of the beasts were just inches behind him. The animals dug their claws into the uneven terrain, dragging themselves up after the fox.

There! Reach for it! No, what're you—

Instead of grasping what looked like the steady wooden beam rooted deep in the debris pile at the top of the heap, Maxan grabbed the loose one next to it and swung it behind himself in a wide and wild arc, putting all his strength behind the blow. His calculation proved correct. The solid wood struck hard against the leader's skull, who let out a whimper and toppled back onto the next two in his pack. The rest cascaded several more feet down the slope in a writhing mass of furry limbs, tails, and snarling, snapping maws. Maxan had bought himself precious seconds, which he used to rise and stand painfully on the balls of his hind paws, then leap as high into the air as he could and clutch the overhanging edge of the rooftop, pain in his leg be damned.

He dangled from the edge, then hauled all his weight up, over, and onto the rooftop, where he lay sprawled, his chest heaving, his amber fur matted with sweat. He stared up through the clear night straight into Yerda's Wound. He imagined that his other voice—the other Maxan, who often invaded his thoughts—was living on that distant world, and was right now staring up from that crater, right back at him. He extended his arm to the sky and waved, smirking.

"Told you so!"

Fine, his thoughts conceded. *Save your own damn self from now on, then.*

Something slammed against the wall beneath his rooftop haven, then set to scratching at the wood. Then came another impact, and more scratching. The growling resumed, more furious than before. If the wolves had not been Stray, if they still had mental faculties, the ability to stand upright, and the desire to see this chase through to its bloody conclusion, then Maxan would surely be dead.

But they've completely lost their minds.

Still, probably best not to test the Strays' environmental adaptability.

Agreed.

Once again, the rooftops of Crosswall proved to be Maxan's truest friends and protectors. He painstakingly rose on his hind paws and limped away. There would be no more running or climbing for this fox for quite some time, it seemed.

The bedroom door crashed open from the kick Rinnia gave it. Sarovek could not afford to pay for wasted time with any more drops of her blood. Muttering curses, the fox heaved the semi-conscious hawk and the heavy plate armor she wore onto the large bed in the room's center, and she gradually let her fall on her back atop the sheets, careful to extend the delicate bones of Sarovek's wings behind her. The house rule was to come and go as silently and softly as air through a cracked window (her master's very own words, in fact), but rules be damned.

"Saghan!" Rinnia had called her brother's name a dozen times at the top of her lungs since she'd first entered the main hall on the floor below. He had been there when the owl brought the pen and everything else crashing down upon them. An uneasy feeling gripped her stomach as she imagined him crushed and buried in that rubble, but she knew that it wouldn't be enough to stop Saghan. The master would never allow his son to fall so easily.

"He's not here," she reasoned aloud. "So where is the—"

Then she knew. Not where he was, but where he was going, and the anxiety gripped her again and would not let go.

"He'll get to it before me. Then what?"

The hawk drew in a sudden, shuddering breath, breaking Rinnia's contemplation. Bypassing the traps and triggers of the house's main entryway had proven tedious, costing precious time. Panicking would only cost more. Rinnia would have to find Saghan's spare vials of panacea. But first...

"Sarovek, can you hear me?"

"Yes." The hawk's eyes remained closed, and her voice was a labored whisper.

"I'm going to get panacea. I want you to focus on unstrapping this ridiculous armor you insist on wearing until I get back. Can you do that? That's right. Here's the strap. Give me your other talon."

The hawk worked the first buckle at her shoulder out of its loop, then slid her talons across her chest to the next.

"Good. Get to work. I'll be right back."

Satisfied the task would keep her friend conscious, Rinnia dashed out of the room and headed for Saghan's quarters. The house was immense, being one of the tallest structures in Crosswall's western district. Some elk lord's house, she was told, who had gone to war to exterminate the insects decades ago, taking all his sons and daughters with him to their deaths, ultimately leaving this fine estate and brick manor, enclosed by a high wall topped with shards of glass, to neglect and ruin. Though expensive beyond measure in Leoran estimation, the cost was negligible for the brotherhood. The massive house, overgrown gardens, and courtyard with the three-tiered fountain at its center served as an isolated training ground and a secure base of operations whenever affairs brought them to this sprawling city. The traps and false panels they had built into the house had done well to spread the rumor of it being haunted. Neither the Stray nor desperate looters had dared trespass during this past year of quarantine.

Rinnia found the nondescript wooden panel that served as the secret door to Saghan's room, recalling how they had once returned here a few years ago and found a severed, rotting calico cat's tail in this very spot in the hallway, confirming that the traps—most of them—worked as designed. The intruder had kept her legs, though, using them to rush straight out the way he or she had come. Rinnia remembered how her brother had picked up the tail, smirking. "One life down, as many as eight left to go."

Rinnia reached up and touched the low ceiling where the panel ended, pushing the disguised buttons in the correct sequence with the tips of her claw. She heard the snap in the wall behind her, indicating that the hidden scythe blade would not be swiping at her legs, and then she pushed the panel into the hidden passage beyond.

Her brother's room was impeccably clean, as always. Every beaker was arranged in meticulous classifications of size and utility. The dregs of some concoction still pooled in the bottom of one, which signified the snake must have brewed the substance in an uncharacteristic hurry. By contrast, everything else in Saghan's room was orderly. The blankets and sheets on his bed were smooth and level. His books on chemistry, physics, genetics, and thermodynamics were arranged on shelves by the color of their leather spines, with his favorite collection of ancient fables kept separate. His sets of thin swords and daggers displayed on the wall rack followed some perfect arrangement Saghan had devised based on their centers of gravity and balance. A few of these blades were missing, as was the finely crafted armor from its stand.

She saw Saghan's vial satchel hanging from its peg across the room, and Rinnia took the most direct course to it, scrambling across her brother's bed, tearing the bag from its peg, and dumping its contents on the rumpled blankets. She clutched the only remaining pink panacea vial in Saghan's collection and ran back through the corridors. She bounded up the staircase quickly (but not so quickly as to step on the eighth and eleventh steps) to Sarovek's room.

The hawk lay as Rinnia had left her. Rinnia's bloodstained cloak, which she had held against Sarovek's side less to staunch the blood and more to prevent it from leaving a trail, had fallen away from her side, and red now flowed in rivulets down the shining plate. Her chest, covered as it was by the solid metal armor, gave no indication of rising and falling, but Rinnia could hear the faintest intake and exhalation of breath through the hawk's beak. Sarovek was alive, but she had lost consciousness during the unfastening of the third buckle just above her waist.

Sarovek was more than just a sister of their ancient order. To Rinnia, she was family.

Rinnia frantically finished the job of unfastening the armor's straps, then peeled away the heavy layer. It fell with a clang on the floorboards. Like the blankets on the bed, the quilted padding and white linen Sarovek wore beneath the armor were soaked in crimson. Rinnia unsheathed one of her short swords from its scabbard at her lower back and expertly, painstakingly, sliced up the side of this fabric to reveal the numerous leaking wounds the hyena's hideous weapon had put in the feathered side of her dearest friend.

Yacub's weapon was not meant to inflict death, only pain. Anguish. Suffering. The sole purpose of that sword, if one could even call it that, was to bleed its victims slowly. It was curved like a devil's smile, with jagged devil's teeth that thirsted for blood. She hated it, and she hated him. Hated his entire species.

Because she knew what it all was really for, Rinnia hated the whole world.

While she was also trained to kill, with every life she ended, she hated herself most of all because killing made her a part of it.

"Now's not the time." Since the moment she learned the truth, Rinnia had wasted enough of her life lost in her rage. She uncorked the small vial of pink powdered panacea, and with one arm, she gently rolled Sarovek onto her side and lifted a line of quills to inspect the wound underneath. She counted seven holes in the hawk's skin, all in a straight line. She plucked the ruined feathers from Sarovek's flank (knowing they wouldn't help the hawk fly) and tapped the powder out of the vial over each hole, where the medicine sizzled for a few seconds, then cauterized the opening. Within a minute, Sarovek's wounds were completely closed.

After stripping her sister more thoroughly, dressing her in fresh bandages, and administering an intravenous medicine drip (cursing more than once at how hard it was to find a Corvidian's veins beneath all the feathers), Rinnia finally let her sword belt drop to the floor and her exhausted body slump into Sarovek's favorite cushioned chair. She began piecing together all that had happened today and all that would have to happen tonight, indulging in her bad habit of thinking out loud.

"If Saghan didn't come back here, then where…"

She closed her eyes and tried to picture second by second exactly what happened at the beast pen. She saw the two enemies' heads Saghan had taken, the bomb he'd set off at the wolf's feet, how the wolf turned it away just before all became fire and dust. Rinnia had caught a glimpse of her brother being swept away with everything else, but when she later pulled herself and Sarovek from the wreckage, he was gone. "Or buried," she muttered, but she knew that wouldn't matter. No toppled ruins in the world were heavy enough to keep the snake contained forever.

"No," she surmised, "he made it out. And he… *STUPID!*"

Rinnia sprang up from the chair and scrambled to refasten her sword belt. "How can I be *this* stupid? The hyena told the wolf where it is. Even I heard him. If Saghan heard him… No, if Saghan gets the artifact before me, then everything I've done is for nothing."

She sprinted to her own room for a fresh cloak, then to the top floor and the trapdoor, adding up the times in her mind while her body moved automatically. It had taken her an hour to drag Sarovek here, another half hour to tend to her wounds, and five minutes to think. She accounted for the extra time it would now take her to inquire about such a stupid inn's name from the locals.

Back on the top floor, she carefully untethered Saghan's shrapnel cartridge from the latch of the trapdoor to the roof, then flung it open, revealing a clear night sky full of twinkling stars. Yerda, her belt, and her wound dominated the stunning view she did not pause to admire. She neglected to reset the booby trap as she bolted into a sprint across the Crosswall rooftops, faster than she had ever run before.

Maxan limped along the rooftops and abandoned balconies back toward the center of the city, away from the westernmost areas that the Stray had claimed. In the dark alleys and thoroughfares below, he could hear scratching, growling, barking. He could hear the chase of predator after prey. Down there, any animal bigger, healthier, or more vicious than another would pursue that animal at the first sign of weakness. Down there, there was no natural law or hierarchy. There was no order or sense. It was just blood spilled for the sake of spilling.

Yet Maxan blocked it all out. There was no one else in the entire city of Crosswall that had seen more of the Stray than the fox shadow stationed in the western district.

He ignored the sound of skittering claws that faded into the distance seconds later as he scrambled up and over a low plank separating two buildings. He painstakingly picked his way across the wide wooden rafters of a building whose roof had caved in, wincing a little at the throbbing in his leg, but more so at the sluggish pace it forced upon him. Something important had happened—*No, is happening*—and he should be racing toward it.

As was his habit, Maxan had been carrying on the conversation in his head for quite a while as he attempted to answer a single question: *What should I do?*

At this very moment, he could picture the armed and armored guards badgering their captain, Chewgar. "The shadow's not back," they would argue. "Caught by the Stray, finally." And no doubt they would add "What he deserved, the bastard." And the rhino would smile at these chides in that friendly and gentle way he had, which somehow never ceased to unsettle and terrify his subordinates. (They had all witnessed what Chewgar could do to those who made him their enemy.) And so the other guards would stow their feelings, for a time, and Maxan's life as the guardhouse outlier would go on.

Why does Chewgar protect me?

I don't actually know.

I don't deserve it.

Maybe we could run away. Again. Is that what you want?

Maxan felt invisible strings pulling him in all directions at once. Beyond the walls. East, back to the Denland forests where he was born. Or west, to Peskora. He had always wanted to see the glittering blue sea, to feel the white sands of its beaches scratch softly at the pads of his hind paws. Or he could run north, to live and die by his wits among his natural enemies the tribals, who might mistake him for a rebel. But instincts told him a clever enough fox could make a coin or two and a life of adventure there.

A short life. But a fun one.

What about south? He paused beside a crumbling brick chimney and craned his neck toward that horizon, imagining the dark patches of shadow between the deep green tangles of Leora's jungles.

He sighed, knowing he wouldn't really go anywhere. Ultimately, there were only two strings he knew that were real. One was pulling him back to the guardhouse. To his duty. To report what he had seen. To finish the mission. To be a shadow.

And the other…

Damn shame you can't overcome that curiosity, Max. What did they say about curiosity and foxes?

They say nothing. Because that's cats.

Don't try to dodge this, Maxan. Admit that you want to see this treasure.

He gritted his fangs in agitation. One part of his mind, it seemed, knew him better than he knew himself, giving voice to those dark thoughts he hated to admit were true.

Fine! I want it. I confess. So what? After what I just went through? I deserve to know.

But what if we'd died? Actually, forget that. What if you steal it and actually get away with it? What then? Oh, you're not thinking…

Oh, but I am.

They're dead, Max. Let it go. That was your life then, this is your life now. There are no more foxes.

Well, turns out that's not true.

What? Are you going to ask her *to join you in your new little thieves' guild? Maybe start with the little weasel kit from this morning. He could be your second-in-comm—*

"Rrrraaaaahh!!" Maxan thrashed his paws angrily in the air before clapping them against his fanned ears. He felt an urge to just tear them off, anything to silence the agitating voice. "Shut up!" His outburst echoed across the emptiness below, suddenly hushing everything else around. The thoughts quieted as well, and he slowed his breath in the stillness.

But it didn't last for long.

I'm just saying, one of us has to think it through. And if you won't, I will. Think, Max—you're hurt. What can you do with that leg?

Maxan, the inner voice pleaded, *Listen to yourself. You're crazy.*

"I am," he said aloud, nothing around to listen but the sky. "And maybe I am." He cinched the makeshift bandage around his thigh tighter, worked the joints in his knee and ankle. His leg throbbed, felt heavier, hotter, but the bleeding had stopped. The thing still worked. He moved on.

If I *survived the blast*, Maxan reasoned, *then I assume the others did as well.* The white wolf would have probably fled to nurse his nasty new scar. As Maxan knew quite well, and as this night had already reminded him, crossing the western district at night with an open wound attracted a deadly sort of attention, and he doubted Feyn would be much of a climber with that arm.

And what of the hyena and the hawk? The snake and the owl? And the fox? Again, assuming they had not been entirely consumed by the churning storm of structures, they were no doubt in just as much need of repair. The mysterious and well-armed newcomers at the meeting wouldn't dare try for the Aurochs' Haunch inn with those injuries, expecting to take on or sneak by whatever was left of Yacub's vicious cackle of raiders.

So your mind's made up.

Finally, the voice in his head faded to silence. Whatever quips it still held in store for him fell apart like shattered manacles.

"Listen to me," Maxan whispered.

He dropped to a crouch over a wide avenue to scan the hundred figures packed together into the space below. He had passed their improvised barricades a few streets ago, finally putting the Stray's territory behind him. With all the houses and shops packed to capacity with afflicted animals, most of the folk below had no choice but to huddle under blankets against the facades for warmth. Some had turned market stalls into ramshackle hovels.

Pressed on one side by a city that didn't want them, and on the other by the slavering, roaming packs that would eat them, a kind of civilization had sprung up here—it had to. Many animals volunteered to keep watch over the barricades on the ground, and so they paid no mind to the rooftops above their heads. Some stood in packs around braziers or makeshift fires, conversing or commiserating quietly into the night, perhaps plotting their rebellion.

"How long can we keep doing this?"

The whisper was already out before he even knew what he meant by it. *Doing what? Keeping the Stray out? Cramming more and more together? Lining up? Looking away? Fighting? Surviving?*

No, he realized. *Hoping.*

Maxan's mismatched eyes roamed over the forms of the herded animals below. For anyone who had seen what he'd seen, from the unique perspective he'd seen it, there could be no doubt it would all end in fire and death, sooner or later. He knew because fire and death had almost taken him before. Twice.

"I have to get out."

His gaze came to rest on a wooden sign depicting the flank and back side of the most common burden-beast in Leora, the aurochs, swishing its tail futilely against the swarm of flies that it attracted.

And that's the door that gets you out.

He reached below the eave of his perch, found a hold that could support his weight, and swung himself easily, silently over the edge.

FILE 002: "CONFESSIONS"

Time: 003271/11/10-[06:42:25-06:46:07]
Location: Castle Tower
Begin audio transcription:

I should probably regret what I've done. But...

Do you? Regret anything?

We're not so different, you know. Murderers. The both of us.

I see maybe you disagree? Well, I know I'm a murderer, but I learned everything I know about murder from you. I never could have found it in me to ... set all this in motion if you hadn't first shown me, shown all of us, that we had such potential.

You were always so inspiring. Your speeches were ... glorious. I wonder, any speeches now?

Nothing to say?

Huh. Well, I remember being there, in the great hall. You called every one of us, every Monitor, from every corner of this little world, to announce our next campaign. Zariel and I, we noticed the unusual lack of details as we left our post. We speculated the whole trip. You were always quite elaborate with these sorts of things, you know.

Never could we have guessed that the proposal—forgive me, your word was solution—would address what you called "the Thraxian Problem." I remember those words.

And they all agreed. Every. Single. One. Why?

Why? Tell me why.

SPEAK, damn you!

What are we to you?

Just lifeless ... what? Clay? Or meat? Soulless ... what? Vessels?

I know. We're just animals.

You gave your blessing to centuries of slaughter because you never let yourself see that we could ever be anything more than that. Just animals.

We made all of this. Together. Every brick, every grain of dirt, every speck of dust. The sky, the sea, the city, the very air you breathe. Every atom. All of it, because we thought it could break the circle of history.

Do you still believe none of this is real? That the real you is just sleeping somewhere? That this thing you call a body is ... what? Expendable?

Huh. Expendable—another of your words I remember well. That part of your speech... about how none of us matter. Despite all the death, you said, life continues. How like a murderer, I thought, to so easily forget all the lives he's already taken. All those lives. Those bodies we cut, mangled, burned, poisoned, crushed, drowned. Just ... soulless, mindless meat.

But I knew, there was a soul. In everyone.

I can see you still don't believe it. Look at me.

LOOK AT ME!!

I will make you see. You think we're animals?

I'll show you what we are.

We are murderers.

Chapter Three
The Aurochs' Haunch

MAXAN IGNORED THE THROBBING IN HIS LEG and willed his sore muscles to hold firm as he balanced precariously just outside the third-story window of the Aurochs' Haunch inn. He was relieved to find that the windows here were very familiar to him—basic, therefore easy. His old thieving instincts were taking over. He slid the tips of his claws silently under the frame and, just as he remembered to do with this particular type of fitting, lifted first with his shoulder to eliminate the window's usual grating noise.

He glided through the opening as silently as a sleeper's breath and closed the window carefully behind him. A barrage of potent scents invaded Maxan's snout: sweat, rust, and rot. He managed to stifle the sound of his retching and the rising contents of his stomach.

With the edge of his cloak over his snout, he turned about and found himself in the corner of a wide-open common room lined with rows of bunks for guests who lacked the coin for the private lodgings on offer. The only light in this place was the dim glow cast along the floor from under one of these doors, but it was enough for Maxan to see that the common room was a wilderness of tossed bedding, torn sheets, the spilled straw innards of mattresses, and shattered pottery.

What is that smell? Spilled beer? Excrement? Or worse?

He saw that the tattered sheets hanging down from the top bunks were stained with it, and then he knew.

Blood. Blood everywhere.

Maxan locked his eyes on the shadowed floorboards, looking away from the splatters on the sheets, still glistening and fresh, trying to imagine that somehow a Stray had done this. It made it a little easier. He padded silently through the mess toward the sliver of glowing light beneath the doorway. If he was going to find what he came here for, he would need more light. Thankfully, it seemed the place was abandoned. Yacub, if he was still alive, hadn't returned to this place after... *After whatever happened.*

His left low paw landed in something sticky. He drew it away instinctively, then stumbled sideways in horror.

Just to his left, around the edge of the bunk closest to the window, a hyena sat slumped on the floor, his hind legs splayed out before him. A heavy scimitar was lodged in his shoulder, splitting his chest nearly to the heart, pinning him upright to the thick wood of the bed. Maxan's illusion of a Stray attack faded instantly. The hyena's own sword lay before him, split in two pieces across his lifeless lap, telling the story of how this hyena had perhaps raised it to block the killing blow, but the killer had just been too strong. Strong enough to cut through: iron against iron.

Maxan choked audibly, bit down hard on his cloak, and clamped his muzzle with his paws, suppressing what might have become a horrified cry.

Baynay.

The name from Yacub's story.

A shadow passed across the dim glow beneath the door, and some creature moaned painfully on the other side. The moan became a chuckle, then a gurgle. Through his lower paws pressed on the floor, Maxan felt claws scraping, something dragging. Something heavy thudded against the floor, then silence.

Maxan crouched low between two bunks across from the mangled hyena's corpse, focusing every effort now on controlling his breathing. Sweat trickled between the rows of raised fur down his nape and spine.

The door opened, and the candlelight glow spilled into the wider room, reflecting off the shining pools of blood. A figure stood in the doorway, hooded, with tall and slender limbs encased in form-fitting fabric, or perhaps a full-body suit of thin leather armor—it was near impossible to tell in the shadows. But most of all, Maxan was drawn to the stranger's eyes as they swept slowly across the common room.

Those eyes were smoldering fires that seemed to siphon all other light around them, burning all the brighter as the rest of the world grew dim. At their centers were two vertically slit pupils of deep black, curved like butcher's blades. Their shape, their color, spoke a single idea to Maxan. *Power.* It was power that ignited those flames.

Maxan stared, fixated on those eyes, for in his world they had become the only source of light for miles all around, like signal fires on a mountainside in the dead of night. The paw he thought to tighten on the hilt of his sword he found trembling instead.

The newcomer's gaze swept over the room, casting a narrow beam of orange light like the aperture of a thief's hooded lantern. Something clattered below them, from the ground floor, and those eyes snapped toward the staircase. The dark figure descended.

Now or never. Go. We can make it out.

Maxan ignored the voice of reason. He ignored the calculations for opening and ducking through the window. He heard only the sound of his controlled breathing as he stepped out from his hiding place between the bunks. His eyes flitted from object to object strewn about the room, trying to recall what Yacub had said about the artifact.

Red light, he said.

And Ulbur, he said, lost an eye. And Baynay...

He crouched to the side of the split corpse. Gravity had already drained its blood from the shoulder down. *Baynay. What did Baynay do?*

They left it... tucked in...

Maxan reached a paw into the hyena's vest, feeling something solid. Slowly, he unfurled his claws, then frowned at the apoth figurine. "This?" he breathed, his face scrunching in confusion.

The hyena Baynay slid forward, off the blade pinning him in place, folded over, and lunged for the fox. Maxan gasped, fell back, felt his paws skate over the slick blood, lost his balance, and slammed onto the floor, the figurine clattering away. A coldness crept over his body, from the tips of his ears to the end of his tail—a numbing, freezing fear. All the sound in his world was hushed. The silence lengthened, until he was aware at last that the hyena was still dead, and he could hear himself breathing again.

Some pulse of light grew by the corpse's side, tearing Maxan's eyes away. A golden intensity spread underneath the white sheet covering the hyena's paw, then faded to nothing, then pulsed again, and faded again, rhythmically. Maxan inched closer, clutched the sheet in his trembling paw, and drew the cloth away.

The golden light filled the room.

"No," he said, taking the thing in his paw. And again, witnessing the light wink out, he said, "No."

I've seen this before. In ... a dream.

Or in a... m... m...

A pain lanced Maxan's skull, behind his golden right eye.

Memory.

He doubled over, the end of his snout nearly touching the floor. One paw pressed against his head firmly, the other gripping the artifact tightly. He winced through the pain, watching as the light pulsed again, flooding the entire room in gold.

It was a metal rod, polished to an impossibly reflective finish, as long as his forearm and as thick around as the hilt of a great sword, though lighter than any metal he knew. Thin channels ran up and down its length, and a few golden beads of intense light, yet no bigger than raindrops on a pane of glass, shot through these in a constant, steady circuit, illuminating everything in a brilliant, limitless shimmer. Once the first bead of light reached the end of a channel, a new one appeared at its start, chasing after it, then another, on and on, endlessly.

The world fell away it seemed, and everything Maxan thought he knew about it fell away with it. He stared, entranced, at the pulsing and fading light in the glass, and at the green-and-gold-eyed fox that stared back at him from the polished metal reflection. He forgot himself for a moment. As the pain in his mind subsided, he became someone else, some other fox, who knew exactly what this thing was.

"Aigaion," he whispered, and an angular room of tall, sloping shadows and white panes of glass flashed across his vision. "The relay."

He looked up, blinking, but saw only the bloodstained common room of the Aurochs' Haunch. The eerie sensation faded, as though he were waking from a dream, and some other, instinctual sense took control, rooted him to the floor, and raised the fur at the back of his neck. He felt eyes upon him. Fear slithered over his body.

A bead of light ran its course across the glass on top of the artifact, sending a momentary flash into the darkness, framing the slender shadow at the top of the staircase, and revealing the face of a green-scaled snake.

It's him, Maxan. The voice of the other fox informed him before he made the realization himself. *The same. From before.*

The golden glow faded, but the snake's fiery orange eyes remained lit.

"Know what you have there, boy?"

The eyes moved in the darkness, weaving between the bunks, drawing closer to the fox. The artifact pulsed again, and Maxan saw the snake's hand reaching behind his back.

The snake's hand shot forward just as the golden light faded, and something in Maxan took over, some sense beyond his nature, more powerful than mere instinct. It ripped him from the freezing grip of his fear and rolled him sideways into a crouch. It saved his life. The dart that sailed over his head would have planted itself in his heart. Another object hissed by, sparked, and exploded in midair with the sound of several rattling, clinking chains, shooting a web of razor-sharp threads in all directions that nailed themselves into the frame, the ceiling, the floor, and inches in front of the nearest window, covering it like a net.

Maxan rolled farther, his momentum carrying him down and backward in a somersault, and he sprang up directly against the web of fine metal fibers cutting off his escape.

"My, my. But you are fast and sprightly." The snake took another step forward, drawing a very thin sword whose blade gleamed in the brief golden flash. "Set it down gently, boy, and step away."

Maxan glanced at the artifact, long enough to see the next bead of light set off along its channel. Somehow, somewhere within his own mind, something buried deep was restored, and he recalled precisely how it all worked.

The snake watched Maxan intently. He read the look on the fox's face, saw the recognition in his mismatched eyes, but it was too late. "NO!" he yelled, lunging forward with his sword.

Maxan's claw had already caught the bead of light, slid it forward to the middle of the channel, and held it there as the next bead merged with it, and then the world flared in glowing, pulsing red. Red that washed away all other colors. The snake's green skin, his shadow, his black armor and blades, and his orange eyes, everything, drowned in the inescapable red that poured from the artifact in Maxan's paw.

"Survival of the fittest," Rinnia muttered under her breath, scanning the masses of animals packed into the avenue below the roof where she perched. She heard them cough, heard them groan. Sickness and hunger would take some of their lives, and the rest not strong enough to fight their way into more secure shelter would fall prey to the Stray. Or become Stray themselves. Soon.

"No, Rin. Just nature."

She had been traipsing across the rooftops of Crosswall's western district all night, stopping only to read the hanging signposts of inns, hoping finally she might find the one she'd heard the hyena tell the wolf.

"The Aurochs' Haunch," she scoffed. "What a stupid name."

The fox had much to be angry about. Since her and the other Monitors' arrival in Crosswall three days ago, they had chased after rumors that the artifact had been found, or that this or that collector or black market broker was interested, and she had not slept more than thirty minutes between each dead end. And at last, just hours before, when the last lead yielded results, she had nearly died, her throat cut by her own blades. Her sister had been grievously wounded, and their brother had gone off alone.

"Not his choice," she reminded herself. "Not Saghan."

She let out a long breath, a plume of mist carried away on the wind of the chill night. "I've no choice either." She swung her legs over the roof's edge, resigned to rouse some of the locals, ask if they knew about the Aurochs' Haunch, and so chase rumors and likely false leads all over again.

But then she froze. Two hundred yards out, she spied the thick bloodred glow on the underside of a low passing cloud. Then it started. The howling, the scratching, the screams. The stink of fear and hunger and violence. Everything her master had warned them of.

Below her in the street, all at once, the red light flooded every crevice of the city, and every single animal shifted beneath their blankets. Makeshift shelters toppled over. Their bodies writhed as one, grunting, snarling, screeching. Eyes snapped open and slathering mouths pulled tightly back, baring sharp fangs. The peace of slumber was forgotten. All rational thought fell away. There was only chaos. Only beasts. Only Stray, tearing each other to shreds.

And there was Rinnia, who was caught in the same frenzy but felt nothing.

She scrambled away from the churning violence below. By the time the first blood was drawn, she was already racing toward the red light's center.

The snake fell to his knees. His thin blade fell beside him. His slender, trembling fingers pressed the sides of his smooth, scaled head, covering its small ear holes, as though he were struck by a deafening cry.

Maxan stood over him. He felt nothing except the rush of blood and adrenaline in his body. He heard nothing except the clash coming from the streets all around the inn.

The red light did not fade into darkness like the soft golden light had. It burned steadily, unyielding. It filled every angle of the room, hanging heavily, suffocating like smoke. Whatever the light was, Maxan knew it was the root of all the violence. The red light was violence itself.

The raving Drakoran dug his black nails into the floor, dragging himself closer to the fox, inch by inch. But Maxan didn't move. His fear froze him in place. That, and disbelief. The snake reached for him with a wobbling arm, and he recoiled from the touch, able to back away at last.

Why can I move? Why am I not crazy? Like him?

His back collided with the plank of a low bunk, set against the far wall beside the window.

No time for that. Time instead to move! Get out, Max!

The black nails lashed out, fast but clumsy, and found only the wooden frame where the fox had been a second before.

Maxan rolled away and came up beside the window where he had broken into this place not even five minutes ago. He clutched the red thing in his left paw and reached for the window frame with his right. He pulled it away suddenly, remembering only too late the web of razor-thin wires that had exploded from the Drakoran's device. Even in the red light, he saw the slashes in the glove over his hand and the dark red blood welling there.

Maxan whirled about and found the snake fighting his way up the side of the bunk frame.

"Wait." The creature's voice was hardly more than a whisper, yet it seemed to resonate with that same power that fueled his wild, burning eyes.

Maxan drew his short sword, leveling it at the Drakoran as he sidestepped away, hoping there would be another hall, another window, anywhere away from this corner.

"It'sss ... *MINE!*"

The snake lunged suddenly at Maxan, tossing another dart drawn with frightening speed, but Maxan unexpectedly found himself batting the thing away with his own weapon before his mind could even register the movement. The dart twanged upward and sunk deep into the ceiling.

"Did I just... *Huh?*" The fox stared dumbly at his short sword while the voice of sanity screamed inside.

Run, idiot!!

Maxan leapt across the pile of torn and bloodied bedding toward the hall around the corner, and spied another window at its end.

"*I SHALL HAVE IT!*" the snake wailed, crashing against the door just a few feet behind Maxan. One arm clutched his head, the slender fingers scraping at his scales involuntarily, but with the other he reached again behind his back.

RUN!!

Even the lightning-quick thought in Maxan's mind lagged behind the sudden surge of energy in his body. Before he could finish the thought, he was leaping, forming himself into a ball, flying directly at the glass windowpane.

The force of the explosion rattled his bones. Next came the heat, turning his cloak and the tip of his bushy tail to ash. And then he felt the pain. Searing hot, igniting his entire being as the rippling burst of air popped his eardrums and turned the hallway and half of the inn behind it into luminous, swirling bits.

Maxan's smoking body was shoved through space by a jet of bright flame, erupting through the window in a shower of glass. It shot him straight out across a narrow alleyway and slammed him hard against the adjacent building, from which he fell in a smoldering heap atop the cobblestones below.

THE ARTIFACT

IT TWIRLS. END OVER END. LIGHT, CHROME, IT cuts through the heavy night air.

How did it get here?

Mother. She brought it. Kept it hidden. Then she threw it away. The artifact…

Its golden channels illuminate the mud-packed walls of the foxes' den, the whole clearing the mother and kit called home, their garden, the towering fortress of trees that protected them. Shadows and light frolic across their broad trunks as it sails by.

It sinks into the rushing river, and the tumbling currents swallow its light.

The river, where we drew our daily water.

Only the torchlight remains, held by the ones in black. Assassins, with slender swords. They ring around the mother fox, who holds only a simple hatchet.

Panting, the kit raises himself onto the high rock at the edge of their clearing. He sees the twirling light, and the sight of it sears into his memory, but he buries it along with everything else. The ring closes around her.

One dives after the light. Another brings its fire inside their den.

She told you to run, you fool! Why aren't you running?

"Mother." The little fox chokes on her name. Tears well in his large eyes, one green, one gold. He shivers in the cold. His tail squirms. "Mother," he calls louder.

No, Max! Shut up and run!

I left her to die!

What could you have done?

The assassins' blades cut his mother down.

"Mother!" he screams.

The assassins' heads turn, and the kit sees their faces. Walls of whirling flames in their empty hoods. Their eyes, needles of white fire. He hears his mother's voice one last time, the last thing she told him.

Run, Max...

And so he runs.

And the killers follow.

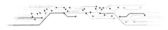

Behind closed eyelids, the vision stayed with him. The burning faces in his pursuers' hoods cast a searing heat upon his back. In his dream, he ran, but in reality, he squirmed, and his claws scraped on the hard ground beneath him.

Maxan's eyes snapped open. He twisted and wriggled about, gibbering like mad, grappling with the very real flames that clung to his cloak. Somehow, in his frenzy, he managed to unclasp the thing and scamper away until his back hit a wall.

And that's when he saw the Aurochs' Haunch had been engulfed in fire. An enormous circular wound where the window just above him used to be gushed spirals of unraveling flame. Enormous pillars of roiling black smoke rose into the night sky, lit with a shifting orange glow.

His brief nightmare, reliving his worst memory, was a peaceful respite compared to the horrors and brutality he'd seen in that place.

This is real. It all happened.

"And I'm alive."

And you're lucky to be. Twice in the same day.

He had seen the opening door, made a choice, taken a risk, and won.

Inexplicably, he felt his body relax at the realization, every part of him but the paw that still clutched the artifact. Its red light had faded. Not even the golden beads were racing through the channels. It was inert. Just a rod of polished metal.

Something crackled and snapped inside the ruined inn. Pieces of it sagged, toppled over one another, and then caved in at the structure's center. An enormous burst of sparks rushed up toward the sky, swirling about the pillar of black smoke. The fire was consuming everything from the inside out. The green snake—the murderer, the one who said it was his—could not have gotten out. *Gone,* Maxan assured himself. *Has to be.* Eaten by the very fire he'd set.

Maxan hated fire, ever since the night it had taken everything he loved. *Not just once,* he thought, his gaze dropping to the glove covering his right arm. He could see the ruined skin through the cuts and burns from the snake's deadly devices. Before his mind could make sense of the words *granary* and *commune*—and the name Safrid—that came rushing back, that same right arm was pushing him up, his back scraping against the wall for support. Moving, running, always helped him forget. *No more time for dreams,* he thought. *Or memories.* He was on his legs again, and they carried him with as quick of a limp as they could, eastward, toward the center of Crosswall.

He left the smoldering cloak, and he forgot his sword. It lay a few feet away, the light cast from the inn's raging fire gleaming on its naked blade.

Rinnia was closing in—just one more gap between her and the Aurochs' Haunch—when the explosive shockwave knocked her flat on her back. She rolled aside fluidly and recovered in a crouch as she had been trained, just in time to see the rain of flaming sticks, splinters, and bits of brick.

By the time she leapt onto what little remained of the inn's sagging tiled roof, the hole the blast had opened had become a widening mouth filled with angry, flaming teeth, chewing through more and more of the structure's second and third stories, vomiting a plume of black into the sky. Rinnia padded her way around it, peering into the chaos for any sign of her brother. The flames ate the support just underneath her, and she dived aside just as ten more square feet of the inn were swallowed.

She spun around on her rump, her forearm shielding her face from the intense blast of rising heat. Sweat matted her amber fur, soaked through her clothes and armor, and rose in steam from the thin cloak on her back. She wiped it away from her muzzle and eyes, blinking through the haze for any sign of Saghan. Then, in a pocket of clear air between thick puffs of smoke, she caught a brief glimpse of a figure, the green scales of its arms untouched by the destruction, for now.

"Saghan!" she cried, but the name drowned in the roaring fire.

There was no time to scan for a safe route through. There was no safe route. Her eyes locked on the body, lying inert on some floorboards between two rising walls of fire, and she plunged straight through the vortex of heat and smoke, crossing the gap and rolling on the floor far below. Only her bushy tail caught fire. She quickly doused the flames with her cloak before turning back to Saghan's body.

He was alive, despite all the odds, but then she recalled what he really was. "Of course you're alive," she said, and she couldn't stop the relief flooding through her.

"But we're both going to burn here if you don't *get up*!"

Rinnia was not strong enough to lift his body on her shoulders, let alone carry him out a window or up the smoldering structure to the roof. She had no time to puzzle out how such an impossible plan could work anyway. The flames had chewed several more inches closer.

"Saghan!" she screamed in his face. "GET UP!"

The snake's slitted eyes snapped open. His limbs flailed as if tugged by tangled puppet strings, slamming Rinnia hard against the flaming wall. She lunged forward again just before a cascade of charred debris toppled upon her. There was no way she could grapple against Saghan's enhanced strength, and he was likely to bring the rest of the place down if she could not make him see he was himself, in his own body again. She had to try.

She slapped both sides of his V-shaped head at once, screaming his name right into his face as she did. His widened eyes ceased rolling in his skull and centered on hers.

"Get up!" she screamed. "Now!"

His forked tongue grazed the fur about her muzzle, and he groaned. Soon she had his thin arm draped over her shoulder, and the two crept down the ruined hall toward the staircase. The rest of the inn had thus far been spared from the conflagration, and at moments, Rinnia was kicking the heavy front door wide, releasing a trapped stream of thick smoke into the night.

The wide avenue was filled with Leorans of all species, all in a state of pandemonium, many pinching gashes in their sides or across their faces, wounds left by the claws and fangs of their fellow outcasts. Many were on their knees, wailing over the dead. Blood streamed in the gaps between the cobblestones and pooled against the ruptured bodies. The sour stench of them hung thick in the night air.

Rinnia held Saghan up against her shoulder and guided him around the inn into a narrow alley. She eased him down against the wall of the adjacent building.

"Rinnia," he wheezed, "where am I?"

"Somewhere in Crosswall. Some blasted inn." Her eyes traced the singed edges of his ornate Drakoran armor. Her claws opened the charred flaps and ran along the scaled skin beneath. If there had been any wounds, they had already—miraculously—stitched themselves back together. "Literally blasted! By one of your new little toys," she scolded him. "What were you thinking?" It was too late. The question was already out. She saw the hurt in her brother's eyes before they looked away. "I'm sorry."

Saghan shoved Rinnia's paw away. "When he comes for me, I remember. I sssee everything."

"Tell me you… he…" Rinnia kept her voice level, hoping to keep her desperation hidden. "Tell me you got the relay. At the very least." If Saghan had it, she could take it. She could run. Leave it all behind. "After all this."

"Unless you just felt it under my armor, it's not here."

Even more of the Aurochs' Haunch split inward and sagged, crashing on top of itself, and a brilliant flash erupted behind the cracking panes of glass. More of the flaming mess spilled into the alley, mere feet away from Rinnia and Saghan. The snake watched the embers creep nearer the soles of his feet, indifferent.

Rinnia pretended to misunderstand her brother's look. "We can return and sift through the ashes later."

"No. It's not here."

"Who—" she started, but then she realized whoever held the artifact now didn't matter. "Father will kill us," she said instead through clenched fangs.

"Father wouldn't waste all his work. Not you. Not me. But he'll kill *somebody* for our failure."

Rinnia pulled her brother up and moved in the direction of the safe house but stopped. Something glinted in the firelight farther down the alley. A short sword, standard issue for the Crosswall Guard. She cradled the weapon in both paws, ran a claw tip through the flakes of dried blood on its channel. "The wolf's," she muttered.

"You know a snake'sss senssse of hearing is shit," Saghan hissed, coming to her side, his weight on the adjacent wall to steady himself. "What did you sssay?"

She handed him the weapon, seeing that he knew whose it was as well. "I said we're not going to fail." Rinnia's gaze landed on a smoldering mass of thick fabric. A cloak, *his* cloak, cast aside perhaps only a few moments ago. Her blue eyes darted to and fro around the alley. There were too many ways out, and no further signs of his passing. But it didn't matter.

Saghan flicked his forked tongue as he read her expression. "You know where it isss."

"No." She sighed. "But I know where it's going."

To the west, he glimpsed the dark orb of Yerda just over the rooftops. In moments, it would disappear behind the other side of Herbridia, heralding the new day. To the east, Yinna was not far behind.

In the gray-blue haze before dawn, Maxan entered the square with the dried fountain at its center where he had first spied Yacub's raiders with the weasel boy's help nearly a full day before. Across the way, closer to the central wall of the cross, the green-robed Mind initiates were already gathering, piling, and sorting the foodstuffs that would be today's giveaway for the innumerable masses of desperate, hungry exiles who had already begun organizing themselves into lines. Maxan wondered if any of these had partaken in the violence in the avenue outside the Aurochs' Haunch just a few hours before—if they had just shrugged, folded their ragged blankets and shirts over the wounds they had suffered, and fallen back asleep until it was time to fall in line.

They have no choice, if they want to eat.

Maxan was in terrible shape—he looked as bad as, if not worse than, any of the animals gathering here. He couldn't bear to put weight on his right leg; the wound in his thigh still seeped a thick, viscous red through its blackened bandage. And he was fairly certain some of his ribs were broken or bruised all along his right flank where the force of the Drakoran's bomb had slammed him against a building. Most of his clothing was intact, however, as it had been his cloak that suffered all the damage from the heat.

Hobbling his way around the perimeter of the wide-open space, staying close to the buildings on the southern side of the square, he knew two things for certain. *One: Word of what happened will spread. They'll tell the guard, tell the Mind. Tell each other, all over the district. They'll get desperate, try to break out, throw themselves at the walls, anything to get away from the Stray that overran them.*

And two... His paw fell, clutched the metal rod tight against his hip, and concealed it beneath his trouser. *This thing made them all lose their minds.*

But not you, Max. Not you.

All the fear from the previous day and night was gone. The fear of a slit throat from the blue-eyed fox's blade or from the green-scaled snake's. The fear of rushing in among the throng of killers and shouting something about being a guard. The fear of all the blood he'd seen. All of that was behind him. The only thing that scared Maxan now was the uncertainty.

Why not me?

What frightened him most of all was knowing how to activate the artifact and knowing that its power did not affect him. And not knowing how he knew. He ground the heel of his paw into his right eye, trying to scratch and soothe away the sudden pain that was knifing the inside of his skull.

He took a deep breath and reexamined the gathering crowd in the square, plotting a mental course through and back to the guardhouse. Just over a year ago, these very same spots were crowded with merchants and vendors opening the shutters and awnings, pulling out tables and piling their wares and goods on top. The Leoran folk of the western district came out every day to purchase the essentials, comforts, tools, and maybe even diversions, perhaps on their way to contributing to society at their own places of employment for an honest day's wage.

And this thing can bring all that back to nothing.

The history of this world was violent and bloody. It was the story of five nations—mammals, reptiles, birds, ocean dwellers, and insects—and hundreds of species, splintering into tribes, forming alliances, plotting betrayals, claiming territories and rulership, winning, losing, hacking, killing, enslaving … for hundreds of years. Until the Thraxian hives swelled beyond their borders, invaded Drakora, and eradicated great swaths of the reptile species there. The four remaining nations had no choice but to band together and exterminate the insect race for good, before the hive swept over the whole of Herbridia.

And now, twenty years later, that peace between Leora, Corvidia, Peskora, and the remnants of Drakora still held. Everything was new. Every system of trade and every law was a cog in the machine. The sprawling city of Crosswall was proof that Herbridian civilization worked, that all the species in all the kingdoms could live together without tearing one another's throats out, that difference didn't automatically make disharmony. And all of it—the whole societal bulwark that kept barbarity at bay—was built by the Mind.

But the Stray were changing everything. With every Herbridian that showed signs of going feral, that faced exile to the quarantine zone, or that lost their rational mind and lashed out, the Mind—in fact, the entire civilization of this world—lost yet another piece that kept the machinery of society turning. Soon, once word reached the Mind of the sudden and widespread outbreak of violence last night, that machine would break.

Maxan came within twenty yards of where he had last seen his guard captain, Chewgar, just the day before. The small troop of ten armed and armored guardsmen that had accompanied the captain—the same band Chewgar had promised Maxan would be ready once the fox delivered the whereabouts and activities of Yacub's cackle in the western district—was now nowhere in sight. Neither was Chewgar. Two soldiers blocked the small gate that led to the rear courtyard of the guardhouse, one a wide-bellied, orange-haired orangutan, the other a skinny and spotted leopard, both decked out in the standard long white and black tunic and ringlet armor of the Crosswall Guard's uniform. Neither of them seemed particularly vigilant. So engrossed were they in discussing the latest list from the arena, rattling the dice in their clay cup, and pushing their carved figurines across the apoth board between them that they didn't notice Maxan limp forth until his shadow fell over their game.

The leopard, Anda, wrinkled his snout at the scent of singed fur and clotted blood. He looked up and saw who it came from, then tapped the orangutan on the shoulder, inter-rupting the ape's toss of the dice. Neither guard greeted Maxan.

"Where's the captain?" the fox said finally.

The orangutan, Breg, spat out a long, wet wad that landed just an inch shy of the fox's hind paws.

The leopard sighed. "Whose captain?"

Feeling the exhaustion and rage welling inside him, Maxan dug his claws into the side of his leg. It was all he could do to restrain himself from digging Anda's eyes out. Anda and Breg exchanged a conspiratorial smile.

"Chewgar," Maxan said at last.

"Oh. Him." Anda leaned to the side, catching a glance of Maxan's singed tail. He took a look at the fox's bandaged thigh, but he made no comment.

"Where is he?"

"Oh, he was here. Hours ago. With the rest of us. Waiting for word from our shadow. But we gave that useless bastard up for dead. Right, Breg?"

The orangutan grunted.

"Right tired we are too," the leopard finished. With a shrug, he turned back to the apotheosis dice, rolled them alongside the board, and moved his figurines.

Maxan stood over the pair, watching their game, imag-ining what it would feel like to shove the game pieces down the leopard's throat and hold his muzzle closed with all his might. For as long as he had been stationed at this guardhouse, Anda especially saw to making the fox feel like an outcast at every opportunity. The other guards misunderstood the duties of a shadow and, therefore, misunderstood Maxan. Over the years, that misunderstanding had rotted until it was a lump of disdain, then a caustic loathing. To the other guards, the fox was just a coward who watched from the rooftops while they fought and bled to keep the rowdy citizens of Crosswall under control, while they ducked and dodged through crowded streets after cutpurses they would probably never catch, while they stood watch year-round, bored, through the summer heat or the winter chill, next to drafty city gates or putrid sewers, playing apotheosis or taking bribes from criminals, thieves' guilds, and corrupt merchants. And all the while, the aloof fox would whisper something in their captain's ear and send them off in pursuit of dangerous thugs or miscreants, which earned them no coins on the side.

In short, they hated the fox. And Anda hated him perhaps most of all.

And maybe he's right to, Maxan told himself. *You were, you are, and you always will be an outsider, Max.*

Maxan was tired of this. Tired of Anda, of Breg, of being an exile in the one place that he should've called home. The fox's lips curled back into a vicious snarl. His brow furrowed, his head lowered, and he looked down at the leopard with a murderous glare, his whole body tensed to strike.

Breg noticed first, hesitating to throw for his turn. Anda, his back turned, recognized the worry in his partner's eyes. He turned about, countering Maxan's scowl with a thin smile. "You don't look well."

Maxan stepped forward, the tip of his snout nearly colliding with the leopard's. "Get out of my way."

"Breg," Anda said over his shoulder, his eyes locked on Maxan. "Did you see that?"

"I did."

"This fox bared his fangs a bit just now."

"He did. Just so."

"And his shoulders seem a little curled in. Think he's going astray?"

"Look at his claws, Anda. How soon 'til he crawls?"

"Any moment now, Breg, I'm sure." Anda stood and unsnapped the loop holding his long sword secure in its scabbard. "Poor soul. Kindly rejoin the rest of your kind in the square."

"If you're going to kill me—" Maxan cut himself off. He was suddenly aware of the artifact pressing against his leg. He remembered the screams and howls outside the inn. He thought of what he could turn all the animals for miles around into. He thought of what some of them, like Anda, already were. He thought of what he was too, and the sudden shame washed away all the anger.

Anda saw all the fight leave the fox, and the leopard's spotted features curled in a sadistic smile. He stepped closer, coming face-to-face with the fox. "Not yet," he whispered. "Not while the noble rhino still rules. But how much longer can that last?"

Suddenly, Anda stepped back. "Besides!" he shouted, taking his paws away from his weapons and throwing his arms up proudly. "I'm a Crosswall guard. Paragon of the king's love and justice. Eh, Breg?"

"What's a paragon?"

"Though if you suddenly *lost your mind*," Anda said, ignoring his counterpart, his eyes intent on the fox, mistaking Maxan's backsteps as a display of fear. "And you lashed out at us," Anda continued, oblivious to the immense gray-skinned creature rising behind him from the guardhouse gate, "as a true Stray is wont to do, well then I would have to defend myself." The leopard inched his long sword free. "Clearly, citizen, you've been bitt—*aaaaAAAAHHH!*"

A massive three-fingered hand fell on Anda's shoulder and squeezed, twisting the sinews and rearranging the leopard's bones as easily as crumpling a parchment.

"I see you've found our shadow," Chewgar said flatly. "Breg, you can go. Anda has proved so vigilant this day that I trust the next watch to no one else in the company."

The orangutan nodded nervously, then beat a hasty retreat, scrabbling through the gate as fast as he could, on both feet and both knuckles, leaving his game of apotheosis unresolved.

"Good work, Anda." The huge rhino released the leopard's shoulder, likely bruised and all but useless for a week. Anda crumpled in pain, his eyes squeezed tight, which was all the affirmation Chewgar needed.

To Maxan, the rhino said "Inside," ducking through the gate and beckoning him to follow. To anyone else within earshot, the order sounded gruff and agitated. But Maxan alone heard the relief in his old friend's voice.

Maxan stepped gingerly over the writhing leopard.

"Don't eat so fast, fox, or you'll make yourself sick!"

Maxan caught his breath then sipped his next gulp of the steaming, salty broth methodically. At first, he had tried to refuse the bowl of wild fowl stew, claiming that the need to deliver his full report exceeded that of filling his empty stomach, but Chewgar would not budge until the haggard-looking shadow he had presumed dead or captured had something to eat.

The fox and the rhino had taken a corner bench in the guardhouse mess hall. Yinna's morning light filtered through the windows high on the eastern wall. Firewood popped pleasantly in the large pit at the room's center, filling the place with warmth. Over the fire hung Chewgar's bubbling stewpot, filling the place with savory fragrance. A playful smirk crossed the rhino's rough gray face as he watched his culinary masterpiece help Maxan recover from his night-long ordeal. Atop the table, he crossed a pair of muscular arms as solid as the masts of a Peskoran trading vessel. The towering broad shoulders of this famous captain of the Crosswall Guard could strike a fearful silence upon every Herbridian in sight, but Maxan knew the rhinoceros's heart was as soft and warm as the bowl of stew he had just finished.

"Good, isn't it?" Chewgar beamed.

"It's so ... so terrible," the fox replied with a straight face, but he couldn't hold it. A wry smile spread across his face as he watched the rhino's confidence falter.

"I haven't had any Hundred Isle salt for months, so I've made do with the local lowland river stuff. *Stuff* is too nice a word. Sludge, more like. Don't give me that face, fox!"

"Chewgar! The stew's fine. How many years have you known me? Get a sense for sarcasm already. Now shut up before I bust this empty bowl against your gigantic, empty skull."

Had Maxan been anyone else, any of their fellow guards, he would be slapped either with additional duties and patrols or by the broad palm of a massive gray hand. Even now, as Maxan glanced around the room, he saw several observers at other benches who had been reprimanded for their tone, or questioning of orders, or other insubordination before. They took great offense to the shadow's friendship with the captain. Maxan knew his closeness with Chewgar made him a target, yet it was the only thing keeping him safe the last five years.

What the others didn't know, however, was that the fox was not just another guard to Chewgar. In fact, he was the rhino's oldest friend.

"More likely to ... bust that tiny little paw if you tried," the rhino replied, though he'd had to chew over his words before assembling them into speech.

Even though the two of them were out of earshot, Maxan saw more than a few species present in the mess hall renowned for their sensitive hearing. He waited until the perked-up ears of the bobcat and the jackal turned away before he spoke again, now in a whisper.

"I need to tell you what happened."

"Very well. Start with Yacub. Where did he go, and where is he now?"

"I … lost him."

Chewgar's huge arms unfolded slowly. He laid his palms flat on the table. His voice was steady, but stern. "I guess something else caught your attention."

Yeah, Maxan thought. *Something did. Rinnia.* He imagined her sea-blue eyes. But his vision became a pair of knives flying through the air, the white wolf controlling them. His hideous scar. The owl, the lights under the Aigaion. The power that she called from the sky.

"Some … *things* happened," he stammered at last. "Things you won't believe. I can't tell you, not here." Maxan's paw came to rest on the solid metal tube held against his thigh beneath his trouser. He absently wondered if the racing golden beads had returned. "I have to show you."

Chewgar grumbled and rubbed a hand over his broad jaw, a clear sign of deep thought Maxan knew well.

After a moment's deliberation, they stood up from the table and crossed the common room toward the staircase that wound in a spiral up the southeastern corner of the guardhouse. They took the steps up past the sleeping quarters, training areas, and armory, all the way up to the landing at the top floor, whose ceiling was just pure blue sky. The day promised to be clear, though the easterly winds were pushing a blanket of high, thin clouds in from just over the horizon. Maxan could see the snow-covered caps of the Corvidian mountains that way, and some dark line in the sky just over their peaks. The Aigaion.

"Now," Chewgar said, after dismissing the sole lookout who had been stationed up here, a wolf whose name Maxan did not know but who nonetheless glared at the fox as he passed and disappeared down the stairs. "Before you give me your report, I'd like you to know that we waited well beyond the time you requested. The boys don't like standing about, weighed down by their gear and weapons, only to have the promise of cracking some hyena skulls go unfulfilled. They blame you for that." The rhino lightly jabbed the fox's shoulder with a finger nearly as thick as the fox's wrist.

"If the Aigaion were to drop on Crosswall, they'd blame me for that. I don't much care. Especially not after last night. Chewgar, listen, I ..."

There's so much to say, Maxan realized. He hadn't had time to think of how much he should share: the pack of murderers that fell upon him and the owl that blew the place apart. Would Chewgar believe she had brought the Aigaion to a standstill?

And then there was the artifact. *No ... the relay.* His vision of it. His familiarity with it. His nightmare. How his mother's final act had been throwing it away.

One thing had become frighteningly clear. This "treasure" he'd managed to steal out from under the snouts of the hyenas, the wolf, the owl, the other fox, and the murderous green snake—the thing he'd risked his life for, his escape from this life in Crosswall and return to the other side of the law he'd dreamed about—he no longer wanted it.

His mother would not have wanted him to have it.

"I ... don't know where to start."

"Start with Yacub."

Maxan sighed deeply. He knew he couldn't keep this to himself. And if there was one person Maxan trusted, it was Chewgar. Besides, making an official report was his duty, and Chewgar was a stickler for duty. So he went over every detail, from the moment he spotted the hyena raiders in the square with the weasel kit's help, to his pursuit from the rooftops, to their arrival at the abandoned beast pen.

Maxan recreated the conversation as best he could, mentioning how the scarred white wolf spoke of an escape from the animal inside, a promise that brought the brash and wild hyena to tears, how all Yacub had to do was deliver something.

Maxan drew in a deep breath and saw the concern in his captain's—his friend's—eyes. "Some treasure," he confessed finally. "But Yacub didn't have it. He left it somewhere. He told Feyn where it was, and that's when I chose to leave, thinking I could steal it out from under both of them."

"Back to your old ways, hmm?" Chewgar hadn't meant to sound accusatory, but Maxan felt shame flush through him anyway. "Sorry, Max," Chewgar added, seeing the fox look away.

"Well, I never got the chance. They had some uninvited guests drop in." Maxan thought of the hawk. "Literally." He recreated the silhouette slinking through the shadows across the way and described the fading light beneath the Aigaion flashing on his attacker's blades, the feel of them against his throat. How she'd let him go. And then how he'd chosen to follow her down into the pen.

"I had to save her."

"Dammit, Maxan!" The rhino loomed over him, huffing with disappointment. The jab at Maxan's shoulder was not so light this time. "Observe. Report. *Never engage!* You should have hightailed it back here the *second* you heard the inn's name. It's what I'm here for."

"Maybe," Maxan said, shoving the thick finger aside with the strength of both paws. "But something told me this was important." Chewgar cocked an eyebrow expectantly at that. "*More* important."

Maxan didn't feel like explaining the mystery of his disappearing species (Chewgar knew well enough anyway, as most Leorans did) and what seeing another living fox had meant to him. So he tried to change the subject, taking his own turn at jabbing a claw point against his friend's immense chest.

"I know what I'm doing. You need to trust my judgment a little more."

Maxan went into as much detail as his sleep-deprived mind allowed. He started with the piercing screech of the hawk knight, how Yacub's cruel ripper had bitten savagely through her plate armor, and how the wolf had paralyzed her with just his claws. "This Feyn … Chewgar, what he did to the Corvidian … I think he's a … caller."

The rhino shut his eyes tightly and shook his head, the massive horn unique to his species swaying side to side. "Those are just stories," Chewgar huffed.

There were stories, long ago, that a great number of species throughout all five kingdoms could manipulate objects with the power of thought alone. The most powerful among them could rip trees up from their roots, command winds, call lightning from the clouds, and even control others like puppets. "There's no such thing as a caller," the rhino concluded, rather decisively. Then he frowned a little, adding, "Or at least not anymore."

Maxan considered pointing out that until this day, he had never really believed the legends either. That a gray owl's word and a wave of her talons could uproot city blocks. *But it happened.* Still, he sensed his captain would likely not budge from this belief.

He wasn't there. I can't tell *him anything he'll believe. He has to be shown.*

So he said instead, "Well, I was knocked aside, left unconscious, and when I woke up they were all gone."

"Wonderful work, Max!" Chewgar threw up his massive arms, and Maxan could've sworn he felt the guard tower sway with the motion. "No doubt you lost Yacub's trail? They got to the inn before you, and … and … what is *that*?"

Maxan brought out the relay during his captain's tirade and held it up in both paws. It had returned to its golden, glowing state; the beads of light racing their never-ending circuits were bright enough to see even though the whole world was awash in Yinna's rays.

"This is what they wanted."

And it's what drove everyone mad.

Maxan swallowed the bile rising in his throat. He heard the screams that came through the windows of the inn. He felt the heat of the snake's eyes. He heard the Drakoran's words: *"I SHALL HAVE IT!"*

Chewgar scraped his flat teeth together, furrowed his thick gray brow, and folded his massive arms over his chest. After a moment of deep thought, the captain still had nothing to ask beyond the obvious. "What is it?"

"I don't…"

Liar.

"I … don't know."

Maxan's eyelids fluttered. He felt his body meld with the sunlight and heard his voice fade against the ringing in his ears. A sudden wave of nausea set him off balance, and he fell against the rampart, nearly losing his grip on the artifact.

My mother… Maxan wanted to tell Chewgar. *She… When they came for her…*

But he couldn't.

Chewgar bent over the fox and shook him gently. (Of course, a gentle shake from a rhinoceros could topple a bridge spanning the Radilin River itself.)

Maxan felt the rattling in his bones, and his eyes soon refocused. Then he saw Chewgar staring curiously at the metal thing gripped in his paw. He drew it away quickly, clutching it to his chest.

"I don't know how it works." He said this more to himself than to Chewgar, but it was a denial. Somehow, a deeper part of his mind was working without his consent, piecing together the observations he had made when the green snake went mad with something that felt like memories of a life he never lived. And in the flash of insight, one certainty was branded into him: the artifact caused absolute chaos. It fueled some violence that could not be contained. It severed whatever lines tied an animal to his or her reason and capacity for…

For what? Decency? Morality?

"Chewgar," said Maxan, standing and resecuring the artifact against his thigh, "we can't keep this thing here. If one of them got their paws on it, mishandled it…"

"Can we destroy it somehow?"

"Maybe, but if we put any kind of pressure on it, and it turns out we can't…"

"Throw it in the river, or the ocean?"

You know that won't work, Max.

"We…" Chewgar rubbed his broad chin and ground his flat teeth thoughtfully. Then he blurted, "We bury it! I know of some loose baseboards in the storeroom basement. Tonight, we creep down there and—"

"No. It won't work. If you found some loose baseboards, then someone else will eventually find them too…" The fox trailed off as a memory of golden lights against a wall of trees in the night flashed through his mind. *Nothing stays buried forever.* "Whatever this thing is," he carried on somberly, "someone tried to get rid of it before, yet here it is."

Both the fox and the rhino sank into silence. Chewgar kept his eyes on the planks of the tower's floor, probably devising other spots in the guardhouse below where they could bury the thing forever. Maxan meanwhile squinted toward the eastern horizon, to the city he saw bathed in the white light of the morning sun. Just then a bank of clouds obscured part of Yinna's radiance, and one of the three points of the Aigaion drove a black wedge into her side.

And Maxan saw the answer, clearly, across the city.

"I know where to bring it," he said.

FILE 126: "CONFESSIONS"

Time: 003280/11/19-[16:11:57-16:16:01]
Location: Castle Tower
Begin audio transcription:

You know, before all of this started, I considered ending my own life. I mean after I'd killed all of the rest of us, of course. Brought us all to justice. Made us all answer for our crimes. These ... perversions we created.

But I didn't.

How simple it would have been. Just switch the true for the false. One last time. What's one more life on top of ninety? But I was at an impasse. I couldn't do it. I suppose I lacked your level of conviction. Ha!

Do you think me a coward?

No?

Then tell me this... If it had just been the two of us left, the last Monitors, and you tore me to shreds, what would you do then, all alone? Rebuild everything? No. I think you would sit somewhere for a long time and have yourself a good think on all this. I wonder how much of what I'd done would sink in. Through that thick shell of yours. Ha! Ha!

Hmmm... Ahahhh... Hmm.

Tell me, are you capable of change?

No? You won't speak to me?

No. You won't speak to me. I should have expected as much. Well, have a think on it right now, then.

BLACK ROBES

CROSSWALL WAS A CAULDRON OF CULTURE. The kingdom of Leora boasted the most diversity of all the four kingdoms. While Corvidia was filled with graceful beings of the sky, Drakora with the slithery species of the swamps, and Peskora with a multitude of beings from various depths of the sea, all of Herbridia's nations and the species that populated them had gathered in this grand city for the last two decades, making it the mapped world's center of trade. This place became a symbol of rebirth after the death brought upon the world during the Thraxians' invasion—and their ultimate extermination—twenty years ago.

Maxan and Chewgar had avoided drawing too close to the center of the cross, packed with throngs day and night, sealing trade contracts, buying and selling goods, attending festivals, and bringing grievances to the courts just outside the palace steps. But mostly, it was the arena at the very center of Crosswall that drew the biggest crowds. The structure dominated the very heart of the city, and even from this distance, nearly half a mile away, Maxan's sensitive ears picked up the applause, the collective gasps, the howling laughter of the animals in the stands. Between him and the arena stretched a sea of animals, flowing between market stalls, demonstrations, and new buildings under construction. Smoke from cook fires filled the air with delicious scents of roasted field fowl, spiced and charred to perfection, mingled with simmering stews.

The fox and the rhino fought against the current of bodies flowing by. Maxan mostly stayed in the pocket of space created by the massive rhino's passing, but the closer they drew to the main thoroughfare leading to the arena, the smaller that pocket became. Just when the tide was tightest, there was a commotion to their left. A sounder of boars grunted and stamped; one cried "Thief!" and one punched out, misunderstanding his mate. A smaller, hooded figure dashed off toward the arena, drawing Maxan's full attention. The white tip of its bushy tail swished with its cloak. Then it was gone, merged with the crowd. Chewgar dipped his arms into the mass of bodies and parted them, meaning to pursue. The rhino took one step in but grunted and stopped short, frowning down at a scratch in his thigh where someone had pressed too close and nicked him with a claw. The sea of animals rolled around them.

"Chewgar," Maxan said, raising his voice over the querulous boars. "Whatever happened, we can't." He pressed a paw against his chest, feeling the thing concealed there under his shirt, to remind the rhino why they were here in the first place.

The boars protested as the two guards passed them by, hollering something about their betting and big chances at the lists. Chewgar hung his head and wouldn't meet their eyes. Maxan hoped the shrug and raised brows he paid them would suffice, then quickly caught up to his captain when the boars lowering tusks indicated they wouldn't.

The two guards made it through the throng of Crosswall's center and were just on the outskirts of the northern district—the "lords' district" it was also called—making their way eastward. The animals up here were clearly cut from more decorative cloth than any other in the city. These were the highborn families dating back generations, whether the offspring of war heroes and arena champions—those living and dead who'd earned enough fame to be immortalized as apotheosis figurines—or honored officers who served in the king's army. Here, one resided in an opulent mansion and strolled through lush gardens. Here, one could afford to blind the eyes of the Crosswall Guard if the first signs of the Stray started to show in your family. One could turn the Mind away if they came calling in the name of research. Maxan glanced north toward the cluster of extravagant buildings and wondered how many of these households had hidden chambers in their subfloors where those Stray relatives were caged. It wasn't so hard for the fox to picture their construction, having broken his way into dozens of those places in a former life. His eyes were snagged by nearly every gilded coin purse or decorative sword worn on the belts of the highborn strutting by.

"Max!"

Chewgar called to him from several yards farther down the cobbled street. Maxan hadn't realized that he'd fallen so far behind (again), enrapt as he was by the opulence of the lords' district.

"What? Your one giant stride makes, like, ten of mine." The fox trotted forward at an exaggeratingly slowed pace as if to prove his case. "See? It's just math. I can't help it!"

They came around to the eastern side of the central square, the high alcoves of the arena rising at their backs. The boundary here wasn't a wall like the one keeping the Stray trapped in the western district. It was a long line of water, a canal dug by the Mind's division of engineering and development nearly a decade ago, back when they first set about transforming the capital city. The beavers in charge of the project—if Maxan remembered correctly—had diverted the flow of the Radilin River, drawing the water north of the city to irrigate the farms there, then south to cut straight between the central and eastern districts before rejoining the river once more. Beyond the canal, the Mind's campus had grown to claim nearly all of Crosswall's eastern district.

As Maxan and Chewgar reached the apex of the arched bridge spanning the canal, the view of the eastern district took the fox's breath away. From wall to wall, the industry and complexity of the Mind's sprawling campus filled every inch of this place. To his left, crenelated towers and buttressed halls, galleries, and auditoriums squatted on the land, with grassy hillocks and graveled footpaths spaced randomly between them. To the south, massive wheels turned in the artificial current where the canal broke off, their slow revolutions turning whatever machinery the great blocks of buildings housed. Rising over all these were smokestacks spewing a never-ending stream of vapors—most of them black as night, but some laced with color: red, blue, green, pure white like the steam made from snow.

One color for each of the Mind's robed followers, Maxan realized. And here, the Mind's followers were everywhere.

Nearly every animal here wore a robe, cut to fit the size of the wearer's species and dyed to distinguish their role in the hierarchy. The Mind's followers swarmed every open space, bustling to and fro on some business, guiding carts packed with freshly printed books and scrolls or rattling with newly forged devices, gears, apparatuses, and utensils. A train of broad-shouldered gorillas in green initiates' robes hefted crates full of more objects and tools. Maxan spun about and observed another gathering on a hill not far away, where a red-robed scholar presided over a rapt audience of blue-robed students, many of whom scribbled marks into notebooks with pens or claw tips dipped in ink. Some more students walked past, miraculously weaving through the traffic without incident though their snouts were drawn down to the pages of the books they held in front of them. They drew Maxan's gaze back the other way, toward the center of the campus, where the enormous symbol of all the Mind's power rose to scrape the ceiling of the sky, like a giant's scepter stabbing the world.

If there's anyone who knows what to do with this thing, they'll be there.

"The Pinnacle," he murmured.

As though saying its name had woken the thing to action, its shadow angled away from the dumbstruck fox at that moment. The brightness of Yinna spilled over the Pinnacle's top and stung Maxan's eyes, casting everything around him in a hazy darkness. He shielded himself from the light and tried to search the crowd before him for the massive frame of his rhino captain, but some other glob of shadow crept from the lower side of the tower, drawing his gaze. Far away, sailing now just over the peaks of the Corvidian mountains, the Aigaion wandered into view. His golden eye twitched.

A sudden spear of pain brought Maxan to his knees. He caught himself with both paws and felt the rod slide down his flank toward his belly. His paw shot up to secure it just before it fell from the folds of his uniform.

If this hits the ground…

A red eruption of violence tore through Maxan's mind, with him at its epicenter—a vision of all these civilized, learned, studious animals clawing one another to pieces, snarling, growling, lapping blood spilled on the paved paths of the campus.

The spear wedged in his brain twisted, and he clutched the artifact tighter. A thought tried to form. He could feel it. A voice called out. He could hear it inside his head, but the meaning was all a jumble. Nothing made sense.

And then, as suddenly as it had struck, the pain was gone.

Something's not right. With who? With myself. I can't … think. I can't … think of the other side, what the other me would say. Something's…

"Something wrong, pal?"

This came from Maxan's left. Still on his knees, the fox could manage only "Ahh!"

"Hey, guy!" Each word was high-pitched, squeaky, shot rapidly in a string, yet exceptionally articulate. "I said hey, guy! Can I help you with something?"

"I… I…"

A pair of tiny paws hooked under Maxan's armpit and tried to heft him up, but the strength in them was minimal. The paws belonged to a young red-robed squirrel who beamed with pride once he saw Maxan regain his footing, even though he hadn't really done much of anything.

"Yer cloggin' the bridge, friend."

"I… ah, sorry."

"No problem!"

Before he could say more, Maxan felt a pair of massive feet storming down the bridge, and once again, he was covered in a towering shadow.

"Why can't you keep up, Max?" Chewgar glanced down at the squirrel boy. "Who're you?"

"I'm Pryth!" The juvenile rocked forward on the balls of his hind paws, rising a few inches higher, but he was still just a pebble against the boulder of the rhinoceros. At least his wide, bushy tail rose above Chewgar's belt. "Guards, hmm? Nice…" The squirrel spun his paw around as if trying to draw the right word to him. "Regalia!" he exclaimed, wide-eyed. "White and black. Official looking. Sharp! Anyway. Where you headed? Maybe I can help!"

"Not sure. We—" Maxan began, but Chewgar's voice rose over him swiftly.

"We've a delivery to make."

"Okay, I can take it," Pryth said, his tiny paw shooting out comically fast.

"I don't think so, little one," Chewgar said, a warm smile creasing the flat line of his mouth. "What we have is very…"

"Sensitive," Maxan finished for him.

Quite literally.

"For the Mind's leadership only."

"Is there a *high scholar*," Chewgar clarified, "or somebody we can speak to?"

"Yes! Sure! You semi-fainted in front of just the right squirrel scholar today, my red-furred fox friend! I know 'em! Follow me!"

Pryth was off, skittering across the bridge. Maxan and Chewgar looked at each other, shrugged, then followed the squirrel boy's bushy tail as it bobbed between the crowds, straight down the campus's main thoroughfare, and across another bridge that spanned the moat encircling the Pinnacle Tower.

The three of them stepped through into the grand hall. From the tall latticed windows just above them, Yinna's early-morning light streamed in and reflected off the polished marble floor, which was laid out in intricate symmetrical designs of white and black stone that repeated around the entire space. Along the north and south walls, two grand staircases coiled up and disappeared into the tower's next level, high above. Giant statues of behemoths—legendary beasts of immense size and no discernible species, which in ages past had been hunted for sport to extinction—served as supports for these staircases, all in various poses, from crouching beneath the stairs' lower landings to cradling the midsections to lifting the immense weight of their highest heights over their heads. Maxan stared wide-eyed at the monstrous pillars long enough to realize these behemoths were amalgamations of all five Herbridian species.

At the hall's western wall, an enormous iron wheel revolved steadily—no doubt attached to the water wheel that matched its movement in the canal outside along the tower's base. Its motion spun an intricate network of several hundred gears embedded in the tower's walls and floor. Several of the Mind's students observed machines encased in boxes of glass, which trapped purple streams of lightning that scratched ceaselessly at their transparent cages in a vain attempt to break free. Black cords attached to these contraptions stretched all around the grand hall; most were bolted to the walls or disappeared into the spaces between the room's giant slabs of stone. But some of these cords ended at the tops of tall lamps, diverting the lightning into glass spheres that glowed an unnatural blue. Combined with Yinna's golden brilliance shining down from the tall windows, the light cast everything in surreal outlines, and Maxan felt as though he were walking in a dream.

The turning of the great iron wheel also activated a series of pistons, which rose and fell rhythmically at both sides, pumping the canal's water through some unseen filter before feeding it into a sprawling network of tinkling streams set into the floor and the pipes of four small gurgling fountains that ringed the Pinnacle's circular center.

Maxan craned his neck upward and saw that the entire tower was hollow. The ringed levels high overhead formed a cone of empty space between their round balconies that became narrower as the tower's walls came closer together above. Long banners of green, blue, and red were fastened to the edge of every floor and swayed lazily in the air, all of them emblazoned with embroidered golden shapes—eyes, books, paws, candles, flames. *And triangles. Of course.* Maxan saw there were even two banners that appeared to depict Yinna surrounded by perfectly symmetrical waves of fire, and another resembling Yerda surrounded by her chaotic and scattered belt.

"Hey, pal." Maxan felt Pryth tug at his sleeve then reach up to close the fox's jaw, which had been hanging slack in amazement. "First time here? I know, I know. Never ceases to amaze!"

Maxan ignored the annoyed looks the short squirrel was drawing their way with his high-pitched voice. He pointed at the iron wheel, then the nearest glass sphere. "How do you …"

"We call it *electricity*!" Pryth beamed. "I know, I know! Sounds weird, right? Who comes up with this stuff? Not me!"

Inside the Pinnacle, there was not as much of a press of bodies as there was outside, but Maxan saw a series of cloisters carved into the wall ringing around the hall that were lined with bookshelves and filled with blue-robed figures, themselves a diverse collection of species, all with their eyes and ears focused on the scholar delivering a lecture or marking on a chalkboard. They were mostly Leoran—grayish-brown wolves from the Denlands, black rats, sleek-coated and dappled jaguars—but there was no mistaking the yellow or green or purple scales of the handful of Drakoran reptiles among them, nor the size of the folded wings on the backs of a few gathered Corvidians or the silver-scaled Peskorans sitting next to them.

"What are you all learning here?" Chewgar asked Pryth, his eyes on the same group as Maxan.

"Ha! What *aren't* we learning?" The boy rambled on enthusiastically, bending a claw back for every subject on his list. "Forces. Ethics. Economics. Botany. Biology. Laws. Mathematics. Rhetoric. History. Electromagnetism. Elements. I dunno. I'm probably forgetting something. Yes, I'm forgetting … astronomy! That's a new one. My favorite. Did you know Yerda's night glow comes from her smoldering core? I've seen it up close! Come back at night! We got these new lenses—*Hey! It's Principal Harmony!*"

Cold fear seized Maxan's stomach. *Did he say...*

Pryth pointed at a group of six figures on a raised circular dais along the central alcove wall between the two grand staircases. Three of them wore dark blue armor trimmed with solid gold and polished to a mirror shine, and on each of their faces was an ornate mask depicting a lion's furious face and flowing mane. Maxan recognized the soldiers immediately. Few Leorans in Crosswall wouldn't. *The king's personal guard.*

The other three wore long robes of the deepest black, entirely plain except for the Mind's triangular sigil stitched in gleaming golden thread over the rim of their pointed hoods. Maxan could see the design clearly on two of the figures—one lounging on a cushioned wooden chair with wheels, the other standing at its side. If it hadn't been for the set of long, curling claws emerging from the seated figure's sleeve, Maxan might have easily mistaken the frail thing as simply a robe tossed over a wooden frame, like a frightener used to keep pests away from a farmer's field. The standing figure stood over the other's shoulder, its paws clasped behind its back. Both had their hoods drawn so low that their faces were obscured in shadow.

But the third... her hood was thrown back, revealing a head of sweeping gray feathers, some of which rose above either ear like horns. Her black robe fell in a strip down her back, between a pair of folded gray wings.

Maxan tugged feebly at Chewgar's tunic. "We have to get out of here."

The rhino looked down at him, puzzled.

"From yesterday," Maxan whispered. "It's her."

"That's her!" Pryth told them, as high-pitched as ever. "Principal Harmony. Over there, see? Your lucky day, guys. They're not usually down here—not all three at a time. But seems we got a special visitor. The king. His own grand self! Oooh! But we better wait."

"No," Chewgar said flatly, laying a mighty hand on Maxan's shoulder, understanding the danger. "We better not."

The two guards wheeled about, meaning to blend in with the Mind's followers milling about the grand hall (as well as a rhino nearly twice anyone's height here could blend in) and make their way to the entrance. But the Mind's own armed and armored guards had already filed into the crowd, some massing at the tall doors, many surrounding the fox and the rhino.

"Nowhere to go but forward."

The gray-horned owl's calm voice froze Maxan's paws to the marble floor, froze all the blood in his body. Fear tingled in his paws. It stole his will. It pressed his ears against his head. Harmony turned about before the others on the dais, or rather her head swiveled around before her body, bringing the unnerving gaze of her wide, unblinking globes of abyssal dark upon the three of them.

He could not look away from those eyes.

Her movement brought the attention of the other five. One of the king's armored bodyguards took a heavy step forward. "Well, well." The voice was muffled by the lion-face mask, yet was so deep that it seemed to drown all other sounds in the hall. "I was wondering when we would meet again, boy."

A searing pain speared Maxan's brain behind his golden eye. He pressed a paw against the side of his muzzle. If not for Chewgar's firm grip on his shoulder, he would have toppled over. A tinny agony flooded his ears. He knew, somehow, that he should be thinking of something.

No... Something I should be thinking... Someone should be ... saying. Telling me. Trying to ... tell me something. Tell me that, it's him. It's...

But the thought never fully formed. Even if it had, it would have been wrong. The armored lion descended the steps and stood before them. But the knight was clearly more interested in Chewgar. Although the rhino was taller and broader, there was something in the way the lion held himself now, some power, that matched Chewgar evenly. There was an immensity of unspoken violence in the mere inches that separated them.

The knight removed his helmet. Beneath it was a lion with brilliant golden eyes, his face an identical copy to the mask but scarred. Horribly scarred.

"Chewgar," the lion purred.

"Locain," the rhino answered.

Oh...

The spear point of pain drew back just enough for Maxan's thought to complete itself. *Locain.*

King Locain.

"Tell me." The lion drew back his shoulders as he spoke up at Chewgar, his fangs flashing at the final word of each sentence. "You are still stationed on the west side of the cross. You must have passed the arena to get here. Did you join the lists? Did you seek me out to tell me yourself?" His gravelly voice rumbled, it seemed, in the very stones of the Pinnacle Tower, and with every word, the hulking rhinoceros seemed to shrink, smaller and smaller. "Finally ready to accept my challenge?"

The world seemed to pitch under Maxan's paws. A sudden dizziness swept over him. The strips of light cast from the tall windows high overhead seemed to double their pace across the floor and choose that precise moment to shine in his mismatched eyes. He lurched away involuntarily. The movement made it seem like he was beating an awkward retreat. Before he could stop it, a whimper dribbled quietly from his lips.

All eyes fell on Maxan then. Even Chewgar shot the fox a quick glance. The gray owl's serene, unflinching glare was most unnerving of all. Still, none of them moved. King Locain's bodyguards—who were truly his body *doubles*—flanked the seated black-robed figure, its curled claws clicking rhythmically against the armrest of its wheelchair.

Despite the ringing in his ears, Maxan heard the squirrel juvenile cough, then mutter, "Sheesh, pal…"

The king spared a chuckle at the reeling fox, then turned to the rhino again. Some of the intensity between them had dissipated, but he clearly expected an answer. "So. How many years has it been, boy?"

Chewgar's jaw clenched so tight it could've snapped an ax blade in half. "Fifteen years."

"Fifteen years," Locain repeated, drawing out every syllable. "And perhaps you'd hoped I wouldn't recognize you anymore?"

When Chewgar made no reply, the corners of Locain's mouth lifted like curtains, showing an empty space in the row of fangs that aligned perfectly with one long scar. "I will never forget you. I know your line like I know my own. Not a coward among them. Honorable warriors, all." Locain stepped back. His smile faded as he looked the rhino up and down. "All but one, it seems. I have waited. Patiently. For resolution. Tell me, boy, that it is why you've come here. To seek me out, so we can put an end to this … question."

Chewgar's huge hands squeezed so tightly, the muscles all along his arms seemed ready to burst. It seemed for a moment that he would ram his fist so hard against the Leoran king's chest that the plate armor would simply disintegrate from his fury.

But the moment passed. The tension in his arms released. Chewgar's eyes fell away from the lion's. His great horn dipped, then his whole massive frame lowered. Chewgar kneeled before the king of Leora. That's when Maxan realized, despite the throbbing pain in his head, that a hush had come over the entire grand hall of the Pinnacle Tower. The Mind's guards, its scholars, students, and initiates, animals of every species in robes of many colors, were ringed around the two guards from the western district, which might as well have been a whole world away, watching.

"Locain," Chewgar said, his head still bowed. "My king. I must apologize. Because the business I bring is not for you."

Now it was the king's turn to seethe. The lion's eyes narrowed. Razor-sharp claws slid out ever so slightly from the ends of his broad paws. But Chewgar barely noticed. It seemed like he'd already forgotten the king.

Although he understood little, if anything, of what was going on between them, Maxan had never felt more pride for his friend the rhino. The feeling helped chase away the fear crawling under his skin and the pain behind his eyes.

Chewgar raised his horn and settled his sight on the gray owl, Principal Harmony. "I've come to see what the Mind can do about the fires that burn in the western district, to request more resources—or some strategy at least—to ensure we preserve as much of Crosswall as we can while we wait for the affliction to subside. Just last night, an inn beyond the safe zone burned to the ground. This fox under my command was the sole witness. We had no choice but to let it burn.

"But that's not the worst of it," Chewgar went on, rising to his full height and stepping around the king. "The destruction left a hole in the district's defenses, and the Stray flooded in. The guardhouses in the western district lack the numbers, equipment, and training to make headway into the Stray's territory. Each day, we push more afflicted one way into quarantine, while the Stray push them from the other. We cannot count how much of the city is lost, how many dead…"

Chewgar trailed off. He averted his eyes and appeared to be a little choked up. Maxan glanced around the grand hall.

Every animal in the vicinity—the Mind's three principals, the king's bodyguards, even King Locain himself—everyone seemed to hang on the rhinoceros captain's plea. Maxan realized then where the pride he felt truly came from.

This is the greatest con I've ever seen.

"How many more have to die?" Chewgar swept a hand behind him, indicating the lion. "King Locain is well aware, I'm sure, of what's happening within the walls of his capital. But nothing is being done. This is why I've come before you today.

"Perhaps," he went on, turning to lock his eyes with the king's once again, "when I know the folk in my district are safe from danger, hunger, and persecution, the business I bring will involve you."

Silence reigned. The only sound was the subtle rumbling of King Locain's every breath. For seconds that seemed like hours, no one moved. Then the black-robed figure in the wheelchair raised its arm. It hadn't made any sound—Maxan's ears would've picked it up—yet, as if she had eyes in the back of her feathered head, Harmony's gaze swiveled around, and she answered the figure's summons. She leaned in close to its shadowed hood, then stood and clasped her taloned hands before her waist. Before she spoke, she swept her unblinking eyes across the whole hall, and all the work and study of the Mind immediately resumed.

"Thank you, Captain," she said in a soothing voice. "You have moved us. Deeply. Something will be done. Soon.

"And to you," Harmony said, turning her attention to Locain before Chewgar could even bow in gratitude, "you will kindly resume your campaign to quell the Denland rebellion. I trust that you have everything you need to end it once and for all, and there will be no further need to visit the Pinnacle on such business."

Locain—a titled, celebrated warrior, king of all Leora, the Golden Lord himself—suddenly seemed so small, so petty, in the presence of the Mind's principals. The lion likely meant for his few retreating steps to signify a kind of disdain for those towering over him, but anyone could see that the movements were a little too hasty. But there were very few onlookers now.

No one's ever spoken to him like that, Maxan thought. *Not since his reign began, and how long ago was that?* Maxan's eyes widened as the clues fell into place. He looked at Chewgar. *Fifteen years.*

Locain motioned for his identically armored body doubles to join him. He donned the golden lion-faced helmet as the pair flanked him at the bottom step of the dais. The king shifted his weight, as if about to stride away, but stopped. He turned instead back to Chewgar, his rumbling voice barely above a whisper through the mask. "You may have convinced them, for a time, that you're something beyond yourself. They don't know what you chose. But I do. I know who you really are, boy."

The king nodded to the three black-robed principals, turned, and disappeared into the bustling crowds of the Pinnacle's grand hall.

Maxan knew Locain was smiling under his mask. His farewell seemed to diminish the pride that had swelled in Chewgar just a moment ago. The rhino seemed somehow shorter, somehow weaker. He ran a rough hand across his broad chin and up the side of his great horn as if trying to rouse himself from a nap.

Are you okay? Maxan wanted to ask, but being in this place, in the presence of the Leoran king, and bearing witness to his own friend exposing that king's smallness, had shocked him into silence.

"Golden Lord? Pffth!" Maxan's ears fanned out to catch Pryth's hushed, parting commentary. "More like golden butt." The juvenile squirrel looked up at the fox, shrugged, and smiled.

If Harmony had heard him, she gave no indication, only stared curiously at the pair of city guards like they were a pair of purple leaves that had blown into her tower. The seated figure behind her stirred and coughed, its heavy, curling claws clicking against one another. The shadowed hood of the one standing turned to regard this.

Pryth cleared his throat dramatically, though it was more like a squeak. "Well, so now!" he called jubilantly, clapping and rubbing his paws together. "Seems like nothing left to discuss. Off you go, guys. Nice speech by the way. Someone oughta—"

Harmony raised her taloned hand, and all the playful nature in the squirrel was blown out like a candle in a hurricane. Pryth's jaw went slack. His eyes drooped visibly, his enormous bushy tail sank to the floor, and his tongue lulled. It was all so sudden, as though an invisible hand had twisted the squirrel boy's brain around inside his skull. His body spun about, and he slunk away without another word.

With all that had happened since the two guards crossed the threshold to the grand hall, Maxan had somehow forgotten what he had seen the gray owl do not even one day before. And he had forgotten the decision he and Chewgar had made together on the top of the guardhouse.

"I know where to bring it," he had said.

How could I have known?

Maxan expected his inner voice of reason to chime in any second, to assure him, to warn him, to say anything, however insipid or insightful. The pain in his skull had seemingly cut his mind in half. Only clipped thoughts screeched through.

Wrong.

Maxan shook his head.

Go.

But Harmony had already started speaking.

"Your friend," she said to Chewgar, her every word like a lilting breath of wind, "he is not well."

The seated principal coughed, and the coughing became a terrible, rattling, scraping fit. Overcome with concern, the standing principal brought both paws from around its back and laid them on the handles of the wheelchair. The fur on those paws was white as snow.

"We know... ," Harmony said, letting her words hang an uncomfortably long time, "that it is not fire you came to speak of, Captain."

"No," Chewgar admitted. He glanced nervously at Maxan.

Harmony's unsettling gaze locked on the fox. "What is your name?"

Maxan tried to reply but found his voice unable to rise above a murmur. He cleared his throat and tried again. "Maxan."

"No doubt you told your captain what happened? What you saw?"

Maxan knew she wasn't asking. He knew that she knew the answer already.

"I assure you," she continued, swiveling her head back to Chewgar and blinking, the first time Maxan had ever seen her do so, "he identified himself as a guard. And he performed his duties admirably. However, he engaged with an enemy of Crosswall. Of the Mind itself. Our greatest enemy. Long have they sought the means to destroy us, to undo our great works, and so bring ruin to our world." Harmony turned back to the fox. "I assume, Maxan, that you must be upset about what happened. I assure you that if you were meant to die in that place, you simply," she blinked again, a sign of how sincerely she meant what she said, "would not be here. You're very lucky."

"What about Yacub?" Chewgar asked. A trickle of sweat ran down the rhino's face.

Not sweat, Maxan realized. *Rhinos don't sweat. It's a tear. His eyes are watering.*

"The hyena?" Without moving her body, the owl swiveled her head around to regard the other two principals, relaying the question to them.

The snow-white paws pulled back the wolf's black hood. From the side of his hideously scarred face, Feyn's breath rushed as he came to Harmony's side.

"Not so lucky," he said.

Harmony stared at her fellow black-robed principal as if she expected Feyn to say more. The wolf's icy blue eyes narrowed at the owl. He heard the agitation grating in his throat.

"I suppose," Harmony said, once again turning back to the guards, "you are wondering why we met with such a nefarious individual. That it might call into question our motives."

"We were a little curious," Chewgar said, exchanging a look with Maxan.

"Fate, as it turns out. Specifically, the hyena's. He found something of immeasurable value on his ... travels. When word reached the Mind of his discovery, we acted quickly, lest the artifact fall into the clutches of our enemy."

"Who were they?" The words were out before Maxan could even consider holding them back. "The Corvidian. The..." He swallowed his rising fear. "The Drakoran."

"And the fox." Harmony's black eyes bored into him.

Feyn took an impetuous step forward, his paw snapping out at Maxan, claws upturned, a thin line of red staining the bandage on his forearm. "Enough," he snarled. "You have it, don't you?"

Just then, a massive shadow crept over the sky above Crosswall, snuffing out the beams of sunlight falling through the Pinnacle's tall windows, one by one. Even the electric lamps seemed to dim in the artificial twilight. Feyn closed his eyes and raised his muzzle, sensing the unseen power, his nostrils flaring as he savored the air.

"It's... ," Maxan stammered. He clutched the thing under his shirt instinctively at Feyn's advance, squeezing it tightly, recalling all the chaos it had caused, and imagining the marble floor of the Mind's tower splashed with blood. "It's ... the Aigaion. Isn't it?"

Harmony laid a gentle talon on her fellow principal's out-stretched paw. The wolf reeled about, fangs bared in fury, as if to bite her feathered throat. But he didn't. His snarling faded as the owl held him in her abyssal gaze. He relented and drew his paw away from Maxan.

"You know much," she told the fox.

Maxan wondered then, *If Corvidian beaks could smile, would she be smiling now?*

Harmony's eyes shined in the dark that shrouded the grand hall. The dying horizon light of the world outside limned each latticed window in an orange glow. Her gaze fixed on Maxan's chest knowingly. "It is the means to bring ruin."

It... Maxan wanted to say the words aloud, but found he could not. *It ruined my life.*

"You saw, did you not?" Her voice was soothing. "You want to be rid of it, do you not?" She calmly opened her taloned hand before him.

I do.

That was it? No objection from the voice of reason? Is this what Maxan wanted?

He produced the artifact, the relay, from the folds of his tunic. The golden, glowing lights raced in their perpetual circuit, casting mesmerizing shafts of radiance and shadow in tandem all around.

The gleaming chrome was so cool against his paw. It weighed almost nothing, yet he struggled to lift it any closer to Harmony.

"Have no fear, my child," Harmony said. The fingers of her talon closed around it. "This belongs with the Mind."

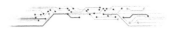

The roar of the crowd was deafening.

Even with her back turned on the spectacle of violence far down in the center of the arena, the noise crashed against Rinnia like rolling waves. She shuddered, pulled her hood even farther down her muzzle, almost to the tip of her snout, and pressed her ears even flatter to her head. Her futile attempt to escape only seemed to make the savage crowds cheer all the louder.

But when it came to finding a good vantage point where one could observe the central gateway to the Mind's campus, there was no better option than the outermost high wall of Crosswall's arena, at the city's center. Although she had not slept in more than two days, her blue eyes were alert. They swept across the sea of green and blue and red robes coming and going over the massive stone bridge spanning the canal that surrounded the triangular tract of land the Mind had claimed for itself. The ebb and flow of bodies was ceaseless.

"The enemy never rests," she grumbled to herself. "So why should I?"

Rinnia's tired eyes didn't linger on the Mind's members. Her gaze constantly shifted to those animals caught up in the mass of movement who were not covered in colored robes, searching for a pair of uniforms in the blinding white and jet black of the Crosswall Guard.

"They sure make an odd pair," she mumbled aloud.

"What's that, sissster?"

Behind her, Saghan leaned lazily against an arched support. Although his body faced the raucous carnage of the arena, his slit eyes were focused solely on the grilled leeks he held in his hand, wrapped in a wide lily leaf paper and imported from the outskirts of Drakora. The pungent vegetables were a delicacy in his homeland. His sharp nails pinched a leek. His forked tongue caressed it to savor its flavor, and his wide mouth engulfed it, bite by bite. She wanted a bite for herself, but she wasn't sure if he'd cleaned the bane poison from his nails yet, and she didn't feel like asking.

"Talking to yourself again, I sssee," he said between bites when Rinnia made no reply.

Another roar of applause quaked the ancient bricks of the stadium. Rinnia felt it surge through the pads of her lower paws and rattle in her bones. She shuddered. She wished she could just lie down, sleep. Somewhere far away, quiet. Forget everything she had done.

Her reptilian brother Saghan had made a full recovery from the damage his firebomb had inflicted last night. All of the shrapnel wounds had stitched themselves closed. All the bones had reset. Besides the shredded pieces of his dark red armor, there was no trace that the snake had suffered any damage whatsoever.

By contrast, her Corvidian sister Sarovek had struggled to pull through the night. Despite the miraculous powers of their order's secret panacea formula, the hawk had been wracked by fever and fits, thrashing and squawking all the night through. After dragging Saghan back to the safe house, Rinnia refused to abandon her sister's side. She knew Sarovek would do the same for her.

She could have really used the hawk's acute vision right about now. A snake's eyesight was shit, after all, and a fox's wasn't much better. Rinnia's fanged mouth split open for an enormous yawn, but the sudden eruption from the crowds over her shoulder nearly made her choke. Without thinking, as if drawn by an invisible leash, she spun about to see the commotion.

A falcon knelt at the center of the pit. The blood spurting from his thigh stained the sandy floor red. This was Bennis the Sunspear, leader of the Corsairs, a troop of Corvidian warriors who had been earning glory in the Leoran arena for the last several months. His apotheosis figurines had just been minted, and his name had been demolishing its way to the top of the lists ever since. But the falcon's fame wouldn't last much longer.

Only a few strides away, a warrior encased in plates of dark blue armor etched with shimmering gold discarded his barbed whip in the dust, satisfied with the wounds it had left in the falcon's knee, the ruins it had left of the Corvidian's wings. They looked like the dying trees of autumn; the leaves were the Corvidian's feathers and the branches his bones.

The warrior's face was hidden behind a mask of solid gold shaped like that of a lion. A halo of long golden fur spilled onto the animal's armored shoulders, and the crowd erupted into a frenzy that could be heard for miles.

Flattening her ears as best she could, Rinnia could not look away. She finally understood the crowd's relentless furor today.

Locain, the king of Leora, tossed his priceless golden mask over his shoulder. It landed in sand spattered red with the blood of Bennis's Corsairs. They were the lucky ones. Their deaths had been swift. Locain had shown today why he was a legend of the lists, why his rule was absolute. His cruel whip had snatched the Corsairs from the sky, one by one, dragged them close, and broken them upon the spiked tower shield at his side. It was a fighting style that had earned the lion one of his more popular titles, the Anvil.

Bennis fell onto his side, scrabbling for his spear, screeching in anguish as his useless wing snapped even more degrees the wrong way. He swung his weapon in a wide arc, trying for Locain's ankles. The clang of its bladed point against the lion's steel rang through the arena. Locain hefted his shield high and brought it down on the shaft of Bennis's spear, then again on the thin bone of the falcon's forearm, biting both to bits with a sickening crack. The crowd howled wildly. The species here were of one mind. They slathered for more blood. They chanted Locain's name and demanded Bennis's death.

"It's probably not even him." Saghan's long neck had brought his head around to rest on his sister's shoulder, his forked tongue snapping at the hood against her flattened ear. He had to shout to be heard. "The real Locain fights with a great sword."

Rinnia shrugged away from him and returned to her vantage point over the Mind's campus. She felt disgusted—by the spectacle, by the crowds, but mostly by herself for allowing it all to draw her in. Behind her, the hysteria died down to a kind of breathless anticipation as all the animals focused on the lion pacing around the falcon.

"This world was made to bleed," Saghan said, observing the souring look on his sister's face. He slurped his last grilled leek and dropped the wadded lily paper at his feet. "Even with the imprints of their masters gone, the violence is esssssential. It's in their nature."

"You talk like we're any different."

"We are. Because *we know*."

Rinnia tightened her jaw, crushing the argument rising within her before she could scream it. She'd already said too much. She knew what she really was, what all of this really was—the kingdoms, the city, the arena. The species, the weapons, the blood. She'd already spoken her mind countless times to Saghan, trying to get him to realize the truth: that it was all just a game.

But it was useless. Saghan had been made for a singular purpose—to be an indestructible vessel to host his master's undying mind whenever, wherever, for any reason, for as long as it took. There was no escape for him. Not like there could be for her. For all the jealousy Rinnia felt over Saghan's body's ability to heal, she often wondered if he felt the same of her mind. She had been born free, with no imprint, no strings, no voice, no will but her own.

She was sure of it. She had to be.

Rinnia observed her reptilian brother, wondering if it was really him right now and not their master who was nonchalantly cleaning his sharp nails.

A maddening roar ripped through the air. She didn't have to see to know that the armored lion, perhaps the king's impersonator, had satisfied the crowd's demand. With a sigh, she resumed her watch over the expanse of the Mind's campus. And she found what she'd been searching for.

"They're coming back."

Saghan was at her shoulder. "I see them."

"How much longer does the rhinoceros have?"

"No telling." Saghan's membranous brilles blinked over his eyes as he stared out over the crowds. He shrugged. "He's a big one."

"We should've hit the fox."

Rinnia didn't look away from the two guards wending their way through the crowds, but she felt the snake's eyes turn on her. She heard the flicking of his forked tongue.

"And they say *I'm* cold-blooded."

II

THE TOWER

CHAPTER SIX
THE WILD HUNT

THE AIGAION HAD PASSED THE CITY HOURS ago. The afternoon had come and gone while Maxan and Chewgar worked their way westward, chasing the arc of Yinna as she drew closer to a horizon painted the deep purple and blue of twilight. Their pace slowed, the feeling of urgency from the morning hardly remembered. Doubt seemed to cling to Maxan's heels.

"This belongs with the Mind," she said. He repeated Principal Harmony's words with every step he took away from the Pinnacle Tower. Every time he heard them, he hoped he would suddenly believe it was true.

Why can't I?

Kill them. He remembered the wolf, Feyn, the blood running from his forearm. The ferocity in his voice. *Harmony, kill them all.*

And then she did. Or she tried to.

It always *felt* different when Maxan's inner voice of reason spoke to him. Even though the thoughts were flowing now without pain, without interference, hours after leaving the Mind's campus, he felt abandoned.

If there's one place in all Crosswall, in all the world, where the relay can be safe, it's with them. Right? With the principals, the callers, who tried to kill me. Right?

His downcast eyes watched the cobblestone street slip by under his hind paws. He didn't care much to look up and see exactly where he was.

Ahh! What's the use? It's out of my paws now. If I can't trust the Mind, I can't trust anybody! Maxan grimaced. He told himself it was true, but the doubt still gnawed at him. *They help us. They feed us. They give us hope. They make us better than what we are. Don't they?*

He looked up just in time, nearly colliding with Chewgar's bulk as the rhino leaned against a building. They were somewhere in the center of the cross, nearing the western wall, though still very much in view of the arena. All around them, merchants and bookies in service to the daily lists were packing up their wares and scrolls and dumping the small fortunes they'd won that day into their moneybags under the watchful eyes of their bodyguards. A few more minutes' walk and the two guards would pass the quarantine gate and soon be home.

But looking at Chewgar, Maxan was sure it would take them longer.

"Hey," he said, the first word either had spoken for hours, "you all right?"

Chewgar grunted, scratched at his leg, and wiped away the moisture seeping from his eyes. "I'll be fine," he said at the end of a very long exhalation. "Something I ate."

Maxan had seen Chewgar devour the strangest dishes by the bucketload for years in the guardhouse mess hall, and never once had the rhinoceros suffered from an upset stomach.

I've never seen him suffer from any illness, come to think of it.

"Let's rest for a moment. Over here."

The fox led the way around a corner into a long alley separating two taverns that catered to the daily revelers who couldn't afford entry to the arena and instead turned to their apoth boards and dice for amusement. With the contests closed for the day, the taverns were all but empty, and the alley between them was lit by the dim glow of the dying hearths behind their grimy windows. Chewgar sank against one brick wall and splayed out his massive legs, long enough to touch the other tavern. Maxan flicked aside his bushy tail and sat cross-legged at his side.

Chewgar's eyes closed, releasing a fresh runnel of tears that carved a dark line of black across his dry gray skin. Seeing him like this, one might find it hard to recall how easily the rhinoceros had reduced the king of all Leora to a whimpering kitten.

"Chewgar," Maxan said. The rhino pried his eyes open with some difficulty.

"Huh?"

"Ah… So, how do you know King Locain?" Maxan swallowed, deciding to ask the question he really meant. "What was all that about a challenge?"

The rhino's chest swelled, and he let out a great gust of a sigh. The question seemed to rouse him. "You never told me about your arm," he replied at last. "Why I never see you without that glove."

Confused, Maxan held up his right arm and flexed his paw. "What does this have to do with anything?"

"You've never told me because you think there's some reason I don't need to know. I've respected that for years. I stopped asking. But I remember very well the first time we met, long before you showed up at the guardhouse. I remember your arm wasn't wrapped up like that. Something happened to you. Something you don't want to talk about."

"So this is how you tell me you don't want to talk about how the king of all Leora knows *who you really are?*" Maxan's best impression of Locain's throaty, rumbling voice fell flat, but not as flat as the attempt at humor behind it.

"I haven't ever wanted to," said Chewgar, drawing one leg closer to hold up a massive forearm. "Sometimes I'd see a grass-lander looking at me. A kudu. A cheetah. Heh, even another rhino. Whoever. Just staring. I'd know they knew me, maybe knew my father. But I think most folk have forgotten who I was. What I was. And I think… I don't want them to remember."

Maxan recalled the vendors on their way to the campus who had gladly offered the passing rhinoceros skewers of meat earlier that day, or slices of ripe fruit, even swatches of fabric, all free of charge, but Chewgar had graciously declined everything. At the time, preoccupied as he was with the dangerous thing tucked into his uniform, Maxan assumed they'd all mistaken the captain for some famous contender in the arena.

"But I've known you long enough now," Chewgar went on, "longer than anyone else I've ever known, actually." The rhino wagged a finger at the fox. "If I tell you about Locain and me, you tell me what you keep under that glove."

It could have been an order from his superior officer, but Maxan knew better. Chewgar was his friend.

"Deal," he said.

"Huh. Oh. I didn't think you'd go for it." Chewgar took the deepest breath Maxan had ever heard him take, held it, and released it with a gust that could have powered a Peskoran skiff for miles downriver. "Locain killed my family," he said flatly. "One after the other. In single combat. In a single day. Until it was just me." He left a long gap of silence after each confession.

Maxan listened to everything, unsure of what to say that could fill the deepest silence of all that followed.

Chewgar continued at last. "It's our way. Up north, in the tribal lands. After the Thraxians were exterminated, Locain returned to Leora as our most honored hero. The king before him had fallen in battle somewhere in Thraxia when all the trouble first began. But the war did a good job of distracting everyone for a time from the question of who would lead Leora when it was all over. And then it *was* all over. Most tribal warriors returned to the north, battered and broken, and Locain saw his chance. He didn't rest like the other soldiers. Just went straight to all the tribes of the Golden Grasses and challenged every chief who wouldn't kneel before him. Well, they all did. All except my father."

Chewgar glanced sideways at the fox. "So that's it."

"Do you hate him?" was all Maxan could think to ask.

The rhino's jaw flexed, his flat rows of teeth grinding over each other thoughtfully. "It's our way," he said. To Maxan, it sounded like a kind of reassurance the rhino told himself.

One which he doesn't necessarily believe.

"I should say," Chewgar went on, "it's *their* way. I'm not tribal anymore. Haven't been since the day I left. Before that day... All of my memories of my father are of his gentleness, but I saw him from time to time bring justice to the enemies of our tribe. I knew he could fight, but not like the lion. My father knocked Locain so far across the dust and charged, his horn leading the way. I thought it was over. But..."

Chewgar's eyes focused blankly on the dying light behind the windows across the alley, yet only saw the bitter memory replaying, leaving Maxan to fill in the unspoken details.

"In the tribes," the rhino resumed, "when the chief falls, the next in line becomes chief. Male or female. So it was with my mother. My father's corpse wasn't even cold, and Locain asked her if she would pledge our lands, our people, to his united banner. She refused. Then my brother refused after she fell. Then my sister. And so it was up to me."

Maxan watched Chewgar's hand ball into a fist tight enough to crush stone into dust. The veins in his giant gray arms swelled until they looked like cords threading under his skin. There was no doubt now that the tears flowing from his eyes were real. "Locain was hurt. My family had done its work well, but not well enough. I should have finished it. I could have… but I was afraid."

"I …understand." Maxan wasn't sure his friend would take the remark for the pure truth that it was instead of just some sentiment to fill another long silence.

The night I ran from my mother's den… the night the fire ate the granary…

The moment I let go, and the owl took it away…

Yes. All of it. I was afraid.

"Locain knew I was afraid. I was five years old, maybe. I mean, big for a five-year-old, you know." Chewgar meant to chuckle but coughed instead. He spat out a wad of phlegm that sailed down the alley. "The Golden Lord may be a skilled warrior, but he is not without honor. In front of all my… all my *father's* people, our whole tribe, he said that he would wait for the day when I was ready. But he had me taken away from my home, like a prisoner, to be raised in Crosswall, trained as a soldier and guard."

"Yovan," Maxan whispered. He hadn't thought about the stag—with his great, long spear and his great, tall antlers—in a long time. Yovan was a Denland knight the two of them had known, though the rhino was far more familiar with him than the fox was.

"Yovan," Chewgar echoed. "The night we first met, Max, he and I had been on the road to Crosswall for nearly a week already. After Locain and all his warriors left, when it was just

Yovan, waiting 'til I was ready, I didn't want to leave my home. But I think the stag knew my people, knew how they saw me after my family fell and I refused to fight. I had to leave. Everyone there told me exactly what I was."

For as long as Maxan had known Chewgar, there had always been an edge of humor to everything that came out of the rhino's mouth. However slight it might be, and even in the gravest of situations, somehow his captain—his friend—found some shred of lightheartedness others could never see.

But it was not so now. Chewgar's voice was hollow. "A coward," he confessed.

"You're not a coward. You made the smart play."

Chewgar only stared sunken-eyed at the fox.

"I'm serious," said Maxan. "Better to be a living coward than a dead hero."

The words were already out before Maxan realized his mistake, and his cynical self suddenly sprang to life there to chide him.

A living coward, huh, Max? But a coward all the same.

"I didn't mean it like that." He fumbled for the right words as Chewgar turned his eyes away. "What I mean is… what's the point? Bravery and fear. Heroes and cowards. You want them to cut a figurine of you? Scrape you across a game board? Build a statue of you? Chisel some title onto it? It's all shit! Dead is dead. You're alive, here and now, because you made a choice, and this city—your *real* people—we're grateful for the good you're trying to do."

Hey, that sounded pretty good.

You should know, Max. It's what you tell yourself.

"Is being a coward something you can grow out of?" the rhino said. "If you're a coward once, just once, but then brave your entire life afterward… if you die doing something brave…

are you always and forever a coward who's just pretending to be something else?"

The silence this time spanned the memory of Maxan's lifetime. *My mother. My escape. Yovan. Desperation, starvation, thievery. The Commune. The granary.* His whole story played itself out in an instant.

What am I? What ... made me?

"They set fire to my gang's old hideout." His mouth seemed to move automatically. "We were called the Commune. Foxes, all of us foxes. All of us thieves and burglars. Pretty good at it too. I would have died without them." Maxan heard himself say this last bit and huffed at the irony.

And I'd have died with *them if I hadn't chosen to walk away. I remember. The day I chose not to kill.*

Maxan felt the phantom of the dagger she pressed into his palm. He had looked up from it, saw her eyes. Was she really asking him to do this? Her eyes told him she was. Written in those eyes was the order, the demand. Plunge the blade hilt deep. Prove you belong. Because this is who we are.

He remembered her name. *How could I ever forget? Safrid.*

"Who were they?" said Chewgar, and Maxan knew he did not mean the foxes who had saved him, then ultimately damned him. He had meant the ones that brought it all down in flame.

"I don't know. Some animals that had it in for foxes, I guess. Haven't seen any of us around ever since. The night it happened, I'd had some ... disagreement, and I fled. But then I remembered what it was like to be alone in this place, and I went back." *Like a coward.* "And when I tried to save them..."

Tried to save her.

He held up his right arm, and Chewgar understood.

The sky directly overhead had darkened to the color of charred steel, and the stars twinkled like the glowing sediment beneath a layer of ash. Maxan peered down the long alley at the strip of horizon that burned like embers in the forge, the black profiles of the buildings beyond the central wall running in a jagged line against the color. And across the wide avenue just in front of them, atop an arch that connected the two structures on either side of the narrow alleyway, Maxan saw her. Or saw her ghost, rather. Safrid. She watched them with deep sea-blue eyes that lit the twilight darkness.

"Wait," said Maxan, blinking, but the apparition didn't go away. "Chewgar, there she is."

"What? Who?"

"Her," Maxan whispered.

The fox did not move. She merely stared down at Maxan and his giant friend, watching them, silent.

"Rinnia," Maxan said.

Now that she'd finally caught the guards' attention, she rose, balanced expertly atop the arch, and sprang up the side of the building. Three nimble steps and a flip added for style, and she was on the roof. Rinnia spun about, and there was a challenge in the angle of her body, the paw on her hip, the flash of her smile.

"What are you waiting for?" Chewgar rose with a speed one might not expect from a massive, ill rhinoceros.

"Huh?"

"You're a shadow. Time to do your job!"

"By the time I get up there, she'll be go—*oooaaAAAAH!*"

The rhino hooked an arm under the fox's rump, scooped him up, and flung him powerfully into the air overhead.

Maxan soared high and fast, his natural sense of gravity forgotten for the briefest of moments, replaced by the joy young Corvidians must feel at their first flight. And if Chewgar had been off by a single degree, Maxan might have crashed through the windowpane just under the tiled edge of the rooftop where he landed.

The years of training he'd put in with the Commune and the muscle memory he had honed as a shadow commanded his body to fold and tumble and release its chaotic momentum in a centrifugal motion until he regained enough control to come up expertly in a somersault. Without thinking, without planning (though it almost certainly appeared he had), Maxan rolled into a crouch, slammed his gloved right paw on the roof, came to a full stop, and rose slowly to face Rinnia, no more than ten feet away.

Now it was her mouth's turn to hang agape.

"Please," Maxan started.

But before he could finish with "stay," she had already burst into a sprint along the tiled edge, chasing the dusk blooming to the west.

Maxan called down to his captain "What do I do?"

"Follow her, you idiot!" the rhino yelled back, charging with so much force down the narrow alley some of its cobblestones cracked. "And I'll follow you!"

Whether by order of his captain, or that of his own curiosity, Maxan forgot all his aches and exhaustion. Instinct seized his body, and he ran after her, after the bushy amber tail he saw dancing left and right to keep a precarious balance. She was more than just a suspicious visitor to Crosswall to be questioned by a guard, more than the Mind's so-called greatest enemy. She was more to Maxan than just his duty. Rinnia was part of a question he'd had no answer to for ten years.

You're a fox. The first words she'd said to him echoed in his mind.

And you have answers, his thoughts replied.

The two foxes bounded across the rooftops for two minutes as straight west as the path of narrow top beams allowed, heading for the central wall that cut off the quarantined district from the rest of Crosswall. They closed in on a cluster of buildings sprouting from the wall's side. Maxan recognized this place. Knowledge of landmarks—and the calculations of speed, steps, and seconds it would take to reach any of them—flashed by his mind's eye faster than the buildings below. A grand chimney of a gambling house—unironically constructed after its namesake, the Hearth Tower—loomed only thirty yards ahead, and Rinnia was clearly headed straight for it.

She ran full sprint at the brick chimney, leapt, and rode her momentum straight up to its top, grasping its edge and lifting herself effortlessly to stand atop it. The rising smoke from the inn curled around her legs and tail as she observed her pursuer's reaction.

Maxan matched her maneuvers, clambering up beside her mere seconds later.

"Wait," he coughed through the haze of smoke, but she was already gone. Coming through the veil surrounding the chimney's rim, he saw her now turned, waiting on the top of the high central wall thirty feet of precarious, empty space away. She'd made it across with nothing but the bone-shattering pavement of the street below to catch her.

"How'd you get ... all that way...? Huh?" Maxan choked on chimney smoke as he stood up.

"C'mon," Rinnia called to him. "You can make it! You're not doing too bad, considering..."

"Considering *what*?" Maxan replied indignantly.

"Considering you're hurt," she said playfully.

If her smile wasn't so beautiful, he thought, *I'd very much like to kick it off her face.*

The orange burn of Yinna's fading light had almost faded. Gas-fueled lamps flickered to life along the streets below—a contribution the Mind had provided to every district except the western. Lights glowed behind the translucent windowpanes of the buildings around them. Rinnia's sea-blue eyes were twin jewels in the galaxy twinkling over their heads.

Despite the gap, she was so close. Maxan felt he could reach out and grasp her wrist.

And fall to your death.

Or I could tackle her.

And send both of us to our deaths? Why not shove her over the side?

I can't jump that far!

Sure you c—

No! What am I—are you thinking? I don't want to kill her.

Again, she struck her angular pose. The sight irritated Maxan's eyes more than the acrid smoke. As he blinked through it, a flash of silver drew his eye, a taut line spanning the space between them. *A thin rope of some kind.* The metal pincer at its farthest end had bitten into the edge of the stone wall under her; her paw held the rest and fed it into a spool clasped to her belt.

Rinnia smirked at Maxan's puzzled expression and smiled but said nothing.

"What is that thing?"

Rinnia's eyes fell away and traced the streets to either side of the Hearth Tower's chimney. "Your friend. The big rhino. He coming soon?"

"Friend?" Maxan bristled. She was toying with him, stalling. He grappled again for control of the conversation. "Why are you running?"

"Why are you chasing me?"

"I want to…"

Yeah. What, exactly, do you want?

"…to know."

"Know what?" She seemed preoccupied with the thin cord now spooled on her belt. She threw it with all her might at something on the opposite side of the district wall that Maxan could not see.

Since the moment he'd first met her—*With her blade pressed to your throat, don't forget*—he'd thought of so many things to ask her, about her, about the hawk and the snake and their fight with Feyn and Harmony. *And the Mind's leadership, no less.*

About the artifact. *The relay. About where it came from. About how I know what it's called.*

But he forgot about all those questions now. He really had only one.

"I want to know where you were. When all us foxes started to…"

"Disappear?" she suggested. Her expression faltered, for just an instant, but long enough for Maxan to know.

She knows.

Her lips parted to form an answer.

"MAXAN!" Chewgar's voice tore the stillness apart. The rhino had charged through the streets, gotten lost in the twisting veins of the city, doubled back, and finally spied the pair of foxes outlined against the darkening sky. He stopped in the street below them, huffing and wheezing, spitting phlegm, his meaty hands on his knees. He raised his horned face skyward. "What're you doing? After her!"

With a smile, Rinnia stepped backward into empty space before Maxan could react, before he shouted, "Wait!"

She can't get away.

He channeled all his anger, all his bitter resentment at being left alone, all his energy into his legs, and their sudden burst of energy launched him across the immense gap, with a ferocious cry rushing from his throat. Thirty feet, an impossible leap. It was certain suicide.

But he made it.

Well—

His hind legs missed the wall's edge by inches.

—*almost made it.*

His gut slammed against stone, blasting the air from his lungs. His claws scratched at the sheer wall under him, searching for a hold. He was slipping inch by inch.

On the other side, the cord had caught Rinnia's weight, and the device on her belt whirred loudly as she ascended. At the top, she stooped to retrieve the pincer. She could see the other fox's fanned ears just above the top of the wall. She back-pedaled a few paces along the wall, muttering to herself, or to him, "C'mon. C'mon…"

Below where he clung, Maxan heard Chewgar pounding away to the nearest gate to the western district. He was all alone.

Get up! Maxan screamed in his mind. *Not again! NOT AGAIN!*

"RrraaaAAAHHH!" He pulled with all the strength in his arms, the strain nearly ripping them from his shoulders. He clambered over the side a few seconds later, ignored the over-whelming desire to simply lie there and look up at the stars, rolled over, and stood, and didn't even think before launching himself once again over the next gap after her. Lucky for him, it wasn't as wide.

Rinnia did not slow to see him clear it. She had already bolted to this building's edge and leapt onto the next structure. She ran along the edge of some straight, flat rooftops, the rail-ings of balconies, even a short wire of dangling, drying clothes, and she never slowed. Maxan matched her every movement, gaining on her all the while.

I'm faster than her. I have to be.

An enormous dome came into view ahead of the running foxes. The angular building had once been a prominent count-inghouse of some kind for a Corvidian mining guild. Now it was likely crammed with animals seeking shelter from the cold, or from the Stray, like so many other structures in the western district this close to the wall. He was familiar with this dome's particularly treacherous slope and smoothness, having nearly slipped off—*And nearly died*—when he first attempted to cross its surface at full stride, years and years ago.

She ran on, putting all her energy into every stride, flying faster than the wind straight on toward the dome, as he'd suspected she would. In a flash, her silver cord sailed from her paw, uncoiling, winding around the iron flagpole at the dome's apex, and snapping taut just as gravity began to pull at her. Her lower paws found no traction on the smooth surface, but her legs never stopped pumping, swinging her body round the far side of the dome, anchored by the cord.

Just behind her, Maxan watched her form disappear around the bend. He may have lacked her device, but he had experience with this place.

He leapt, folded himself at the waist just right, planted his hind paws straight on the curve, and ran half a dozen steps straight up. He put every ounce of energy he had left into a final burst, buying himself the last ten feet up to the iron pole. He swung around it and hopped onto his rump, holding his bushy tail aside, his paw wrapped around the taut line holding the other, unaware fox as she skittered round the dome below.

Rinnia pressed a button on the autofeeder at her belt, and a jolt sent through the taut line released the pincer. The rope came rushing back, but she was already airborne, having reached the rim of this building and jumped for the next.

But her paws never touched the roof there. Maxan hit Rinnia like a ballista bolt, wrapping his arms around her waist, bringing her down hard onto the tiles with a groan and a crash. They rolled together down the angled slope of the roof, and Maxan wound up on top of her, pinning her arms beside her head.

"I am not your enemy!" he shouted, despite how close they were, the tips of their snouts nearly touching.

Rinnia's blue eyes flitted back and forth between Maxan's green and gold ones. She didn't struggle. "Are you sure," she said, breathlessly, "of what I am?"

"A mystery."

"Oh, I see. I'm … alluring to you, then?"

"Not alluring. Annoying. And Elusive. In equal parts." Maxan shrugged. "Actually, more annoying than elusive."

Neither fox said anything further. But her thin black ears flared out and turned this way and that, catching whatever sounds they could. "Where's the rhino?"

This rankled the fur along Maxan's spine. "Why do you keep asking about *him*?"

There was some glint in her eyes then, an expression Maxan wasn't quite sure he could read.

Pity? Contempt? Joy?

It's a con, Max. She's setting y—

"MAXAN!" Chewgar's booming voice bellowed from below.

"Here!" Maxan called back, taking his eyes away from Rinnia's for a split second.

And Rinnia was suddenly in motion, dragging her pinned arms to her sides, lurching her captor into a forward tumble, which was then aided by the knee she brought up sharply against his rump. He flipped over her and landed on his back with a crash and a cry of pain. Rinnia was back up in an instant.

"We're almost there," she told him.

She backpedaled gracefully along the roof's edge, then turned and jogged—in no apparent hurry—up the slope of the building and disappeared onto the adjacent one.

Maxan lay for a few seconds, groaning. It was clear at this point, at this pace, that Rinnia was leading him somewhere. One part of his mind realized it, but he shoved it aside, buried it under his determination to catch her. She *would* tell him what she knew about their species. He would *make* her. He sprang up and set after her once more.

But they'd apparently reached their final destination. Rinnia slowed, then dropped down the open balconies of a few buildings, until finally she stopped atop the shoddy plank roof of a small toolshed built against a high brick wall enclosing a grand estate. She whipped about to check for her pursuers, then jumped over the wall and into the grounds beyond it.

Maxan knew this place. Or rumors of it, anyway, exchanged among his Commune of thieves. This was once the estate of an elk—a stag like Yovan, maybe Yovan himself—some wealthy lord who had marched his whole family off to war, where they had all fallen to the Thraxians. The widow he had left behind, crushed by the weight of her grief, died soon afterward, and the place was said to be haunted. Not even the fox's guild of thieves had dared to venture inside. He'd heard of an infamous burglar—a calico cat, he thought—who'd made an attempt, however, and been maimed somehow.

Maxan came to a halt on the toolshed roof and caught his breath for a while as the rhinoceros came charging up the alleyway just behind him. Somehow, he knew Rinnia would be waiting for him beyond the wall.

"Chewgar," he said.

The rhino skidded to a halt and looked up at him. By now it was nearly pitch dark, and if Maxan had not been waving, Chewgar might have searched for the small fox's shadowy outline until the break of Yinna's light the next morning.

"I'm here," he rasped. Chewgar leaned heavily against the toolshed, hacking up and spitting out chunks of bright green.

The rain-rotted planks of the shed's roof threatened to snap. There was no time to ask if Chewgar was all right. Maxan needed his help. Capturing Rinnia was all that mattered. "Pace around the path to your left," the fox ordered his superior officer, "and wait for my signal. Break through the little gate over there if you have to. I'll try to press her to it."

Without waiting for affirmation, Maxan ran straight up the wall, gripped its edge, and hauled himself over.

The perimeter of the courtyard was perhaps a hundred feet around. The circular three-tiered fountain at its center was decorated with ornate carvings and scrollwork, though cracked and flaking from years of neglect. A solitary torch was the only pinpoint of light in the dark of night that had fallen at last.

Rinnia held it. She waited for Maxan beside the edge of the fountain's wide bottom basin. Once he dropped softly down, she leapt gracefully onto the second basin, then to the top of the fountain, her amber-furred tail swishing to keep her balance. With a deep, exhausted sigh, she rested her rump in the top basin and dangled her hind legs over the edge.

Her body language communicated her intentions pretty clearly. *I think we've concluded the chase,* Maxan thought, but he approached her with caution all the same. His old thief's senses came back, looking for discolored or misaligned bricks in the pavement, or patches of leaves and debris in his path. Also, he had seen what she could do with those short blades of hers, which he saw belted at her hips. He thought about putting his paw on the pommel of his own short blade, and then he realized he actually hadn't seen it since the previous night at the inn.

Then he thought better of it all, knowing full well that if she wished him dead, he would be already.

"You're pretty fast," she pointed out.

"Just had a lot of practice. Running."

"Running," she scoffed. "And stealing."

"Stealing? From who? From Yacub?" Now it was Maxan's turn to scoff. "I have a feeling he stole the relay from someone, too. Someone dead now. And they stole it before him. Because it belongs to no one!"

Rinnia's legs had stopped moving. She sat in stunned silence for a long time, staring at Maxan as though really seeing him for the first time. "How do you know what it is?" she asked finally. "The relay. How could you possibly know that?"

I just know.

A voice told me.

A needlepoint behind his eye made him wince, but he held her gaze. "If I knew *how* I knew, I'd tell you."

Rinnia's pointed ears twitched ever so slightly. "If that's your friend lurking just beyond the gate there, you might want to tell him to lift the gate up before knocking it in," she announced rather loudly.

Maxan had to admit asking Chewgar to be stealthy was like asking a Corvidian to hold his breath as long as a Peskoran. *But that's actually possible. It's more like asking a Peskoran to fly.*

"Come on out," Maxan called. "You make more noise than a hyena in heat."

There was a grating sound, and the squealing of old, rusty iron. Two gray fists hoisted the enormous frame of the gate up and guided it inward. Chewgar glanced to his left, reached into the overgrown blanket of vines that covered every inch of the wall, tore away a hinged lattice that would have swung three sharpened spear points into an unexpected intruder, and tossed it aside.

A part of Maxan wished just then the rhino had held onto it. It could have made a decent weapon in a pinch, but Maxan knew that mattered little if Chewgar had to engage in a fight. Even without his massive battle ax, the twin blades of which were as broad as the fox was tall, the rhino was one of the deadliest animals in the Leoran kingdom. Besides, the thick black horn embedded at the end of Chewgar's broad face meant he was never truly unarmed.

And yet the other, wiser part of Maxan could tell that Rinnia was perhaps just as deadly. *And certainly more unpredictable.* But right now, he worried less about losing his life than he did about losing the answers to the questions that plagued him.

"Chewgar," Maxan said in a level voice, "stay where you are."

"Yes," Rinnia said, pointing to Chewgar. "Stay exactly—"

There was a sharp hiss. A silver streak flashed and was gone.

"—where you are," she finished.

Chewgar winced. His brows knit together. His massive hand slid up his chest and yanked out a sliver of metal, a dart thinner than a Corvidian hatchling's quill.

Chewgar considered the tiny thing cradled in his palm. His eyes shifted slowly, accusingly, to the fox perched on the fountain, and then they turned red. The veins of his giant, muscular arms and neck came alive like ropes pulled tight to halt a runaway beast. And in the next instant, a runaway beast was exactly what Chewgar became.

THE BROTHERHOOD

CHEWGAR LOWERED HIS GREAT HORN AND charged, roaring louder than all a lion's pride in unison. The unstoppable rhino barreled forward, shaking the ground, ramming into the fountain, and pulverizing the stone into gravel and dust. Chewgar bucked his neck skyward to gore the puny fox, splitting the upper tiers in two.

Rinnia leapt away just as the basin beneath her fell into chunks. But her surprise at the rhino's fury and her severe underestimation of his speed set her maneuver off a fraction of a second. Her hind paws hit the far edge of the fountain's lowest rim, and she stumbled, then fell against the low wall encircling the fountain.

Chewgar hoisted a giant slab of the ruined fountain and turned on her prone body. He had her.

"NO!" Maxan called out.

The rhino hesitated. His meaty arms shuddered beneath the weight of stone over his head. Chewgar turned his glare on Maxan. The rage in his eyes dissipated, but the eyes themselves still burned a bloodshot red. And where tears had streamed before were now lumps of thick green pus.

Chewgar groaned. The slab crashed to his side. He fell to his knees, trying in vain to steady himself on what little remained of the fountain, but only bringing more of it down in a pile all around him. Maxan saw that the veins constricting every swollen muscle of the rhino's body pulsed with a sickly, unnatural green that matched the color discharging from his eyes.

"No! No! No!" Maxan leapt to his captain's side. He laid a palm on Chewgar's swollen neck, and recoiled immediately. It was like grasping a torch at the wrong end. He tried to loosen the straps that held the captain's guard uniform in place. He didn't know what else to do.

"Wasssted effort." A hiss, a whisper, rushed through the court like a short-lived breeze.

The green-scaled snake dropped to the ground in complete silence from where he had hidden among the vines high up the brick wall. "Nothing to do but let nature take its course," he said.

Maxan's arm moved, grabbed for the hilt of the weapon he had forgotten wasn't at his side. Before the realization registered, Saghan had his own dagger free. Its naked blade pointed directly at the fox. The snake pinched another long, delicate sliver between two black nails of his other hand.

Chewgar blinked, breaking the membranes forming over his eyes, flushing out small chunks of the hardening pus every time he did. He tried to rise, huffing and groaning with all his strength, and he managed to straighten a single knee before his balance gave out. He toppled over like an avalanche onto the landslide of stones that used to be a fountain.

"What did you do to him?" Maxan cried, rising toward the snake.

Rinnia stepped between them. She pressed a paw firmly on Maxan's chest, and slapped Saghan's scaled hand away.

The snake's eyes narrowed. His forked tongue flicked. But he sheathed his blade all the same and tucked the sliver into the bracer on his wrist.

Maxan had only seen him in the drowning red light of the relay. But now, in the light of the torch Rinnia had cast aside, Maxan saw the artistry of Saghan's armor. He wore the same fine dark red material all over his lean, wiry frame. Designs were branded in black along every inch of its trim. A stiff collar rose halfway up the length of the snake's long neck. His V-shaped head at the end of it turned down, high above Maxan's own head. Traditional, perhaps ceremonial, Drakoran armor was an extreme rarity these days, since much of that nation's treasures were lost—alongside more than half of its population—with the Thraxians' genocidal invasion of the reptilian nation.

"He's dying," Maxan said.

"We all chase death." The snake shrugged. "Your friend's only chasing it faster now. That's all."

Maxan's eyes fixed on the bracer where the sliver was concealed.

If I move now, at this distance…

"I was told you are called Maxan," the snake said. He turned his arm away from Maxan, clearly reading the fox's silent calculations. "I am Saghan. She, as you know, is Rinnia."

Something's not right. Maxan looked away, winced at the confusion. There was something in the way Saghan spoke to him now—cool, detached—in stark contrast to the rage that had smoldered in his orange eyes at their first encounter, hot enough to burn the world down.

This isn't the same snake from the inn, he realized.

"What do you want?" Maxan spoke through clenched fangs. He glowered at Rinnia.

Her lips parted, perhaps to answer, then shut tightly. She looked at Chewgar, who had somehow managed to control his breathing. The rhino's big hands feebly gripped the stones around him, trying to control the spasms rocking him. She placed her small, amber-furred paw over his massive gray hand.

The rhino tensed at her touch, then relaxed shakily. He groaned. Whatever had seized up the rest of his body was also locking his jaw. He looked at her, pleading. His breathing gained a little more rhythm. Rinnia gently rubbed her paw over his forearm and hand. She couldn't look him in the eye for long.

Saghan broke the silence. "How can you not know what we want by now?" He flicked his tongue.

"The…"

No, Max!

He stammered, simultaneously certain he should not call the relay by its name, yet uncertain why it mattered so very much if he did. "The artifact," he corrected himself. "I don't have it."

"Oh, we know you don't. You brought it straight to the one place in this world it belongs the least."

The Mind said the same about you, Maxan almost pointed out, but the truth was he didn't care. Only one thing mattered right now.

"Spare him," Maxan said, joining Rinnia at Chewgar's side. He saw an apology in her eyes. "Will he die?" Maxan asked her.

"It didn't have to come to this." Saghan sighed. "I wonder, thief, how much you expected to sell it for."

Maxan ignored him, ignored the guilt that squeezed his heart. "What's it doing to him?"

"Accelerating the earlier dose," the snake hissed.

The sight of a bushy tail disappearing into the crowd flashed in Maxan's mind. *Chewgar, holding his scratched leg. Saying it was nothing.*

"It's called bane," Rinnia breathed, still caressing the rhino's burning arm.

"Can you do something? Anything?"

"Yes," she said.

"But why would we?" said Saghan. "What is he to you? I know plenty of guards in Crosswall who would happily see their captains suffer some gruesome agony."

He's not just a guard or a captain. Again, Maxan bit back his words. *He's a king.*

Chewgar had entrusted Maxan with his past, a part of himself he had hoped could stay forgotten. The fox understood only too well. He would not betray that trust.

"He's my friend."

"Friend?" Saghan scoffed. "Maybe the hyena was my friend." He stroked a slender finger up and down his scaly jaw, smirking. "What was the hyena's name again?"

Rinnia shot him a withering look, but Saghan hardly withered. He only shrugged at her. "What?"

"Brother," Rinnia said. "This is pointless."

"You're right. A fox catching a snake in a lie. How utterly literary. Yacub was no one's friend. But we bought his service, and he betrayed us. The ... *artifact* you stole. He and his chuckling idiots were paid to retrieve it from the Radilin River towns and bring it to us. Right here." Saghan swept his arm over the cracked stones littering the ruined courtyard. "But instead, he marched straight to that *cult's* initiates, thinking he'd get some better price, and his message went all the way to their principals. Who knew a band of murderers would want redemption over remuneration? And he almost got it! He almost bought his way in with the artifact."

Maxan heard every hissing word but fixated on just one. "Murderers? You say it like you're any better than they are. But I saw what you did. At the inn."

Maxan saw the crack he'd made in Saghan's armor of apathy. The snake crossed his slender arms, and his long neck swung his gaze away from the fox. Without another word, he withdrew a few paces from the fountain.

Maxan turned to Rinnia. "Who are you?" Before she could respond, he added, "*What* are you?"

"We're part a brotherhood," said Rinnia. "A very old brotherhood. The Monitors."

"Monitors," he echoed, shaking his head, thinking the idea of brotherhood sounded very familiar. "How are the Monitors any different than the Mind?"

"The Mind," she replied, lowering her head to fix him with sharpened eyes, "is our greatest enemy. There are some things on this earth—dangerous things, things that would unravel the world—that are better off buried, and that the Mind very much seeks to unbury. Get it?"

"Ow," Maxan said when Rinnia's claw prodded him in the chest.

"The Monitors work to keep those things hidden. Forever. Since long before the Thraxian War. But with the Stray driving everyone out of their settlements, with all the order in the world falling apart, animals are wandering into places they shouldn't be. Finding things they're not meant to find."

"Like Yacub."

"Like Yacub," she echoed, and silence lingered a moment.

"But ... the relay," he started.

Rinnia shot her brother a look, but Saghan hadn't heard. He still brooded over Maxan's accusation several paces away, his back turned to them.

"It fell," Maxan said, shaking his head from the sudden ache behind his eyes. "From the sky."

Rinnia's paw fell on his suddenly. "Not here," she whispered.

Maxan looked deeply into her eyes, then to the snake, and understood.

"The thing you found," she resumed a moment later in a normal tone, "was one of those. A piece of the old world. It's like my brother says. We came to Crosswall to get it back, and Yacub betrayed us. By the time we found his trail, he was already with the Mind. And you know the rest."

"Part of me wishes I didn't. In the beast pen, who was the Corvidian? The hawk with the spear."

"She's one of us," said Rinnia, ignoring the more pressing question in favor of answering the simpler one. "Sarovek. She was wounded. Gravely wounded."

At this, Saghan rejoined them. "But she's not yet in her grave."

"And, the white wolf, he was holding her with..." Maxan trailed off, at a loss for how he could describe all he had seen. The rhythmic rise and fall of the wolf's knuckles, the anguish on the Corvidian knight's face.

"Feyn was once a knight-commander in the Leoran army," Saghan said, "if what passed for records back then can be believed. We heard he went to sleep a corpssse and woke up a..."

"A caller," Maxan suggested.

Saghan's forked tongue lashed the air. His lip curled in a smirk. "Sssomething like that."

"And Harmony. The owl." Maxan recalled how her upraised talons had pulled the Aigaion to a standstill, how she'd called down the vortex of air from it. As if the universe had read his mind at that moment, a gentle breeze whipped through the courtyard and stirred Maxan's cloak.

"That one," Saghan went on, exchanging a look with his sister, "is a mystery to us. Sarovek knows her."

"Knows *of* her," Rinnia corrected. "Only that she came from a lower Corvidian house but quickly earned her rank in the Mind once she got to Crosswall."

"How do they…" Maxan waved his paws around to illustrate what his words failed to do. "Harmony and Feyn…"

"It's the Aigaion," said Rinnia. "Callers draw from its energy. Like a gust of wind bends a flame, and its heat trails behind it. Invisible."

"My sister's quite the poet," Saghan said. "But the comparison oversimplifies their tricks for your understanding. All you need to know is that the Mind has uncovered a very old, very forgotten, very forbidden way to … bend the flame. Like she said, some things are better left buried."

Rinnia's eyes widened, and she turned her face away from Saghan.

He heard her, Maxan realized. *He might have heard everything. She wants to keep something from him.*

Saghan, however, didn't appear to notice. Or perhaps he didn't care. "We'd like very much to bury it again," he said. "Though it's probably too late."

Maxan saw Rinnia was watching him closely, judging. There was something in her eyes that he couldn't read. It wasn't contempt—*Not anymore, anyway, so there's that.*

Is it…

She has to trust you, Max. She has no choice.

"You're not old enough to have been in the Thraxian War," Maxan pointed out, eager to change the subject. "Neither of you."

Chewgar groaned and fell over to his side, clutching at his chest with fingers that seemed to have lost all their strength. Maxan suddenly felt his guilt crushing him. Here he was, running some investigation while his friend was dying. It was true that these questions had burned in his mind for more than a day—some for years—but his need to know was nowhere near as fatal as the bane that burned in his friend's veins.

"You've got to help him," he said, falling to his knees at the rhino's side.

"Oh. *Ssso sssorry,*" the snake hissed. "I wasn't aware we had an obligation to do so."

"Saghan," Rinnia said, reaching for his shoulder.

He shifted away before she could touch him. "Fine."

Saghan squatted beside the rhinoceros, his long whiplike tail coiling around his ankles. He pulled the metal sliver from his bracer and pinched it between his two black nails. "As soon as we come to trussst one another—"

"If you touch him with that," Maxan warned.

"—but no sooner," the snake finished unperturbed, tucking the sliver away, his wide, flat mouth leering.

Stay calm, Max. It's some kind of medicine.

Some kind of aurochs' shit! All of this! There's no play here. Nothing I can do.

You can fight.

But Maxan knew he wasn't much of a fighter. Also, he'd seen just what this snake did to fighters.

Chewgar was watching Maxan, his eyes half-closed, crusted with green pus. The look in those eyes spoke for him. Heat radiated from his gray skin, still steaming with sweat. In all the years he had known Chewgar, he never could have imagined a way the giant, proud warrior could be reduced to this so quickly.

"Will he be all right?" Maxan asked.

Saghan regarded the slumbering gray hulk and flicked his tongue. "No. He will still die. But on this tiny world, we're all built for death." He paused to look at Rinnia. "Well, most of us."

She turned away. Maxan saw some evidence of an unspoken disagreement—*One of many, it seems*—between them.

"His pain will return, stronger than before," Saghan went on, "before Yinna's light breaks on the horizon. No one even this strong can fight bane for long."

"You know that's not true," said Rinnia.

"Fine," Saghan conceded. "No one besides her."

Maxan ignored their bickering.

There's no play here for us, his inner voice surmised. *You were right.*

No choice but to do what they want.

"We need to go," said Rinnia, rising over Maxan.

"Go where?" he said.

But Rinnia ignored him. "Coming?" she asked Saghan.

"Afraid not." The snake shrugged. "You know I'm not much of a climber."

FILE 211: "CONFESSIONS"

Time: 003280/11/19-[16:16:11-16:18:29]
Location: Castle Tower
Continue audio transcription:

Oh. Before I go, I remember why I came to visit today. As it turns out, I miscounted. By two.

You remember the squid? Forgive me. Whatever. I forget sometimes that we did not opt for squids. So many other thousands of species. Only the dangerous ones, hmm? More ... fun that way, I guess.

Anyway, he escaped. Can you believe it? Ha! I only found out a few days ago. The slippery bastard chopped some of my agents to bits. I don't know what he wants.

Also, I was wrong when I'd told you your favorite pupil died. Even after I'd buried my knife so deep in her eye that it struck bone. Wouldn't go any farther in, and I couldn't pry it out! Huh.

That roar of hers, though! The energy from it! The power! You'd have been very proud, I think. It brought the whole cave down on us. I sometimes wake in the night, and I still feel the tingling her force left in my bones. Well...

She's alive too.

Seems she's found a way to outrun the poison. Long enough to start some little cult in Leora somewhere. She likely thinks it will protect her. From me.

You know, I don't mind that she got away. I almost feel bad. Thinking about what the bane will do to that body of hers. She's dying. A little more each day, I'm told. Pieces of her, just ... falling off. And soon...

Hmm.

Only dark.

Listen. I want you to do something for me...

If there is an afterlife I'm not aware of, then I want you to tell her something for me, once you're both there. Tell her the poison was never meant to kill her. Tell her that I let her go. That I wanted her to suffer. Most of all, tell her that all her planning to prolong this ... sad excuse for a world...

Tell her what you once told me. That all this is a lie.

And the beast cannot be stopped.

CHAPTER EIGHT
THE PINNACLE OF KNOWLEDGE

MAXAN WAS USED TO CLIMBING IN BURSTS OF energy, straight up the cracked and wrinkled faces of structures that time, neglect, and the ever-shifting Herbridian seasons had eroded. The only good things these invisible, inexorable forces left in their wake were good footholds. Spots where the clay had worn away, revealing strong, wooden support beams within. Jutting floorboards. Missing bricks. Fissures and cracks. Dangling ropes. Even overgrown weeds that clung to buildings, sucking life from the vertical rivers that flowed in rainstorms. Any of these could hold the fox's weight well enough to be useful.

He knew them well, every crevice and crack, all across the western district. It wouldn't stretch the truth too far to say the young fox shadow was the foremost authority on vertical travel in the western district, for not even the bird-men of Corvidia would go there.

But *this* was not the western district. Far from it.

Don't look down, Max.

"Don't look down," he whispered as if saying it aloud would make it more convincing.

But Maxan looked down anyway. And imagined himself plummeting, hundreds of yards, taking in the vast sprawl of twinkling city lights one last time on his way to meet the solid ground that would blast him to bloody, wet pieces.

He hugged the cold stone wall as tightly as his outspread limbs could, regaining his balance, swallowing the rising vertigo.

"Don't look down," said a voice below him, barely louder than the biting wind that whipped Maxan's cloak and rushed in his ears. "Keep going."

Unlike their race across the rooftops earlier that night, this was a race with Rinnia that Maxan didn't care to win. She was about ten feet below him. She periodically anchored herself to the immense wall by shoving her pincered cord between the narrow crevices in the gray stone slabs, then retrieved it with the spool device on her belt when the line ran out. Maxan heard a *buzz* and a *fwip*, and he knew she did this just now.

Wish she'd brought an extra one of those things.

His only "safety line" was the more conventional kind of rope, knotted about both of their waists, so that one might catch the other if either fell. Of course, if he slipped... *What good would this really be?*

It's more like a set of manacles to make sure you don't escape.
She knows if I escape, Chewgar's as good as dead.

Maxan craned his neck back and cast his eyes skyward. The seemingly endless plane of the Mind's Pinnacle Tower stretched beyond, disappearing into a soft blanket of clouds above. The clouds dispersed for an instant, and Maxan gazed beyond the black emptiness of space above them, beyond the asteroids in Yerda's Belt, straight up into Yerda's Wound, that nebulous dark hole in the side of the spherical moon. The pinprick of yellow light at its center gazed back at him, always watching, wondering if he'd fail. He felt the tower sway, or the whole world of Herbridia turn beneath him, or both at once, and his grip slackened, his paw slipped, his claws dug gravel from the stone that showered onto his companion below.

"I said keep going. Maxan! Do you hear?"

Maxan's claw found a small crack where the mortar had worn away ever so slightly. He dug it in and hauled himself up. Brick by brick, he made his way up the tallest structure in Crosswall. The climb was arduous and slow, but thanks to whatever that red pellet was that Rinnia had ordered him to swallow, the acidic fatigue that had seeped into his muscles dissolved in an instant. His heart pumped blood hot and swift and steady, and despite the occasional vertigo, this exercise was nothing at all.

Of course, the extra energy in his body came at the price of the expeditious thoughts chattering in his mind.

What're we doing here?

I'm saving Chewgar.

No. What are we doing here? We're supposed to be smarter than all this. Clever. Sly. Witty.

What does being witty have to—

Pay attention! The best plan you—no, no, I'm sorry, you TWO—could come up with was to scale the symbol of all the Mind's power? And hope the relay's still up there?

It's up there.

None of this would've happened. If you'd just listened. To reason.

Listened to your reason. Never engage. Go home. Wait for Anda to slide a blade in my neck. Wait for the Stray to overrun us. Wait for the king to burn it all down.

There was no rebuttal to that. The rhythm of his body lulled him into a deep focus— reaching, grasping, holding, pulling, again and again—over which his thoughts raced freely. He hadn't even realized Rinnia had begun to struggle to keep up.

I made a choice. A door opened. I stepped through. And we're here now. I brought us here. Let me own it! I'm done waiting. I won't wait while Chewgar dies.

There was a sudden stillness in his mind. But after a moment, Maxan's inner voice asked another question, less critical and sarcastic than its other remarks, but no less important.

So what's the plan when you drop over the rampart up there? Assuming you don't drop down *and drop* dead *first.*

The plan is to improvise.

Improvise, Max?

Improvise. Time enough to be witty and sly once I get inside. Stay out of my head and let me get us up there so I can make you proud. 'Til then, shut up!

It seemed to work. Maxan's focus was sharper than an executioner's ax as he made the rest of the way up, with Rinnia—perhaps literally—in tow.

Maxan didn't have much of a plan, true, but nonetheless he had allowed for the possibility of an armed conflict with the Mind's soldiers once he reached the top. *If. If I reach the top.*

As he dropped over the edge of the rampart, his paw clutched the hilt of his guard-issued sword, which Rinnia had returned to him. When his hind paws touched the floor, he was surprised to find it was made of soft, finely trimmed grass and not solid planks of wood.

Illuminated by Yerda's moonlight, the garden atop the Mind's Pinnacle Tower was breathtakingly beautiful. Maxan's eyes swept over manicured hedges peppered with brilliant, blossoming pink and red rosebushes, yellow tulips, and white garlands. A long row of small trees, whose twisting trunks and clipped branches made them appear like dancers forever striking a pose, ran all around the edge of the tower's rampart, which must have been nearly three hundred yards in circumference. At the center of the garden stood a three-story manor, itself rising like a tower from the massive structure on which it stood. *The true Pinnacle*, Maxan thought. His ears perked up at the pleasant sound of gurgling water, and he spied a fountain not twenty feet from where he now crouched, at the center of the path leading to the manor's double-doored entrance.

How did I get here?

You climbed.

No, I mean... Maxan's brain throbbed with the rhythm of his heartbeat; both were racing under the influence of the strange red pill Rinnia had forced him to swallow. In the ten seconds before she would follow his lead up and over the rampart and crouch beside him in the grass, his mind relived a dozen jumbled memory fragments of the recent conversations he'd had with the Monitors.

"We are the vigilant eyes," Saghan had said. "In the night, in the day. Our eyes never close. Our watch never ends."

"Tell me about the relay," Maxan had said later to Rinnia's back as the two foxes stalked their way eastward across Crosswall's rooftops, toward the campus. "Tell me what it, ah... *relays*."

"You saw it," she had said, stopping in her tracks, waiting until Maxan stopped, too, and met her eyes. "Death," she had said.

"Your brother's right." Maxan frowned and folded his arms. "You're quite the poet."

She let out a deep breath. "The desire to hurt, to damage, to destroy. To kill. We all ... *feel* it. But mostly, we're in control. The relay's light takes our control away."

"Like the Stray."

She nodded. "It just unlocks what's already sealed up in one's own heart."

When he asked her if there were any more relays, she simply glanced skyward and said no more.

Soon after that conversation, the two foxes made their way down from the rooftops and slipped into the grand canal, which would ultimately carry them to the center of the campus, right to the ever-turning gigantic water wheel at the Pinnacle's foundation.

The seconds were catching up with him now. As he crouched, feeling Rinnia tug at the rope cinched around his waist, waiting for her to drop over the rampart beside him, a smile came to his muzzle. Here he was, a shadow alongside another shadow. *Making a difference. No longer alone.* He stared blankly ahead at the soft glow coming from behind many of the manor's windowpanes, lost in his thoughts.

"Maxan," Rinnia whispered, crouching near him in the grass. "Maxan!" She laid a paw on his shoulder, startling him from his reverie. She noted the wild look in his mismatched eyes, remembering the first time she had taken the red pill and sprinted nearly fifty miles across some treacherous Drakoran swamplands in a single night.

"We made it," Maxan said unnecessarily.

She clamped his muzzle shut and scanned the immediate vicinity. As far as she could see, the garden was empty. They were alone, besides the hundred or so fireflies bursting in yellow luminescence from time to time. A part of her couldn't help but be charmed by his carelessness, but now was not the time for carelessness.

"Remember," she sighed, withdrawing her paw, "they may know we're coming, but they likely won't know from which direction. So we start from the top and work our way down."

"I know a thing or two about trespassing," he murmured as the two of them snuck quietly behind a flowering hedge just to the side of the main walkway. "On rich Leoran estates. I was a thief for maybe ten years before joining the guard."

"Are you trying to impress me?"

"I have no idea," he admitted. The smile he gave her then was the kind charming drunkards flashed when trying to coax another round from the innkeeper. Before Rinnia could stop herself, she found herself smiling back.

The foxes remained crouched beside the hedge for a minute longer. Rinnia's muscles burned with the same level of rampant energy as Maxan's, but she remained in control, darting her eyes about the garden and grand latticed windows of the manor, on the lookout for any shadows, perking her ears up and around for any crunching of gravel, swishing of fabric, shifting of armor, or snapping of twigs. Besides a little water and wind, some starlight and fireflies, she neither saw nor heard anything. Meanwhile, Maxan fidgeted at her side, restless, doing his best to be silent.

At her signal, they leapt over the gravel walkway, from one soft and silent patch of grass to another, and then they climbed the high brick wall to a wide balcony on the second floor of the manor. Every stone surface of this place seemed to be etched with ornamental artwork. The very pattern in which they were laid spoke to some grander scheme or meaning. "And wealth," Rinnia muttered to herself. "And power."

"Are you talking to me?"

Rinnia shushed him.

From where they crouched on the balcony, the glow beyond the floor-to-ceiling windows was much less obvious. Whatever light was casting it seemed to be well within the great house.

"Funny," Maxan whispered. "Before last night, it had been five years since I'd touched a latch with the intent to steal anything. And here I am, doing it again. And I'm after the same prize."

"We don't know if it's here. So we go slowly. Hey. Look at me." Rinnia doubted that Maxan understood enough about the Mind and the true level of peril they were in up here. "Can you stay focused?"

He nodded vigorously, then turned and squinted at the seams of the tall window frame, trying to determine the best place to pry with the blade of his weapon. Rinnia gently pushed him aside and reached for the handle he had failed to notice. She pulled it down gently, then swung the lower casement open.

"Yes. Excellent focus," she remarked.

"Ah. Thanks." Maxan sheathed his blade and stepped silently over the sill and onto a plush rug.

Rinnia watched him, and then she knew. "Something's wrong," she said, reaching for Maxan's shoulder. "This was all too easy."

"That climb was *easy* for you?"

"Yes. And everything else. Something's wrong. We have to find another way."

"There is no other way."

"We can find some disguises. Red scholars' robes—"

"Chewgar doesn't have time for disguises. For questions. For walking up and down the campus turning over every little stone 'til we find it." Maxan wrenched his arm away from her paw. He turned and folded into the shadows within the manor, leaving her behind on the balcony.

Shelves filled with books loomed high overhead, lining nearly every inch of every wall, stretching into the darkness where Maxan could not see. The books stood in rows or lay in stacks that were arranged by the colors of their leather-bound spines. Vases of wilted plants, jars of multicolored minerals and fluids, brass instruments, various other bits and baubles, and even a skull or two rested at periodic points alongside the library's collection, and everywhere beside these things were papers scratched with notes and the fowl-quill pens and inkwells that made them.

The air in this immense space was like nothing else Maxan's snout had ever experienced. Herbs, both fresh and dried, and woodsmoke mixed with something chemical, cooked, and cloying. As he moved through the stacks, he ran his paw gently along the spines of books and guessed part of the scent came from their hardened leather materials and from the abundance of ink on their pages. *But there's something else,* he realized. Something under it all that his snout had never taken in before.

He turned away from the bookshelves and shuffled silently to a railing that ran around the wide-open space of the manor's main floor below. Rich, woven carpets had been thrown down over the floorboards all around this level of the library, but nonetheless, he was careful to test them for creaks before every step, as the Commune had trained him to do long ago. He moved in utter silence, perhaps more a testament to the Pinnacle's solid construction than to his skill at staying hidden, and peered over the railing.

At the other side of the great library, a colossal statue resembling some kind of beast had been built into the wall, rising from the ground floor all the way to the high ceiling. The wide space between its squat, muscled hind legs served as a hearth, where a fire now burned; it was the library's only source of light besides a few low-burning candles arranged on slanted writing desks here and there throughout the place. The beast's legs were carved to resemble a typical Leoran species with the characteristic triple-joined ankle, but curiously, Peskoran fins had been carved along each of the statue's joints and the edges of each limb, all across its massive body. It had four arms, all of which were chiseled to depict the fine lines of Drakoran scales. To either side of the statue, a pair of folded Corvidian wings ran from floor to ceiling, forming the edge of the chimney where the balconies and bookshelves terminated. At the very top, just beneath the steepled rafters, a carving unlike anything Maxan had ever seen formed the statue's head. Maxan had never personally seen a Thraxian, but he knew the legends well. The stone face that stared down upon the Pinnacle Tower's grand library belonged to a Thraxian brood-mother—a queen ant, Maxan believed—who was the source of all life and leadership in that long-dead society.

It's like one of the legendary monsters, Maxan thought. *A behemoth. And every kingdom in Herbridia is part of it.*

Set before the hearth were four of the writing desks, each with a pot of ink and an assortment of quill pens, weights, razors, and other tools resting inside a built-in tray. Affixed to the side of each desk was a set of glass lenses, and underneath each of these was a large volume bound in rich red leather. A candle glowed in every desk's corner, leaving a long trail of wax running down its tall wooden legs.

In front of all these desks, just a few feet from the hearth, were a grand wooden rocking chair—with a pile of crumpled blankets draped over its back and seat cushions—and a small table with a basin, a pitcher, and some rags.

And the relay!

Maxan's eyes widened, and his body's first instinct was to leap over the railing then and there to seize it.

He shifted around, suddenly aware of a presence at his side. It was Rinnia. He exhaled, watching the dull glow of the hearth sparkle in her eyes as they came to rest on it too.

He followed her over the edge and dropped to the floor. The pads of their lower paws absorbed the impact, and their trained joints bent perfectly to absorb the rest. The only sound that came from the foxes, perhaps, was the soft fluttering of their cloaks.

Rinnia moved immediately to crouch behind one of the desks. She kept it hidden beneath her cloak, but Maxan somehow knew that her paw held one of her razor-sharp weapons. *At least one.* She remained there as Maxan moved past her, silently, from desk to desk toward the table where the inert relay rested. The thing that was worth the life of his friend was only ten feet farther, in an open space lit by dancing firelight.

He took one slow step past the last desk, out into the open.

And something creaked. The rocking chair swayed forward, then back, just once, just one inch, and Maxan saw the pile of blankets stir. He froze just inside the light, his shadow stretched out far behind him.

Something that looked like a thick, wet pelt of brown fur draped loosely over bones emerged from the folded cloth. Curling black claws came to rest on the arm of the chair with a *clack.* The dozing creature lifted its head, its face obscured by the folded black robes, except for the long brown muzzle with a huge black snout at its tip. Its nostrils flared as it drank in the foxes' scents. A single point of light twinkled from the dark of the creature's hood. An eye, watching Maxan.

The beast's drooping lips parted, and its voice croaked. "My child." It raised its paw weakly, beckoning Maxan. "Come closer."

But Maxan didn't move a muscle. He recognized the creature now. The third principal. "Who are you?"

"I am many things." Every word faltered out of its mouth. "The source of knowledge. I am … wisdom. Law. Society. Truth." A corner of its muzzle lifted weakly in what might have been a smile. "I am the Mind."

"Oh. Ah. Is that all?"

"You can call me Folgian."

"I'm not sure I can. Might be hard to recall, given all your titles there."

What are you saying, Max?

I don't know!

"Did you earn all those in the arena or something?"

Improvising?

Improvising. I guess so.

Somehow Maxan knew that if the red medicine Rinnia gave him weren't throbbing through his body right now, he would most likely be paralyzed in fear. At this point, though, he also knew it was the only thing keeping the blood from freezing in his veins.

And it's making you kind of asinine.

"You may call me Maxan."

"Maxan … you seem very … familiar to me." Folgian's voice was grating. It sounded like metal worn to rust by the elements and time. Yet it was also unmistakably a female's voice, and beneath the caustic surface, there was a softer note of nurturing there.

"I saw you today, when your owl friend took that thing away from me." He nodded at the relay on the table by Folgian's side.

"You gave it…" Folgian's breath rattled phlegmatically. The curling claws stretched apart as if stricken with sudden pain. "Willingly," she finished with a whisper.

"Believe me, there was little to no will involved."

"I do … very much believe you, Maxan. I understand very well the feeling of being compelled. Being a puppet. Powerless … against the pull of its strings." Folgian's claw reached out to her side, coming to rest on top of the relay. "So now … you've come back? Please, child. Allay my curiosity."

"Allay?" said Maxan.

The drooping flesh peeled away from Folgian's muzzle, revealing long, decayed fangs. The sudden irritation in her voice evaporated any trace of that singsong nurturing Maxan thought he had heard. "Tell me why."

The branches of possibility began sprouting in Maxan's racing mind, forming what he hoped was a convincing story. He fought back the urge to swallow, to glance away, to display half a million other tells that a discerning mark could read plainly on a liar (assuming the glint of Folgian's eye could see him from inside that hood). He held his eyes and his voice steady and said, "I knew from the moment I laid eyes on that thing that it would be worth a lord's fortune. But my captain would have none of it. It was either turn it over to the Mind, or he would personally chop my paws off, throw me in a cell, and let me bleed out. But he doesn't know I had a buyer all lined up. Someone who'd do the same, only let me bleed in the gutter. So I'm here, back to get the relay." The smile that came to Maxan's lips wasn't just part of the act. He was quite pleased with the con itself. "I may dress like a guard, I may stalk the city's enemies like their own shadows, but I'm a thief. Maybe Crosswall's greatest. Not even a tower this high can keep me out. It's just in my nature."

"I see." Folgian's grip on the relay relaxed, but her paw remained settled there as she spoke. "Somewhat convincing. Although there are several points ... at which I could prod your story to find the truth it conceals, I need only ask... Who told you this is called a *relay*?" Folgian's snout swayed to her left and sniffed. "The fox ... with a blade at my back. Hmm?"

In a blur of motion, Rinnia's form darted into the ring of firelight just to the side of Folgian's chair, her short sword thrusting in an arc straight at Folgian's heart.

And then it stopped. The weapon hung in the air, suspended, frozen in time, and all of Rinnia's strength seemed to collide with an invisible wall.

She let go and rolled away, coming between Maxan and Folgian. She was up in a flash, her second blade drawn and striking out as she leapt once again at the seated figure.

Rinnia's chest crashed onto the point of her sword's pommel, crushing the wind out of her lungs as it, too, froze in midair. She toppled, breathless, onto the floor, leaving both her short swords to hang in space, pointing at Folgian from both angles of Rinnia's failed attacks.

Maxan crouched at Rinnia's back, drawing his own weapon and holding it out at Folgian. Rinnia propped herself up against him, holding her chest and heaving to regain her breath.

Folgian's laughter scraped its way out of her throat.

A black-robed figure emerged from the shadows at the corner of the library where Maxan's eyes had swept earlier (perhaps too hastily) and seen nothing. One snow-white paw was extended to "hold" Rinnia's weapon, and the other drew the hood away from the wolf's head, the scar along his muzzle pulling his lips into more of a leer than a smile.

The first of Rinnia's swords floated lazily into Feyn's grip. He plucked it from space and stood beside Folgian's rocking chair. The other still hung in the air.

"Harmony," Folgian rasped as loudly as she could. "Come down from there."

Maxan craned his neck to the ceiling and saw two bright needlepoints of light piercing the darkness above one of the rafters. A fluttering of wings brought the black-robed, gray-feathered horned owl softly down to the library's floor before the hearth. Harmony took Rinnia's other sword in her talons and stood at Folgian's side, across from Feyn, watching the two foxes with her unflinching eyes.

"Two callers," Maxan remarked, still pointing his weapon at Folgian even though he realized the futility in it. "Any more on the way?"

"Oh yes," Folgian said. "Though finding an animal ... in full control of its own will is rare. And rarer still is the animal among us ... with the strength of focus to ... *feel* the Aigaion ... to *bend* it to its will... But yes, child. More *are* on the way."

Folgian's next intake of breath crackled in her throat. It might have been intended as a laugh but wound up as a hacking cough. Feyn spun toward her, his mask of violence becoming a look of true worry. But Harmony didn't seem to care, keeping her gaze locked on the foxes.

When the coughing subsided, Folgian let out a sigh of deep resignation. "There are so few of us left. And fewer still, it seems, who remember our legend. Worse, there are those who do remember but refuse to believe the miracles they saw were real."

"Miracles. Sure." Maxan waved his sword at Harmony. "Miracles of urban demolition. What if there were families hiding from the Stray in that beast pen?"

The owl stood as unmoved as the towering behemoth behind her. The only sound in the room came from the crackling embers of the fire between the statue's legs. Maxan didn't need to hear her answer, though. He saw the emptiness of emotion in the deep wells of black that were her eyes. He knew. *She doesn't care.*

"And you," he said, sweeping the tip of his sword to Feyn. "What you did to the hawk, you paralyzed her somehow. Why can't you do that to me?"

The wolf laughed and brought his free paw up. Before Maxan could even consider tightening his grip, his weapon slipped from his paw and floated away into Feyn's. "Do I need to?"

Maxan dropped his paw and shrugged. *What else is there to do?*

"Bind her at the wrists, with that," Feyn said, gesturing to the rope device on Rinnia's belt. "And sit down."

Maxan glanced at Rinnia, but her eyes were too busy darting between the two callers and Folgian to notice him. She reluctantly moved her arms to the small of her back.

"Keep your paws in sight," Feyn growled.

She complied, and a moment later, Maxan had extended an adequate length of the thin rope from the winch, seeing for the first time how delicate it was, yet feeling the strength of its material.

"What about me?" he asked, tying off the rope on Rinnia's wrists.

"Ha." There was the mocking snarl on Feyn's ruined face Maxan had learned to hate. "Tighter," the wolf told him.

"You." Folgian's raspy voice drew out the syllable. "You are … different. I cannot … *feel* your mind, child." Her head lolled sideways at the owl. "Harmony, my dear, would you kindly…"

The owl raised her talons toward Maxan and slowly twisted her wrist like she was carving a circle into wood. Maxan recalled how the squirrel, Pryth, had suddenly, uncharacteristically, shut up and wandered away. He recalled how a hyena had inexplicably slit his own throat. He swallowed the rising anxiety.

But in the awkward seconds that followed, Maxan felt nothing.

Harmony dropped her arm. Her head swiveled to Folgian. "Nothing," she said and twisted her gaze back to the foxes.

"Nothing," Folgian echoed, sounding as if she didn't comprehend the word's meaning. "No *imprint*. Not even the trace of one. As though your brain were designed … differently. As though your body were born … *free*."

"What?" Maxan looked back and forth over the three principals. "What do you mean *imprint*?" When none of them answered—or even visibly acknowledged he'd spoken at all—he tried to catch Rinnia's eyes, but they were downcast.

"The female's as well," Feyn said.

"How utterly ... fascinating." With some effort, Folgian's paw closed around the relay. The golden lights raced rhythmically under her curled claws, casting waves of shadow all across the grand library. Maxan hadn't realized until that moment just how much of the dim light in this place emanated from the shining chrome object. "You know, don't you?" she rasped quietly. Maxan could see only the glint of her eye in the dark, but he knew she spoke only to him. "This ... such a little thing ... could destroy us. We have only to activate it, and we, the Mind's principals, we will lose ... everything. We'll tear one another's throats. But you ... without an imprint..." She lifted the relay in her trembling paw and pointed it at one fox, then the other, slowly speaking her next words.

"Not ... you..."

The silence hung heavily. The unknown scent filling this place still tickled Maxan's nostrils. His eyes swept over everybody else once again. They all seemed enrapt by some drama he failed to understand. He felt the anger flush through his veins, prickling his fur up and down every limb. He dug the points of his claws painfully into his palms.

Chewgar doesn't have time for this shit.

"I don't have time for this shit," he said loudly. "I don't know what you're talking about. I have nothing to threaten you with. I'm not here to kill you. I don't even care about you! Just give me the damn thing and let me go!"

Maxan had taken more than a few steps toward the three principals and was standing now directly before the glowing hearth. His fangs were bared.

Folgian had withdrawn her paw, still clutching the relay, and weakly held it up to Feyn's chest, halting the wolf's advance toward the fox. Feyn's icy blue eyes looked up at the fox from his lowered head. His scarred face was wrinkled in ferocity. The fur he'd tried to slick down along the back of his neck stood up in spiky patches. He seemed ready to shred Maxan to pieces, but the gentle touch of his master calmed him. Feyn seemed to regain his composure. His gaze fell to the shining thing pressed against his chest, and he shrank back to his place beside Folgian.

"Tell me why," she said to Maxan. "Again. Why do you want it? And the truth this time, if you would."

"It is the truth," Maxan lied. "I came here to steal it. Also, I enjoy a good climb. And what better way to challenge myself than with scaling the Pinnacle itself?"

Folgian's ugly, rotten fangs had withdrawn into the dark of her hood. Maxan couldn't see it, but he knew she was smiling at that.

At least I'm amusing her.

"My wolf," Folgian said after a time, "has your sword. The very same you wounded him with. I'm sure he'd very much enjoy cutting into you with it. Feyn?" The glint of her eye turned toward the wolf beside her. "You would enjoy that. Wouldn't you?"

Feyn's knuckles tightened on the grip of Maxan's sword. His icy blue eyes fell to the floor as a spasm of snarling overcame him suddenly. He seemed to be wrestling with the idea, fighting to control the urge to hack the fox to pieces. Folgian's words had brought him back to the brink of violence. Maxan could see that it was a kind of test for the scarred white wolf.

And she'll keep testing her pet if I don't give her what she wants.

Maxan sighed. "The truth is… The relay. I saw what it can do. How perfectly normal, rational animals can lose their minds, lose control, and just become … savage. I've seen enough to know. The relay, whatever it is…" His words drew the wolf's gaze. "It makes us Stray."

Before Folgian could answer, Maxan lifted a paw to Feyn. "I hope you leave my arm, and the rest of me, like it is." He couldn't help but smirk. "Nothing personal."

Feyn's only answer was a scowl.

"I believe you," Folgian said finally. "I believe you think you're doing the right thing. I believe you want to ensure this … weapon's light never shines again. But you must know … the relay is but a small piece of the grand machine … that would destroy us all. I believe you worry that it will. And I believe most of all that you … misunderstand exactly where you are … right now. Exactly who *I* am."

Maxan wanted to indicate that he'd already suffered through her grand list of titles, but managed to keep his scorn in check. At least for a few seconds.

"You're the Monitors' greatest enemy," he blurted, adding a new title to the list.

"Ha!" Folgian wheezed. "Is that what she told you?"

The rotten brown-furred muzzle swung to Rinnia. The glint of Folgian's eye smiled at her. "What else do you know about me, girl? Hmm? What else, did your … *master* tell you?"

"You were one of us," Rinnia muttered, guilty, like a kit who'd been caught stealing from a market stall. "A Monitor. Long ago. But you betrayed the brotherhood."

"LIAR!!" Folgian's booming roar shook every brick and echoed from every wall in the library. Maxan slowly rose from where he'd cowered, and there was no doubt in his mind that the withered old creature could have blown them, the tower, the whole campus below into dust and gravel.

Folgian's frail body was suddenly animated. She came forward in her chair, gripping it with all the strength left in her, her sharp, curling claws scratching at the armrest. "Liar," she repeated between deep, calming breaths. "Has he never told you of all he's done? Of all the blood he's spilled?"

Rinnia was the only one in the room who had weathered Folgian's rage, unmoved. Maxan was certain he had seen Feyn wince, and he was half-certain even Harmony had blinked. Only Rinnia seemed unaffected. She glared defiantly at the frail, angry figure in the rocking chair, and added, "He told me you spilled far more."

The light of the fire seemed to die just a little, and the candles burning in sconces and upon desk corners all around the library seemed to fade like distant stars behind passing clouds. Maxan felt himself tense. *Be ready,* he told himself, despite the fact he knew there was little chance for him if Folgian wanted them dead.

But the Mind's supreme master said nothing. Her only reaction was to relax her ruinous grip on the armrest and ease back into the cushions of her chair. Then her claw rose weakly and drew her hood away.

The face beneath—and the smell, the source of that mysterious tinge in the air—made Maxan cringe. Green and yellow veins threaded across a single drooping milk-white eye. Green pus crusted along its rim, while a slow discharge from the gaping, swollen tear duct streamed ceaselessly, thickening it. Where the other eye should have been was a well of red shadow sunk deep into her skull. The pale skin and brown fur above and below it had fallen away long ago, so half of Folgian's broad head was bare yellow bone. What few strands of fur remained were greasy, and the little skin left was either an irritated red or a diseased and splotchy green.

Folgian was a grizzly bear, or had been. Maxan took in every detail of her horrible face and somehow did not look away. A word came unbidden to his mind.

Bane.

"Do you see me, child?"

Rinnia's defiance broke. She turned away.

"You do. You see me. You see what he's done to me." Folgian's claw rose to her shoulder and unwrapped the folds of her black robe there, revealing the stump of her other arm. "His poison has eaten me. *Eats* me. It chews this body, limb to limb, bone to bone. It drinks my blood. Turns my spittle, my tears, my puke and shit, everything ... green. And the pain ... oh, the pain I endure. I could have you thrown from my Pinnacle a thousand times, to have your bones a thousand times pounded to mush by the ground below, and still, you'd know not the pain I endure. For twenty years ... twenty years I have lived. That is my only betrayal. That I would not die when ... Salastragore told me to."

Folgian seemed unaware of how tired her wasted body and how ragged her voice had become. She shivered visibly without the thick black robe wrapped about her head and shoulders, the frail bones audibly clacking and scraping against one another beneath the sagging, heavy pelt of brown fur. Maxan had seen corpses in the streets of the western district, their guts torn away in the night by the fangs and claws of the Stray, and still they seemed healthier to him than the creature before him.

Feyn moved in to cover her again in the warmth of her robe, then tried to pull the black hood once more over what remained of the bear's head, but she shook away from him.

"I am not dead," she rasped, quieter now, her words like the gibbering of a maniac as she falls asleep. "But I am finally ready to face the oblivion I know awaits me when this body dies. There is no coming back for me. Not anymore. Not for any of us. We live just one life, and though his poison ate my flesh, it could not eat my mind." Folgian's milk-white eye darted blindly about in its green-crusted socket, as if she could see the vast library of books surrounding them all. "This is my gift. My knowledge. With it, this world will live. Armed with wisdom, virtue, and civility that we can be better … than the beasts that we are."

Maxan followed her gaze across all the rows and stacks of books, over the scrawled notes and papers and scrolls covering every desk and heaped on every table. He grimaced, trying to picture how any of it would help anyone fare better in a fight against a Stray.

"Books?" he said with an incredulous squint.

"Education," she corrected. "This world's only *salvation*. We must learn to be better. *How* to be better. And *why*. You've seen it, haven't you, my child? How we're dying. All of us. Turning on each other. Clawing and biting and … eating. Hating. Like poison. In time, hate will tear us all down and there will be nothing left … of our better selves. Until we become only animals. *Real* animals."

"We're already *real* animals," Maxan pointed out. He threw up his arms in frustration, looking wildly around at the owl, the wolf, the other fox beside him for any indication that he wasn't the only one hearing this craziness. That's when he knew.

They all know. And I don't.

Do I?

The headache squirmed again behind his right eye.

"No," Maxan said almost automatically. His gaze was lost in the glowing embers of the hearth. His mind dazzled as the light of knowledge dawned on him. "We're just … bodies."

"Vessels," Folgian corrected. "Empty, mindless flesh. Soulless."

Maxan no longer heard her. From somewhere deep within him, from a consciousness not his own, a word, a name, that he'd never heard before was rising. In a trance, he whispered it.

"Epimetheus."

Rinnia, with her eyes wide open, backed away from him slowly. But the Mind's three principals were so fixated on the other fox's uncanny recitation of this world's most deeply buried secret that they paid her no mind.

"But ... the signal," Maxan said. "The mind ... from beyond the stars. It's—"

The festering mass of pain exploded in his skull. He fell to his knees. Visions flickered in his mind. Floor of glass. Pillar of glass. Racing golden lights. Everywhere. But only the empty dark above.

I stole it. Before. Didn't I?

Not you.

Did you?

Folgian's claws had carved lines in the armrest of her rocking chair where she'd pulled herself forward. Feyn had dropped both the foxes' weapons and set his paws on his master's shoulders. Rinnia had backed so far away, she probably could have made a run for it, but Harmony's gaze followed her.

"You." Again, Folgian lengthened the rasping word, her voice just a tired whisper. But her tone had changed from accusatory to captivated. "Who are you?"

The visions were gone, and the pain with it, leaving a hollow in Maxan's mind. He could not recall the last ten seconds of his own life. He struggled then to recall even his own name. "I'm just... ," he murmured, looking up at the Mind's supreme master. "Just a thief."

"No, my child. I've met thieves before. You're something else entirely." Folgian let Feyn ease her back into the chair. Her claws spread apart again as her whole body was flushed with pain. She gasped and wheezed, fighting for every breath.

"Enough," Feyn growled at the pair of foxes. He advanced on them, but a curling claw wrapped around his arm and held him in place with surprising strength.

"No," Folgian rasped, the word hardly more than a weak waft of air. "Keep them ... alive... I will know ... how he knows..."

Her claws slipped away suddenly. Feyn wheeled about. Even Maxan thought she was dead, but a moment later he saw the tension in the wolf's shoulders relax.

Only asleep.

And dying. Slowly dying.

From...

Finally, the gray owl detached herself from her position by the master's side, and seemed to float across the floor toward the foxes. "Time to go," she said, her voice like a pleasant song, a strange humming amid all the tension.

"Wait," Maxan said, feeling a resurgence of the red pellet's effects flush in his blood. His bushy tail swept agitatedly over the soft carpet. His muscles tensed and relaxed. His mind raced to form some kind of plan.

How many seconds to rush the bear? Snatch the relay? Duck the inevitable swipe from the wolf and from the owl and then spring up or spring away? And what if they fling a desk at me and ... what about Rinnia?

He watched Harmony's daggerlike talons dig into Rinnia's shoulder.

No, Max. There's no play here.

The owl lifted her with surprising ease and spun her about to walk down the central aisle of desks.

It was his turn. Feyn stood before him, Rinnia's swords gripped again in either of his paws. The wolf didn't grab him or force him as Harmony had Rinnia. He simply barked, "Move." Maxan expected to see at least a trace of some triumphant leer within that scar, but Feyn somehow seemed less than committed to escorting the Mind's prisoners.

There is a play. There is. I just have to...

Maxan stood where he was, looking beyond the wolf at Folgian's ruined face, considering ... suddenly aware of what he could do.

If you do that…

Rinnia will never forgive me.

"Move!" Feyn said. "Or I'll move you."

"Wait," Maxan said again, louder, speaking beyond the wolf's shoulder, to the wasted grizzly bear wheezing in her chair. "Wait. Master Folgian. Please. The truth." He swallowed, unsure if she'd actually heard him, but she turned her eye upon him.

"Too late," she sighed. "Time enough for truth … when we tear it from you."

"I'm here because of my friend," Maxan went on, sidestepping the wolf's lunge with a sword's pommel. "He's dying! Like you! Exactly like you, in fact!"

Rinnia had stopped and turned to listen, Harmony as well. Feyn stood between Maxan and his master, but had ceased reaching for him.

"It's bane, isn't it?"

The withered form in the chair stirred. "What of it, boy?"

"There is a cure."

"Maxan. Don't." Rinnia's voice was threatening.

He saw her grinding jaw, her glaring eyes, and he ignored them. "I don't care about your war. Monitors or Mind. None of you matter to me. I care about my friend. Please. I need the relay to save him. I cannot leave here without it."

"The rhinoceros," Folgian muttered.

"He's a…"

You really going to do this?

"…a king."

"We know," Harmony said flatly. "But Leora already has a king. One of the Mind's favorite pets."

"We feed Locain blood," Feyn explained, "and he feeds us the affairs of this entire kingdom."

"I'm sorry, my child," Folgian said quietly. "But there is no cure." She waved her feeble claw dismissively. "Your friend is already dead."

Feyn laid the blade of one sword on Maxan's shoulder, waved the other toward the doors at the side of the library.

"No, wait!" Maxan shouted, ducking away, skirting around a desk to the side of Folgian's chair.

Rinnia took a step closer.

She'll never forgive you, Maxan's inner voice reminded him, and he ignored it.

"I'll tell you where they are! The Monitors." He put his paws up as Feyn rounded the desk, the sword raised to strike. "They have the cure. They have to. I'll take you there right now."

Feyn lowered the weapon slowly. He looked to his master.

Folgian nodded.

"Take her away," Feyn barked at Harmony. "*This* fox and I may yet have some business this evening."

The gray owl reached her talons for Rinnia's shoulder but closed around nothing but air.

Many had forgotten how quickly, how seamlessly, a caller's command of gravity and the unseen forces could bring change to the world. But even still, there was no creature alive with the speed to match the fury of this fox. The step, the leap, the spinning kick that Rinnia slammed into the back of Maxan's skull was faster by far than any caller's trick.

Not even Maxan, with his mind still racing under the red drug's influence, had enough time to fully grasp the sensation of pain or the reason why his vision suddenly went dark.

THE TWIN CALLERS

THE FOREST STRETCHES ITS FINGERS TO SNARE the young running fox, but it only scratches as he sprints through. The trees' branches are whips that lash his face and sting his body. Their old roots are traps that send him tumbling, knocking him down so suddenly that his fangs smash into the grit of the forest floor, and he rises with the taste of blood and fallen nettles in his mouth.

And he runs on. Frantic. Frightened.

And the shadows run after him.

If you must go, go slowly, his mother warned him. *Silently. Be a shadow at night.*

And now she is dead.

Maxan tries to make the kit slow down. He sees the deep underbrush where he could hide. He wants to see through the fear, to heed his mother's words.

This is a dream. And dreams are the past. You can't change the past.

Maxan hears the young fox painting for desperate breaths and the snapping of twigs. He sees the kit stumbling, slowing down.

If *anything happens to us,* she had told him, *to me … then you go to the village. You follow the river.*

Rushing water and the thudding wooden wheel turning at the mill break through the stillness of the forest. The boy hears it, too, and breaks through the dense veil of leaves, glimpsing tiny lights glowing in windows and torches lighting the streets.

He scurries onto the rickety bridge spanning the small tributary that irrigates the village fields, and he slams right into the sturdy armored leg of a knight, regaled in white and black. He falls hard on his rump. An enormous, mighty stag towers over him.

I remember. When he said…

"What's the rush?" The stag takes a knee to help the fox stand. On the other end of the bridge, a rhinoceros boy grips its railing. Their eyes meet briefly.

Is that … sorrow?

I remember. Chewgar's eyes were filled with sorrow.

So were yours.

The little fox squirms in the stag's arms. "They," he pants, and as though the word alone summons them, three thin assassins materialize from the shadowed tree line, wrapped head to heel in black armor. Their eyes shimmer in the dark. They bring the fire with them.

The stag knight lets the kit go, stands tall, pulls aside the oiled cloth from the blade at the end of his spear. The three shadows fan out, drawing their thin blades.

"Boy," the knight says without looking away from his enemies, "take this, follow the road, and when you find yourself in Crosswall, find those in white and black, and speak my name. I am called Yovan."

Maxan remembers the coin pressed into his palm by the stag's strong fingers.

"Now run!"

And he does, sharing one last look with the rhino as he darts across the bridge.

Soon, there is the clang of steel and the cry of agony.

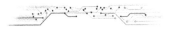

"I'm surprised he yet lives."

Sarovek stood with folded arms and folded wings to the side of the ruined fountain. She nudged a loose rock with a taloned foot, observing the tiny avalanche it made. Because of the panacea and a few other vials of potent nutrient concoctions the Monitors alone knew how to make, it had taken only one day's time for the hawk to make a full recovery. She had left her armor in the manor house and now wore a white linen tunic to conceal the bandages wrapped about her waist.

"I'm not," Saghan replied, lounging against a chunk of the ruin, watching the great gray hulk slumber fitfully amid the wreckage. "I didn't give him a killing dose. Didn't have enough," he added under his breath.

Her snake brother always forgot that a hawk's hearing was nearly as sharp as her vision. Whether Saghan lamented the rhino's survival or was merely stating a fact, Sarovek ignored his statement's ambiguity. She clacked her beak shut (her method of coping with irritation, while Rinnia's was rolling her eyes) and approached the rhinoceros.

She splayed her three-fingered talons against the rough skin of his shoulder and felt the intensity of the heat. It felt like she was scraping the sunbaked sands of Thraxia. She clacked her beak again.

"How long?" she asked.

"I don't know."

"Speak true. I've never known you to be less than utterly precise when you tip your little darts with that ... foulness. And

I've never known you to target an animal at random." Sarovek paused, then simply said, "I know you, Saghan."

"Fine. He'll be brain-dead when the sun comes up, and moments after that, the neural signals to his heart and lungs will—"

"Enough!" Sarovek closed her eyes as she imagined the horror that was to befall this wondrous creature, this mighty and powerful warrior, as the microscopic invaders in his body tore him apart cell by cell. She couldn't stand to hear her brother's description.

"Give him the antidote," she said firmly.

"The bear lived, somehow," said Saghan, as though to himself. His wide mouth fell in a smug frown. "Maybe our friend will be jussst as lucky. Then again, if it had been *me* that poisoned her—"

"Give him the antidote!" Sarovek ignored the biting ache beneath her bandage as she spun on her brother.

"I can't. Salasss—" Saghan broke off. His long neck turned his gaze away. Sarovek knew he was a jumble of emotions when it came to his father. He hated the sound of that name. "He'll kill me," he said quietly.

"Oh, please. Spare me the lie, brother. It doesn't work anymore."

"Fine. Call it punishment, then. For meddling in matters of state. He'll know it was my needle that did this. Did you know our friend here could be a king?"

As though Chewgar had somehow heard him, the rhino's arm twitched and spasmed in response.

"Rinnia overhead them talking," the snake answered Sarovek's unspoken question. His slender hand swept gently over Chewgar's feverish brow, down to the horn at the end of his face. He pressed a finger against its tip, hard enough to draw blood. "Better to let him die," Saghan concluded, watching the scale over his flesh stitch itself together.

"Then give me the needle—the *right* needle—and begone. I can fly away a lot easier than you."

Saghan shook his head, closed his eyes. "I don't have it."

"What?" Sarovek's talons dug into the snake's high collar and jerked him closer. She felt the sutures in her side tugging painfully, but didn't care. "What did you say, you slithering bastard?"

"All I can do is stabilize him." Saghan put his hand over hers and wrenched it away with ease, as if it were no more than a patch of molting skin. "If there is a cure, then you know who has it.

"Besides," he added after a tense silence, "are you forgetting why we poisoned him? Hmm? Are you forgetting our sissster is, quite literally, in the *damn bear's den*? If this lumbering fool stands a chance, it's as good a one as Rinnia stands of getting the relay. Which is to say…"

"Rinnia will succeed."

Another silence passed; the only sound was the rustling leaves on the vines clinging to the courtyard's walls. And far to the west, very faint, were distant howls, and maybe screams.

"It's too late," Saghan said at last. "She's not coming back, Sarovek."

"She will," the hawk said, blinking her wide saucer eyes. She looked eastward, imagining the Mind's campus sprawled across that enormous portion of Crosswall, and the Pinnacle Tower at its triangular center. When Saghan had informed her Rinnia had insisted on going with the fox to climb that towering monstrosity, she had almost taken to the sky immediately. But the snake reminded the hawk that of all the Monitors in the brotherhood, she was the least stealthy and, therefore, the most likely to be killed first. And therefore the one who would get them all killed.

"She will," Sarovek repeated, even though she believed it less this time.

"Fine. But think on what we will do if she doesn't. Hmm? There will be nowhere to escape his wrath. Oh, I know! You can fly us to the Aigaion. I heard you know a Corvidian who's crazy enough to think that's possible."

This time, Sarovek didn't simply clack her beak. She struck his jaw with all her strength. Being Monitors made them brother and sister of a sort, but to a Corvidian there was no higher family than one's own house, one's own blood, and there was no honor more sacred or in need of preservation.

"You dare to speak of my brother so." She seethed and took a step forward. "If I could kill you, if you were not our master's … *abomination*, you would be dead where you stand."

Saghan's forked tongue whipped rhythmically as he stroked his bruised jaw. "Well, I'm *sitting*. But, yes, I … apologize." The last word sounded more like a question, as though he needed clarification it was the correct one. Then his voice grew lower, grating. "But don't ever call me that again. I can't change what I am."

Sarovek didn't empathize with the reptile the same way Rinnia did. She'd meant every word. She knew it was the only way to truly hurt him. But she also knew that now wasn't the time. Sarovek let the matter go and kneeled again by the rhino. She ran her talons gently over the topography of his bare muscular arms. Chewgar's breaths had grown heavier, and there was now a rattle, a distinct sign that fluid had begun seeping into his lungs.

"Such a waste," she said. "Of a warrior. Of a king. Do you think…" She caressed the gray skin beneath the rhino's eye, which looked up at her, helpless. "Saghan, do you think the Mind would trade his life for the relay?"

"Ha!"

"They have a perfectly good puppet already, don't they?"

Saghan's laughter ceased. He slid closer to his sister, his forked tongue lashing the air inches from her face, as though it could snatch her thoughts from the air.

"Why don't we," she continued, "*educate* him?"

The hawk's eyes picked up everything. She stared into the snake's slit black pupils as they widened and contracted, watching the scenarios and ramifications playing out in his mind. What would it mean if a warrior with a claim to real power—a king puppet that the common puppets would follow—were to suddenly know the truth of this world, of the game that was played? Of the game still being played? Of the real players?

"Yesss," Saghan conceded at last. "We will need to hold him down somehow."

"I don't think there are any chains long enough, or strong enough, in the house." Her keen eyes reassessed the gigantic ridges of Chewgar's muscles. "I doubt the two of us could lift them if there were."

"That's why we have," Saghan reached a hand around his waist and brought it back with a flourish, holding a small black sphere, "technology!" He rubbed the side of the device, and its locking mechanism popped with the release of its pressure. A thin web of long chains shout out harmlessly in all directions, with much less force than the sphere he had thrown the previous night at the Aurochs' Haunch's window. He set to work passing the tiny, incredibly durable chain through the metal rings on the black sphere, and a moment later the neck of the rhino who would be king was leashed with a terrible explosive.

"Puppet shows are most convincing when you can't see the strings." From the bracer of his ornate red armor, Saghan pulled a metallic sliver free. "And when there's no trace of the puppeteer."

Tiny drops of water trickled down the bricks of the cell. Farther along the dank corridor, a single torch provided the only illumination in this part of the Mind's dungeons. In the dim light, Rinnia tried her best to count the drops as they carved deeper and deeper into the stone.

"Time," she reminded herself. "And water."

She pictured the Pinnacle Tower, the campus it stood upon, the cult itself—relatively young as far as the entirety of Herbridian history was concerned—all of the Mind pitted against the inexorable forces of nature (in this case time and water) and how those forces would eventually eat the whole intellectual empire away.

A part of her wanted to fully embrace this notion, to apply it to her own life and the purpose that had brought her here. "What's it all matter?" she asked herself, in a whisper so low it was outmatched by the rhythmic, pattering drip that had soaked the fur of her bushy tail.

But the other part, the part she considered the true Rinnia, answered, "Because I'm here, now, in this time, and I'm still alive. And while I'm alive I can still do something."

She lifted her arms from her lap and felt the weight of the chains that attached them to the wall. She peered at the four heavy bolts embedded in the bricks that fastened them there and estimated they were as thick as the bones in her thighs.

Rinnia dropped her arms heavily. She was considering giving up hope for herself, perhaps, but not for Sarovek and Saghan. Maybe not for the rhino either.

"But what about you?" she called through the iron bars, across the darkness of the corridor, and into the shadows of the small cell that matched her own. Even in the dim light thrown by the torch farther down the way, she could see the other fox well enough.

Maxan lay in a heap where the Mind's jailers had thrown him, facedown on the dirt floor, breathing heavily. His deep sleep was as much an aftereffect of the red metabolic pellet she'd given him as it was of the kick she'd planted at the base of his skull. In a way she was envious of the idiot; she had only rested for what she guessed was no more than one hour while he'd snoozed for several.

"You brought us here," she mumbled. "*Your* choices. It never would have come to this if you hadn't interfered."

Maxan pushed hard, suddenly, against the ground and rolled over. Rinnia thought he had somehow heard her and would retaliate, but he only mumbled something about a coin before falling again into unconsciousness.

"That idiot saved my life," Rinnia whispered, resuming the conversation with herself after a moment. She knew it was true, even the part of her that didn't want to believe it. If Maxan had run away, if he hadn't jumped into the beast pen and slashed at the wolf, she would be dead. Sarovek would be dead.

"And the principals too," she breathed. She knew they couldn't stop Saghan. No power they could call would be great enough if their master chose to possess her brother...

"He would have it. And would have brought it home. And undone," she whispered, her lips shuddering as if afraid *he* would hear, "everything I've worked to protect."

As far as everyone was concerned (her brother, her sister, even the Master Monitor himself), Rinnia was dedicated to the mission of retrieving the relay—that piece of the great satellite that was stolen long ago—and doing her part to reset the signal that kept the great game running. But none of them had any idea that she knew the truth—several layers of it, in fact, deeper than perhaps even Saghan, the master's own son, did. Rinnia didn't just know of the game's existence; she knew why it had to be played.

Here and now, however much it stung her to admit, she also knew that she was thankful to Maxan for more than just saving her life. If he hadn't been brave enough to strike at Saghan at the inn, if he hadn't been tough enough to get blown through a window, if he hadn't been determined enough to get back up and run with the relay...

"Then he *would* have it. And we'd all be doomed anyway.

"But Maxan betrayed me," she shot back at herself.

"Sure," she countered, "to save his friend.

"But I can't forget." Her mouth parted again to add *I can't forgive*, but she couldn't give it breath. After all, the two of them—perhaps testaments to the natural inclination of the fox species—had a knack for betrayal.

With everything she knew, as much as she hated to admit it, the world might still have a chance with the Mind. If something wasn't done to prevent species from going astray, Herbridia would quite literally eat itself within a decade, and this planet would be nothing more than a never-ending, violent cycle between predator and prey. Maybe Folgian wasn't crazy to think that educating the common people could keep their inner beasts in check.

But then Rinnia reminded herself that when all the true power was held by the few, who were free to decide which parts of the truth to reveal and which to conceal, the world would fall into a much more vicious cycle. Of all the books in Folgian's library, scribed by all her scholars, read by all her students, preached by all the initiates she sent out across the world, Rinnia doubted any of them knew the real truth.

"That none of this is real," she muttered, remembering Old Four Swords's revelation when he had found her as a girl. She remembered how those words had devastated her.

She wondered if he would come to rescue her now. It wouldn't matter how many hundreds of soldiers the Mind could throw at him. They could empty every bunk in every barrack at every corner of their sprawling campus and he would slice them all to pieces. But no, Old Four Swords wasn't coming. It wasn't a question of numbers or skill, but of location and tactics. He had only survived these last twenty years on the run, he had told her, by never allowing himself to be backed into a corner, and if this dank dungeon was anything, it was clearly a corner.

"No one's coming," she admitted, drawing her legs up to her chest and dropping her head onto them, curling her damp tail around herself for warmth. Her eyelids felt heavy with resignation, so she gave up on holding them open.

The next thing she knew was the raised, squeaky voice that echoed from the corridor.

"Principals said so!" it said, high-pitched and incredibly impatient. "We got questions! They got answers! You gotta skedaddle, pal! Couldn't be more simple!"

Rinnia found herself on her side, covered in dirt (at least she hoped it was just dirt), and realized she must have slept. She rose quickly and moved to the bars for a better look, but her chains snapped taut with a clink.

"Hear that? They're awake! Excellent! Dismissed!"

"Hey! Hold it!" This was the gruff voice of her jailer, one of them anyway. Rinnia remembered the gorilla's distinct, rough quality; when they had first met, he had seemed delighted to point out how he would administer the interrogation once Harmony gave the word.

But whomever the gorilla was hollering at didn't hold it. Rinnia heard the patter of little paws and saw a small shadow pass across the corridor's wall. A moment later, a squirrel juvenile no taller than her waist came within her view beyond the bars. He wore the red robes of a Mind's scholar, the triangular sigil etched in yellow thread on his chest.

"Heya!" he chittered through the bars, his head small enough to fit between them. "Rest well? Thoughts all clear? Good morning. Early morning, I mean… No Yinna. Not yet. No matter! I'm Pryth!" As the gorilla came into view—his knuckled, meaty forearms pounding the dirt—the squirrel added, "And *he's* just leaving! Right? On your way out, pal. Scram! As ordered!"

"As ordered?" The gorilla's big fist thumped his chest. "No one's to—"

"Chop-chop!"

"Principal Harm—"

"Off ya go!"

"She said—"

"Thirsty?" A small bottle of clear liquid sloshed in the squirrel's tiny paw. He must have pulled it from the sleeve of his robe while Rinnia blinked incredulously. She was trying to catch up with her sluggish thoughts, which were trying to catch up with all this tiny juvenile had said.

Pryth held the bottle up to the gorilla. While huge in the squirrel's paw, the thing was only as big as the nail on the gorilla's smallest finger.

"Hold on a—"

"You *look* thirsty. You feel thirsty? You do. Take a swill. A quaff. A guzzle."

"No!" the gorilla erupted. He swiped angrily at the tiny bottle in the boy's paw, but missed, again and again, as Pryth's arm pumped back and forth, back and forth, and each time the boy insisted with a new synonym.

"Swig. Swill. Gulp. Drink."

Then Pryth said, "Enough!" and wheeled on the tiny pads of his paws with one final dodge of the furious gorilla's swipe. The juvenile's bushy tail prickled up proudly from his rump as he stalked a few paces away, clicking his tongue in disappointment.

The only explanation Rinnia's addled brain could conjure was that the Mind had chosen her, its most valuable prisoner, as the test audience for its latest comedy routine. Whether it was from her fatigue or from sincere enjoyment, she found herself smiling at the little creature.

A shadow shifted on the wall of the corridor, and a moment later, a second squirrel appeared, absolutely identical in wardrobe, size, and appearance, save for the strikingly angular, feminine shape of her eyes.

"Pram! Ugh, *finally*... Try to keep up, sis!" Pryth held out the bottle. "The monkey doesn't want to drink!"

The gorilla huffed in protest. "Monkey? I'm not—"

"Thirsty! Look, pal. I told you. Yes, you are. Agh, forget it! I'll never get the mind-control stuff ... Pram? He's thirsty. Isn't he, Pram?"

In the next blink of her eye, Rinnia was certain the jailer's rising, massive arm would crush the boy's bones against the bars of her cell, but the girl raised her arm faster, the tips of her tiny claws spread out, and the gorilla froze in place. The pose was unnatural. The gorilla was so still, it seemed more like time itself had locked him in place.

"Pram. Don't forget this time. He's gotta breathe, Pram!"

The girl remained still but moved her fingers slowly. The gorilla's arm lowered itself, and his massive barrel-shaped chest expanded with air once more. At the flick of her finger, the gorilla plucked the tiny bottle from Pryth's outstretched paw—which the boy had uncorked—and lifted it to his black lips.

"Finally!" Pryth sighed, flicking the cork at the gorilla's broad forehead, pegging him directly between the eyes. "Now go! Lie down somewhere. And let the big boys and girls get to business. Mkay?"

Pram drew her arm away and pointed back down the corridor, and the gorilla did as he was told. She easily lifted the jingling key ring from his belt as he passed.

"Make sure he forgets, Pram. Or we're in trouble. Deep shit, got it?"

The girl spun around to face her twin brother, closed her eyes, and dipped her head in a solemn nod.

The boy twirled around to Rinnia's cell and cleared his throat. "Now then. Shit! Again! Sorry for that. Did I already say sorry? Did I just say *again*? Sorry. Forget it. *You're* Rinnia." This last observation came with an emphasizing point of Pryth's claw tip and a wink of his eye. "We're here to let you go. Not really. But kind of. You're coming with us."

Rinnia realized her jaw had gone slack as the comedy routine wrapped up. She finally closed it, swallowed, and said, "Wait. Who are you?"

"I'm Pryth. She's Pram."

"I gathered that. I mean who *are* you?"

"Uh. Squirrels?"

"No, I mean, what are—"

"We're twins!"

"Yes, I see th—"

"So what're you—aha!" Pryth pinched part of his red robe and held it up through the bars. "We're Mind scholars!"

Rinnia rolled her eyes. "No! *What are you doing here?*"

"Oh! Right. Setting you free! Er, letting you go? No! Wait... Didn't I answer this already?"

"Why!" Rinnia yelled, startling the young squirrel several feet off the ground. She took a step backward, allowing for just enough slack in the clinking chain to reach a paw up and pinch the fur between her eyes, which she had squeezed tightly shut. "I mean why are you here to collect me?"

"Both of you," said Pryth, ignorant of the more vital part of Rinnia's question. "Him too." He jerked a thumb at Maxan's cell, smiled wide, and winked again. Before Rinnia could clarify, Pryth turned to his sister and said, "C'mon! C'mon!"

Pram unslung a pack from her shoulder and brought forth two red scholars' robes. She tossed one between the bars of Rinnia's cell.

"And these?" the fox said, holding up her chained wrists.

"Oh," said Pryth, "that's my department." The squirrel boy gestured at the metal plate bolted to the bricks behind her, and with the flick of his wrist, the chains' first few links glowed a dull red, then intensified to a brilliant white before dribbling to the floor in hissing clumps.

Rinnia felt the scorching heat even several paces away. The molten slag left a cloying smell of burnt dirt and dust in the air.

Pryth beamed, rocking back and forth on his ankle joints. "I got elements. Well, er, one of 'em anyhow. And Pram's got the... what's it...? Whatever! The whatcha call it."

"And what am I supposed to do?" Rinnia asked, frowning at the lump of cooling metal the chains still attached her to. "Carry all this under that robe?"

"Oh! No! No, no. Sorry. No. I just wanted to see, y'know, if I could rip it out. Okay? Here's the real stuff now." Pryth clapped his paws together, and Rinnia felt the manacles around both her wrists vibrate. Then his arms exploded outward, and the iron locks tore themselves apart and shot into the cell walls. Rinnia's chains fell in a heap.

"Boooom!!" Pryth shouted, loud enough to wake the dead, but not Maxan. Pryth's tiny claw tips covered his lips, his eyes rolled, and he whispered, "Oops ... Shit ... I mean ... *boom* ..."

Rinnia swept the red robe around her shoulders. "How do you know I won't knock you both unconscious and find my way out of this hole on my own?"

"Whoa! Lady! No need for violence. Do we look violent? We're *children*!" Pryth took a step back and snapped his fingers at his sister. As Pram approached the enormous lock that held the sliding bars of her cell in place, Pryth added, "Besides, my sister'll make you smash your own skull against the wall until it cracks like an egg."

The squirrel girl cranked the key until the bolt creaked back, then slid the bars along their frame and stepped away to tend to Maxan's cell.

Rinnia stepped into the corridor and stood next to Pryth. The two of them watched Pram unlatch the lock and slide the bars away. The fox within still slumbered, oblivious to all the commotion.

"Oh!" Pryth spurted suddenly. "I get it. Brother and sister?"

Rinnia shot a scathing look down at the little squirrel, but his cute smile only beamed wider.

Waking the fox from his deep sleep proved to be more of a challenge than any of them anticipated. Pryth ordered his twin sister to try her "trick," then asked politely when Pram scowled at him. After a few silent attempts, in which she raised her arm and worked the tiny points of her claws through a variety of movements, Pram shook her head, confused and agitated. So it was left to Rinnia, who told the squirrels she had a trick of her own.

She straddled Maxan's chest and slapped either side of his muzzle, lightly at first, and then twice more with rather liberal force. His eyelids fluttered for a few seconds, then closed again, so Rinnia slapped him a final time to make certain they stayed open. And they did.

"C'mon, you two," Pryth said, leaning in close over the two foxes. "Master's waiting."

Maxan made a sound, something like "Whazza," and he lurched upward onto his rump. His bushy tail swished left and right in the dirt behind him, working out the stiffness of being lain upon for hours. Every muscle was sore, as though he had run for a hundred miles without rest. For some reason his memory could not explain, his muzzle felt sorest of all.

Maxan set to rubbing the throbbing pain away, until Rinnia tossed a red robe in his face.

"Put this on," she said. "Now."

"What the—" The question died in his throat when he pulled the robe away, when he saw two young squirrels and Rinnia standing over him, when he realized he was on the dirt floor of a cell. He cleared his throat and finished, "What's going on?"

The fast-talking squirrel jumped in then. "Remember me, guy?" Pryth introduced his sister, and told Maxan all about their ingenious jailbreak with flourishing *bams*, and *whooshes*. It took him fifteen seconds, but none of it seemed to register with Maxan, who stared blankly with a slack jaw as Pryth finally blurted, "Mkay?"

Rinnia took over and simply said, "We're getting out of here. Get up."

She, who kicked me in the head—I think it was her, anyway—now offers to help me stand.

Maxan put his paw in hers and rose to his feet. He pulled the red robe around his shoulders, concealing the white-and-black guard uniform beneath.

Three times in ... whatever days. Three times, I've been knocked out cold.

Whatever kind of sleep he seized when Rinnia put him under didn't necessarily help him fully recover his mental faculties, so he had neither the capacity nor the desire to formulate some kind of plan to get away from his two little escorts. Pryth said he had a way out, and Rinnia didn't seemed opposed to the idea—*Yet*—so Maxan resigned himself to see where it led.

Cell's wide open, he surmised. *So off to a good start at least.*

They went in single file down the corridor, a procession of four red-robed scholars. As they passed the gorilla slumped over on a table and snoring loudly, Pram delicately looped his ring of keys on the hook of his belt and retrieved an empty vial from the table.

This branch of the Mind's dungeons was isolated from the rest. Every cell they had passed so far stood empty, with no evidence—or smell—to indicate that they had ever held prisoners. They took a few turns, passed through a few barred gates—whose sentries seemed to have inexplicably forgotten the important visitors they had let through an hour ago, a fact Pryth now happily reminded them of—and ultimately came to a more populated portion of the latticed network of corridors and cells. The smell was certainly stronger here, and Maxan pulled the edge of his red hood over one side of his muzzle to filter it when he breathed. It did little good.

Every cell they passed now was occupied. Some of these prisoners grasped the bars and pressed their muzzles through to plead, wild-eyed, with the passing scholars to let them go.

Some others paced their cells quietly, gibbering to themselves like madmen and scratching at their fur with claws caked in their own dried blood. Most of these moved about their tiny cells on two legs, but some did so on all four, and these latter prisoners bared their fangs, growled, and raked at the dirt floors with their paws. All of the prisoners were Leorans, and all of them, Maxan saw clearly, were going astray.

As they passed one cell in particular, Maxan was captivated by a pair of green lights glowing in the shadows beyond the bars. Rinnia shoved him aside just as a tiger's striped arm swiped between the bars, a powerful blow meant to snag the red-robed visitor. A thunder rumbled in the tiger's throat as she faded slowly back into the dark.

Besides the Mind's sentries—who were all larger Leoran species like boars, bears, and gorillas, and were all wearing studded leather armor embroidered with the same triangular yellow sigil—Maxan and his escorts passed small gatherings of blue-robed students who huddled just outside cells, posing questions to the captives, dipping quill pens in ink, and scrawling notes upon bundles of parchment. Some were even dripping fluids from small vials onto raw shanks of meat and goading the more afflicted specimens to ingest these. Some other clusters of observers held torches aloft to cast better light upon the most feral Stray, while their counterparts sketched illustrations of their altered physiology and gait.

So it's true. Stray get dumped in the western district, or the Mind kidnaps them.

But why? To help?

What kind of help is this? Are these students going to recite Folgian's books to that tigress and expect her to get regain her better self?

Maxan remembered the flickering hate in Saghan's eyes, the light from them burning through the darkened inn's second floor. In that look, Maxan had seen the snake wavering on that edge, between being an animal and being…

Being what?

Being human, Max.

The word arrested him, rooted him to the packed dirt floor. It was a word spoken inside his head with his voice but not his will. Just like another he'd spoken to Folgian. He had no idea where these words came from. How could he know them but not know what they meant?

My head's starting to hurt.

"Maxan." Rinnia glared at him from farther down the corridor. Some of the students here had taken notice of the higher-ranked scholar standing dumbfounded in their midst.

"Ah," he said with an august gesture, glad to forget his own, painful thoughts. "As you were."

At long last, the four scholars passed a final gate into a wide entry chamber, climbed a broad staircase, and stepped into the grand hall at the lowest level of the Pinnacle Tower's interior. "Electricity," Maxan mumbled, seeing again the arcing streaks of light scrabbling within their glass cages. As quiet as he'd been, Pryth's little ears perked up, and the energetic squirrel just couldn't resist the urge to ham it up.

"Ah! Yes, indeed, master! An ancient marvel. Electricity. Yes? Am I right? Right. This way, mast—*OW!*" Pryth squeezed one eye closed and swept a paw over his face as if someone had just thrown a pie at him. "What'd you do that for?" He wheeled about to face his twin sister.

Maxan looked to Pram. The caustic look she gave her brother could have wilted a field of wildflowers.

"Just … getting into character, y'know?" Pryth looked around at all the crowds about the grand hall, who had taken no notice. "I got a reputation to keep 'round here, y'know."

He shrugged. "Besides, Pram ... *fun*! Y'know? Remember what *fun* is?"

Pram stormed away into the bustle, moving toward the great doors. The two foxes exchanged a glance, shook their heads simultaneously, shrugged, and followed her.

They walked casually across the campus for nearly twenty minutes before abandoning the main thoroughfare to wind along the smaller pathways between some outlying buildings and even a cluster of pens and corrals for livestock and beasts of burden. Maxan soon realized that not once had he seen a black-robed principal among the hundreds of cultists they had passed. He wondered how often any of the common initiates and students, and perhaps even scholars, saw Harmony or Feyn. Or Folgian. *How much do they really know about their leadership? Do they know about the Stray imprisoned in the dungeons?* If any of the captives below were the mothers, fathers, brothers, sisters, sons, or daughters of any of the robed followers above, Maxan wondered if these initiates would still proudly wear their colors and willingly be a part of the Mind, a part of the system that kept their loved ones in chains. *Would any of them object to being prodded, observed, drugged, and dissected if they felt themselves going astray?*

Even as the pathways they walked became less crowded, Maxan occasionally spotted a small group of the Mind's robed animals laughing, smiling, sharing stories, or debating issues they considered important, and he sincerely wondered if what Folgian had said was true, if learning truly could prevent the violence in their hearts from being set loose. But then he remembered there was at least one thing—one dangerous thing—that their supreme leader had kept from them, and there were likely hundreds more.

Maxan shuddered as he thought about the relay's drowning red light, imagining it spreading across this vast space, staining the green fields and gardens and hillocks of the campus with blood.

By now the dark gray blue of the early-morning sky had filled with the white shimmer of full daylight. Enormous gray clouds, a storm burgeoning them from within, were sweeping in slowly from the west, on course to overtake Yinna's rays in a matter of hours and threatening to wash Crosswall with rain. But Maxan had no time to appreciate the glorious weather while it lasted, or to ponder the possibility of escape, as the four of them had arrived at their destination.

They had meandered about the campus in a generally westerly direction, and had come nearly a full mile from its center to a large manor house whose fenced and gated grounds ran right up against the high wall surrounding the Mind's triangular tract of land. The place was likely as spacious as the haunted estate the Monitors called their safe house, but unlike that gaudy structure with its crenellated edges and high-steepled rooftops, the architecture here was simpler and sturdier.

Pryth led the way up the path to the large front door. Without losing a step, he waved his paw, and the door creaked open wide enough for them to enter one by one.

Just beyond the threshold, they entered into a large room with a high vaulted ceiling, a floor dug three feet belowground, balconies at opposite sides, and a pleasantly crackling fire pit at its center. The smoke from the fire escaped through a grated circular hole between two thick rafters that must once have been mighty Denland trees. Arranged neatly around all of this were woven rugs and plush, cozy furniture of the finest artisanal craft.

Principal Feyn stood from one of these chairs as they entered and beckoned them to join him, gesturing at a low table where a skinny green-robed initiate was just finishing laying out dishes of seasoned salads, grilled strips of meat, bowls of ripe fruit, soft loaves of bread, and decanters of steaming teas.

"Sit," the white wolf offered. "Eat."

"Sure!" Pryth said quickly, bounding to the closest bowl of greens and lifting pawfuls of its contents to his mouth.

Pram followed her brother's lead at a slower pace, but the two foxes remained frozen just within the manor's doorway.

"I don't need to tap into your minds to know what you're thinking," Feyn told them. Maxan sensed a sincerity in his words—*Something new for the wolf*—but the scar dragging the edge of his maw into a permanent snarl made it hard to believe.

He's dangerous, Maxan's inner voice reminded him. *Among the most dangerous. Be ready.*

Maxan scoffed, somewhat tired of these circumstances. "Not going to throw that nice couch at us if we do something wrong, are you?"

"This isn't a trap. You're free to go. But you won't leave. Not until you hear what I have to say. First, eat."

Maxan's growling stomach made the decision before the rest of him could object. Feyn had a point, it told him. *And if we're going to die, might as well do so with a bellyful.* He hopped down the stairs into the recessed den and took a place next to the squirrel boy, then snatched a strip of grilled meat in either paw and tore into them greedily, before even considering if Feyn had poisoned it all.

But he said it wasn't a trap. He stopped chewing.

Exactly what someone who's laid a trap would say.

"If I wanted you dead," Feyn said, "then I'd simply smash your skull with something heavy. Or I'd have left you in the dungeons."

Maxan gulped down a wad of food nervously. *I thought he couldn't—*

"And I don't need to feel your mind to read the concern on your face." The other corner of Feyn's mouth smiled in equal measure with his scar.

Maxan eyed Rinnia, framed by the light from beyond the open door, as she balled her paws into fists and lowered her center of gravity, ready to bolt away at the next bat of the wolf's eyelash. She remained there for a few breaths, just watching, waiting, unsure of her next move or what this all meant.

"Folgian is wrong," Feyn called to her. "Go, if that's what you want. But you'll never get what you came for out there."

"How do you know?" asked Maxan.

The white wolf settled back into his lavish chair, his wrists emerging from the wide sleeves of his black principal's robe, the claws of either paw touching to make a steeple. His icy blue eyes closed, and his nostrils widened, sucking in a deep breath. He remained still for several breaths, long enough for Rinnia to finally join them. Even Pryth managed to stop fidgeting in the silence.

"When she found me," Feyn began slowly, opening his eyes and fixing his gaze on the foxes, "I was wild. Lost. Covered in filth and blood, some of it mine. And this." His claw traced the line of his scar, from the base of his ear to the corner of his mouth. "She … saved me. She reached inside my mind and found the … self, that I wanted to be. Not this … *animal*. And she brought me back. And that's when I saw *her*, you understand? A once-proud bear reduced to withered flesh and fur. Withering more by the minute. Folgian needed me as much as I needed her. Together, we built the Mind. Everything you see. It's *ours*.

"But…" He trailed off. He stood, ascended the small stair out of the sunken floor, and stood with paws clasped at his back by the tall windows facing the high outer wall of Crosswall and a yard full of flowers.

Maxan realized that in the short time he'd known Principal Feyn, he'd never imagined the wolf could carry himself with such dignity. It was hard to picture him now with his claws around Rinnia's throat, calling on the Aigaion to hurl her own swords back at her.

"I can live this lie no longer," Feyn stated. "Folgian, my master, my savior, she is wrong. The Stray cannot be stopped. Culture, education, laws and justice, codes and punishments… Society itself will only *slow* the inevitable. The beast will always win. Always. It gnaws upon our rational brains, consumes our thoughts, leaves only the baser lusts and instincts. It eats our identity, until only the true animal remains."

Maxan suddenly understood. "You're Stray. *Still* Stray. Aren't you?"

"We all are." Feyn turned his head, looking sideways at his guests with one icy blue eye. Framed by the light streaming in from the windows, he seemed hardly more than a shadow. "It's in our nature, to destroy ourselves."

"So what, then? If you're saying we're all doomed, and that the Mind can't do anything to stop it …" Maxan waved a skewer of half-finished meat in the air, suddenly at a complete loss for words. *Then what are we—what am I—still doing here?*

He tossed the skewer down with the rest and stood up. "I have to go. And see if my friend's *already dead.*" He spat the final words—Folgian's words—venomously, spun around, and started for the door.

"You told her that the relay makes us Stray," Feyn called after him, freezing the fox mid-step. "How did you know that?"

"Because I saw it. With these." He turned and held two claws dramatically up to his mismatched eyes for emphasis. "And your master said it herself; it's a weapon. Maybe it is better off here." He looked to Rinnia, for what he thought would be the last time. "I'm sorry. We failed. *I* failed. And I have to see Chewgar."

"The relay is not a weapon," Feyn cut in before Rinnia could say anything, circling the recessed lounge, his eyes fixed on Maxan. "It doesn't have to be. When I call upon the Aigaion's raw power, to shape this world, there is always … an emptiness." Feyn snarled in frustration, failing to come up with a phrase a non-caller could understand. "An illusion. Like the strings I'm reaching for are not as far away as I feel them."

Maxan's eyes drifted over the twin squirrels as their principal spoke. The girl sat straight-backed, her paws folded in her lap, watching her master intently. The boy's claws hovered over a bowl of greens, his eyes flitting between the fox and the wolf as if unsure he had permission to take another bite. But when Feyn spoke of illusions and strings, Maxan saw the affirmation in their eyes.

But I still don't know what this has to do with me. Or Chewgar. Or anything.

He cleared his throat. "Okay. So?"

"So," Feyn grumbled, "when the relay is near, that emptiness is filled. And more than that … the beast inside—the part of myself I loathe, which would claw its way out and have me rip your eyes out …" Feyn grew quiet, even as Maxan flinched. "It is silent."

Rinnia sprang up from her seat and nudged Maxan aside to face the wolf directly. "That is not possible."

"And what would *you* know?" Feyn turned the scarred side of his maw sideways and stared down at her like she was nothing.

"Stop it, will you?" Maxan came between them, afraid the principal of the Mind and the Monitor would settle what they started in the beast pen little more than a day ago. Rinnia shrugged away from Maxan's paw, but went back to her chair instead of the door, folding her arms and tapping the tip of her tail on the stone floor in agitation. *Well,* Maxan thought, *at least she didn't leave.*

But Feyn's right, Max. How can she know?

Because she knows ... something.

His suspicions would have to wait. "So why are you telling us all this?" he asked Feyn flatly.

"Because I believe that the relay can save us."

Maxan considered again how the snow-white wolf had been carrying himself differently ever since they got here. His stance, his tone. *How about the fact that he sprung us from the dungeon? To reason with us. He wants something.*

"You really mean it," Maxan said, breaking the silence that had fallen.

"I *feel* it."

"Tell me why you let us go."

"Because we share a common enemy." Feyn paced slowly to the chair beside Rinnia's, drawing her seething gaze. "The Mind," he said to her, almost pleadingly. "And the Monitors."

Rinnia glanced at the wolf. Then she looked at the squirrel twins.

Callers, Maxan realized, eyeing them as well. *And more on the way,* Folgian said. *But...*

And then he knew what Feyn was getting at. Or rather, who.

"Harmony," he said.

Feyn nodded slowly. "The gray owl. The Corvidian. The outsider from beyond our border, who would rise to principal, who would poison the supreme master's convictions with falsehoods. Your brotherhood may have once done its work on the bear's body, but the owl would poison the Mind itself. Harmony is powerful beyond measure. Beyond me. Beyond them." Feyn glanced at his red-robed pupils.

Pram's gaze fell to her lap, as if ashamed by the truth that Feyn spoke, as if she herself had somehow let it happen. Pryth's little tongue stuck out, and his eyes traced the ceiling, as if he were solving a mental equation. Then he shrugged and nodded. "Yep," he said.

"Harmony invaded our campus five years ago, claiming her Corvidian house had fallen from prominence because of her *curse*. That her connection to the Aigaion made her an outcast in Corvidian society." Feyn's voice fell further and further into a guttural growl the longer he talked about his fellow principal. "She proved her connection to the Aigaion, easily. It wasn't long before Folgian recognized her strength and gave her the black robe, and with it, control. Of our very nation."

"Jealousy."

Feyn snapped his scowling face toward the fox that dared to say it.

"I was jealous of my brother once," Rinnia went on. "Of *his* gifts. Of *his* place in our brotherhood. Always at the master's side, while I was … Anyway. I get it." She rose from her chair. "Be careful. Or else it will turn you into someone you really don't want to be. Maxan, let's go."

"Wait, Rinnia." He grasped her by the sleeve and held on even when she tried to shrug him off. While she had been talking, trying to get a rise out of the wolf just to spite him, the pieces of the puzzle had been arranging themselves in his mind.

Maxan turned back to Feyn. "You don't want her to have it, do you?"

"Folgian will die. Soon. The Monitors saw to that. And once she is gone, I fear I will not be not strong enough to keep Harmony from using the relay to do as she desires."

"To do what?" Maxan prodded, the full picture becoming even clearer.

"Start a war," Feyn said.

Maxan felt Rinnia relax in his grip.

"Even now," the wolf went on, "she conspires to weaken Leora from the inside out. Until yesterday, I had no real evidence. No real proof. Only suspicions. But then, when your captain asked the Mind to help stop the fires from spreading, to rebuild the western district... Harmony and Folgian, they lied to him. I overheard them, later, discussing the irony of his request. They mean to burn that place to the ground. And everyone in it."

Maxan's paw fell away from Rinnia's sleeve. He suddenly felt as if the world had fallen away beneath him.

"And as the panic becomes a pogrom, as more and more Stray are rounded up, Harmony will disappear with the relay, leaving the Mind in disarray, leaving the Leoran throne empty. And so, the knights of Corvidia will swoop in to claim dominion, as their great houses feel is their natural right."

Maxan thought about all the time he'd spent on the rooftops of the western district, all his years as a shadow, sprinting and climbing, waiting, observing, reporting, never engaging. Hearing the Stray howling, finding the shredded, eviscerated remains from their passing. He imagined the endless lines of the afflicted and accused, shuffling their feet, starving, sleeping in the cold, despairing, dying.

All of it. All my time. For what? So they can burn? So they can run even as the eagles ram spears in their backs?

Guilt surged in him as he recalled how he'd once longed for an escape, how he'd wanted to steal the relay and sell it and run away. Run away again, like he had before, just turn his back on all of it. How he'd leave Crosswall behind, for good, and start a new gang of robbers and thieves.

And be no better than raiders like Yacub.

And he imagined Chewgar, keeping the sole watch in the courtyard of their guardhouse after all the rest had abandoned him, the lone defender of his district, even as the Stray charged in from the west, and the flames advanced from the east.

Run. Or serve. Or die. But what else can you do, *Max?*

Maybe ... with Feyn... Maxan looked at the wolf's face, seeing beyond the hideousness of the scar, looking deeply into the wolf's icy blue eyes, to the goodness that dwelled there beyond the animal. *Maybe with him, I can do something.*

"You have it," he said firmly. "Don't you?"

Feyn reached into the folds of his robe and withdrew the relay, its golden lights bathing the walls and ceiling in shimmering golden light, more intense than the bright sunshine spilling in through the windows.

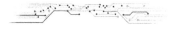

There it was, just within her arm's reach, the very thing her master had sent her to Crosswall to retrieve. The thing Old Four Swords had said should never find its way into his scaled fingers. But Rinnia only exhaled, forcing her rising adrenaline to settle, knowing there was no move she could make fast enough to outrun the squirrel boy's command of heat and fire, or the wolf's will to bring the house down upon her.

"So what now?" she said, her voice sounding as bored as she'd hoped for. "Are you just going to give it to us and let us be on our way?" She even snatched up a skewer of meat from the table to hide the trembling in her paws.

Feyn set the relay on his thigh, ran the tips of his black claws along the polished metal, and considered Rinnia's words. Maxan looked worried, like he expected her to pounce on the wolf and spear him with the skewer. Instead, she raised the meat to her muzzle, tore off a chunk, and sank back into the cushions of her chair, chewing hungrily.

"There is a rumor," Feyn said only to her, "that, far across the mountains, on the shores of Lake Skymere, a great tower is being raised. Taller than the Pinnacle. Allegedly, a way by which a Corvidian may reach the Aigaion. Is it true?"

Rinnia shrugged. "You'd have to ask a Corvidian."

Feyn leered at the fox, seeing through the poorly managed bluff. "It is true. You know it, may even have seen it. Your master is building it, isn't he? With Corvidian money and stone. And Drakoran labor."

She stopped chewing. The food was sand in her dry mouth. The little bit she'd forced herself to swallow felt lodged like a boulder in her stomach. "Mostly right." She tossed the half-eaten skewer back onto the platter.

"Hey!" Pryth moaned, flicking her stick aside from the others. "Germs!"

"You will take me there," Feyn said, ignoring the juvenile squirrel like everyone else. "To meet him. To meet the Master Monitor, Salastragore."

Rinnia clenched her paw into a fist at her side, stabbing a claw into the soft pad of her palm, anything to keep from shaking. "And then?"

"He will take me ... home."

CHAPTER TEN

THE WATCHER FROM THE WELL

MAXAN FELL BACK A STEP TO SEE IF RINNIA would even notice. She might as well have been walking alone, he realized, as her gaze remained fixed ahead. She was like a spear, carving her way through the crowds. He had felt this sullen, furious energy radiating from her since they left Feyn's manor. From there, they'd passed under the campus's gates, through the eastern and central districts, then over the western wall, posing as the Mind's scholars the whole way before finally tossing their red robes on the smoldering embers of an abandoned cookfire in an alley just a few minutes ago.

We're almost there. Ask her something, anything, right now.

About what? Dead foxes? Defecting principals? Dying kings? Callers?

Maxan took a deep breath, trying—and failing—to halt the onrush of questions. *The Aigaion?* There were just too many. And he knew all the questions really boiled down to just one question. One word.

Human.

He watched Rinnia's back, his mouth open to speak, but he realized he didn't know how to even start. He still didn't know how he knew anything.

Ask, Max. You may not get the chance again later.

I may be dead later.

Such a clever fox, you are. Full of clever excuses.

Nothing had turned out according to their expectations. They should have retrieved the relay, made the climb back down the Pinnacle the same way they'd come up, and been back at the safe house hours ago. Saghan by now should have already given Chewgar the antidote he'd promised.

And then what? Back to the guardhouse? Back to being a shadow?

The truth was, he knew none of it mattered anymore. One door had closed, and another had opened. Feyn had sprung them from prison, and before he let them go, he had instructed them—*all* of them, the Monitors and the Crosswall guards who'd meddled in their affairs—to meet him in two days at Renson's Mill, a town along the Radilin dozens of miles to the east, at a tavern called the Red Well.

Callers can't seem to control our minds, Maxan mused. *But we're just as much in Feyn's power anyway.*

Still, as you say, better off than being dead.

Maxan smirked at the low-hanging charcoal-colored clouds as they scudded across the sky, glimpsing the last ray of sunlight before they sealed the world away. He cleared his throat. "It may not have gone like we'd hoped," he called to Rinnia's back. She didn't turn, didn't slow, but he knew she'd heard him. "But at least Yinna's shining."

Rinnia stopped so suddenly that Maxan nearly collided with her back. An angry thunder rumbled in the cobblestones under him, prickling his skin.

Maxan came around to face her, found her seething, livid eyes still locked forward. He took a deep breath. "What I mean

is, we got it back. In a way. I thought you'd be a little more …
satisfied than, well… Unless…"

Unless what? he asked himself, realizing that the thought
made no sense, led nowhere. "Never mind." He wished he'd
never stopped her, never said anything.

"Unless what?" she insisted.

"Unless maybe you never expected—or wanted—to get the
relay back. The way you talked to Feyn about it, it sounded like
you believed it was a terrible idea to bring it to—"

"Why are you here?" she snapped.

"Ah, there's a lot of ways to ans—"

"No. Here. With me. With the Monitors, going along with
all of this. Why? Why don't you go home, get some rest, wake
up tomorrow, and get some new orders or shadow some new
set of criminals or rebels?"

"If your *brother* hadn't poisoned Chewgar—"

"I'm not talking about your friend." Rinnia's voice had
gained intensity along with the fury in her eyes, and the tip of
her claw jabbed Maxan's shoulder hard. She drew closer until
their muzzles nearly touched. "I'm talking about you."

The raindrops had swelled from the size of a grain of sand
to that of a pebble, and he could feel the damp spreading
through his cloak and uniform. White light suddenly washed
everything he could see, then faded before he could blink, and
another enraged rumble of thunder followed.

"Even without Chewgar, you'd still have climbed all that
way," she went on. "Admit it. It's the reason you do what you
do. You think I haven't realized by now you used to be a thief?
I've seen the way you move, how you went for the window on
top of their tower. But you didn't just steal the relay because
you expected some big payoff."

Well, about that, he wanted to say. But he couldn't
say anything.

Because she's right, Max, the voice of reason told him.

"You want to do the right thing. But *wanting* to do right doesn't mean you *can*."

"You're wrong," he sputtered, his brow furrowing in confusion. His fanned ears flicked uncontrollably at the falling drops of rain. "The Stray. It's all about the Stray. If we could just ... put a stop to them. And with Feyn, now we can." He said it again, latching on to the strength it gave him. "I can."

"Listen to me, Maxan. You're not making a difference. You've almost thrown your life away, more than once. I almost cut your throat myself. And after all of it, the actual *good* you've done is zero. Some people work their whole lives toward something and never achieve it. And yet when they die, they die proudly, thinking that just because they tried, their life had value. They're idiots and fools. They're worse than worthless."

For some reason, the image of the weasel boy catching his half-eaten apple flashed in Maxan's mind. He gazed at a puddle as though waiting for the lightning to strike it.

"But maybe it's not their fault," Rinnia went on. "Maybe they were led to believe that what they did would matter. Do you see this?" She slammed her fist against the bricks of the alley wall, then her own chest, and then gestured at the stormy sky. "All of this. None of it matters. Because none of it's real."

She paused, putting a paw on his shoulder, which drew his mismatched green-and-gold eyes up to her blue ones. "It's a game, Maxan," she said, just loud enough to be heard over the rumbling thunder. "We're inside a game."

All right, then, he realized. *Rinnia is insane.*

No, Max. He felt the headache creeping in again behind his eye. Always when there was something he was supposed to know, but didn't. *Listen to her.*

Absolutely not, he countered, shaking his head, wishing his contrary thoughts would fly out of his ears once and for all and never come back.

He wriggled free from her touch and shot back, "Don't you see them?" He flung his arm wide, indicating all the afflicted animals, all the families that had been exiled, crammed into every street and building nearby. "Their hunger, their suffering, all of it is real. The Stray are real. As much as I wish it was all just a bad dream. Chewgar, my friend, he's real. As real as the bane that's killing him, right now." Now it was his turn to jab her shoulder with his claw. "You're going to tell Saghan to give him the cure. I don't care what the damn bear said. There *is* a cure. The snake has it. He has to."

Maxan hoped the rain masked the tears that were welling in his eyes. He withdrew his claw. "I'm coming with you. To see this through. All the way. Don't tell me I can't." He turned away from her, but Rinnia caught his arm.

"Saghan won't kill Chewgar."

"He's a killer. The hyenas, he…"

"It wasn't *him.*" Her voice was barely audible above the noise of the falling rain. "He didn't do those things."

I saw him! Maxan almost screamed it in her face, but there was something in her tone that gave him pause.

"He didn't," she said again.

She's telling the truth.

"What do you mean?" he said, but his voice was drowned in a deafening peal of thunder and blinding flash of light. Suddenly, he knew what she meant anyway, somewhere in the back of his mind. The snake's mind wasn't like his, or hers. Saghan wasn't free like the foxes were like Folgian had said.

At the inn. It was an imprint. Another mind.

By now, the plummeting raindrops had swelled to the size of coins and felt just as heavy on his shoulders and the back of his head. His pointed ears and bushy tail sagged with the damp soaking into them. Water streamed down from the slanted rooftops to rush against their ankles.

Whether she had heard him or not, Rinnia nearly had to shout her response. "Do you know your own way back from here?"

"What? Why?"

"Feyn might have had us followed." For just an instant, Rinnia's eyes flitted down and to the left.

Maxan knew a con when he saw one. He did all he could to keep his gaze and his voice level to hide the realization.

"Right," he said. "I know the way. I can go roundabout. Let's split up."

Rinnia nodded.

Maxan watched her go, drawing the soaking wet cloak about his shoulders. When she faded at last into the storm, his eyes scanned the closest wall, calculating the maneuvers he'd have to make and the time they would take him.

"It wasn't completely a lie," Rinnia told herself, hardly able to hear her own voice in the crashing torrent of water all around. She knew they had, in fact, been followed, though not by Feyn nor by the Mind. She knew very well who was following them. After everything the Monitors had done in Crosswall, Old Four Swords would expect a word with her. He would want to know how it was possible she could fail so miserably again and again to recover the relay and disappear for good, as he had ordered.

Rinnia headed due east, away from the route to the manor house, then wove her way northward toward the city's outer wall, then cut west again and pushed far into Stray territory, avoiding any animal bold or opportunistic or simply hungry enough to scavenge away from the larger groups. She soon emerged from an alleyway and found the fresh carcass of a rabbit in the street's gutter, his paws and hind legs still twitching in the air above him, and the entire cavity of his chest and guts eaten away. The rain had washed his insides so thoroughly that the red carried away to the drain was hardly perceptible.

Rinnia clapped a paw over her mouth to keep from retching and tore her eyes away, only to see four more bodies just like it littering the street beyond. She drew in a deep breath, composed herself, and stepped among the dead, keeping her eyes forward, ignoring the frenzied marks that the Stray had left on the corpses.

She finally reached the small circular well that served as one of Four Swords's drop points. Normally, if she ever had news for him, this was one of many spots in Crosswall where she would deliver it—in this case by scrawling it on a small note, stuffing it in a bottle, and tossing it down the well. Right now, she was fresh out of paper, and besides, he had been following the foxes since they left the campus, a sure sign that he intended to meet her face-to-face.

Her body was soaked to the bone, her hind paws especially so, but she pushed on through the downpour all the same instead of seeking the makeshift shelter of a nearby threshold. The well was in the center of a small courtyard surrounded on all sides by conjoined housing structures where farmers would come to rest and be with their mates and offspring after a tiresome day of tending the fields north of the city. She scanned the boarded windows and doors of the houses around her, from high to low.

In an instant, her paw shot around her back and gripped one of her swords.

From where she stood, she could clearly see the tip of a long black-furred muzzle resting on the ground just at the edge of the well. Whoever it belonged to was lying prone, perhaps waiting to spring an ambush. Her eyes focused on the animal's nostrils, but they neither twitched in the rain nor sucked in breath. Something wasn't right.

Inch by inch, Rinnia crept to the well. The head had once belonged to a rat and was sliced clean from his skinny neck. The rest of him lay in a heap a few feet away.

Rinnia tried to relax the grip on her weapon's handle but found she couldn't. Her flesh prickled beneath her amber fur, and her ears fanned and twitched all around but heard only the rain. It wouldn't have mattered, she told herself inwardly. If Old Four Swords had wanted her dead...

Rinnia slowly turned.

He towered over her, completely shrouded in his black oiled cloak; the unique Peskoran substance laced into its fibers repelled the rain. The cloak's deep, wide hood extended across both of his shoulders and was pulled low over his bulbous head, but the two long gray-blue tendrils that jutted from the bottom of Old Four Swords's chin hung out from the darkness onto his chest and writhed in the rain.

Rinnia called upon all of her will to force her body to relax, and it seemed to work on everything but the fur along her spine and tail.

The tall, gangly octopus said nothing, but he compressed his gel-like leg muscles to lower himself to her eye level. The Peskoran's eyes were twin pools of reflective silver. Rinnia was unnerved by his gaze, as she had been at all their meetings, and she looked away.

"I saw her," she said. "Folgian. Last night. She was there, in her tower. You told me what he did to her, but I never thought..."

She trailed off as a blunt blue appendage peeked out from the fold of Four Swords's cloak and drew upward to the edge of his hood. The muscles at its tip hardened, pinching the oiled fabric between two suction cups, and drew the hood away from the octopus's head. Then, from a concealed space just beneath the writhing tendrils on his face, Four Swords's beak-like mouth spoke in a harsh, resonant clack, "The relay."

Rinnia looked down at her paws, empty but for the rain. "Feyn has it."

The higher pair of tentacle arms rose from his sides, swept the cloak up over both his shoulders, and folded across his chest, affecting a pose of disappointment. The lower pair rested atop the pommels of two of his four elegantly curved swords, attached to the harness strapped across his otherwise naked chest.

She knew almost nothing about the old octopus. She didn't even know his real name. But he once told her that he had been a Monitor long ago, before the brotherhood fell, and Rinnia knew that everything Old Four Swords had ever told her had turned out to be true, including what he had warned her the bane would do to his former partner, Folgian, the withered bear.

Most importantly, he had been the one to tell Rinnia who *she* really was and what the grand liar masquerading as the Master Monitor meant to do with the missing piece of the Aigaion.

"We're going to get it back," Rinnia said. "We have another chance. The wolf wants to bring him the relay, personally."

"Where is the wolf?"

"Hold on," she said, hardly believing what she was about to say. "When the wolf brings it to him, finally, after all this time, we'll have our chance. *I'll* have my chance. I can kill him. I can end this."

"No."

"I can!"

"He will come back in a new body. You know this."

Rinnia remembered what Saghan had said when she had pulled him from the fiery jaws of the inn, how *Father wouldn't waste all his work.*

"What else, then? Huh? Answer me! I just steal it, and you whisk it away under the sea and hope he won't find it again? You know as I do that won't work. Not forever. He'll find it. If it's true he lives forever like you say."

"It is true."

Something inside Rinnia was crushed all over again, just like it had been the first time the octopus had found her and told her everything. She knew he was right, but the weak, vulnerable side of her that for years she had struggled so hard to stifle suddenly emerged. Before she could swallow the words down, she whimpered, "But he killed my father."

Rinnia knew Old Four Swords didn't care. He wasn't the type to console lost little fox girls. She hated herself for being weak, so she pressed her useless emotions back to the underside of her heart. She straightened herself and shook the tears away, letting them merge with the falling rain.

She saw herself in his silvery gaze. And he watched her silently, for a long time. "Go with the wolf," he said at last.

"What about Salastragore?"

"Remember, I am the only one he fears."

Their time was up. Old Four Swords drew the hood over his face, drowning his silver eyes in shadow, and pulled the cloak about him again. Then he glided over the edge of the well and disappeared into the darkness below.

Rinnia glanced a final time at the rat's severed head, then found the path that would take her back toward the Monitors' safe house. Saghan, Sarovek, and maybe even the rhino would have expected her a while ago, and she hoped that Maxan had taken his time getting there.

He certainly had.

So intent was Rinnia on getting to the well, so loud was the drowning crash of the storm, so skilled was the shadow that watched her and her Peskoran friend from the rooftops, that she never suspected Maxan had seen everything.

III
THE DENLANDS

FILE 764: "CONFESSIONS"

Time: 003292/01/07-[09:49:27-09:55:15]
Location: Castle Tower
Begin audio transcription:

Oh! Ha ha! See the technique? The artistry in her limbs and movements?

Very good, my dear.

Again!

Watch her now. Ahh... I see it in your eyes. That recognition. You know her, don't you? You know why I brought her here. Just a moment. Let's speak in private.

Stop! That's enough.

Gather your blades. Bow to our guest before you go.

Now go.

You know, don't you? You know exactly what she is, who she is. She's just like him, I assure you. Down to the last chromosome. All but the eyes. He wanted those to match his mate's.

Don't look away from me! What's the matter? Oh, please. After all I've done, THIS is what you resent me for? Now that is ironic. After all these years... finally, some glimmer of emotion. Some feeling from you. And it's resentment.

Well. It's a start. But you know I'm holding out for remorse. We'll get there. I'm sure. Eventually.

You know what I feel when I see her? Admiration. Respect. Pride.

Hmm. Pride most of all. I am proud. You see, she is him, but she isn't him. She is my daughter. Not his. She's known me since the moment she was... Well, since she took her first breath.

I've made her into everything he was supposed to be. Reliable. Trusting. Loyal. She will never betray me. She may be his mirror image, but her heart ... it's all ... reptile. Ha ha!

Ah. Look at you now. Not just resentment, hmm? Perhaps ... disgust.

If she has the gall to ask me later, "Father, who was that in the tower?" What would you have me tell her? Hmm?

"My dearest child, he is this world's oldest living god. And you... you are its youngest."

I'll say, "With the strength of my conviction, with the power of my intellect, I brought that old god low, so that I could raise you up.

"I took this world from him...

"And soon, I will give it to you."

CHAPTER ELEVEN
THE ROAD OF SILENCE

THE DAWN CAPTIVATED MAXAN, LIKE IT always had. He slowed his pace, then stopped, the dust from the road carried on the breeze past his ankles, his eyes locked on the eastern horizon as Yinna's rising, bright, perfect golden circle peaked just above the perfectly straight black edge of the Aigaion's triangular form. Within minutes, the shapes would merge, light and dark coming together. He wasn't a Mind's scholar or anything, but he reasoned all the same that a phenomenon like this—the precise moment when Yinna and the Aigaion seemed to share the same space and time—occurred perhaps just once in any Herbridian's lifetime. He wondered, were there even any animals awake to see it? Were they watching? And if they were, would they even feel … something?

The fox looked at his traveling companions to see if any of them were animals like him, if anyone else had stopped like he had. But the hawk, the snake, the other fox, and even his friend the rhinoceros kept walking along the dusty road leading away from Crosswall. Nobody said anything. Nobody stopped. Nobody even noticed he had. After all that had happened to them in the last few days—all the brushes with death, all the secrets—every one of them was too occupied with brooding.

With a sigh, he gave the eclipse one last glance and caught up with the others.

They had left the Leoran capital early that morning, hours before dawn, setting out along the paved main artery of trade between Crosswall and Corvidia across the mountains to the east. The Denland Road it was named, after the territory of Leora that it cut across, the thickly forested region that stretched for almost a hundred miles from where the Radilin cut north after rounding the great city, to the slopes of the mountains that marked the Leoran king's border.

Less than a day earlier, the Denland Road had suffered the weight of a thousand marching paws, hoofs, and feet, whose owners had something other than trade on their minds. King Locain had departed his city soon after leaving the Mind's Pinnacle Tower, having mustered a fresh contingent of troops to bring eastward, confident he could crush the rebellion once and for all.

Maxan had observed the occasional red spatter on the road's uneven cobbles, had caught the scent of blood in the air. *Those killers couldn't wait for the bloodshed to start,* he thought. He imagined the Leoran warriors squabbling among their ranks, scratching with their claws over petty disagreements or boasts or lost wagers concerning arena champions or apoth games. Locain hadn't returned to Crosswall to gather food, supplies, or building materials. No, he had come for the Mind's blessing, and to find and enlist his most vicious volunteers, animals that were well trained and eager to kill.

Not so different from the Stray.

Crosswall was now nothing more than a black line set against the dark horizon behind them, and only now did Maxan realize that he hadn't thought to say goodbye to everything. The sprawling city had been his home for almost fifteen years, and yet he realized he had never truly considered it such. It hadn't been his home for the first year when he stole to survive, living on scraps and trash he found in the gutters behind the markets. It hadn't felt like home when he stole trinkets and coin purses as a proper thief with the Commune of foxes that had taken him in. And even when their hideout was burned to the ground—when he sought out Yovan and found that the great stag knight had died years earlier, but his replacement, a young rhinoceros captain, recognized the fox and the coin he carried in his amber-furred paw—even then, being a guard, taking the oaths, and donning the white and black had never made the place feel like home either.

The only place he had ever truly considered his home...

Is the very place we're heading to.

Renson's Mill.

He imagined the bridge over the creek outside the village, the forest path he'd taken to get there, and farther back, miles away, the river by his mother's den. He imagined the flames. He felt his dread of fire amplify with every beat of his heart. Out here on the road, with no one to talk to and nothing to do but walk, he couldn't keep his mind from wandering into bad memories.

He shook his head and tried to recount the more recent past that had literally brought him here. Everything had been a whirlwind since the moment he and Rinnia had arrived back at the Monitors' safe house in the western district. After Maxan had hurried back across the rooftops to wait for her, panting for breath just outside the walls of the abandoned manor, all the questions he couldn't ask about her meeting with the Peskoran had so dominated his thoughts that he hadn't even considered the situation that awaited him when he got back there. What if Chewgar was dead? Would Saghan be there? Would the snake approve of the arrangement the foxes made with Feyn?

He was glad he'd waited for Rinnia. The uncertainty made for an effective lie when they met up again by the vine-covered wall.

She looked so tired.

The foxes pushed through the squealing iron gate into the courtyard and found the toppled fountain, but no rhinoceros, no snake. Maxan and Rinnia found them inside with the hawk, the three of them sitting in silence beside a low-burning fire in the house's enormous hearth. No one told him how, but Maxan figured that Saghan had given his friend the antidote.

Chewgar said nothing to him, not even when Maxan threw the little twigs he called arms around the rhino's comparatively boulder-sized shoulders. He patted the fox's back, grunted something, and shrugged out of Maxan's embrace. The rhino seemed out of sorts somehow, but Maxan assumed it was just a lingering effect of the bane, perhaps.

Saghan, on the other hand, had plenty to say about their failure at the Pinnacle, and even more hissing anger to spit when he learned that the relay had wound up in the white wolf's paws. Maxan watched in muted silence as the snake flicked his forked tongue and pointed accusingly at his sister, then at him, and back again, his scaly tail whipping around behind him to work out the fury. Most of all, he watched Saghan's orange eyes, thinking back to what Rinnia had told him. There was no fire, no glow, behind them.

And he didn't threaten to stick his dagger in my eye, Maxan surmised. *Gotta be a relationship milestone there.*

Rinnia—soaked to the bone as was Maxan—had simply closed her heavy eyes and waited for her brother's tirade to subside, then she calmly, tiredly, relayed Feyn's deal to the rest of her small brotherhood. "We're not lost yet," she had said.

Do I tell them?

Not even Maxan's sensitive ears could pick up her words with the blue octopus over the crashing downpour.

Tell them what, Max? You couldn't hear what they said.

Maybe he's one of them.

No. He's not.

Maxan had suddenly felt as if his brain had shrunk to half its size yet sagged with twice its weight.

Who would I tell anyway?

There wasn't much to talk about after Rinnia spoke. They all watched her disappear into the dark corridors of the manor. Saghan and Sarovek looked at the pair of Crosswall guards, the ones who'd bumbled their way into their brotherhood's secret war with the Mind, and it was the snake who told them they could plan to leave Crosswall as Monitors the next morning, or they could die. Chewgar said nothing, only stared at the fire. Maxan knew the snake was really only speaking to him. "The guard captain," Saghan said, nodding at the rhino, "in uniform, will essscort us through the city's eastern gate. No questionsss. No fusss."

The hawk and the snake finally left them alone. Before she departed, Sarovek said something about deadly traps all around the manor, but Maxan had no intention of moving from the sagging couch he'd picked out across the room. Maxan stripped himself of everything but his skivvies and leather sleeve, set his soaking cloak and uniform to dry on the furniture closest to the fire, and sank into the couch. He tried to get Chewgar to speak about what had transpired here.

But the rhino had merely grunted. "I'll be all right," he said.

Maxan yawned. "What did they tell you?"

Chewgar was silent a long time. "Nothing."

Maxan, although only half-awake, knew Chewgar was lying. He knew then that the distant stare wasn't only from the fading bane in his blood. But the fox let it go, pulled the tattered and dusty covering over his body, and was soon snoring.

It felt like only a moment later when Saghan had prodded him with his tail, hissing that it was time to go. "For you," the snake had said, setting a bundle of drab-colored clothes and a tin plate of some kind of cake-shaped paste on a small table beside the fox's couch.

The clothes fit surprisingly well. They might have belonged to the elk's son and likely hadn't been used in decades. But they were fresher than the sweat-and-mildew-scented uniform that hadn't dried so well by the dead fire. Ultimately, when the companions left the manor house a few moments later, he chose to leave the white and black garb by the smoldering hearth, and no one had cared to object.

The "food" was much less pleasant than the clothing, however. It had the consistency—and practically the taste—of clay, and seemed just as hard to snap into edible pieces. Once in his throat, it transformed to a stiff kind of slag that scraped his innards. Chewgar, meanwhile, consumed his double portion without protest, staring wordlessly at the single point of dying light amid the cooling embers in the fireplace.

Sarovek had assured them the stuff was enough to make up four full meals.

Now that they'd been on the road for a few hours already, there was no denying how right she had been about its energy supply.

The stuff really works.

The shadow of the Aigaion had swept over them hours ago, and the great city to their backs was lost behind the mid-morning haze and the tall, swaying grass beside the bends in the road. Ahead, still miles away, the land rose steadily into lumpy hills, crowned with a dark green line of trees. Maxan ran his eyes to either side, seeing nothing but plains. The sight caused a rankling along his fur, a fluttering in his heart. *No walls*, he realized. The familiar buildings of Crosswall were gone. They had always been there, within reach, like shields protecting him at either side. All he had to do was jump and latch on and climb. And run.

Everything's different.

His nostrils flared, sucking in the fresh air. The smell of the city, the cloying scent of work and unkempt fur and sweat, mingling with the pungent ale and roasted food wafting from the inns—it was all gone.

Everything's different, but I'm still alive. Chewgar's still alive. That hasn't changed. And neither has Yinna. Maxan squinted up at the sun, creeping closer to her zenith over his small world. *She's still the same. Beautiful. Bright. Warm.*

Sure, Max, his sarcastic self countered. *And she still doesn't care about you.*

With that sentiment, his eyes were drawn to Rinnia.

Exactly what I was thinking, Max! How'd you know?

It was no use. No matter what Maxan thought about— pretty sunrises or prettier foxes, recent events or the long-dead past, terrible failures or more terrible food—he could not prevent his inner voice from pestering him.

"Maybe I should just speak to myself," he muttered, at a volume he was certain no one else could hear. He saw Rinnia's fanned ear twitch in his direction, and he quickly abandoned the idea. He didn't want to talk to her, didn't want to hear how he was an idiot—*less than worthless*, she had said—for believing he'd been making a difference in the world. He glanced at Sarovek and Saghan, deciding he knew nothing about one and remembering the other had tried to blow him to pieces.

He tried to recall the last *real* conversation he'd had with someone.

Maxan looked from Chewgar's broad back to the leather sleeve covering his right arm, to the buckles and straps keeping it tight, then back again to his friend. His claw started picking at the buckle on his shoulder.

"Chewgar," he said a minute later, coming up beside his friend, holding out the furless, whitish-pink arm crisscrossed with scars.

For the first time since their time in the alley, when he'd shared his story with the fox, Chewgar looked at Maxan, at his arm, at his eyes, and really saw him.

"My fur's never grown back," Maxan said, tossing the leather sleeve to the side of the road. He flexed the claws of his scarred paw, bending his arm at the wrist and elbow. "Not since it happened. And I can't feel anything."

To Maxan, now, it was fine that Chewgar said nothing. The rhino's eyes told Maxan that he understood. Maxan smiled. He was glad that his friend was still here, that he could honor his part of their agreement, to fully share his past.

"You're not the only one with ssscars." Even while he walked forward, Saghan's long neck brought his wide, scaly face around to observe the commotion behind. His tongue flicked the air. "We've a ways yet to go, fox."

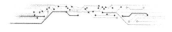

The road was completely deserted, which was highly unusual. Under normal circumstances, caravans of tradesmen and their guards would lead teams of burden beasts westward, hauling stones from Corvidian quarries or other goods from the kingdom of birds. Or there might even be villagers on their way to or from the capital to buy luxuries, visit relatives, or renew their licenses to peddle wares (one of the many forms of "order" introduced by the Mind, which arguably made ordinary life outside the city more tedious).

But war changed everything. Many times that day, they had passed overturned carts and ransacked outposts where the main road crossed with the dirt paths leading to villages north or south. Maxan suspected that the damage of Locain's troop's passing would be just as evident even in those remote places. He knew for a fact that many of the smaller towns for hundreds of miles outside of Crosswall had been emptied long ago anyway, since the Denland forest-dwelling species had chosen to side against the Golden Lord in the rebellion. Locain wouldn't care if his loyal soldiers helped themselves to whatever was left behind there, or set fire to it for fun. Even now, Maxan's snout caught the phantom of smoke on the breeze.

When they finally settled that night to make camp among a grove of trees just south of the road, Maxan came to the conclusion he was willfully going along with the Monitors now. For all intents and purposes, he was one of them. *They haven't killed me so far, so likely they're not going to.* The notion sat about as comfortably with him as his rump sat upon the barbed leaves and nettles on the forest floor.

Saghan used a device no bigger than a pen to easily ignite a bundle of twigs he had gathered, and soon there was a pleasant, snapping fire at the center of their clearing. Sarovek dropped her pack, announced she would take the first watch, spread her mighty wings wide, and shot away into the air, which brought a few curses from the snake, tending to the flames at the time. Rinnia disappeared beyond the tree line without a word, leaving just the three males behind.

Maxan's stomach grumbled audibly, but he refrained from inquiring about food. He, of course, hadn't had the chance to pack any provisions and was completely at the whim of the Monitors' supplies. He watched Saghan rummaging through his satchel, hoping there might be something to eat on its way out of there soon.

"What did she tell you?" the snake asked, looking up at Maxan, bringing one of his black metal spheres from the satchel.

Maxan frowned. "Who?"

The snake whirled the slender fingers of his other hand and his jeweled dagger suddenly appeared in his grasp from nowhere. He flicked his tongue and smiled at the fox's astonishment, then worked the dagger's point into the side of the sphere. "The bear," he said. The device popped open with a hiss of pressure. "Folgian."

"She said…" Maxan began, then trailed off into silence. *A lot of things.* He glanced at Chewgar, who sat with his back against a fallen oak tree. For some reason, Maxan suddenly thought he was dead, but the rhino let out a great, huffing breath.

"She said there was no cure," Maxan said.

"Hmm," Saghan replied. "Not for her, anyway."

"Why'd you save him?" Maxan tucked his legs under himself to lean closer to the snake by the fire, meaning to fix him with a serious look, but recoiled awkwardly from the sensation of the fire's heat along his fur. "You didn't know if we were coming back. Or if we'd have it."

Saghan's long neck turned his head in Chewgar's direction. "The next king of Leora could make a powerful ally."

"Next king?" Maxan looked at Chewgar again. The rhino hadn't moved.

"Locain knows nothing. Less than nothing, in fact. The Mind's principals keep him ignorant of all the secret places, all the old power that sleeps under his very own city, across his kingdom. And rightly so. All the lion wants is violence. It's sport for him. And so long as the Mind can turn Locain's violence to suit their own ends, like crushing rebellions or purging animals that've lost their way, well… But once it's time to rebuild upon all those ashes..." Saghan drew a finger across the base of his neck and smirked at the fox.

"And you'd have Chewgar step in?"

"Only if he wantsss."

Both the snake and the fox peered at the rhinoceros. In the dim firelight, Maxan saw the outline of Chewgar's hand ball into a fist.

And behind him, in the pitch black, Maxan saw eyes, drawn by the firelight, glowing faintly. A dozen feral eyes. Just waiting, perhaps, for the light to go out. If Saghan saw them, too, he didn't seem surprised, but he snapped another branch from the fallen oak and tossed it on the fire all the same.

"It won't come to that," Maxan said. "We'll get the relay back where it belongs."

"Hmm." Saghan delicately plucked the top half of his sphere off the base and set it beside him, then wound a dial inside with the tips of his nails. "Folgian told you about the Aigaion, did she? I asssume it wouldn't matter, if she'd meant to kill you."

"Feyn did," Maxan corrected. "After he saved us from her."

"Have you ever thought about the Aigaion?" the snake asked, setting the base of the sphere down in his lap. "I mean truly thought about it. So very few have. And rightly so. Why question the nature of something that's been with you all your life? It's like ... language. Have you ever thought about where your words came from? When they formed? Who decided what they would sound like? And why—not how—you learned to speak them? Why speaking is essential to survival?"

Gotta admit, Maxan wanted to say, *it's a little overwhelming.*

But he said instead, "I suppose not."

"We are puppets, Maxan. And the Aigaion is where the puppeteers live." Saghan shrugged, turned his attention again toward calibrating the spherical device. "Or *lived,* anyway."

"Hu…" Maxan breathed the sound, but couldn't bring himself to finish the word. Because he still didn't know how he knew.

Humans.

And the visions of glass flashed in his mind.

Floor, pillars, and the racing golden lights.

Epimetheus.

His eyes snapped up as though they could discern the great, shadowed ship itself passing overhead.

Tetrahedrons. Chambers. Sloping shadows. White cells. Cages.

But it wasn't there. Only the pinprick glow of Yerda's Wound and the scudding clouds veiling her belt of asteroids.

Maxan shook his head, the words and visions already slipping again. He caught Saghan's slit orange eyes narrowing at him from across the firelight. "So our choices don't matter," he picked up quickly, hoping to deflect the snake's scrutiny.

"They don't. But what's worssse? Not deciding your own dessstiny, or being obliviousss to the fact that the decision was never truly yours in the first place?"

No, the other fox rang out in the recesses of Maxan's mind. The fur on his shoulders and back rolled in spasms, as though his body subconsciously felt for the points where his puppet strings attached. *It's not true. Your choices, Max—our choices—matter. They've made all the difference.*

Then he remembered what Rinnia told him in the rain.

But have they?

"Either way, choices are *meaningless.*" Saghan brought the word down like a hammer upon a nail. "Or, at least they *were* meaningless. There's a reason why animals of all five nations, all species, cannot recall their history before the Thraxian extermination. There's a reason why they never bothered to record anything before that time. You see, as that war drew to a close, the strings were severed. The relay was disconnected, the signal cut off. After years of being controlled, the animals' minds were set free. They … *woke up*, all at once, for the first time, in their own bodies, as if from a bad dream."

"Only the … *imprint* of the…" Maxan trailed off. He glanced up, saw that the snake was watching him intently. Saghan had meant to teach *him* something, perhaps, only now Maxan had revealed he already knew quite a lot. "Ah, Folgian said a lot of other things," he lied.

"Yesss. The imprint the parasitic mind left on the host body. How to eat. How to walk on two legs. How to speak. How to live. But even still, that animal is just a puppet whose puppeteer has lost hold of the strings."

"Harmony and Feyn," Maxan said, staring now at the fire, understanding dawning. "They can still feel those strings."

Saghan nodded, then swung his head toward the rhino. "A point our large friend here vehemently tried to deny."

"No such thing as callers," Chewgar grumbled, but the tone of his voice betrayed his uncertainty. Maxan realized then that nothing he and the snake were discussing was new to the rhino, that he had heard it before, that the Monitors had told him.

But they hadn't told Chewgar everything, for after a long silence, the rhino said, "Who's Folgian?"

Saghan's only response was to lift the point of his dagger to the sky as the line of his mouth bent in a grin.

Maxan understood. "She's one of them."

"One of who?" Chewgar huffed, not at all happy that he was being left in the dark.

"The puppeteers," Maxan said, almost in a whisper.

"At the Pinnacle," Chewgar said slowly, his flat teeth chewing over the thought. "When we saw Locain. She was there, with the principals. She sat between them."

"She *is* the Mind," Maxan said dramatically, recalling how silly he had thought that title was at the time, thinking perhaps it wasn't so silly any longer.

Saghan finished whatever internal checks he was making to the spherical device and locked the two halves together. Maxan's ears jittered involuntarily for a second, barely picking up a tinny burst. He looked into the darkness beyond the firelight, watched the glowing eyes wink out suddenly like candles.

"What if I tried to run?" Maxan said impulsively. Take all this ... *truth* to the Corvidian houses, or to the Peskoran guilds? What if I say 'Shit on the Monitors' and 'Shit on the Mind' and just tell everybody?"

"Then we'd kill you."

Maxan's head followed his ears to the voice behind him. Rinnia had been as silent as the still night air. She stepped into the ring of firelight, a decapitated wild meadow deer over her shoulders.

"I was just, ah, asking."

Rinnia ignored him, dropping the carcass by the fire. She retracted the cord back into the spool on her belt, which had been keeping the flesh together. "Stole it from some Stray," she said, answering Maxan's unspoken question. "Why didn't you prepare the spit?" she asked Saghan.

The snake just shrugged. "I didn't know your intention."

"Makes two of us," she said drily.

"Besidesss, I like my meat raw."

Rinnia rolled her eyes and set to stripping the pelt from their dinner with a small hunter's knife.

"Don't suppose you could go fetch another of those," said Chewgar, nodding at the deer. He was ultimately disappointed when Rinnia ignored him.

Maxan ran the edge of his paw up and down the side of his muzzle, contemplating the last thing Saghan had said. "Raw meat," he mumbled. Then, a bit more loudly, "Like the Stray."

"You don't know many Drakorans," the snake countered, almost laughing. His dagger flashed up and skewered a hunk of red meat Rinnia tossed at him. He pulled the portion off, held it up, tilted back his long neck, and lodged the entire thing in his throat with one swallow.

Maxan watched the bulge in the snake's green-scaled neck work its way down, then disappear beneath the collar of his armor.

Rinnia sawed several strips from the deer's thigh and arranged them on wide green leaves, then set those near the fire.

"How was the relay lost in the first place?" Maxan asked. He knew part of the story already. In his mind, he saw again the image of his mother tossing the glowing golden relay end over end into the river, just as the assassins cut her down. "At first, I mean."

"Our master—" Rinnia began.

"Salastragore," Maxan cut in. "Feyn mentioned him," he said, answering the quizzical look crossing the snake's face.

"Yes," Rinnia went on. "While the Thraxian campaign kept the world busy, he hunted down your so-called *puppeteers* here on Herbridia, one by one. He would have killed them all, but they locked themselves behind a door that can't be opened. And they stole the means of control, the relay, and hid it."

As she spoke, Maxan could tell that her words were just a recital, that she didn't believe what she was saying. He almost cut in again, wanting to say *That's not how it happened. They didn't steal it.* But he held his tongue. His head was starting to hurt.

"They knew that without it, in time, down here, we would…"

"Eat each other," Chewgar said somberly, rising from the fallen oak.

"Destroy ourselves," Rinnia countered. "It sounds more digestible."

"Does it?" Chewgar grumbled, stooping to check the meat by the fire.

"Did you even know," Rinnia groused at him, clearly disliking his meddling with her cooking, "that the rhinoceros, by nature, doesn't eat meat?"

"Ha," Chewgar said, grinding a strip of venison between his flat teeth. "Lies!"

"It's in all our natures," added Saghan, his forked tongue flicking at the air again. "To destroy ourselves."

Don't believe it, Max.

I don't. It doesn't have to be.

"So Salastragore means to finish what he started," Maxan concluded.

"Yesss."

"To finish Folgian."

"She is the lassst."

"And then what? All that control will be just left behind when she's gone. You going to crash the Aigaion into the ocean? Peskorans might have a problem with that."

"The Monitors keep the secrets of this world hidden," Rinnia said, repeating what she had told him at a time that seemed like so long ago but was only the day before. "Without the Aigaion… If it falls, the sky literally falls with it. Storms forget how to form. Every bead of water suddenly forgets how to stay stuck in the ocean. The air we breathe dissipates. We can't live here without it. So, we're sworn to guard it. To keep it beyond reach. Forever."

"But how do you guard it from yourself?"

Rinnia and Saghan exchanged a glance.

Maxan could tell it was a question neither could answer. He reached out to stab a steaming strip of venison with a stick.

Chewgar stabbed the remaining six, then put two back on the leaves when Rinnia scowled at him. "Should have fetched two deer," he muttered. "That's all I'm saying."

Rinnia's scowl melted into a smile. Then she chuckled alongside the rhino's full-throated laughter.

Maxan couldn't help but smile at the two of them. It was good to see Chewgar break free of the dismal cloud that had seemed to hang over him after recovering from the bane. He wondered how his friend could laugh so easily, despite the fact he and Maxan were leaving their lives as Crosswall guards behind, despite discovering all they had thought true about their world seemed to be based on lies.

When you lose everything, even your illusions, you've nothing left to do but laugh. So he tried to laugh with them, but couldn't.

"We seem to be defeating the purpose of sending our hawk to watch for danger," the snake remarked, unamused by the others' laughter, "when we're so intent on attracting it."

As though Saghan's observation had summoned her, there was a sudden blast of wind directly above the fire, which sent leaves and embers in all directions across the clearing, and Sarovek's taloned feet and armored knees slammed onto the dirt.

"I hope you all enjoyed your rest," the hawk said, rising, "because Renson's Mill is on fire."

Chapter Twelve
THE RED OF RENSON'S MILL

SAROVEK COULDN'T TELL THEM ANYTHING more when they pressed her for the finer details. While they packed up their things and snuffed out what little remained of their scattered campfire, Sarovek recounted all she had seen from her vantage point several hundred feet in the sky.

Theirs was not the only campfire. There were many points of light scattered among the trees along this tract of the forest's edge. Most likely, she reasoned, those lights belonged to refugees hiding out in the woods, who preferred to risk an encounter with the Stray over Locain's army. The hawk's keen eyes hadn't caught any figures lurking in the dark spaces of the forest. After perhaps half an hour of spiraling outward from where she began over the Monitors' own campfire, Sarovek was satisfied that no one posed any immediate danger to her companions, so she decided to gain altitude and push farther eastward to scout the road ahead to Renson's Mill.

That's when she spotted the orange glow hanging over the otherwise pitch-black horizon. Had her keen sight not been busy piercing every shadow, her eyes darting after every rustling leaf below, she would have seen the fires much sooner. She flew closer to be sure it wasn't just an outlying farmhouse or isolated incident, and ultimately, she discovered that the entire town had been set ablaze; from the historic sawmills along the Radilin that had given the place its name all the way to the northern edge of town, everything was engulfed in a swirling red.

Sarovek had flown directly over the burning town, low enough to see the firelight reflecting off dozens of bloodied weapons and to hear their clashing. Then she caught the current of rising heat and rode it a thousand feet or more into the sky. She pitched her wings to the side and dived at a steady angle all the way back to the Monitors' camp, as though Yerda herself had loosed an arrow from where she hung in the sky above.

And now, Sarovek was back in the air. *And the rest of us are running like mad beneath her,* Maxan thought, stringing whispered curses together with almost every stride he took through the tall grass along the side of the eastern road.

Thankfully, Rinnia had restocked her supply of the small red pellets before leaving Crosswall, and she had practically forced one down his throat, insisting it would carry him the remaining miles to Renson's Mill.

Rinnia ran just ahead of him, having taken her dose also. Saghan glided through the grass at the lead with ease, his neck, tail, shoulders, and waist moving fluidly to compensate for the rapid motion of his legs and tail. Chewgar brought up the rear.

"Hold!" Saghan halted suddenly, half a mile before Renson's Mill. The others came to a stop with the snake, but Sarovek, barely more than a swift shadow overhead, darted on toward the town. Ahead of the Monitors was a line of red with a cloud of black rising above it, and they could see one another perfectly well by the glow the fires cast into the night sky.

"Why'd we stop?" Maxan said, finding that he was hardly winded and eager to race on.

"We need to split up. Avoid conflict. Find the relay. Then find each other. Come away to this distance on the town's other side. Yesss?"

"What about Feyn?"

"Inconsssequential," hissed Saghan.

Maxan read the implication in Saghan's slit eyes easily enough: *Feyn knew the risks.* And *The relay is all that matters.*

"And what about you?" Rinnia added.

"The Leoran ruins." The long line of the snake's mouth curled in a grin. "I'll be there, keeping to the first tenet of our brotherhood." He looked again at the fox and the rhino as if they'd never been this close to bloodshed.

Mostly true in my case, Maxan thought nervously.

"Locain brought his fire here," the snake said to them. "He's long suspected Renson's Mill to be harboring the rebellion's messengers, who move between the Denlands and the capital." He regarded Chewgar. "Will it trouble you, killing your king's soldiers?"

The rhino dropped his head, the point of his great horn dipping low into the grasses where he crouched. Despite the fact they were clearly out of time and more of Renson's Mill was catching fire by the second, Maxan watched his friend intently. Chewgar's answer was an important one.

"Locain has never been my king." Chewgar looked at each fox then the snake as he spoke. "If any of them try to take the lives of my friends, then they've already killed themselves."

"Then arm yourself," said Saghan.

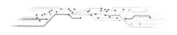

The rhino stepped directly into the wild, double-pawed swing of his comparatively puny opponent's battle ax. The wildebeest hadn't been expecting the big rhino's burst of speed and was sent crashing against the stucco wall when Chewgar's boulder chest slammed into him. The wildebeest twitched, but didn't get up. Chewgar tested the weight of the ax he had snagged from the soldier, spinning it around with ease.

Guess he's armed himself.

Maxan smirked, watching his friend in the street below from his perch on the roof of an adjacent building. Rinnia had clambered onto a roof on the opposite side of the street and already disappeared into the chaos of swirling black smoke and the hungry flames eating that side of Renson's Mill.

The impact of the wildebeest's horns against the wall attracted the attention of some of his fellow soldiers. They had been stripping coin purses, weapons, or other spoils from the fresh corpses they'd made farther down the street. Maxan couldn't tell if the dead there were rebels or just townsfolk defending their homes against the killers paid by their own king. Maxan gritted his fangs.

There were four in all—two more wildebeests, a cheetah, and a young lioness. They readied their weapons and fanned out around the rhino. They were all draped in layers of linked chain armor and the yellow-white tunic that matched the Golden Lord's banner, and all had a bloodthirsty twinkle in their eyes.

"You there," Chewgar boomed. "Slain any wolves with snow-white fur tonight?"

The question went unanswered, and the cheetah was the first to spring, spinning his curved saber in a feint, then coming back in fast with a vicious overhand swipe.

Chewgar had trained with all sorts of weapons, and with opponents of every size and species, and was not so easily fooled by the maneuver. He stood his ground, caught his attacker's sword in the groove between the blades of his ax, then simply stepped one foot forward to send the thin cheetah off balance. The cheetah had a chance to escape the counter if only he had let go of his sword. But he didn't, and Chewgar brought the heavy, broad steel down flat atop the cheetah's skull, not enough to break bone, but enough to send him into mental oblivion.

The cheetah crumpled in a heap. His saber clattered away behind him. He must have been the most reckless of the four soldiers—certainly the fastest and the most eager. Had the other three closed the distance as fast, Chewgar might have been in trouble.

"Please stop where you are." Chewgar swayed the massive ax head at the lioness, who was closing in on his left, but Chewgar found his request unnecessary. Locain's soldiers had already frozen in uncertainty, just out of range of the rhino's weapon. "I've nothing of value, and I really am in a hurry."

"The white wolf," one of the wildebeests grumbled. "He your friend?"

"You've seen him?"

"Nah. Hmm. Maybe. Seen plenty of Denland folk. Wolves, maybe."

"The Red Well!" Maxan called down from his perch, finding that his paws could finally ease out of the tense fists they had balled themselves into while watching Chewgar fight. "Where is it?"

"Boys, don't wind up like your friend here." Chewgar nudged the limp cheetah at his feet. "Don't look up there. Look at me. Now, the Red Well. Do you know it?"

While flames still gutted parts of Renson's Mill all around them, the three soldiers exchanged a silent look with one another. Even from where he stood, Maxan could recognize its meaning well enough. *They're stalking like predators, circling to strike, figuring out the angle.*

Before he could warn Chewgar, the three of them rushed the rhino with their swords drawn. And before their shorter blades could come within effective striking distance, Chewgar's much longer ax was rushing at them from the side. It bit clean through one wildebeest's chain armor and deep into his flank, then carried his dead weight over to the next wilde-beest, charging from the middle, sending the second attacker careening backward several feet.

The lioness had made it through, far enough to jab several inches of sharp steel into the rhino's side, then draw it back wet and red. She jabbed again, but Chewgar's giant hand swatted the blade away, sending it flying into a collapsing storefront engulfed in flames. The same hand closed around the lioness's scrawny neck and lifted her entire body, bringing her face-to-face with the angered rhino.

Chewgar snorted fiercely, locking his gaze with the terri-fied soldier, then brought the blunt side of his horn crashing down against her skull. The lioness went limp in his hand, and Chewgar tossed her aside like a wet rag. The rhino clutched at his side, where red had bloomed on the white of his Crosswall uniform.

"WHY?" Chewgar's full-throated cry echoed from every wall still standing along the street. "Why couldn't you just listen?" Only the second wildebeest was conscious enough to answer, but he was finding it hard to regain his hoofs at that moment.

"Chewgar!" Maxan dangled his hind paws over the edge of the building, readying himself to roll once he'd dropped down.

The rhino held up his hand, and the fox froze. "Max," he called back, "why are you still here? Find the Red Well, or what's left of it. I'll be fine."

"You sure?"

"Go!"

The wildebeest was standing now, shaking the last bit of daze out of his horned head. He gripped his sword, and his body tensed.

Chewgar let the haft of his heavy ax fall into his opposite hand, and he lowered his great horn at the defiant soldier before him.

Foolish soldier, Maxan thought, rising again and taking his first few strides away across the rooftops, leaving the wildebeest and the rhino in the street.

Dead soldier, he corrected himself, leaping across a gap between two blazing buildings, the sound of clashing steel echoing behind him.

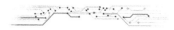

The orange glow of Renson's Mill was far behind him now; the patches of flames between the trees looked like shards of glass suspended in space. Everything this far east of the burning town was dark and still.

Saghan hadn't intended to kill the two stragglers from Locain's army—a pair of hyenas, male and female. Both of them had stripped out of their king's colors to engage in some post-slaughter reproductive rites, and he had encountered them just as they were apparently finishing the act. From where he had crouched in the thicket, he had been polite enough to silently count sixty slow seconds, assuming—maybe also hoping—that they would move on from the small, flat clearing on the forest floor they occupied, a perfect spot for completing the task he had set forth to do.

But they hadn't moved on. And now Saghan was cleaning their blood from the blade of his dagger with one of their yellow-and-white tunics. Apparently, he had become something of a hyena killer lately, so he had been informed. He took no pleasure in their deaths. Killing them had just been a necessity.

He rolled the corpses over, covered their nakedness with the stained uniforms, and set the device he'd retrieved from his satchel at the center of the clearing. He ensured it rested level on the forest floor, then depressed the button at its center. Tiny flaps snapped open sharply, tiny servos whirred within metal joints, and plates unfolded like spider's legs, revealing a dozen hollow glass beads across their length. These began to flicker blue with electricity, and Saghan stepped away.

The current intensified, and a ghostly blue light erupted and hung in the air above the device, swirling and crackling at first, then coalescing and taking shape, and finally projecting a clear figure: someone, draped in a fur-mantled robe with his back to Saghan, bent over a table, tinkering with something Saghan could not see.

A moment passed, and Saghan clenched his slender scaled fingers into fists, feeling the agitation rising with every cold thump in his bloodstream. He knew the robed figure was aware of his call. He resented being made to wait as though whatever was on the master's worktable were more important than any news he had to deliver.

Finally, a word rattled through the hexagonal lattice at the center of the spider-legged projector. "Speak."

The order did nothing to loosen Saghan's fist or his anger, but he said, "We're on the Denland Road, east of Crosswall, returning in two days' time."

"The relay?"

"We'll have it. Soon."

The ghostly blue image ceased its work. It turned its profile to Saghan, flicked its forked tongue, and regarded him with one narrowed slit eye. "You try to hide your repeated failures from me."

"There's still time. I have not failed yet."

"Where is it?"

Saghan looked away. It was just a projection, he knew, just a ghost. The master was more than a hundred miles away, yet his presence was real, unnerving. Powerful. Saghan's scaled throat swelled as if to swallow, but his throat was dry and cold. He would have shivered then if he had been warm-blooded.

"Feyn … the Mind's white wolf. He has the relay."

"Ah yes," the image said. "The cannibal."

"He means to betray her. To defect. He wants to bring it to you personally."

"But the wolf isn't with you. Is he?" Even across a vast distance, even without the invasion of Saghan's mind, the snake in the projection could easily read Saghan's thoughts.

"There are complications. The Mind has sent Locain to finish their little war. So he's burning everything, the entire forest, on his way to the rebels' stronghold. My guesss is Feyn is with him or captured. We don't know."

The projection stood to his full height and brought the other side of his head, and the empty eye socket there, to face Saghan fully. The ghostly blue light from the device seemed to shift upward so that the snake towered over his son.

"Must I intervene in *all* your affairs?"

"No. Please." Saghan hated himself for it, but he could not stop that word of such weakness from escaping his mouth. "There's still time. I can retrieve the relay. I can. On my own."

"No. Not on your own. Why sssay there's no time when you clearly have time for these games? You need help. And you called me for it."

Saghan said nothing. He clenched his fists tightly, driving the tips of his sharp claws into his own flesh, drawing a trickle of cold blood that dripped between his slender fingers. He hated it all. This place, this mission. He hated *himself* for failing. And hated *him* most of all for knowing it. For knowing everything. Every time.

"Three hundred. I shall send all that can be spared." The blue image of the snake turned his back on Saghan and resumed his activity at the worktable. "Kill them all," he commanded. "The lion. The wolf… I tire of the Mind's little Leoran drama."

"And the fox?"

The snake lifted his head again. "Hmm," the voice crawled from the metal plate like a rusty blade dragged across a slab of stone. "Bring the fox to me."

The minds of living things know when they are beaten. When the fangs have sunk deep enough into their necks. When the claws of their killers have torn enough flesh away. When enough blood has been spilled. The mind knows when to let the body die.

But the tiger—a fierce knight-commander of Locain's army, who stood unwavering in a corner just outside of the Red Well tavern—*his* mind, at that moment, was not his own, and despite many lethal injuries, his body would not fall. Blood streamed from the horrible gash atop his head where his left ear used to be. It ran down over his wide-open eyes, staining his beautiful stripes red. A hatchet had claimed that ear, the same hatchet that had cleft the tiger's jaw apart just under his temple so that the bone now hung slack, his mouth open in a kind of wild, lopsided, laughless leer. That same hatchet was finally at rest, now buried in the tiger's shoulder, deep enough to collapse his lung.

The hatchet's owner, a small coyote half the tiger's size but perhaps twice his speed, had been a loyal soldier in the tiger's regiment. Cutting pieces away from his own knight-commander had been the last thing he had ever done, however. At the bidding of his body's new master, the knight-commander lifted his spiked mace away from the coyote's crushed skull and kicked the corpse with such force that it flew up and onto the heap of other corpses that fenced him into the corner.

Beyond that wall of dead soldiers—all tribal species, all loyal and savage killers in Locain's ranks—four more of the knight-commander's soldiers stood, clutching their weapons tightly, exchanging nervous glances, wondering if everyone among them was thinking the same thing. Why hasn't the commander gone down?

When one of them, a hyena, finally spoke, it was to ask a different question though, yelling and chuckling it right in the tiger's face. "Why you protect *her*?"

The tiger had no reaction. He was just a machine now, a vessel, damaged beyond repair, and the young squirrel girl that stood behind him in the corner, with her eyes closed and her paw stretched out at his back, was straining every ounce of her will to keep that machine working. If the tiger's body came apart any more, she would lose her grip on his mind, like a puppet master whose tired hands had twisted her puppet's strings.

"Step away, sir." This from the warthog, the biggest species among the four. "We've orders to detain her like the others."

"She's special," the hyena chuckled.

The tiger's vacant eyes remained fixed on some point beyond his soldiers as they spread out in a half circle, readying themselves to strike, stepping over the heap of their comrades that had tried to get the squirrel before.

"No one's gotta know if she winds up dead. Right, boys?"

Pram's claw tips twitched, and the tiger raised the mace over his head.

"Hey!" a voice called, and the soldiers craned their necks toward the fox above them. He stood at the edge of a low rooftop, just inches higher than the soldiers' heads, framed by firelight. He held out both paws and said, "Don't—"

The mace came down against the distracted hyena's skull, crushing bone and pulping brain and putting an end to his startled chuckling before Maxan could finish. Pram could feel that her puppet's time was nearing its end, so she wouldn't hesitate to thin the ranks of her attackers when she could.

The blood spatter and silenced laughter got the warthog's attention, who whirled back on the tiger and struck at his side. The blow was strong enough to cave in the metal plate armor, but not enough to bite through it. The tiger toppled onto his side, pinning the mace beneath him, and Pram's hand jerked as though batted aside by an invisible force. She tried to push back against it, to make the tiger push himself upright, but the warthog's sword came down again, chopping the knight-commander's skull clean in two and clanging against the hard ground beneath.

The squirrel girl's eyes snapped open. They were deep black pools that rolled upward into her head, like a receding tide. Her outstretched arm fell to her side, a line of red gushed from her snout, and she slid down the corner and lay there, unmoving.

"NO!" Maxan cried, his arms reaching out as if the gesture could have stopped the whole thing.

One of the soldiers just below him, another hyena, reached for Maxan's legs. The coyote beside him was too short to do the same, and lashed out instead with his hatchet (a standard weapon for his species). Neither found any part of the fox, as Maxan launched himself up and over both of them and landed with a kick at the base of the warthog's skull.

The big soldier staggered and fell onto the tiger's corpse, but he managed to keep himself conscious.

Maxan followed the momentum of gravity into a roll, sprang up on his hind legs between Pram and the warthog, and drew his short sword.

Leave her, he wanted to say. He wanted to shout, *She's just a girl!*

But "CHEWGAR!" was all that came out of his mouth, and its sound was drowned out by the flames roaring and the buildings collapsing across Renson's Mill. He screamed his friend's name again anyway.

As the hyena and coyote came forward, the warthog regained his footing, shook his head, and rubbed the back of his neck. He snorted and stamped, and every muscle along his powerful arms pulled taut as he let out a furious roar.

Oh shit.

The warthog lowered his tusks and charged.

In the span of the single second Maxan had, he could have considered dodging the attack. His muscles might even have considered it a good plan and moved on their own. Instead, he spent that second—*Wasted it more like*—thinking of how the unconscious girl behind him could be spared. And so he stood his ground, almost by accident, and would have died.

But there came a terrible screech just as the warthog took his first furious step, and now that sound rose as Sarovek plummeted from the sky over the burning town, driving half the length of her spear through the warthog's back and deep into the ground. His heart exploded onto the pavers beneath him, and his immense weight wobbled against the strength of the metal spear that impaled him.

He let out a final squeal, which turned into a dripping red gurgle, before finally slipping down the length of Sarovek's weapon.

The hyena was ready for the hawk knight; Sarovek had announced her attack with her shrill battle cry, and as she turned, abandoning the spear and drawing the sword at her belt, his sword came down and hit the delicate radial bone of her feathered wing, nearly cutting it away altogether.

Sarovek screamed and snapped it back, the pain igniting her instincts, and raised her sword to lock with the chuckling hyena's next strike.

The short coyote, roughly the same size as Maxan, came around these two and leapt at the fox, his hatchet leading the way.

Maxan brought his sword across and intercepted the blow, the metal of their weapons scraping as they connected, then disengaged. The coyote swung his hatchet again and again, from overhead, or at Maxan's side, and somehow the fox managed to beat each strike back. But he was purely on the defensive and soon found himself backing into the wall.

Like Yacub, this hyena proved more savage than skilled, swiping repeatedly at Sarovek. But unlike in her fight with Yacub, there was no caller interfering with her brain, so none of his wild swings found their mark. Though the hawk knight had countered and slashed at every opening, and her attacker now bore several deep cuts along the unarmored fur of his arms and thighs, the hyena persisted, maniacally laughing with every heaving breath.

The coyote grew impatient and threw all his weight forward, locking Maxan's blade just beneath the curve of his hatchet and tackling the fox to the ground. His free claw raked three lines across Maxan's muzzle before Maxan could snatch and hold it away. The fox strained to toss his attacker aside, but every attempt to do so was aborted in favor of avoiding the drooling jaws that snapped at his face from above. He was pinned, and he knew at any second the coyote would bite or scratch or chop him to death.

Then, suddenly, the weight was lifted. A powerful gray-skinned hand closed around the coyote's tunic, hoisted him up, and tossed him skyward more than a hundred feet. The coyote soldier let out a surprised yelp as he sailed over the burning buildings of Renson's Mill and disappeared into the swirling walls of smoke beyond.

Chewgar smirked at the prone fox then stepped away to help the hawk.

But the rhino found she didn't need his assistance. The hyena had crumpled to his knees after the tendons in his legs were sliced apart, and he had dropped his sword when his arm had suffered the same. Sarovek's sword opened his throat, finally ceasing his insufferable stream of laughter.

Maxan rolled onto his stomach and saw the squirrel, Pram, who hadn't moved since he'd seen her collapse in the corner. He rushed to her, cradled her head, pressed his palm to her heart, and felt only a flutter. He bent his ear to her snout and felt the faintest of breaths.

"She's alive," he told the rhino and hawk standing over him. "We have to get her out of here."

"What about the wolf?" Chewgar said.

"Captured, I think. The soldiers said so right before I found her."

"There is nothing here," Sarovek said, sheathing her sword. She gripped her spear firmly and wrenched it from the warthog and the blood-soaked ground beneath him. "Nothing but death."

"Where's Rinnia?" Maxan asked her. "Did you see her?"

"Rinnia can take care of herself." Sarovek nodded at the squirrel child in Maxan's arms. "Can you carry her?"

Maxan stood, holding Pram with both arms, happy to find she didn't weigh very much. Her bushy tail hung limp, brushing against his knees. "Think so."

"Then we must go. Now. East, beyond the town."

Chewgar pointed to the white chip of bone that protruded from the brown feathers of Sarovek's wing. "Can you fly with that?"

Sarovek's head snapped to her side. Her sharp eyes focused on the wound as if it were the first time she had noticed it. She blinked, then snapped her head back to the rhino. "Yes. I could, but I'll remain here with you." She added flatly, "For your protection."

Chewgar's wide mouth curled into a grin, then opened to let out a single booming "HA!"

Maxan was sure that if Corvidians could smile, Sarovek certainly would have been.

Rinnia picked her path carefully through the forest, careful to avoid the patrolling soldiers bearing the Leoran king's colors, which at times seemed almost as widespread as the trees. Species from the tribal lands to the north—hyenas, coyotes, lions, and more, those who made up the majority of Locain's army—were not as blessed with acute hearing as species from the Denlands. But judging by all the fresh corpses she had passed along her way so far, there wasn't many of the latter group left alive within miles. Even if a raccoon, wolf, bear, or any other Denland species heard her, they no doubt had more to worry about than catching one of their own slipping by.

Rinnia was bound for the ruins of the old Leoran station. She couldn't recall this particular site's callsign; there were so many like it scattered about the five kingdoms, places where the vast tunnels, chambers, and conduits far below Herbridia's surface helped perpetuate the lie that was life for everyone above. They were dug into the mountainsides of Corvidia, drowned under the oceans of Peskora, and even buried beneath the layers of ash and sand in old Thraxia. Not even Rinnia could be sure of how many stations there were on this tiny planet. Salastragore claimed to have buried every one of them with explosives when the Extermination War began, when he rose against the masters of their order when he hunted them all down and satisfied his bloody vendetta against them.

With the old Monitors overthrown, he had been free to establish a new order. Though they were significantly fewer in number, their first mandate remained the same: to watch. It was this first tenet, above all else, that had given the brotherhood its name, after all. Keeping the entrances to these stations secret was the chief duty of the Monitors. All their lives, Rinnia and Saghan had been raised to believe that the technologies they concealed would bring too much power to any who stumbled upon them, and in time, that power would corrupt—as Salastragore taught them power always does—and the world would find a way to destroy itself. Simply put, if anyone ever stumbled upon the secrets, it was the Monitors' sworn duty to silence them. For the good of all Herbridia.

It was the sole reason the Monitors had fought the Mind for the last twenty years. Folgian, like all the other old Monitors, had become corrupted; but unlike the others, she had escaped Salastragore's justice, fled to Leora, and spilled just enough of her secrets to the powerful lion warlord who would soon be king to gain trust, spread influence, amass wealth, and ultimately achieve sanctuary in her Pinnacle Tower beyond even the Monitors' reach.

Yet for some reason, Folgian had left this station so close to her base of power untouched. Perhaps the dying bear had been lying about sharing all her knowledge; Rinnia could only guess at what "facts" she had told her scribes, what words they had scrawled onto the pages of all those innumerable books in her library. The Mind had clearly taken liberties writing this world's history any way it saw fit.

Rinnia had no idea what was buried below the stations. Not even the old octopus would tell her. She had asked him once long ago when he had approached her during a mission after she had separated from the others, and he had ignored the question. She remembered the wet, rattling sound in his chest, how she had figured then that the octopus knew that if he planned on keeping the fox girl's confidence, he would have to tell her something. So he told her that Folgian was once a Monitor, after all. Like himself. Like Salastragore. Their order had once been one hundred in number, but the three of them were now all that remained.

Rinnia, Saghan, and Sarovek were the new generation, the new order.

But Rinnia knew now that, like so much else, everything they believed in was a lie.

She hated history, if only for the fact that it was poisoned, and those in power would work tirelessly to ensure it always was. History was the gilded tray upon which the masters served the slaves their sustenance, and for centuries, they had eaten, blissfully stupid, pleased to perpetuate the cycle of slaughter. Part of her wished she could return to their ranks, to forget the truths Four Swords had told her, to climb back down into that dark cave of ignorance and just join the war and live and kill and die and be done with it all.

But then who would avenge her father?

She spoke his name. She thought about him every day. He was the reason she could not forget. He had stolen the relay. He had stopped Salastragore once. She would stop him again, forever. She would finish what he started.

Rinnia's path to the station had been roundabout, which meant it had taken her half an hour to travel what otherwise would have been ten minutes east beyond Renson's Mill. She hoped the others would be safe. No, she knew they would be. Sarovek would see to that. And the rhino. As for Maxan, well, he had proven himself resourceful by surviving this long.

"Lucky," she corrected her thoughts in a hushed voice. "Not resourceful."

The only reason she had not stayed in the burning city to help them find Feyn and the squirrel twins was because she knew the callers weren't there. There were too many coincidences—the rebellion, the king's march, the fires he had set, the station. It all pointed to the white wolf's involvement. Feyn had betrayed them. She knew it. The Monitors had walked right into the Mind's trap. Her only hope to retrieve the relay and escape was to come around at the wolf's back while her friends, if they still lived, drew his attention.

At last, she spotted the bare hilltop through the trees that surrounded it, an unordinary landmark but one specifically designed for the Monitors to recognize. The place was surrounded by the camp of Locain's honor guard. Points of torchlight glimmered in the distance, and Rinnia could clearly see the yellow-and-white standard set into the ground at the hill's base billowing in the night breeze.

"It's here," she whispered, watching the soldiers mill about their camp.

She recalled how the rebellion had uncovered this station's existence months ago when seeking a defensible stronghold in the Denlands. Someone had stumbled upon the cave and somehow disarmed the traps and seen through the diversions as they uncovered more tunnels, pressing farther down until they found the door. The Monitors' normal response when the proximity alerts were triggered was to travel to the station and silence the stumbler. But after Yacub recovered the relay, and after the botched exchange when the hyena raider decided to betray the Monitors in favor of working for the Mind, it was clear that she, Saghan, and Sarovek had more pressing matters to attend to in Leora.

Also, she didn't necessarily care to keep the brotherhood's tenets anymore. It didn't matter if the Denland rebels knew. It didn't matter if they cleared the way to the deepest chambers, if they bypassed the automated security, if they found some old tech, studied it, and somehow utilized it to turn the tides of their war with Locain. She didn't care about any of it because if the relay ever found its way to Salastragore's scaled fingers, they were all doomed anyway.

"Where is he?" she whispered, drawing to the edge of the tree line and sweeping her eyes over every figure she could see in the camp.

"Bad time to be talking to yourself, Rin," she whispered back.

She detached the voice amplifier cord from her belt, looped it around her neck, and lodged the receiver against her collarbone. She had already been unsuccessful in reaching her brother, but she decided nevertheless to try again. She pressed the node against her throat and spoke his name. There was no response.

"Rinnia," she asked herself, "tell me again, what's insanity?

"Repeating mistakes, expecting a difference."

She was about to rip the receiver from her ear when it subtly vibrated with incoming static. "Talking to yourself," Saghan hissed in her ear, "is pretty insane."

She nearly shouted but said in a measured voice, "Where are you?"

"Nearby, if you are where I think you are."

"The station's crawling with Locain's army." As if her observation had summoned them, a line of armored tribal species emerged then from the mouth of the cave (which she noted had been significantly widened since she'd last laid eyes on this site), dragging several Denland prisoners bound together by a long chain. "Oh no," she whispered.

"What is it? Rinnia…"

She remained silent, watching in horror as the soldiers forced the rebels to their knees, ten in all, and at the gesture of their knight-commander, swung their sharpened blades at the rebels' necks, separating heads from bodies. She brought her paw to her muzzle and bit hard, stifling her scream. The horror quickly turned to rage. She wanted nothing more than to draw the swords at her back and rush the murderers—the detestable, evil, grinning, and giggling monsters that delighted in the act of slaughter. But the dead were already dead. And if she would even be lucky enough to add the soldiers' bodies to that count, there would only be more to take their place, and add hers, too, soon enough.

"Rinnia!"

She closed her eyes and concentrated on Saghan's voice in her ear. "I'm here," she said.

"You need to be far away from the ruin."

"But…" She wanted to tell her brother that she couldn't go. That the relay was everything. She wanted to trust him. But she couldn't, because it might not actually be Saghan hissing in her ear. "Why?" she finally said.

"I've … taken care of it," the voice in her ear responded. There was a kind of sadness she could detect even over the artificial, electronic link fed through the Aigaion. "We can find the relay after."

"After what?"

There was no response.

"After what!" she repeated, seething. "Saghan, what did you do?"

Blood.

It ran from the fresh cuts from where they'd battered his face. As they dragged him out the back door of the Red Well tavern and knocked him powerfully on the skull, he felt the blood soaking into his snow-white fur and staining the clean commoner's clothing he'd chosen when setting out from the campus, likely for the last time.

A moment later, Feyn blinked away the stars bursting in his vision. Someone lifted him onto his knees. Something clinked behind him. He felt the weight of chains there, binding his wrists just above his tail. The blood had clotted, dried. He saw the red color hanging on a strand of disheveled fur before his eye. Despite the throbbing pain, Feyn smiled, feeling some shred of dignity, knowing that the blood was all his.

When Locain's soldiers had surged through the door of the Red Well, Feyn had managed to blast many of them away. Their bodies, thrown back like rag dolls, shattered the tavern's windows on their way into the street—or in the case of a barrel-chested warthog, demolished the wooden wall of the inn itself. But the yellow-and-white clad soldiers kept flooding into the inn from every entranceway, including the new ones Feyn's power had made. Howling and whooping, they chopped every other patron of the inn to pieces, sparing only the Mind's three callers.

Pryth, for all his idle chattering, was never one for improvisation, and the fear the little boy felt in that moment had paralyzed him. He seemed rooted to his chair, unable to call on any of the forces Feyn had helped him hone his senses for. As the soldiers overpowered the wolf, beat him, and set the iron manacles about his wrists, Feyn realized then—almost smiling at the thought—that he had never seen anything strike Pryth so silent.

Pram, however, proved to be the craftier of the twins, as she always had. Unsurprisingly, she said nothing. She never did. But Feyn saw her large, round eyes close and the tall tiger knight's glaze over, and he knew. The squirrel girl's claws tensed and released as the knight-commander guided his tiny captive out the back, drawing several puzzled looks from the soldiers in his charge who were too afraid to question his orders nonetheless. *If only she could make her puppets speak,* he thought. *Oh well.* If she survived this, Feyn knew her power would only grow.

The soldiers hoisted Feyn onto his hind legs and hauled him through the streets of Renson's Mill as Locain's animals pillaged and razed every building in sight, and put every inhabitant—grown or young, fighter or farmer—to the sword. His mind was addled from the blows they had dealt to his skull. He couldn't feel the connection to the Aigaion's energy. Even if he had wanted to howl and blow the entire city to pieces, he simply couldn't sense its signal. He was nothing without it. Just an animal.

Then, suddenly, he heard a call of a different sort, not from the sky, but from within his own body. An urge. A quickening of his heart, a rumbling in his belly, a tug at the edges of his maw that so wanted to curl away into a fanged snarl. A hunger. His icy blue eyes darted about, then locked on his captor's neck, seeing the rhythmic pulse just under the short fur there. His ears perked at the thrumming sound it made.

Blood.

Feyn's pupils dilated. His mouth watered at the thought of it. His throat thirsted for the taste of it. How easy it would be to just give in to the call. To rip and tear. To drink. To feast. Oh, how he hated the beast inside him. He hated the soldiers for waking it. But he hated himself most of all for wanting to give in.

He clamped his jaw tight and turned his gaze away. The spittle drooling from the scar at the edge of his mouth drew the ridicule of his captors, a pair of leopards, male and female. But he swallowed his hate and kept pace with them. He glanced to his side and saw Pryth being carried like a sack over the shoulder of an antelope with horns as tall and straight as swords. The boy had regained his penchant for gibbering like an idiot. Feyn twisted his gaze around as far as he could, but there was no sign of the squirrel's twin sister.

They marched through the town and witnessed the slaughter. They passed bodies skewered by javelins and severed limbs littering the ground. Had it just been for the glory of battle and the conquest and their king's vision for a unified Leora—had there been some *reason*—Feyn might have understood what drove these animals to kill. But it was their cruelty, their reveling in the bloodshed, that he could not stomach. He watched in horror as a father, a weasel, was pinned under the muscular paw of a laughing leopard and made to watch his own children thrown onto a stack of burning hay. Their mother lay nearby in a spreading pool of blood, her heart thankfully carved out already, sparing her from the sight. Pryth fell silent as they passed this atrocity by.

The smell of smoke wafted through the woods beyond the town, and Feyn knew as they moved onward that Locain's troops were setting more than just Renson's Mill aflame. Whether by the order of his own master Folgian or simply for the chance to indulge in his violent nature, the king would slaughter his way westward, and in time burn all the Denlands to the ground.

They came to a broad hill, the top of which rose above the canopy of the forest surrounding it and was conspicuously barren of trees. There was a cave carved into the side of it, and the soldiers led him down into the narrow torchlit tunnels below. Roughly half an hour since they had first been taken from the Red Well, Feyn, Pryth, and their captors finally emerged into an enormous chamber deep underground, dimly lit by torches discarded on the ground. Glancing about at the rough stone that almost seemed to grow like mold over the tarnished, smooth metal walls, and feeling that the ground here was uniformly level beneath his legs, Feyn suddenly knew exactly what this place was. He remembered how Folgian had mentioned that such underground vaults existed throughout Herbridia, that they were part of the secrets she had once sworn to guard, and that she would gladly take the knowledge of their locations to her grave.

The bodies of several armored Denland species lay on the floor along one of the walls—a stag with broken antlers, an old badger, two raccoons, a young bear, even a pair of dark-furred wolves—all their wrists bound behind their waists, all their throats slit, all slumped in fresh pools of blood. All rebels.

The male leopard shoved Feyn down beside them. Feyn tried not to meet the frozen, glazed eyes of the dead. The scent of their blood filled his nostrils. He choked on the sweetness of it, struggling to control the urge scratching within his heart.

The tall-horned antelope tossed Pryth hard onto the ground next to Feyn.

"Ow! Hey! That hurt! You wanna—"

"Be silent!" Feyn cut the boy off with a stern whisper.

The soldier who'd been about to box the squirrel's ears instead turned and joined a group of his comrades across the chamber who were carefully picking apart a mound of fallen stones blocking a tunnel. Judging by the trail of Denlanders' corpses left battered and bloodied along the way there, Feyn surmised more of the rebels must have fled and caved it in behind them.

"Principal Feyn."

The white wolf narrowed his eyes at the approaching torch-light. It reflected brightly from sculpted plates of pure golden armor, shimmering on the ceiling like light bouncing off water.

"Locain," he said, the scarred side of his face drawing into a snarl more hideous than normal.

The lion king passed the torch to one of the two masked, identically armored body doubles flanking him. The other held the king's own lion-faced mask.

"I received a runner from your master just this morning," Locain said. "She said you'd run off unexpectedly. Left witnesses at the campus who swore they spotted you on the road out of Crosswall, crossing the Radilin, headed west. To Peskora? Hmm. But Folgian, she is a crafty one. She knew better. She knew all along that you'd go east to help these Denland rabble orchestrate their rebellion." The lion swept his arm to indicate the line of corpses. "And that it was likely I'd find you here among them, bearing a weapon that could turn the tides in their favor."

Feyn concentrated on keeping his silence. He focused on the stillness of the ground beneath his knees. He thought Locain might simply flash that pompous, triumphant grin of his and move along. But the Golden Lord held out his paw. One of his bodyguards placed the relay in it, and Feyn couldn't help but bare his fangs and growl. Part of him had hoped they'd burn the Red Well to the ground before searching his room there, and that he could later find the relay in the ashes. If he lived.

"Folgian's messenger said that she demanded I abandon the campaign and return this … thing to her, to guard it with the full strength of my army, with my very own life." Locain's smile died. "Tell me, Feyn. What am I to the Mind? A warrior? A king? A courier?"

Feyn saw the king's paw tightening around the shining metallic tube. He remembered the master's warning. He could feel the beast inside, urging him to leap at Locain with snapping jaws, to forget about what could happen if the lion mishandled the artifact. He closed his eyes and felt his animal instinct suffocate under the weight of his rational mind.

Feyn exhaled deeply, steadily. "You're a fool," he said finally.

The lion's broad, handsome face wrinkled in fury. His fist tightened around the relay until the veins along his golden-furred arms bulged.

"But it's not your fault," Feyn said, trying to sound reassuring. "Rather, you've been made a fool. Because Folgian would keep you ignorant. Like me. What are you doing here, Locain?" Feyn shifted his wrists, clinking the chains that held him. "You think I'm involved with the rebellion simply because of my species? Simply because Folgian told you what to believe."

There it was; Feyn saw that ember of doubt flare hotter in Locain's eyes than the king's smoldering rage. The wolf had set the lion's emotions on fire, and now he needed only to redirect the heat. "She's lying to you. You've always known that it's true. She's using you. And the moment I leave the Mind behind, to bring you the truth, she sets you after me like you're her servant."

"I SERVE NO ONE!"

Locain's roar shook the chamber. The soldiers clearing the tunnel stopped their work, then nervously watched loose gravel and dust fall from the ceiling as the thunder of the king's voice faded. Pryth bent forward at the waist, his tiny nose nearly touching the dirt floor, his bushy tail trembling and wrapping around him in fear.

Through it all, Feyn remained composed, upright, staring hard at the unmasked lion. The scar on the wolf's face helped him conceal his gratified smile. "Folgian demanded you kill me, didn't she? And yet you haven't. Why?"

Locain looked away. His grip on the relay relaxed.

"Because you're not a fool," Feyn persisted. "Because you're the king. You're the one I expected to find here. I came here to find you, Locain. Long before I served the Mind, I served Leora."

"So I've heard," Locain said, a glimmer of respect igniting in his eye. "Feyn. Knight-commander. You even earned yourself a title. It's been so long. What was it?"

"What about me?"

Both the wolf and the lion spun suddenly toward the squeaking voice. Pryth had recovered his courage, it seemed, and had been growing steadily more agitated with each seed of the lie his master was sowing. He hopped suddenly onto both lower paws.

"What about my mom? My dad?"

"Silence," Feyn barked at his pupil. Unlike himself, the wolf knew the squirrel's anger did not spring from his animal nature. Pryth was pure emotion, and Feyn knew there was little that reason could do to rein that emotion back in once it had been released.

"You burned them alive," the boy spat at the king, ignoring his master. "My home! Gone! Ashes! You took everything! From me! From my sister! We saw you throw the torch!" Pryth ducked under one of the masked bodyguard's reaching arms. "Or one of these assholes anyway," he said, spinning away lithely despite the heavy manacles binding his wrists at his back. "You left us to die! Remember? *Do you even remember?*"

Feyn could not feel the Aigaion's presence, but he could feel the presence of his apprentice's mind scrambling maniacally over every particle in the chamber, desperate and invisible, to gather enough energy for … what? If the boy attacked the king, the soldiers would tear them both apart.

"Do you?!" Pryth screamed, standing before the king, his head no higher than the height of the mighty lion's waist. Feyn saw Pryth's small claws curled in anger, and the faintest spark flicker and die and flicker again along the iron manacles binding his wrists.

Feyn had always admired the boy's spirit. He was fascinated by how easily Pryth could rely on emotion to ignite his command of combustible elements, to so effortlessly call on that part of the Aigaion that controlled those forces. He knew the squirrel twins' story well, having found them in the ashes of their village, taken them in, raised them, felt their rare natural connection to the Aigaion and guided them to their powers. Their broken lives were simply collateral damage to Locain; they were just more orphans of war who would be swept away in the wake of the Golden Lord's campaign against the Denland rebels. Feyn had hoped Pryth and Pram had been too young to remember the king and that their trauma would be enough to erase their desire for revenge.

Clearly, that wasn't the case. Right now, the boy's impetuous spirit and those flaring powers of his would do no more good than the Denland rebellion had done for the bloodied corpses beside him. Feyn closed his eyes, inhaled deeply, and reached for the invisible strings of the Aigaion's power, willing the very air to be his fist and knock the boy aside.

But the scent of freshly spilled blood stole his focus.

He felt nothing.

It didn't matter. Locain struck Pryth anyway, the back of his paw slapping the boy's muzzle. The blow was meant as more than a warning; it was meant to harm. The force of it spun Pryth around and sent him crashing against the rock wall where he lay motionless.

"Leave us," Locain roared to his bodyguards and soldiers. The soldiers dropped whatever heavy stones were in hand and shuffled away up the tunnel, leaving their king, Feyn, and the unconscious squirrel alone in the chamber.

When they were gone, Locain squatted, drawing his face closer to Feyn's, the both of them struggling visibly to avoid baring their fangs. "Despite all your wisdom, all your secret schemes, you and Folgian have always failed to see one thing about me. I don't slaughter these animals because you tell me to or because you direct me to from the shadows. I slaughter them because I enjoy it. Because it's fun. Because life without death is so ... boring."

Locain drew a curved knife from the scabbard at his belt, ran the pure golden blade against the white fur of Feyn's ruined face, and set its hooked point against the front of Feyn's blood-stained tunic as he spoke. He spoke so calmly, his voice just above a whisper. "To see the red splash, to see it gleaming on the blade as you slide it from their ribs. To watch the fire reduce all they love most to ashes. It's glorious, Feyn. Don't you remember?"

Feyn's quickening breaths must have seemed like panic to the lion, like fear, and that drew Locain's smile. But the lion didn't know the wolf was fighting himself for control.

Feyn's eyes widened as his pupils contracted, becoming needles aimed at the lion's neck, focusing on the wiry hairs of the lion's mane, seeing them pulse and sway with the thrumming of the blood in the veins buried below their roots. His tongue slithered inside his mouth, sloshed in the hot drool that dripped from the scarred corner of his mouth. But he clamped his jaw tight, his fangs pressing into one another, driving into his gums. He tore his eyes away, settled them on the golden blade held to his chest. He was powerless to stop the lion, but he still held power over himself.

Feyn would not let himself become the animal.

Never again.

"You do remember. You're a killer, Feyn." Locain gripped Feyn by the scruff of fur under his pointed ear and dragged the wolf's gaze back. "You think The Mind has used *me*? No. It's the other way around. Don't you see? You've given me the war I want. And when this war is over, when I'm done with the Denlands, I'll bring a new war to your campus. I'll tear it all down—all your schools, your factories, your tower—brick by borrowed brick. I'll hunt the Stray to extinction. I'll burn their hovels to the ground. I'll forge my army of Leoran warriors in the heat of my own people's pain. They will hate me. But I don't care. I'll see them challenge me, and lose, and find they've no choice but to follow me." Locain let go, pushing Feyn's head aside, and added, "Because they will learn this is who we are. Killers. Every one of us."

Feyn had suffered through every word and every violent shake of his neck in Locain's grip, but he could not ignore the implication. "Follow you where?"

Locain smiled, stood, and sheathed his knife. "It's been too long since we've had a proper war, Feyn. I shall see my banner fly over every corner of this world."

It was Feyn's turn to laugh. "Pride will not lend you power."

The wolf's words stung the lion, drawing a grimace across his handsome golden face. It faded in an instant, and Locain turned to consider the layers of metal, rust, rock, and root overlapping across the walls and ceiling of the chamber. "Power, hmm? I've heard a few things about power. From the mouths of your own scholars, no less. *Knowledge is power*, they teach. This place…" His eyes settled on the collapsed corridor his soldiers had been working to clear. "What's hiding below us? Folgian knows. But she never told you, did she? I wonder why that is.

"*Power corrupts.* That's another teaching." The king found the relay from where he had tucked it in his belt. "What about this?" he said, emboldened at seeing the white wolf flinch as he held the polished device in his paw. "Tell me what you know, and I will let your whelp live a little longer."

Feyn looked at his apprentice, crumpled against a wall, and then at the line of corpses, no more than a few inches from Pryth. All defiance, all schemes, all hope fled from the white wolf, and an overwhelming sense of fatigue rushed in to fill the absence they left. He knew the decision to leave—to betray— the Mind and rely on the Monitors would be risky, the choice to flee eastward even riskier. And to drag the twins into this… He never believed they would wind up buried beneath layers of rock and metal, in whatever kind of tomb this was, the one place, it seemed, where he could not call on the Aigaion.

"Pride is not power," he reminded himself in a whisper. He raised his eyes to the king, ready to admit defeat and buy Pryth more time with the little he knew about the artifact.

But Locain no longer seemed interested. The lion's ears were fixated on the collapsed corridor.

Then Feyn heard it too. A persistent scratching. The muffled clacking of rocks behind the wall. The pattering of loose gravel.

And then, through the cracks between the piled stones, a scream that froze his blood, cut abruptly short. The scratching intensified, becoming frenzied skittering and scraping on the other side.

Locain backed slowly away, reaching his paw to the gold-en-threaded hilt of the tall sword over his shoulder, just as the first rocks tumbled down the pile. Something was pushing them from the other side. Something black, metallic, and incredibly strong. It pushed again—an armored limb reached into the dim chamber, disappeared back into the shadows—and the largest rock tumbled away, crashing to the center of the room, bringing the rest down behind it.

Before Feyn could stand, the first giant ant scampered through the hole into the room, and the swarm of Thraxians followed.

FILE 798: "CONFESSIONS"

Time: 003292/09/29-(18:17:07-18:22:16)
Location: Castle Tower
Begin audio transcription:

Good evening. Pardon the intru—

Oh! My... We need to see to the ventilation in here, don't we? Hmm!

Well. Huh. Hemm. I won't be long.

I wanted to show you... Look what I found in the lab!

Despite decades of neglect, life found a way! Breathtaking, isn't it? An entire colony. Survivors. Extraordinary survivors. Their natural tendency is to thrive, isn't it? They don't need much, I guess. A little dirt. A little darkness.

Go on. Say hello.

Well, I shall leave them right here. Pets. Cellmates.

Look at them in there. Look at those bodies. Remember what we made based on those designs? Scorpions, spiders, beetles ... even the ants! All of them monsters. Beautiful monsters. All their natural weaponry, their natural armor. And their silence? Thraxians always made the best assassins!

Ahhh. Surely you realize you couldn't exterminate them all. They're just too hardy a classification. They were here long before us. They'll be here long after. Always evolving. And now, I've evolved them a step further. Someday, perhaps, I'll let the queen herself pay you a visit. Show you the augmentations I've made.

Look at them skittering around. You never bothered to be one, did you? Not many of us did. I did, once, a long time ago. I was part of the hive mind. I felt their potential. I saw Thraxians for what they really are. The perfect biological expression of order. Organization. Balance. The structures they built and the speed they built them with ... just a marvel.

And your war reduced all their marvelous spiraling castles to dust. Ash.

Were we ... shortsighted in our design? If Thraxians were really a mistake, then who's to say ... we're not?

Well, then! Ha! Pretty heavy stuff, hmm?

Who knows, maybe these little creatures can show you.

Come on out. Don't be shy.

There.

Perhaps, when you're ready, you'll tell them you're sorry.

CHAPTER THIRTEEN
THE RUINED WORLD

THE FIRES SET BY THE KING'S PATROLS WERE as much a force driving them east as the need to reunite with the relay and with their friends. Being stealthy wasn't a challenge for the fox, but concealing the hulking frame of a rhinoceros (with the unconscious squirrel girl over his shoulder) or the wide wingspan and glinting armor of a hawk knight would have proved to be a challenge. Fortunately for the four of them—*Unfortunately*, Maxan thought, *for everyone else in the Denlands*—the bulk of Locain's soldiers had moved on, farther into the forest. Their slaughter of Renson's Mill was complete.

The town, the trees, the corpses—all of it would be consumed soon enough, reduced to ash and terrible memories for any of the Denland inhabitants who had escaped.

If any escaped, Maxan thought. *But how many more were born in fire tonight? Like I was.*

But you escaped, Max.

He looked around at the fire's distant glimmer, still visible between the trees, surrounding them on all sides, herding them in the direction of its choosing.

No, I didn't. Not forever.

Right back where we started.

The light from the fire intensified, moving as swiftly as they did. Having trudged part of their way through smoldering patches of forest floor, the companions were coated in soot from the waist down, to their paws, talons, and feet. The air was cloying, stifling. Smoke wafted like dark curtains in a breeze. Scents of burning wood and hair and meat swirled together, overpowering Maxan's sensitive nostrils, making him wish he had the duller olfactory sense of the rhino or the hawk. *Or at least been knocked out like the squirrel.*

He took a deep breath of slightly cleaner air when they finally came to a halt at a vast clearing. Under a blanket of rolling black smoke that hid Yerda from view, an enormous hill rose before them, hundreds of feet above the tree line, covered in low grass and loose rocks. It was likely the safest place for miles, having little to feed the encroaching fires all around. A few dozen soldiers had figured this, too, setting up camp along the hill's edge under the king's personal banner. A battle of some kind had been fought here, hours ago, Maxan judged, since a group of soldiers farther out in the field between the trees and the hill were gleefully tossing dead Denlanders onto a massive, roaring pyre. From the wide mouth of a cavern in the hill's side, six more soldiers emerged with torches and stood guard at that entrance as two knights in full plate armor followed.

Maxan recognized the lion-faced masks they wore.

Maxan crouched beside Chewgar, who was lying on his stomach below a bush to stay out of sight and tried to massage the pain out of the singed soles of his lower paws. Chewgar tended to the squirrel, almost like a young rhino cub playing with a doll as he gently stroked her brow with his thick finger, trying to rouse her. It wasn't working. Whatever mind trick Pram had pulled on the tiger—*The trick that eventually turned him into a very dead, very carved-up and roasted tiger*—had taken a visible toll on her own body. Her fur was matted with sweat, and she spasmed as though trapped by a nightmare that would not let her go.

Sarovek was keenly focused on the clearing. Her gold-rimmed pupils widened and contracted as they flitted over the king's encampment.

Maxan knew exactly what she was searching for.

"Rinnia," he said, just loud enough for her to hear. "Do you see her?"

Above her shoulder, the hawk knight held up a single talon point, a sign that said either "Just a moment" or "Be silent, you fool!"

Pram's eyes fluttered open, rolled forward slowly, and came to rest on the huge curved horn hovering over her. Chewgar smiled warmly, glad to see her awake. This would probably have startled anyone else into a panic, but the tiny squirrel's expression was serene. She reached up and laid her paw on Chewgar's muscled forearm. The soothing look on the rhino's face faded at her touch. His brow furrowed as though hearing something disturbing.

"We cannot stay," Sarovek said at last. "Everywhere we turn, death awaits us. Behind, we burn. Ahead, we fight, and we lose. Our only option is to circle the clearing, find a way south, and hope the king's fires have not set that path ablaze. We will go now before it does."

"What about Rinnia?" Maxan countered. "She's in there, isn't she?"

Sarovek's only response was a clack of her beak.

"The Leoran ruins," he persisted. "That's what Saghan said. This is it, isn't it? You know as well as I do she's in there."

"And *I* said Rinnia can take care of herself."

Sarovek's voice tried to cut off the debate with a sharpened edge of conviction, but Maxan heard her falter. *She doubts it,* he thought.

"I'm going," he replied, lurching forward a few steps before his own doubt suddenly rooted him to the spot.

The voice of reason chimed in as well. *How, exactly, do you intend to go anywhere?*

Ah...

Maxan swallowed, found his throat suddenly dry, and looked ahead at the well-armed, well-trained killers all about the field.

"You'll die." The hissing whisper behind them voiced the next thought in Maxan's head. "Mossst assuredly." Saghan knelt silently by the hawk, but his long neck brought his face to the fox. "You'd be wise to wait, right here, as the rest of us will."

Sarovek didn't acknowledge her brother's presence. She didn't seem startled or surprised in the least at his silent entrance. But at this last suggestion, she turned to him with half-lidded eyes and clacked her beak tightly. "You'd have us wait for the fire at our backs to push us into the king's soldiers?"

"They won't be alive much longer." Saghan smiled. "Reinforcements are on the way."

Before Maxan could blink, Sarovek's taloned hand shot out, clutched the collar of Saghan's armor, and dragged the snake's face to within an inch of her own. "What did you do?" She seethed, producing a sound that was hardly less than a scream.

Maxan saw a few figures by the hill rise, their ears flicking about, their snouts turning toward the tree line, toward the spot where the five of them hid.

"I held to our first tenet, sister," Saghan hissed, wrenching himself free. "Protecting our sssecrets. Finding that which was stolen." His slender finger stabbed toward the squirrel nearby.

"And what have *you* been doing? I don't suppose she has what we've all risked our lives for."

"Her brother," Chewgar broke in, Pram's paw still resting on his arm, his brow still knitting itself together. "He's there. She feels like ... he's choking ... crushed."

"And Feyn," Saghan reasoned, looking at the girl's paw and quickly understanding who the rhino was truly speaking for. "It's with the wolf. Below." He exchanged a glance then with Sarovek.

Maxan turned to Saghan, ignoring the figures approaching the tree line. "You seem to know where everyone's at. Where's Rinnia?"

The snake's usual arrogance faded. He seemed genuinely disturbed, as though speaking about his sister like she was already dead. "I warned her not to go."

"You've set doom upon her." Sarovek's whisper brought whatever was left of Saghan's self-assured edifice crumbling down.

We may not have much time to grieve, Maxan realized as he counted ten shapes drawing closer, shadows framed by the bonfire of bodies behind them. He gripped the handle of his short sword.

What are you going to do? Rush them? Run around with flailing arms and wagging tail and lead a line of trained killers on a fox hunt?

Wouldn't be the first time.

Maxan saw Chewgar and Sarovek tense, ready to spring into action, and Saghan's hand came out from his satchel holding a small black sphere.

There was a sudden explosion in the field, and the snake hadn't even thrown his contraption yet. A geyser of dirt blew into the air and rained down on the soldiers. They leapt away, startled, and some of them tripped over the holes left behind by the exploding ground as more bursts shot forth all around their feet. Something long and barbed reached up from one of these, snagged a soldier's leg, and dragged him underground.

Then they came out. Maxan knew—yet could not believe—they were real.

Thraxians.

A ceaseless stream of oily-black six-legged insects—all equal in size to the fox watching in shock from the tree line—skittered from each hole, even as new ones exploded open nearer to the hill's edge and more Thraxians engaged Locain's scrambling soldiers. Ants. Once the most abundant species of Thraxia, of all Herbridia.

One or two of them could be beaten back easily, as a broad warthog in yellow-and-white armor demonstrated with two sweeps of his great ax. But his triumph was short-lived, as the swarm he did not see behind him sliced at the tendons of his legs, plunged their knife-sharp pincers into his back, dragged him to the ground, and cut the rest of him to ribbons. The more agile soldiers—the quick-footed coyotes, cheetahs, and even hyenas—fared better against the surprise attack, but the space they put between themselves and their comrades exposed their flanks. It was only a matter of time before half of the dozen or so soldiers that had been caught in the middle of the clearing were torn apart by Thraxians.

Maxan was already up before his inner voice of reason could protest. He somersaulted over the bushes, then launched himself past the edge of the trees and into the clearing at a full sprint, with time only for one thought to cross his mind. *Rinnia.*

His legs never slowed, even when half his own mind protested.

She won't survive this! Neither will you, Max!

She may.

She won't!

I can't be the last fox again. I won't be.

The weight of that notion silenced all thought. His fanned ears turned away from the two Monitors hollering at his back. He became pure focus and calculation as he made his way forward, sidestepping the combatants and the widening holes, where even more ants spilled forth as he passed. Their arms and maws—natural weapons always at the ants' ready—swiped and snapped at his legs, but hit nothing but air.

Maxan caught himself smiling before he even knew why. *Not at all unlike the rooftops of Crosswall,* he thought, jumping onto the broad carapace of one of the larger ants and launching himself high and far before it could shake him off.

But Crosswall wasn't trying to kill us.

That's arguable.

Lit by the glowing bonfire, the field churned with violence, like a scene ripped from the Extermination War. The entire space was equal parts swaying green grass, slashing steel, and shining black bodies that reflected the firelight. Animal howls and screams mingled with insect clicks and screeches.

Maxan landed, rolled, and came up into a sprint without losing speed. He saw the wide mouth of the cave only thirty feet ahead. Led by Locain's body doubles (or perhaps even the Golden Lord himself), the soldiers there were holding their line rather well, adding to the pile of split Thraxian bodies before them with cruel efficiency. But they might as well have been fighting back the rising tide, as the sea of ants still rushed at them in biting waves.

The single moment the fox paused to plan a way up, around, and down was all the time the ant at his side needed to skitter within striking distance. Without any direction from him, Maxan's short sword had already, suddenly, found its way into his paw and was slashing up to intercept the ant's barbed limb.

Wha—

Hit it back! he told himself, but he was already instinctively rolling to the insect's side, trying to break away and reach the cave.

Something caught around his throat, dragged him down hard onto his back. The Thraxian had brought its serrated arm down, missing Maxan's head by inches but snagging his cloak.

The fox rolled aside as the thing's other forelimb crashed onto the ground, cutting deep into the dirt. His cloak still caught in the giant ant's barbs, Maxan swung his arm over the twisted fabric, bunching it up like a rope, and pulled hard, happy to discover a Thraxian weighed hardly more than a bundle of twigs. His short sword plunged deep into the crack between the plates of the Thraxian's carapace. Maxan felt its innards shudder, and then it went still.

As its lifeless body slid off his sword, Maxan sensed a new vibration, this one in the ground. The space between where he stood and the six fighters before the cave was filled with a mass of insects, and half of them had turned away from the soldiers there and focused their antennae in the fox's direction. Now they skittered straight toward him.

Plan, his mind suggested, then the suggestion became panic. *PLAN!!*

He looked about wild-eyed for a way around. The vibration in the ground picked up to a steady pounding as the Thraxian wave closed the distance. With a sinking heart, he realized that there was no plan, that his final mortal thought would be a simple curiosity. *How are all those lightweight ants shaking the ground so much?*

Just as the line of ants swelled about him to strike, the pounding ceased, and the sharp spike of a rhinoceros horn bucked upward, goring two ants and flinging them away into the night sky. At the same moment, the wide, flat face of an ax slammed down just in front of where Maxan stood, shattering five more ant bodies as though they were black pottery filled with oozing pulp.

"GO, MAX!" Chewgar thundered, bringing his ax back for a swing at the ants swarming in to take the others' place.

So, again without thinking, Maxan went.

The Thraxians moved on to the bigger target, leaving the fox free to find the longer way around the battle. He slipped up the side of the hill and knelt in the grass just over the cave's entrance. Three soldiers stood their ground against the onslaught below, none wearing Locain's armor. The corpses of Leorans and Thraxians alike were jammed and twisted together, and Maxan had no time to see if the king's bodyguards were among them. Maxan dropped below, rolled with the impact of gravity, and ran into the darkness of the tunnel without looking back.

If he had, he would have seen a final wave of hard black limbs wash over the three soldiers and drag them away to their doom.

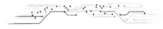

Rinnia found the station's ventilation grate a few hundred feet east of the hill, concealed fairly well beneath a layer of dirt and overgrown roots. She knew all the stations had them, and she knew what to look for. She cleared the debris, pried the ancient metal hatch open, and squeezed through.

She splashed ankle-deep into some wet murk. Her feet had broken through some film of orange grime when she had dropped from the vent, and her breaking of that seal and her general disturbance of the stillness had released a stench throughout the corridor.

A palpable darkness surrounded her. She covered her snout with one paw while the other blindly fumbled the tools on her belt, found the pinlight, and switched it on. Its bright beam cut through the darkness, illuminating metal walls and a ceiling caked with layers of rust and decades of rot. It would be only a matter of time, perhaps a hundred more years, before the decay reached the station's heart. No doubt the same was happening at every other station across Herbridia. The Peskoran sites were likely already drowned in salty ocean water. The ones in Thraxia probably choked with sand. How many more centuries could the geothermal engines connected far beneath these stations keep running before finally shorting out? How much longer did their tiny world have before the systems that kept it spinning suddenly stopped?

Rinnia sloshed forth through the thick pool, aware that she had no idea where she was going. While it was true that to have been in one station was to have been in them all, it didn't stop each from being a labyrinth of corridors, conduits, ducts, and dead ends. Maybe that was part of the design. "Trap intruders in a maze," she observed in a low voice.

"And who's the intruder now?

"*Imposter*'s the better word."

She sighed.

"Rin, stop talking to yourself…"

Thankfully her nose was working harder than her mouth or her memory, leading her left or right, toward what she believed would be a wide central chamber. A scent reached her, some nuance on top of the cloying stench of stagnation. Something salty. Metallic. Even sterile, somehow. And to a killer like Rinnia, familiar.

"Blood."

Rinnia saw the traces of deep red swirling in the ruddy layer of rust on the water's surface. Then she saw the corpses. Denlanders. Rebels. Floating facedown in the murk or slumped against the walls. Bodies, limbs, and heads, ripped and scattered, stretched down the corridor before her. These weren't the elegant cuts from Old Four Swords's blades. This was carnage. Mad, chaotic slaughter.

Rinnia allowed herself a single shuddering breath, then swallowed the horror before it could seize her. She knew what had done this to them. Her impetuous, callous brother had set the Thraxians upon them. No matter how much he hated to admit it, Saghan was not so much unlike his father. He could be just as savage and uncaring as Salastragore, even on his own. It was in his blood.

She picked her way between the corpses, trying not to fixate on the bloody wetness soaking into her fur and skin, trying to feel as cold as a snake. The slaughter here was already over. They were just meat now. Just dead. She didn't have time to feel for them.

Rinnia moved on and soon found what the Denlanders had been running from.

An enormous pile of rocks littered the corridor, rising steadily to a crest just below the metal ceiling that had given out and let go. Rinnia's pinlight revealed a space there where she could clamber through, and her snout drank in the sweeter-scented air flowing in from it.

Something pricked her ears up as well. The clanging of steel. A lion's roar.

She was not too late. There was still time to get the relay, get out, and get to Old Four Swords.

Rinnia's heart thundered in her chest. She felt the rush of adrenaline ignite in her veins. She raced up the slope of fallen rocks and clambered through the open space at its top.

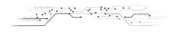

The lion deserved all he had ever earned. His renown. His legend. And in time, his crown. The other animals called him the Golden Lord, a title he had earned in the Extermination War, slaying Thraxians by the thousands, be they ants, wasps, spiders, or any of the other monstrosities that called that desert theirs. Locain had killed them all. He had set fire to their towering hives, collapsed their endless tunnels, and scorched every inch of their homeland until all that remained was a ruined horizon of ash where nothing would ever live again.

That was twenty years ago, and Locain had enjoyed no practice slaying Thraxians since. But he rediscovered the instinct easily enough.

The ground was littered with dozens of cleaved and broken ant bodies. But still dozens more skittered closer, driving him back. Some had scored lucky strikes, tearing away plates of the king's dark-blue armor and striking at the golden-furred flesh beneath. Rivers of red stained his glorious mane, ran down his arms, and dripped from the points of his claws.

But somehow, Locain withstood the onslaught. The pride (perhaps arrogance) that his title and crown had bestowed on him would not let him fall. Not to a foe he had already annihilated. He rose, straightened his back, and heaved the blade of his tall golden-hilted great sword onto his shoulder, ready to strike.

While Locain had been busy destroying the ants at one side of the immense chamber, he had not seen the gigantic scorpion skitter up from the hole it had made in the ground and prowl silently around his flank, keeping its monstrous body low to the ground, its bulbous stinger poised just inches over its armored back.

The few ants Locain had not yet killed inexplicably lost their collective will to fight. As he watched the ten remaining Thraxians slowly back away, some dormant memory woke in the lion's mind—an insight about these creatures' behavior he had learned on the battlefield that saved his life then, and would save him now.

In one fluid motion, he stepped right just as the stinger snapped forward, and he brought the great sword down with tremendous, roaring force. The blade, already slick with the ichor of its innards, crashed onto the middle segment of the stinger and sliced clean through. The scorpion recoiled, emitted a high-frequency screech of pain, and lunged at the lion with both pincers snapping.

On the other side of the chamber, Feyn was fighting a battle of life and death as well. He was grateful to find that his own memory of the ants' behavior hadn't faded much since the war. He knew their shared hive mind always drew them to the more immediate threat, in this case, the armed and armored lion. But while the king was severely outnumbered, the white wolf was severely unequipped. Not only could Feyn not call upon the Aigaion's influence from this deep underground, but also his claws were firmly bound in iron behind his back. All he had were his fangs and his fury. Neither would do him any good against a Thraxian carapace.

The ants' pincers had left his clothes in tatters. Feyn had managed to dart away and kick a few back, but it was no use. They carved bloody streaks into Feyn's legs, and fresh lines of red ran across his white fur. He now stood unsteadily over the unconscious squirrel, determined that the single ant before him, the only one that hadn't abandoned him for Locain, would die before ever harming the boy.

The ant rose, arched its armored back, and came at Feyn with its barbed arm swiping horizontally. Feyn bent at the waist and took the blow against his shoulder, hoping he could draw the thing closer and close his jaws around the stem that held its head. But his fangs shut on nothing but empty space as the ant disengaged and shuffled back several steps, leaving the white wolf to realize the failed maneuver had cost him a bloody gash that wrapped around his shoulder and back.

The pain rushed through him, and he fell to his knees, his arms squirming against their restraints, trying to shake the burning sensation of his freshest—and worst—wound. The ant reared back to swipe again, and Feyn knew he hadn't the strength to rise in time and try for another bite. This was how it would end.

"HEY!"

The shout from somewhere in the cavern was enough to startle the insect, for one second only but long enough for Feyn to spring forward and take half of the ant's head into his wide-open mouth. In the second after, he bit with all his might, felt the plates of the ant's armor break and slide, and the hot, bitter ooze spilled onto his tongue and down his throat. Feyn growled and snarled, jerking his neck with all his might.

Both the ant's arms whipped against Feyn's shoulder, drawing fresh cuts each time, even as the wolf crushed its tiny brain between his jaws.

It was only when the fox leapt onto the ant's back and plunged his sword point straight through its chest that the creature finally shuddered and went limp.

Feyn released the thing from his jaws and spat.

Maxan backed away, sliding his short blade out of the corpse as it fell.

"So—" he started, but a sudden roar of anguish drowned all sound in the chamber.

While the fox's shout might have startled Feyn's lone attacker just long enough to save his life, it had also distracted Locain just long enough for the scorpion to gain the advantage. One massive pincer closed around the lion's waist, punching through his gold-trimmed armor like it was no thicker than paper, and the other caught the wrist of the lion's sword arm. The flare of pain ran through Locain's body, and he couldn't keep his grip on the great sword. He roared in agony as it clattered to the ground.

With its victim firmly seized in the grip of both pincers, the scorpion began pulling them apart as if ripping Locain in two. Its arachnid brain clearly delighted in feeling the lion's bones popping from their joints and his sinews stretching.

Maxan froze, terrified by the sight of a scorpion, a monstrous creature he had never believed he would ever see, not at all unlike the legendary behemoths themselves. He watched helplessly as the king was wrenched apart. Only when he saw Locain's free paw rise over his head—holding something shining, with glowing golden lights—only then did Maxan regain control of himself. Only then did he hear the voice in his head screaming at him.

MOVE!

With all his might, Locain brought the relay down against the scorpion's arm like a hammer, again and again. The racing golden lights halted in their circuit and winked out, one by one, then the relay's red eyes came to life. The light blasted forth from the device, chasing away every shadow. It was inescapable.

A high-pitched squeal erupted from the maw behind the scorpion's mandibles, and the creature's pincers lurched open, dropping the lion. The scorpion skittered several steps away, pinching its claws sporadically as though fighting an invisible enemy. The other Thraxian ants lost control of their limbs, tumbled about, flailing at the air and at one another wildly. Within seconds, their mass of bodies scrambled back into the dark they came from.

The lion rolled over and came up on all four of his paws. He ignored the shattered bones of his wrist, the tightness of the gold armor pressing into his guts, the leaking puncture in his belly. The lion's mind was gone. Only raw instinct remained. The animal saw before it now only the enemy, an adversary that had brought pain, a thing to be destroyed.

Birthed in the red light, the animal in Locain's heart was free. It spurred him into a leap. It drove his claws down as it pummeled the giant Thraxian, scratching away streaks of chitin from its carapace. The lion's claws then found the edges of the scorpion's armored plates, and its powerful arms ripped them back and flung them away, exposing the squishy sacs of organs beneath. The lion shredded these, digging deeper and deeper into the thing's body, each claw coming back more and more slick with the orange of the scorpion's ichorous blood, before plunging in again, and again, until finally the great Thraxian stopped moving, stopped twitching, and lay still.

Maxan watched Locain as long as he could, part of him wanting to keep his distance, part of him urging him forward to snatch the relay that had fallen out of the lion's grasp and rolled away. But the hysterics of the wolf behind him demanded all his attention. He dived aside just as Feyn launched through the air, and avoided the snapping, frothing jaws aimed at Maxan's waist.

The wolf fell hard onto his chest. His brief whimper of pain became a rumbling growl as he spun about. The animal that the principal had become seemed unsure what to do about the iron binding its wrists. It seemed to forget about the bewildered fox and rolled in the gravel and dirt, trying and failing to break free of the shackles.

Maxan backed away, once again caught in a horrid red world gone completely mad. And yet he was completely unaffected. He remained in control of his own mind.

His eyes fixed on the one spot where the world was reddest. *The relay.*

He burst into motion, leapt over corpses, slid on gravel, dived for the light. His paw shot out and clutched the red tube just an instant before another paw swiped in from the other side.

He sprang aside with the relay against his chest.

"Give it to me!" Rinnia screamed, her voice cutting through the high-frequency interference of the squealing ants and the howling of the wolf. "Now, Maxan!"

"You… ," he said, shocked. "You're not—"

"I said give it to me!"

Max, why's her paw on her sword?

And her voice…

There was something in the way she demanded the relay. Some note of desperation to have it that rose above the immediate need to shut off its red light.

"Behind you!" he shouted.

Rinnia ducked just as the lion's paws lashed out with enough power to crack every delicate bone in her body. She tumbled and rolled to her side, drawing both swords from her back as she came up.

A thunder rumbled in the lion's throat. The crumpled armor plates constricting its chest made its pacing awkward. It limped every time its broken paw touched the ground. It moved from left to right, its muzzle wrinkled in anger, its razor-sharp fangs bared. The lion's eyes darted from one fox to another. Locain was deciding, even while the red light was sinking through his flesh, gnawing at his psyche, and swallowing what little remained of his self-control, urging him to just be on with it and leap and strike and bite and fill his belly with meat.

Rinnia drew most of the animal's attention.

Yet, Maxan still seemed to be drawing hers.

"Why are you pointing your swords at me?"

"Maxan," she said, failing to cover up her desperation with her calm words, "give me the relay."

Max, don't ignore—

The lion flattened its chest on the ground.

The fox's claws fell into the channel of the relay.

"Give it to me!!!"

The lion's hind legs locked.

Maxan glanced down—searching for the bead of light he somehow knew was the key to stopping the drowning light—for just an instant.

It was all the time Rinnia needed to strike, her blade slicing into Maxan's right arm, drawing blood from the unfeeling flesh beneath.

And the lion was in the air, its paw raking her shoulder.

Maxan stumbled back and fell onto his rump.

The lion's claw snagged on Rinnia's cloak and dragged her to the ground. The animal was upon her, hundreds of pounds of fury. Its roaring maw lurched at its prey even as a length of steel sank between its armor plates and into its side.

Maxan's claws swept over the channel of red light and the shadows in his drowning vision. He heard Rinnia scream. He felt a vibration, held it, and dragged the bead of light back into its point of origin.

The red dissipated instantly, leaving the chamber dark. Then a glow shimmered on the ceiling as the golden beads emerged, running through their endless, steady circuit. The lion fell sideways, shaking its mane wildly, its jaw hanging slack. It made a sound like a reluctant yawn and closed its eyes.

The white wolf ceased its scrabbling against the ground and lay still.

Maxan came up first, holding the relay away from Rinnia.

"Wait," he pleaded. "Rinnia, it's over."

Her blades never faltered, despite the red spreading along her shoulder.

"It's not over. You don't know what you're doing. Who you're taking it to." She inched closer, her blade rising to his chest. "Maxan, if you don't give it to me, it will never be over."

"I saw you. In the rain. With the octopus."

That narrowing of her eyes just now, Maxan observed, *probably not a good sign.* But he went on.

"Is that who *you're* taking it to? Huh? You and the octopus have a better plan to stop the Stray?"

"You followed me?"

"I'm tired of the secrets! I'm tired of knowing nothing while everyone tells me what to do. Where to go. What to think. Who the *real* enemy is. See this?" He held the relay over his shoulder. "I've given this thing up and stolen it back more times than you realize. But I'm done, Rinnia! I'm done being told to give it up again and run away. You told me I don't make a difference, remember? All the good I've done is zero? How can I choose what's good when I don't know what's true? What's real? Well, now I know. It's not like you said. All of this is real. And I'm making my own choices."

Maxan nodded at the unconscious white wolf. "Feyn wants to help," he went on. "We're not so different. We're tired of being controlled."

Rinnia's eyes, her stance, nothing about her had softened in the slightest.

Maxan swallowed nervously, deciding to try a different approach.

"Who's pulling your strings, Rinnia?"

When she glanced at the wolf, Maxan easily read her intention.

He leapt as fast as his legs could throw him, drawing his sword, bringing it up to clash with the one Rinnia drove at

Feyn's heart. The foxes stood with locked blades on either side of the white wolf. Before she could even consider swiping at him with her other sword, Maxan shoved all his weight forward, sending her stumbling away.

"I won't let you kill him!"

"Give me the relay, or I'll *kill you*!"

He shook his head, stood his ground over the prone wolf, clutching the relay tighter than ever before. "Do the other Monitors know? About your new partner? The Peskoran? Do they know you're not really one of them?"

The questions broke through her hardened resolve, one by one. Maxan saw the anger in her eyes flooding out.

She doesn't even know who she is anymore, Maxan realized.

"If you can't trust your own brotherhood," he said, moving the point of his sword away from her, "then at least trust your own species. Rinnia, you can trust me."

"But you're a thief ... and a liar."

He shrugged. He couldn't hold back the sarcasm in his voice. "Well... I can see the hesitation there."

"You spied on me."

"Ah, well, I'm also a shadow. It's my job."

"And you think I can trust you?"

"You and I," he said, the severity back in his voice, his mismatched green and gold eyes centered on her sea-blue ones, "we are the last of our kind. Aren't we?"

Rinnia turned away from his gaze. Her shoulders drooped. Her arms fell to her sides. She shook her head. "You may think you're figuring things out," she finally said, "but you only have *pieces* of the puzzle. There's still so much of it you don't see."

"So tell me."

"I want to. But I can't trust you. Not until I know how far you're willing to go." With one of her swords, she pointed to the prone wolf behind him. "That one. He's done some terrible things. He's a monster."

"I don't know about all that—"

"Think you're brave, protecting him?"

"All I know—"

"You're a coward because you can't go through with what needs to be done."

Now it was Maxan's turn to be broken by words.

Safrid...

What about her?

That's what Safrid said.

What did she say?

Her words. When I...

Maxan was back in the alleyway. Back in time.

Safrid pressed the dagger against his palm, took his paw in hers, wrapped it tightly around the grip. The pair of foxes, Maxan and Safrid—orphans, friends, thieves, members of the Commune, mates—stared down at their victim, a meek-faced possum still draped in the white and black of the city guard, the very same guard who had once robbed Maxan of his chance at a better life. Maxan remembered the leering grin the possum had worn when he'd shoved him hard into the street, then tucked the coin Maxan had shown him into the folds of his uniform. Yovan's coin.

Safrid had kicked the possum's face until it shattered into a mask of horrific pain. Maxan had laughed with her, heard the snapping of bone, felt the gratification of revenge. He found the coin in the possum's pouch, even after all those years, and wanted to leave the guard to this sudden turn of his fortune. But Safrid refused and made him take the dagger.

"You're a coward," she said. *"He deserves it. Do what needs to be done."*

Maxan turned Yovan's coin around in his claws. He had been parted from it for so long, but here it was, as though it had never been taken. By contrast, the dagger clutched in his other paw felt so heavy.

Back in the dimly lit cavern below the station, now, Maxan glanced behind him, at the wolf with snow-white fur streaked with blood. Maxan believed Rinnia; he didn't doubt that Feyn had done terrible things.

He tried to kill you! the other side of himself quickly pointed out. *Who do you think orders and organizes all the Mind's kidnappings? Their experiments? He's an animal, a monster, like she says.*

But he's trying to change.

Maxan remembered letting the dagger fall in that alley, turning his back on Safrid, suffering her insults as he walked away.

"It's not who I am," he said to Rinnia. "I'm not a killer."

"When are you going to wake up? We're all killers! This whole world! It's who we *are*."

"You're wrong, Rinnia." He shook his head. "It's not who *I* am. And it doesn't have to be who you are either."

Rinnia looked away and was silent for a long while. When she finally spoke, her voice was dismissive, agitated. "You just haven't found anything worth protecting. Something worth giving your life for is something worth killing for. Once that thing is threatened, if you want to save it badly enough, you'll have *no choice*." She prodded him twice with the tip of her claw, emphasizing her final point.

"Is that it? You feel like you never had a choice?"

For a moment, it seemed Rinnia's rising anger might completely fade. But then she turned her seething eyes upon Maxan again, almost barking her next words. "I know what I am, and what I have to do. Give it to me."

Maxan tucked the relay behind him into his belt.

She said she'd kill me.
She could have.
But she didn't.
"You're a killer?" he said.
Don't say it—
"So come and kill me."
Ah. This is not wise, Max. This will probably—

Rinnia's blade cut the thought in half, swiping for Maxan's throat. He gave control over to his instincts, and those instincts saved him, carried him away from the strike the very moment he sensed Rinnia's body tense.

Her second blade followed the first, reaching farther, but Maxan's sword was up, batting it away with a resounding scrape of steel.

He smirked, rather arrogantly. For an instant, he believed he might actually be a match for her. But then Rinnia hopped, spun in a full circle, led with her first sword, and dropped to a crouch to slice across Maxan's abdomen, and the thought perished immediately. He staggered back, felt the muscles over his belly tense in response to the pain, watched a long line of red quickly stain his tunic.

His instincts fell silent, overpowered by the shock that Rinnia had actually hurt him. To say "Huh" was all he could think to do. It was a wasted reaction, as Rinnia's heel shot out, kicking him in the very part of his gut she had just sliced open. He toppled back and landed hard on top of the wolf.

"Ah, Feyn," Maxan groaned, hoping the caller could call on something, anything, to save both their lives. But the wolf lay as still as death.

I'm not a fighter. I'm not a killer. I can't…

He lay there motionless. The chance to get up or strike back or spit or say something witty had already passed. He could only stare up into Rinnia's deep sea-blue eyes as she stood over him.

Just like when we met.

You died already, at the beast pen, when she had you.

Doubtful being a fox'll surprise her into sparing me this time.

Then why is she...

"What're you waiting for?" Maxan said feebly.

Maxan tossed his weapon aside. There was no doubt she could easily run hers through both Maxan and Feyn at once. All she had to do was fall upon them. Maxan's eyes focused on the deadly point of her blade.

Rinnia didn't move.

"You have a choice," Maxan said. "You do."

In the seconds that passed, the metal of her blade seemed to glow, starting at the tip, then running down the sword's length.

Fire, he thought. *Her sword's on fire.*

The weapon warped, melted, bent.

"What..." Maxan trailed off.

Rinnia's hesitation had been more than enough for the squirrel boy to find the connection he had been searching for, to call the Aigaion, to channel its raw power and ignite the particles at the precise point in space he needed. Pryth didn't necessarily need his paws free for this trick, but she had certainly made it easier by keeping so still.

"Boom," Pryth said, and Rinnia's sword burst into a shower of super-heated metal sparks.

She managed to turn her face away, but the sparks flecked her muzzle, her ears, and cloak, burning through cloth and fur alike, down to her skin. Rinnia screamed wildly, fell over, rolled across the rocky ground, and dashed away to the collapsed passage.

She was far luckier than Maxan.

Wounded, prone, hopeless, and ultimately surprised by the phenomenon before him, he suffered the explosion's full effect. He managed somehow to blink, shielding his eyes against the initial blast. The sparks shot against his tunic and trousers, singing through his fur. Then he felt it. On his skin. In his body. A sensation he dreaded to ever feel again.

FIRE! NO!

His paws desperately tore at his face.

NO! NO! NOOO!!

He tumbled over and rolled, kicked, and clawed at the air.

Maxan!

The light behind his eyes was orange, white, red. Coloring the inside of his mind. Bringing buried memories back from the dead. The flames, the snakes, were slithering under the door, up the walls, over his mother. The heavy burning planks were falling on top of Safrid again. His right arm, buried in the embers, was straining to lift them, even as she burned alive.

Maxan! The voice in his head screamed his name. *I can take this away.*

His own scream drowned it out.

The voice resurged, stronger. *I WILL stop our pain.*

He wanted it. Even as his body writhed, his mind wanted it. And it happened.

The fires, the memories, all of it faded to black.

CHAPTER FOURTEEN
THE WHITE CANNIBAL

THE COIN. THE LITTLE FOX'S TINY PAW HOLDS it so tight. He feels its edge press against his bones. The stag that gave it to him told him to run.

So he runs. The ancient roots of the Denland reach up, catch his ankle, and bring the running fox to the ground.

I ran all night. Just followed the road, like Yovan said.

I don't want to remember this.

Yet you can't forget it.

The little fox looks up, sees Yerda's glow behind the leaves of the canopy. He rises. He whimpers. He follows her. West, until the night sky lightens, and she disappears behind hazy clouds. His paw glides over endless rows of wheat to the side of the road, hiding from the throngs of laborers. Then there is no more road, no more field. Only the colossal arched gate of Crosswall.

You never thought it possible. Remember, Max? To pile so many stones so high.

You... you're in my head. But I don't know... Who are you?

I've always been with you, Maxan. I pushed you to get out. I saved your life. I'm the voice of reason. But it was only then—only there, when I brought you to those walls—that you chose to start listening.

Days pass. Cold nights. The little orphan fox curls up in garbage heaps and gutters behind merchant stalls and dining halls, sweating, shivering, retching, his stomach refusing to keep down the rotten scraps his shaky paw shoves into his mouth. The other paw, it clutches Yovan's coin. When the merchants catch him sleeping, hiding, crying, and they beat him away from their wares, his grip on the coin never slips.

Who am I, Max? I'm your teacher. I taught you to watch. To wait. To run. I made you a survivor.

You made me a shadow.

During the first month, the boy's body withers. He's just an amber-furred fox pelt stretched over brittle bones. He's lost the strength to even swish his tail.

Look. See for yourself. What survival looks like.

The boy's dry mismatched eyes dare not blink as they observe the merchant's back. He summons all his will to steady his shaky arm as it reaches toward the merchant's crate. His claws sink into the softness of the tomato. He pulls it free from the others and darts away, energized by the thrill of thievery.

Remember the taste? It tasted like … knowledge. The moment when you knew you weren't going to die. Life. So sweet.

Why did you save me?

I didn't have to. You listened. You learned. You saved yourself.

But you made me … a thief.

Did I? Who made you a thief?

The boy's first year here draws to a close. He does not always outrun the merchants, or their guards, or those in the white and black. They follow him to the one place he thought safe, a small crevice between a shop's awning and the railed balcony just above it. They drag him out and beat him in the street. They break, burn, or steal back everything he took.

Almost everything.

Not the coin.

Yovan's coin is in the boy's palm again as he wobbles his way to the closest Crosswall guardhouse. And Yinna—bright, warm, indifferent—hangs high overhead.

The leering possum in the white and black tears the little fox's palm open, kicks him in the jaw as he dives for the coin, and shoves him back, tripping, tumbling, into the dusty street. All the guards laugh at the show. The possum watches the coin with gratified dark eyes as he flicks it, spinning, into the air.

I remember wishing I had died with my mother.

Remember how long that lasted?

Not long.

The boy crouches and cries in a new alley, far away.

The shadows shift above him. The movement from the rooftops draws his eyes up. The light blinds him. He gazes at the dark figures silhouetted by the sunlight, perched on the edge, their bushy amber-furred tails swishing in the air as they gaze back.

Not long.

Worse than the cut on his leg left by a Thraxian's arm, worse even than the hole in his side made by a Leoran soldier's sword, the hollow in the pit of Chewgar's stomach agitated him the most.

The giant rhino was no stranger to a fight. Though little more than twenty years of age, he had taken part in hundreds of—if not a thousand—quarrels, scrapes, and outright brawls on the streets of Crosswall, doing what he could to subdue the drunken, belligerent, and, more often than he cared to admit, downright savage animals in order to keep the king's peace.

The ordinary, hard-working residents of Crosswall's western district, the area of the city under his charge, thought of the captain as a hero. They were the reason that Chewgar donned the white and black day after day, drilled his cadets in the guardhouse yard, charted the patrols, paid attention to the goings-on and rumors, and ultimately showed up to the kinds of conflicts that only a warrior of his size and skill could resolve. If not for the peoples' gratitude, Chewgar would have hated everything about being a guard captain of Crosswall.

And yet he hated the one thing he was apparently good at: fighting. He hated having to be the one to decide when an enemy would simply not back down or be subdued …

Chewgar hated killing more than anything.

The rhino raised his enormous hand over his horn and rubbed at his brow. Every part of his body felt numb, heavy. Cold. He shuddered. The squirrel had already sewn up the hole in his side the lioness soldier's sword had made.

He had resisted the urge to look, but his eyes were at last drawn to the pile of corpses. Chewgar had made his contribution to it. His kills were the majority, in fact.

Under the lightening haze of morning, he and Saghan had hauled the wolf, the fox, and the lion back up from the tunnel and laid them on the tall grass in the clearing. Pryth did what he could to help if ranting incessantly about the other fox, Rinnia, was his way of helping. It was the snake's first exposure to the chattering squirrel. As he was laying the wolf and fox gently in the tall grass, Chewgar didn't catch what it was Saghan had hissed at Pryth, but whatever it was shut the boy up for good (or at least for a whole five minutes).

Saghan shrugged the lion off his shoulders carelessly and sat down beside him, ripping off plates of Locain's gilded armor with ease and tossing them aside. Chewgar recalled the ease with which the green-scaled snake had dragged his own massive body over the rubble of the fountain at the Monitors' safe house in Crosswall, so the sight of the slender Drakoran shouldering a heavily armored animal with no visible trouble shouldn't have unsettled him. And with all that Saghan and Sarovek had told him just afterward about the miracles of science and technology powering this world, just under the surface of every animal's awareness, Chewgar shouldn't have been surprised to see some of it in action. Saghan had been made that way, he said. The muscles in his body, the blood in his veins. The snake himself was one of those miracles.

Chewgar had tried to convince himself the next rumble in his stomach was just hunger and not uneasiness as he tended to the fox. The rhino had hoped they might be able to rest in the aftermath of the battle, at least until Maxan and Feyn could get their own legs under them again. After all, the fires of the previous night had finally surrounded the clearing on all sides, creeping to the edge of the forest and eating all the trees. Their work shrouded the world all around them in a smoky, suffocating haze. They had nowhere else to go for at least a few hours.

But moments later, a small patrol of Locain's soldiers came through the tree line, perhaps from around the other side of the hill or the Denland forest to the east, forced to seek refuge. They found a clearing full of dead Thraxians and dead comrades. And beside those, a Crosswall guard, a Drakoran, a Corvidian, three Denlanders—a cuffed and bloodied wolf, an insufferably loud squirrel, and a smoldering fox—and finally their golden-maned king, stripped to the waist and battered to within an inch of his life. It was no wonder why the soldiers charged right away. No wonder they refused to throw down their weapons and listen to reason.

And now the soldiers were dead. They were the pile of corpses Chewgar stared at. And the searing guilt in Chewgar's stomach ate away at him a little more.

"Hey, big guy." Pryth's high-pitched voice tore the rhino's attention away. Chewgar realized the squirrel must have been snapping at him for a while. "I said, wha d'ya think?"

"Think about...?"

"Uhhhh," the squirrel groaned. He was less than a quarter of the rhinoceros's size, but he stood before him with a paw pressed to his forehead like a master frowning down at an insipid student. Pryth flicked his claw in Locain's direction. "'Bout him."

Saghan had driven the army's heavy banner deep into the ground and bound the unconscious lion's paws around it with iron manacles. The manacles were easy to find near the ashes of the pyre where scores of Denlanders' bodies had been heaped the previous night.

Even in his unconscious state, Locain's breath was ragged and labored. The lower part of Locain's rib cage had completely caved inward under the impact of the scorpion's pincer, and not even his thick golden fur could conceal the enormous purple welt spreading over his muscled chest. Locain was awake now, still sipping air in shallow breaths, and he stared intently at the rhino.

Chewgar suspected the lion had been watching him for a while already. In fact, he realized everyone else (everyone conscious) was watching him, intent on hearing his answer. Saghan stood up and folded his arms. Pram knelt over Feyn a few steps away, doing her best to wipe the red streaks from her unconscious master's white fur. Even Sarovek, standing watch atop the low hill, had her sharp eyes on him.

"I don't know," Chewgar said—confessed—at long last.

Pryth rocked back and forth on his hind legs, shook his head, seeming on the verge of speaking again before suddenly snapping his mouth shut and turning about to his sister as if she'd called his name.

"I don't know," Chewgar said again. The one thing he wanted least in this world was to have to decide anyone's fate, to pass judgment, and yet it was his duty as a captain of the guard. But this particular decision was different. This life, Locain's life, weighed more heavily on him than that of an unruly criminal who would not back down. He was the killer of Chewgar's family. And yet, by all the laws upheld by his family's tribe, he was Chewgar's rightful king. The king of all Leora. And if he killed Locain…

"The crown." Despite his difficulty breathing, Locain's voice had lost none of its power. His voice commanded attention. "You don't want it, do you, boy? You never did. I used to wonder… why you never challenged me… why you never cared to avenge your father, your family, your name. I thought you a coward. Scared of *me*." What started as a sudden fit of laughter quickly became a hollow, pained wheeze. Locain fought to steady his breathing, squirmed against the banner pole, attempted to straighten his bruised chest. No one made a move to help him. When the wheezing finally subsided, the lion concluded quietly, humorlessly, "It's not me you're afraid of. It's the crown. To kill … is to decide. To decide … is to rule."

Chewgar glanced at Maxan where he lay near Feyn, and he wished the fox were awake to offer his opinion. He saw Maxan's chest rise and fall slowly, his claw points twitch, his eyelids squeeze tightly, then release. The fox was locked in his own inner battle. Chewgar knew Maxan well enough to know that no matter the stakes of that battle, no matter how limited the options, his clever friend would find a way out. There was no reason Chewgar could not do the same.

He looked again at the pile of corpses he'd made not even an hour ago, then to the smoldering remains of the pyre those corpses themselves had made only a few hours before that. Chewgar knew he had killed, but he knew also that, by some weird logic, it did not make him a killer. It did not make him like Locain.

"I decide," Chewgar answered at last, "that there's been enough death."

Chewgar rose to his feet and retrieved the king's golden-hilted great sword from where he had thrust its blade deep into the dirt. Saghan paced away as Chewgar approached the king, his arms still folded. Sarovek turned her gaze away and disappeared down the other side of the hill. As clear signs as any that the Monitors ultimately didn't care what happened next.

Pryth's and Pram's twin almond-shaped eyes had been locked together for almost a minute, an unspoken argument playing out between them. Pryth relented, it seemed, and stepped away silently, while Pram stood her ground and watched the rhino intently.

"At last," Locain rumbled, smiling, his eyes flashing up at his would-be challenger. "You'll keep to the ways of old."

The broad head of Chewgar's new weapon rose high over his shoulder.

The lion's smile faded. "Or you'll keep to your coward's path."

The broad blade bit through the thick pole of the king's banner a mere inch above the top of the lion's mane. The yellow standard fell back onto the muck and bloodstained grass. Chewgar tossed the great sword aside, seized the manacles at Locain's back in one hand, and lurched the lion up to stand. The other hand went to Locain's mane, forcing his head around to face the smoldering Denlanders' ashes.

"Do you see?" Chewgar whispered, bending his head so close to the king's that his great horn almost brushed against it. "The villagers of Renson's Mill. The western district of Crosswall. Even the Stray. All the Leorans you've slaughtered, those who starve in the cage you've made. Your people, every last one of them. My tribe. My family. Even your own soldiers... All of Leora. You will answer for every death. Your fate isn't just mine to decide. You're coming with us. Through the Denlands. I'm not the only survivor of the families you've broken. You have more than just me to answer to."

Chewgar wanted Locain to feel just as disturbed, just as empty, by all the death as he did. He wanted Locain to know that same kind of guilt that gnawed at his stomach even now.

But even as the words rolled out of his mouth, he wasn't entirely sure he believed it was the kind of justice he wanted. After all, here was his father's killer. To say the young rhino had not dreamed of all the ways he could hurt the lion who by the blood of his tribe became king would have been a lie. For years, the young rhino had relived that day, in the dust, outside the ring of combat, watching one by one as his father, his mother, his brothers fell. He saw it again, now, in his mind's eye. He saw their blood turn the dust to clumps of mud. Saw the lion that slaughtered them pressing his paws in it, approaching the rhinoceros boy at the edge of the circle, beckoning him. In Chewgar's dreams, he didn't turn away. He raged, he charged, he gored the lion on his horn. He turned the lion's eyes to pulp with his thick thumbs. He crushed the lion's throat with his flat teeth. He stomped the lion's limbs until they snapped like branches, until the muscles burst like grapes and blood ran like wine.

In Chewgar's dreams, he tasted the lion's blood.

But those had been the dreams of a younger Chewgar. That time was over. Those dreams had stopped haunting him. Those feelings had faded. Chewgar met Locain's eyes, and finally, after all these years, he saw the truth reflected there. Locain was a monster, but Chewgar didn't have to be. He could be better. He didn't have to be a king to prove it. All he had to do was look into the lion's eyes to see the difference.

"I forgive you," he said. "For what you did to my family."

Locain grimaced, whether from confusion, shock, or disdain, Chewgar didn't know. And Chewgar was relieved to discover that he ultimately didn't care.

"Whether the Denlands will forgive you," the rhino went on, surveying the carnage, "or if th—"

"Khhkk."

The lion's body seized suddenly, every muscle tensing, spasming uncontrollably. His arms jerked violently against the restraints at his back, the iron cutting through the fur along his wrists. His eyes rolled upward inside his skull, and his great fangs bit down hard, drawing blood from his gums. The clicking, drowning noise gurgled in his throat. Bubbles and froth spewed from between his teeth and dribbled down his golden mane.

"Kkhhhkkk."

Chewgar held Locain upright, unsure of what to do. He swung his head about frantically, but no one made a move. Sarovek was gone. Saghan crouched on the slope of the hill where she had been standing, his long neck keeping his head just above the tall grass, his tongue flicking indifferently as he watched.

As for the twins ... when Chewgar saw them, he knew.

Pryth's usual, cheery demeanor had vanished. He wore a mask now of utter contempt. His dark eyes seemed to sparkle at the sight of the Leoran king's suffering. For once, the boy had no comment. He stood frozen with folded arms and simply watched.

His twin sister stepped closer and twisted her outstretched paw. Her tiny arm quaked as if she held an invisible leash of some wild, powerful creature. Pram's chin pressed to her chest. Droplets of blood formed below the rim of her wide eyes and ran like tears. Even more blood ran from both her nostrils.

A shadow engulfed them all. All the gray, smoky air went black in an instant as the unseen Aigaion passed overhead, snuffing out the colorless morning light.

Pram opened her maw wide in a silent scream as the power in her swelled.

Chewgar felt both of Locain's shoulders pop from their sockets as his arms strained uselessly against the iron holding them. In the dim daylight, he watched, horrified, as the lion twisted his own neck past its natural limit. He felt the bones at the base of the lion's skull crack and slide apart. Blood gushed from Locain's eyes and frothed between his fangs.

King Locain, the Golden Lord himself, made one final, agonized gargle.

And then went still.

Chewgar felt the weight slipping from his grasp. He let go, and Locain crumpled at his feet.

Pram's eyes closed. She fainted, falling back into her brother's arms. He guided her gently to lie beside their master.

Chewgar's breath seized in his throat. His knees seemed to give out, and his bulk crashed to the ground beside the lion's twisted corpse. He couldn't move. All he could do was stare at it.

"It was a good idea," a voice hissed in Chewgar's ear what might have been a moment later, or a lifetime. "I thought so, anyway. Giving him to the rebels would have given his sssundered army something to rally around. Word of his capture would have spread, attracting all of the Leoran king's might. But word of his *death*..." Chewgar felt the forked tongue flicking against the broad side of his head. He felt a scaled hand clap him on the back. "Now *that* will spread farther, and faster. His soldiers will tear each other apart, trying to gain a name for themselves, to be the next Anvil, or Golden Lord, or … whatever."

Saghan stood up, hauling the rhino's massive bulk up to stand beside him. "Or," he went on, "they will scatter, aimless in the woods, easy targets for the Denland rebels. In any case, that little squirrel brought us the distraction we needed to ssslip through."

Chewgar hardly heard anything the snake said. Saghan's hissing was merely a disembodied pulse of noise over his shoulder. Chewgar's only thought was how, even in death, the king's arms, his legs, the hard and handsome lines of his face beneath the prominent scar… these were the features of a proud and powerful warrior. And now the challenge, the violence, the young rhino used to dream of could never come true.

He lifted his gaze to the twin squirrels and felt his hand ball into a fist.

"Don't be so sssurprised," Saghan said finally. "You said it yourssself. At least, you were going to."

Chewgar looked at the snake, confused, angered.

"The Denlands," Saghan pointed out, nudging his head in the squirrels' direction. "They didn't forgive."

CHAPTER FIFTEEN
THE ABSENCE OF MIND

MAXAN HAD FORGOTTEN HOW BEAUTIFUL THE Denlands were. Their trees were older than any living Herbridian, taller than any tower he had ever seen—*Well, all but one*—and harder than any armor. Some were as wide around as the houses of the rich of Crosswall. It was no wonder, then, why the largest settlements of the forested region were built around clusters of these mammoth trees, above a network of roots that spread far and wide underfoot, or surfaced in tangles to either side of the villages' paths and became blanketed with the fallen leaves of past seasons and years.

Maxan's paws, legs, and muscles had grown accustomed to the dusty, grimy, hard stones of the city. He had forgotten the clean smell of green things. Out here, the fresh rains could bring life up from the ground itself, as opposed to bringing disaster bubbling up from a sewer grate. The leaves scrunched pleasantly under the pads of his paws as the group made its way east through the old forest.

It had been three days of travel. Three days of almost complete, sullen silence. Three days of tasteless rations that settled like stones in their stomachs. Aside from Saghan's periodic order for silence or a shift in direction, no one breathed a word.

For once, the only sounds Pryth made were regular sighs or gasps, accompanied by exasperated glances at his twin sister. Pram often walked with her paw resting on her brother's shoulder. Maxan assumed she not only needed help after her ordeal but was actively keeping her twin's wild voice in check for everyone's benefit.

Their master followed a few steps behind. Principal Feyn seemed to recover quickly from the bruising the king's soldiers gave him. He had washed the dried blood from his snow-white fur in a stream, but his clothing was still torn and stained in places. Feyn had asked the fox about the relay, about what happened underground. Maxan looked into the wolf's eyes and saw that Feyn already knew Locain had activated it, robbed him of control, and ultimately saved his life. The fox cradled the shining metal tube in his paw, remembering the last time he'd given it over to a principal, days ago, at the Mind's Pinnacle Tower. Then, it had been Harmony's talons that closed around it. Now, it was Feyn's paw, and Feyn wasn't a principal anymore. Maxan hadn't told the wolf how he had put himself in the way of Rinnia's sword, how he believed that what Feyn was doing was right, how it was his way of making an actual difference.

Looking into Feyn's ice-blue eyes, he realized he didn't need to. The wolf already knew. Feyn nodded, tucked the relay into his satchel, and said nothing.

And yet, for three days, Maxan's inner voice of reason was there to remind him that in truth he knew so little about Feyn. *Nothing, in fact.* The white wolf was strong, displaying no obvious need for rest, voicing no complaints as the group trekked through the seemingly endless forest. Feyn must have been Maxan's age or slightly older when the Extermination War swept him up and took him south to the front lines of

Thraxia. War had changed him, Maxan reasoned, into someone with unshakable conviction. The white wolf's beliefs were so strong—and the mission that propelled him forward so critical—that he was willing to give up everything he had built alongside Folgian. He had abandoned all his wealth and influence. He had hung up the black robe of a Mind's principal. All to stop the animals of Leora from becoming Stray.

He's saving us, Maxan concluded, *from turning into ravaging beasts.*

Or ... he's only doing it to save himself, he countered.

No, he shot back. *In the cave, what I said to Rinnia about Feyn—I meant every word.*

Would you really have let her kill you, Max? To ... what? Prove some point?

Maxan considered whether he'd rather hit his head with a rock or give credence to what his inner voice was implying. In the end, he did neither. He simply fell in line behind the trio of callers, as silent as everyone else.

Three days had passed, and while it made sense that a mute and a chatterbox mind-controlled into silence would have nothing to say, Maxan expected more from Chewgar. Soon after they had left the station, the hill, and that clearing behind—and even later, when Maxan had finally come to his senses enough to walk on his own two hind legs—the most communication he got from Chewgar was a nod.

Glad you're still alive, fox, he thought it might have meant. *What else does he need to say, Max?*

Three days had passed, and Chewgar hadn't said a word. Maxan had figured out easily enough what must have happened to Locain. He reasoned there was much on his friend's mind, and talking about the lion's death so soon after everything was not going to put any of those thoughts to rest.

On occasion, they would draw near to a Denland settle-ment. The scent of woodsmoke would drift on the wind, and Feyn, the squirrels, or Maxan would be the first to catch it.

The first hint of that smell would send Maxan into a panic, an all too recent memory of Renson's Mill reigniting in his mind, or of Rinnia's sword exploding, covering him in fire. The vision rushed through him, turning his blood hot, prickling his fur everywhere. Of course, he felt nothing along his scarred right arm. Somehow, miraculously, that unfeeling limb had risen just in time to shield him from most of the molten sparks. The new blisters and pockmarks on the pink skin testified to that. The sparks that grazed the side of his face, however, had left painful patches where his fur would likely never grow back. It was the sparks that landed on his clothing, though, that made him lose his mind. The dry fabrics caught fire instantly, and the flames would have engulfed him had he not tossed about like a penniless boar with a tax-collecting monkey howling on his back.

Saghan's forked tongue would flick at the air, the only reli-able method a snake had for catching the scent of smoke, and then he would change their direction, deciding on a new line around the settlement toward wherever it was they were going.

"We're not going to Corvidia," the snake had told Feyn on their first night. They were all huddled in the dark under an overhanging slab of rock, which shielded them from the steady rain.

Maxan expected Feyn would flash his signature snarl. Instead, the wolf asked calmly, "Why not?"

"Rinnia told me why you agreed to come along," Saghan went on, ignoring the question. He lodged a hunk of the Monitors' brick-like rations into his wide mouth. The lump it made in his throat slowly worked its way down before the snake spoke again. "You wish to board the Aigaion. Reconnect the sssignal. Stop the Ssstray. What you heard about the tower at Lake Skymere is true. The Corvidians commissioned my master to conssstruct it. But it won't carry you to your Aigaion, Principal."

At this last part, Sarovek, keeping watch at the edge of the dry ground under their natural roof, turned all her attention to her reptilian brother.

"The Ssspire, as the Corvidians call it, was never designed to sssucceed."

Now Feyn did snarl.

Maxan glanced nervously at the stone jutting overhead, calculating how long it would take to scramble away to safety if the wolf called on the Aigaion to collapse it on the snake's head.

"But there is ssstill a way."

"Where?" both Feyn and Sarovek asked simultaneously. The hawk added an agitated clack of her beak.

The snake's broad head swayed on his long neck between them. He blinked the translucent brilles over his eyes, flicked his tongue, and smiled. "Tomorrow," he said, "we turn south. To the station under the spear." Saghan said this last part to Sarovek, knowing she alone would understand. "Rest well, sis-sster. We'll need your sharp eyes in the morning."

South, Maxan thought, mulling another lump of the Monitors' tasteless ration in his mouth, trying to work up the nerve to swallow it. *To Drakora.*

To the Monitors' castle.
How do I know it's a castle?
I just… We just … know.
I've… We've … been there before?
Me, Max.

Sudden pain seared the inside of his skull. A shower of white sparks burst in his vision behind his squeezed eyelids. He rubbed the heels of his paws into both eye sockets and tried not to think until the pain at last subsided.

Everyone else finished their pitiful meal in the silence and the dark, then lay down and shivered until sleep claimed them.

The jutting rock they had camped under was indicative of the unpredictable terrain of the Denlands. At first, the ground had been relatively level, but the farther into the forest they pressed, the more unexpectedly the land would rise into a chain of rolling hills or dip into a series of valleys. Saghan insisted they continue straight rather than fall into the natural, more leveled paths that slithered between the higher and lower spaces.

Maxan made it to the top of one of those mounds easily enough and glanced down to see Chewgar's progress behind him. A rhinoceros's legs were never meant for such vertical travel. Those thick, muscular slabs were naturally suited to the flat golden grasslands. Maxan could see his friend's exhaustion playing out in his movements, but Chewgar never protested, never questioned Saghan's logic or direction. After all that had happened, it was clear that Chewgar was just falling in line— physically, yes, but also spiritually. He was searching for some direction. While on the surface he'd been dedicated to serving the people of Crosswall, to keeping them safe from harm, all those years, Locain's challenge had always been in the back of Chewgar's mind.

Like a door that was always held open.

And now it's shut.

Maxan lifted his eyes up the steep trail, where he saw Feyn holding the trunk of a sapling and reaching a paw down to help his smaller apprentices. Pryth insisted on clambering up on his own, but Pram seemed to graciously accept her master's extended paw.

Maxan didn't need the power to read someone's mind to have figured out why Locain hadn't survived the aftermath of the battle in the station. Instead, he had posed a question to Sarovek on their first day, and when she gave him a slight nod, that was that.

At sundown, they settled in at the crest of one of the tallest hills of Saghan's choosing for another fireless, shivering, likely restless night.

Maxan lay on his back, gazing through a hole in the high canopy at the trillion tiny, distant lights—stars he had forgotten were there, so diffused with torchlight or smoke or steam was the night sky in the city packed with life. As the rest drifted off to sleep, Maxan absentmindedly watched Yerda come into view overhead, displaying her girdle and her wound prominently. He blinked as a shadow crept into his view and swallowed some of the stars. A dark outline too fast for the Aigaion, he realized, and the thing was plummeting straight down at him.

He rolled away into some bushes just as the wind blast from the Corvidian hawk knight's wings swept over his body, strong enough to extinguish their campfire if they had been lucky enough to have one. Sarovek came to rest inches from where the fox had lain just a moment ago. The armored Corvidian folded her wings behind her and moved away from the sleeping forms, into the shadows of the trees. No one else, as far as Maxan could tell, was disturbed—the rhino especially, as he snored the night away.

Saghan had insisted on taking watch, but he was nowhere to be found.

Maxan crept out from under the bush to follow the hawk. The old instincts of stealth served him just as well on the forest floor as they did on the city's rooftops. He found the two Monitors meeting in the moonlight at the hill's top. He pulled his hood away and fanned out an ear in their direction.

"…sssoon," he heard Saghan hiss. "…at the tunnels."

"Days beyond the king's army… ," the hawk answered. "…scattered…"

"The rebels have archersss…" It sounded like a question.

A silence followed. Maxan could not help himself from creeping closer, slowly, careful to avoid any twigs and dried debris in his path.

"I said it's nothing."

Sarovek folded her right wing over her chest. Something metallic nestled among the feathers glinted in the moonlight. An arrowhead.

"Dear sissster," Saghan said, "this will simply not do."

Maxan's ears picked up Sarovek's sudden, sharp breath. Then a snap.

"All better."

Sarovek's beak clacked. "The rebels are picking them off, pack by pack, with little to no losses. If the tribals had moved in force, as Locain intended…"

"The lion is no longer a factor."

"What does the master say?"

"He doesn't care what happens to Leora."

Although he could barely see, Maxan saw the hawk's intense, unrelenting gaze boring into her reptilian brother, demanding he say more.

"If the little squirrel hadn't done it," he hissed at last, "he would've *made me*."

The snake's meaning seemed to weigh heavily on Sarovek. Saghan finally broke the silence that had fallen between them.

"Any sign of our sissster?"

Sarovek shook her head. "If Rinnia wanted us to find her, she would have left us one. Are you certain the squirrel didn't kill her underground?"

"Ha!" Saghan's orange eyes glowed with the sudden burst of intense laughter. He trapped the rest of it with a hand over his mouth. "Kill her?" the snake asked her facetiously once he'd composed himself. "Unlikely. She simply doesn't want to be found."

"When we arrive, we must tell him."

"We say nothing," Saghan hissed.

The only sound that followed was the rustling of the wind in the leaves and the nocturnal insects. Maxan was utterly silent as he crept back and came to rest in his original spot. The hawk knight arrived moments later. Sarovek lay on her side, drew her knees to her chest, and draped her wings over herself like a blanket, keeping her spear close but the sword still strapped to her side. She didn't even bother to remove her armor, Maxan noticed, but she was asleep in mere seconds nonetheless.

Saghan was apparently still on watch above.

Maxan quietly pulled the frayed edges of his cloak tighter, but it did little to ward off the chill. He had seen enough stars, he reasoned, and tried to catch a little rest. But every time rest came within reach, his mind wandered back to the image of her.

They said she's still alive. Out here. Somewhere.

He saw her in his mind. Rinnia, standing over him, her sea-blue eyes narrowed, her paw squeezing the hilt of her short sword, its point aimed for his heart.

She tried to kill you, Max.

She wouldn't have.

She would've sliced your throat!

But she didn't. She had all the time she needed to run me through, and she didn't.

She would have.

She...

Maxan's eyelids squeezed tightly in anger. He saw red sparks expanding in the darkness behind them.

Would she?

She doesn't know you, Max. She doesn't care about you.

What does she care about?

He was back on the rooftop in Crosswall, after climbing the Pinnacle with her, escaping the dungeon, and meeting with Feyn. After walking by her side, defeated, back to the western district, the rain pouring down on them both. After she sent him off on his own. He had spied on her meeting with the octopus. He tried to recall what he looked like, what they had said, but all he saw was falling water, and all he heard was thunder.

Do they know, he had asked her later in the cave, *you're not really one of them?*

The question had actually struck her, wounded her deeper than a sword buried in her heart.

Why?

Because it's the truth.

Do I tell them? Tell the Monitors that she's ... not a Monitor anymore?

Maxan was ready to lie awake the rest of the night, not because that voice in his head would not stop bantering but because he waited for its answer, and it never came.

Do I tell them?

He closed his eyes and heard the question echo in his mind.

Something nudged his leg, and he stirred. Then something kicked, as hard as it could, which wasn't so hard, and his eyes fluttered open. The deep dark of night had been replaced by the silver velvet veil of pre-dawn, obscuring the tiny stars beyond it.

"Hey. Go time. Time to go." Maxan was awake now, but Pryth kicked him again all the same. "Well, first, eat time. Then go time. Here's food, if you call that food."

Maxan rolled over, sat up, and accepted the strip of soft tree bark Pryth offered him. *Oh,* he realized, biting into it, *just this terrible concoction of the Monitors.* The stuff morphed into a grainy paste in his mouth but went down easily enough. It calmed his hungry stomach and invigorated his dull senses, sure, but he still wished the experience were more pleasant.

He bit off another piece as he watched the squirrel skitter off to rejoin his sister and his master at the base of the hill. Farther still, Chewgar stood with Sarovek, speaking in a low tone not even the fox's keen hearing could pick up. But he didn't need to hear their words to know what they were talking about. Chewgar extended his arm, and the hawk knight clasped his elbow with her talon, an embrace that carried a meaning only warriors who bled together could understand. There was a silent respect in the look they shared, the rhinoceros and the hawk. Maxan remembered how the two of them had fought in Renson's Mill, picking apart the group of tribal soldiers bent on murdering Pram, while he fumbled around trying not to get cut in half. Maxan reasoned that whatever bond they had started forming there was only solidified further in the clearing when he skipped past the hundred Thraxians and the bloodthirsty soldiers, leaving the fighting behind to those two.

He imagined this must have been what the Extermination War was like. Warriors from every nation—Leora, Peskora, Corvidia, and what was left of Drakora—animals that had spilled one another's blood for untold centuries, coming together as one to combat an enemy, to put a stop to a menace that threatened all life, equally. There was something deep in the soul of every animal that didn't care which invisible lines you lived behind, or under what scraps of colored cloth you stood. And when the war was over, the warriors went back to their homes, separated by their invisible lines again, and a peace held. Relations had started to change. This was mostly down to the efforts of the Mind, but Maxan wanted to believe that most of the credit was due to natural decency among living things. Boundaries, treaties, and laws were drawn and agreed, roads were built, guilds were formed, and trade flourished. Tools that would aid in agriculture and masonry were designed and crafted. The young were cared for. The hungry were fed. Cities were built—on the plains, in the shadows of forests and mountainsides, along shimmering beaches, and in tropical jungles—and families grew to fill them.

The Thraxian Extermination War might have been over, but the violence—the desire for it, maybe the natural need for it—never went away. Arenas and fighting pits were carved into cities, serving as central attractions. Somewhere along the way, the Mind introduced the game of apotheosis so that animals could live out imagined violence and glory on a game board. The distractions worked on most animals, but some of those soldiers who returned home to find their lives upended became raiders like Yacub, as a kind of revenge, to take from the world that took from them. For some, the fight itself became their lives, the only thing that had meaning. What was stopping them from reverting to the old ways, the ways that allowed violence as a rule of life?

Me, Maxan thought. *A shadow. A spy. And Chewgar. And anyone else strong enough to see the wrong for what it is and dedicate himself to righting it.*

Maxan realized as he watched Sarovek release Chewgar's arm and lift herself skyward that the Thraxian extermination and the spreading affliction of the Stray weren't all that different. That had been another generation's war. This one was his. Two decades ago, he hadn't been alive to answer the call and march south when the burgeoning insect species threatened to overrun all other forms of life. But he was alive now. He was here, exactly where he needed to be. The one place he could do the most good.

And two decades from now, what will the new war be? Will anything you do really matter? Will anything ever end?

He crushed the last enormous wad of the stuff between his fangs, hoping the mushing sound in his head would shut the voice out. Would silence the questions he knew he could not answer.

Just saying… turns out they didn't get all the Thraxians, now did they?

Later, when whatever little they had was packed up, and Saghan had done his best to erase the signs of their camp, the snake finally spoke frankly about their plans.

"Sarovek says the way is clear. We'll reach our destination by nightfall."

"And what then?" Feyn asked. "At our pace, one more day's journey isn't enough to put the Denlands behind us."

Saghan's forked tongue flicked the air, and a smile bent at the corner of his wide mouth. "You forget, wolf, the Monitors have centuries of buried technology at our disposal, while the Mind has only barely rediscovered the electric current."

"Soooo… can we talk now?" Pryth turned a thumb over his shoulder at his silent sister. "Because, let me tell ya, this one won't shut up!"

Maxan couldn't tell if Pryth was being serious or purposefully ironic. His outburst slammed against the somber mood and seemed to fall flat for five very slow seconds. Besides a few eyes shifting from one to another, no one reacted.

"What?" Pryth pleaded with everyone. Then he wheeled on Pram as if she had flicked his ears with her tiny claw. (For all anyone knew, she might have cast the phantom in her brother's brain.) "Ah, hey, whaaat?"

The mood began to crack. Chewgar's dry chuckle soon erupted into a booming laughter, which spread to Maxan, the squirrels (though Pram, of course, merely smiled), and even Saghan. Only Feyn remained unmoved, having no doubt suffered years of the boy's antics, which rendered him immune.

They were on their way soon enough, descending from the high ground and finally allowed to take the easier paths that wound between the hills. Their elevation declined steadily as the first few hours went by. It was impossible to accurately discern the time of day. Yinna hovered somewhere overhead, beyond the blanket of green, every ray of her light splashing against the layers of canopy until only a kind of diffused haze trickled down to the forest floor below.

Sarovek had gone ahead to ensure their approach was clear. If the hawk's keen eyes caught sight of any danger, she would wheel back and join them. So far, there had been no need to do so, apparently.

Pryth had clambered up onto Chewgar's shoulder, sat down there before the rhino could shrug him off, and thanked him for "helping to save my sister and all that back at the town." And before Chewgar had even opened his mouth to respond, the boy apologized for "her whole killing the king thing."

The rhinoceros stopped in his tracks. The abruptness flung Pryth forward. The tiny squirrel caught Chewgar's horn just in time and swung himself around the rhino's face to land on the other shoulder.

Pram came to his side, drawing Chewgar's attention despite the total quiet with which she moved. The hulking rhino knelt to meet her eyes as best he could. A long, pervasive silence passed between them until Pram, at last, shut her eyes and nodded solemnly. Chewgar wrapped his massive hand around her shoulder and back and drew the tiny girl in for an embrace.

"I'm glad," he told her, "that you did what I could not."

Chewgar scooped Pram up and set her atop his other shoulder as he rose.

"Yeah, but," her twin chittered as the trio moved on, "Pram, you didn't have to make it so gross, did ya?"

For the next several hours, the two squirrels proceeded to pass the time interrogating (out loud or otherwise) the good-natured rhinoceros about his golden-grassed homeland, his tenure as a captain of the Crosswall Guard, his favorite recipes, and everything else.

Maxan marched a good twenty paces behind them, and Feyn brought up the rear. The hunger in the fox's stomach had not returned, thanks to the miraculously filling stuff from earlier. He kept his head down, eyes on the trail, mindlessly following the heavy imprints Chewgar's wide, flat feet left on the forest floor. He focused on keeping his thoughts quiet, keeping all of it out. He tried not to think of Rinnia, the relay, the Mind, the Monitors. He tried to just move ahead, not look back. To go through one opening doorway at the expense of closing all the rest.

"I have yet to extend my gratitude."

The airy, rasping voice brought Maxan out of his trance. He looked to his right and found the white wolf had caught up with him on the trail.

"To say thank you," Feyn clarified, as if the puzzled look on the fox's face called for a lesson on the meaning of *gratitude*, failing to see it as the shock it truly was.

"Thank me? For what?"

"For many things. I feel my world has twisted itself around. That those I saw as my enemies have become my friends. And my friends, enemies." The wolf sighed and turned his eyes back to the trail as he spoke. "I was not sure if I could trust you. When I sent Pryth and Pram to free you from the Mind's cells. When I made the proposal to you. To you both. A pair of foxes, in my own house on the campus. Even then, I thought myself foolish, but I had no other choice. It was my one chance. To trust the Monitors."

Feyn didn't strike Maxan as the kind of creature who would ever want to speak openly about his feelings. He thought it was odd that Feyn had chosen him to be the recipient of these thoughts, this gratitude, just now, out here.

"I'm not a Monitor" was all he could think to say in reply.

"Perhaps not," Feyn conceded. "And that's what I mean to say. I am thanking you … for saving me from a Monitor."

"She's…"

Not really a Monitor after all, he wanted to say.

"Complicated," he said instead.

"Mmm," Feyn agreed. Maxan could see there was some kind of memory playing out behind the wolf's eyes. After a pause, the wolf said, "It takes a certain unbreakable resolve to go against your own species. And a female, no less."

It seemed more of a personal observation than a question. There was some history there in how Feyn had earned it, probably, but Maxan let it go. "She wouldn't have killed me."

"There is no way to be certain, if what my apprentice told me she did is to be believed. Regardless, maybe she'd have spared *you*. But *me*…"

This time, Maxan was sure it was indeed a question.

"She said you were a monster."

Feyn glared at him, or so Maxan thought at first. Then he recalled that the angered look was permanent. His face was pulled into that mask by the long scar.

Maxan shrugged all the same. "Her exact words."

Feyn's eyes were drawn into the forest, fixed on nothing, just the trunks of the trees as they passed. "Do you believe monsters can change? Can an animal deny its own nature?"

"I have to believe it," Maxan said finally. "Otherwise, if we can't change—if we won't, when we know we have to—then we're doomed."

"That's all the Stray really is," Feyn said, turning his gaze upon the fox. "A mirror. When we see what we can become, we have to change. We are all monsters inside."

"I didn't say that."

"No. But you are thinking it."

Maxan clenched his muzzle tight. *Maybe he's reading my mind. Not possible.*

Maxan looked again at his walking companion. Feyn carried himself upright, proud. He seemed like a noble wolf out for a stroll deep in the Denlands, whose eyes had once again been captivated by the scenery as he passed. The wolf's eyes weren't closed, he wasn't locked in rigid concentration with a paw outstretched to grasp the Aigaion's invisible strings, not at all like how Maxan had seen him in the beast pen, or seen Pram and her tiger as Renson's Mill burned all around.

Maybe he's just … better at it hiding it?

No, Max. Not possible. Trust me.

Trust … me?

"That is my greatest fear, you know," Feyn said, cutting through Maxan's confused thoughts. "No matter how I try, I'll never be anything different than … what I've let myself become."

"What do you mean?"

"The king … Locain … the Anvil … the Golden Lord." The wolf said each title slower than the one that came before, as if casting the breath from his mouth into the wind as a memorial. "If your friend had given him over to the rebellion. They would have let him live, thinking they held some great prize, hoping for some bargain. As though his life was worth the price of their own independent nation in the middle of his kingdom. But they would have been slaughtered, every last one, as would their mates and cubs. Their tree fortresses would've been burned to the ground. The Denlands would rise in a cloud of smoke so high, Yinna and Yerda themselves would wonder what had become of our world below."

"Saghan said as much before."

"And do you think what the snake said was true?"

"There's no point thinking about it now. What's done is done."

"But do you think it's true?"

Maxan never expected this tone from Feyn. A ruthless wolf. A powerful caller. A black-robed principal of the Mind, whose very whispers could command a king in his own kingdom. Yet here he was, pleading for an answer from a lowly fox. Maxan swore, just for a moment, he even saw the wolf's scowling mask soften as their eyes met.

He wants me to say yes.

But you won't because you don't believe it's true.

Maxan turned away. "What you're asking is ... can violence prevent violence? Can death prevent more death?"

"I ... have to believe so."

Funny. He sounds like you.

Maxan flinched at the thought.

"The killing here is likely far from over," Feyn went on. "More will die. But with Locain's removal, I have to believe that the rebels—my species, even yours, all creatures in this forest—will live." Feyn's expression hardened again. The scar tightened on his face, pulled the hole at the back of his mouth open again. He let out a long, airy breath. "Pram killed the one, and through his death, she saved thousands. The Denlanders' dream of becoming an independent state beyond his rule—resistant to even the culture of the Mind; proud of their own identity, language, customs; aware of their own place in this world—that dream can now take root. It will thrive. Like the green sprout of a sapling rising from the blackened remains of a forest fire. It is the exact thing the Mind set the lion upon these lands to prevent."

Feyn shook his head, let out a sigh. "Folgian, my master, believed that *difference* leads to *conflict*. And conflict to death. That the only way to survive is for everyone to believe the same things are true. This tiny war among Leorans was supposed to set the precedent. My, how I have betrayed her." He might have been smiling when he said it.

Concerning the Denlands' fate, Maxan thought the wolf's logic was sound. But unless a caller could read the future, there was still no way of knowing this prediction was true.

"And what about Crosswall?" he asked. "Did you consider the king's city, with hundreds of thousands of innocents, afflicted, exiled…?"

"There will be a power vacuum, at least publicly. The lords' district, the merchant guilds, the Mind—they will squabble in Locain's absence for scraps of his leftover power. They might raid the treasury, forge his signature on trade deals or construction projects or the prices of grain. Or—if they're truly mad—they might seize control of the guard regiments. Meanwhile, amid the chaos, the western district eats itself a little more each passing day, as those who are supposed to keep watch over the Stray turn their attention elsewhere. Those who you care so much about will have to fend for themselves. None of what happens in Crosswall concerns them. But, without Locain, at least they will not burn."

Maxan met Feyn's eyes again.

"Locain very much loved his fire," Feyn clarified. "I believe he was always trying to relive the glory of seeing an entire kingdom brought down by flames."

"Thraxia," Maxan muttered.

"Indeed. For him, the fires he set in the Denlands would only be the beginning. An entire district of his own capital was next." Feyn straightened his back, clasped his paws behind him, held his chin high. It was the pose of one who felt justified, Maxan thought. "And now, because of Pram, none of it will matter."

Maxan realized then that he was just a sounding board, that Feyn could have been speaking to anyone, hearing his own voice aloud, working through the reasons why Locain's death was necessary.

"Soon enough," the wolf went on, "with the power struggle in Crosswall, none of it will matter anyway. Assuming your friend chooses to show up with Locain's golden great sword slung on his back."

Maxan's eyes had been wandering as he listened, imagining all the strife and madness in the city when it learned of the king's fate, the weakened patrols in the western district, the freezing, starving exiles there backed farther into a corner they could not escape, all the blood running in the streets. But the mention of Chewgar brought his imagination back to the present and his eyes twenty paces ahead on the trail to the proud rhino who could be king. Carrying a squirrel child on either of his shoulders, their bushy tails wrapped around his biceps. Laughing at trivial things. He had fashioned some kind of strap to sling the lion king's mighty great sword to his back, so that his powerful arms could swing freely or playfully squeeze the squirrels' legs as he walked.

Maxan couldn't say one way or the other what Chewgar would do. He could only say, "He may choose not to."

Feyn lightly coughed three times. Maxan realized it was laughter. "Who rules or who doesn't rule—the beloved rhinoceros returned, or one of Locain's lackeys, perhaps even one of the body doubles from his pride—it won't matter. The Mind controls Crosswall. It has since the first days of a unified Leora. Every Leoran knows this. And if he doesn't already, your friend, should he choose to wear the crown, will learn soon enough."

Maxan nearly tripped as he spun around on Feyn. "How can it be so *easy* for you to manipulate a king?"

"Knowledge," Feyn replied, either oblivious to the accusation in Maxan's tone or ignoring it. Maxan recalled how he sometimes thought he saw a smile in the wolf's scarred face. He was certain he saw it spread there now. "*Secrets*, perhaps, is the better word. Hasn't anyone told you, fox? This life we lead, it's all a game. A grand puppet show."

"Ah. Yeah. Someone's told me a thing or two about puppets." Maxan looked as far along the trail as he could, thinking to catch a glimpse of their Drakoran guide, but Saghan was nowhere to be found.

"How much did Folgian teach you?" Maxan asked after some time had passed. "About the puppet show?"

Feyn's growling intensified.

Sounds like he means "nothing."

"Folgian will get her wish," the wolf said at last. "To die with all her secrets. Almost all. And she will die. Soon." Maxan thought Feyn had meant for his words to carry a tone of satisfaction, maybe spite, maybe a kind of revenge for being kept ignorant. But the sorrow in his voice was as clear as artisanal Corvidian crystal. Maxan knew Feyn meant to say more, but the wolf held his tongue.

"She meant a lot to you," observed Maxan, hoping to keep him talking.

But Feyn was silent for a very long time, weighing and reweighing the meaning of Maxan's words. Maxan believed Yinna was likely to wink out before he ever heard Feyn's raspy voice again.

"I was once a knight," Feyn finally said, after they had walked the next hundred paces in complete silence. "I served the old king, before Locain. I belonged to a pack, a long line of noble wolf lords in the northern Denlands. I had a house, an estate, servants. I had a mate and cubs of my own. But when word of the Thraxians' destruction of Drakora reached us, I left them all behind. Everything. And I took my soldiers south."

Feyn examined the fox at his side then, mentally measuring Maxan from the tip of his pointed ears to the sharp claw tips at the end of his hind paws. "I was perhaps only a few years older than you are now. I … could not tell my mate whether I would return. I said not to fret, for death was the warrior's way of life. I said to remember that wolves are a strong species.

"When the war ended, when we'd watched every last towering Thraxian hive come crashing to the ground, like clouds of fire and sand blown on furious winds, I remember the fool's smile on my face, thinking how I would tell her how right I was about that. How she need never doubt me again. I held the image of her in my mind. It sped me along the roads back home.

"But … when I finally returned … I found my lands ransacked. Pillaged. My house, just a blackened circle in the clearing. My pack of soldiers and I drew our weapons and fanned out, and we found them. Raiders. Some of them had once been my own servants. Some of them wolves, like me. There was no sign of my mate. No sign of my cubs. They had been waiting for my return. I… My mind was unclear. The rage took hold of me. I stumbled straight into the raiders' trap. I remember seeing the last of my soldiers fall. We had taken a number of them with us, but I was the last standing. Just me against … seven, perhaps. That's when they gave me this."

Feyn's claw traced the crooked line of his scar, from the end of his ruined mouth up to the base of his ear. The scar ran like a wide river of ruined pink flesh carving a canyon between the cliffs of his snow-white fur.

"But it wasn't this, or my other wounds…" Feyn trailed off, sifting through the fragments of memories and meanings for the right words to tell this story. "They thought me dead. I felt the blade cutting into my face, but it was something else that fell upon me then. I felt, lifted. *Freed* somehow. Do you understand what I'm telling you, fox? My body crumpled in a heap, plunged into darkness, like a kind of death. But my consciousness, my *mind*, it flew away, into light. Soared, into the sky. And I saw … *everything*. Below, I saw how small our world was. I understood the true feeling of powerlessness. And above, I saw the Aigaion. Inside of it, I floated through endless halls, endless columns of moving golden lights. Glass, everywhere, like mirrors."

"Floor of glass," Maxan muttered. "Pillars of glass. Racing golden lights. "

"Disappearing into shadows above," the wolf finished for him. "You've seen it too?"

"The Aigaion." Maxan winced involuntarily, expecting the pain to spear the inside of his skull. But it didn't come. It seemed both halves of his mind were merging.

"When you died… ," he began, reciting the bursting thoughts as fast as he could, but not fast enough. *When you died, the human mind died with you, leaving the white wolf with just its imprint. A puppet, molded by the hand of the puppeteer.*

"But I didn't die. When I lifted my paw to touch the light, when I tried to take a breath, a desperation seized in my throat. I gasped for air that simply would not come. My consciousness was thrown back, cast down. A weight crushed my chest, and the light—the vision—faded."

Feyn's legs were the only part of him still in this world, stepping along the trail automatically as he spoke. The rest of him was enveloped in the mist of the memory. His eyes cast forward, but he wasn't seeing anything around him.

"When I woke, I woke in a pile of corpses. The raiders must have thought me dead when they struck me and gave me this scar. They had stripped me and my soldiers, thrown us into a pit. And my..." The wolf's voice cracked. Maxan knew well enough what else Feyn had found in the pit, and he expected sorrow. But there was no sorrow in the wolf's eyes, only pure, unchecked rage. "I opened my eyes and found hers staring back at me. For a moment, I thought we were safe, that it had all been just a dream—the war, the fire, the blood ... my departure from her, and the fact I had not truly said goodbye. I reached for my mate's face, only to find that they had removed her head from her body."

The wolf's voice dropped lower and lower, until it was just a throaty growl. "So I gave myself over. To the beast."

Feyn stopped on the trail and slowly closed his eyes. He took in a great breath, his nostrils flaring, his chest arching back. "You were right, Maxan." His eyes fluttered open, came to rest on the fox beside him. "You knew I had gone astray. I can recall the very moment, when my rational mind ... melted in the heat of my instincts. My urges. It was glorious. When you go astray, you see everything as its true nature. The trappings of identity fall away, like clothing burned off the skin, leaving only your fur, your fangs, your claws, your impulses. The voices of reason, of morality, of law... they drown in the screaming of the beast within. Its only language is the hunt. You hear only the thrumming of blood in the veins of your prey.

"My transformation was not gradual, you see. Not like the Stray you've seen in the western district of Crosswall. Not like the ones we've captured in the night and taken to the campus. No, for me, in that final moment, I held my mate's eyes with my own and I was Feyn, and then that moment was over, and

I was something else. For the first time, I howled. I scratched at the walls of the pit with my claws, tearing my way up. And then I hunted them down. The betrayers who had done this to me. But even still, I'm telling you, none of that mattered anymore. They weren't … any better than what I was. They had no names. They were…"

"Monsters," Maxan offered.

"Not even that. To call them such suggests a morality. They were *meat*. I saw the heat of their bodies. They ran away into the forest, and I ran them down, one after another. I sank my fangs into their necks. I drank freely of their blood. I gnawed at their chests until, later, there were only pink ribs cooling in the night air. And when I'd had my fill, I ran on all fours back into the dark.

"And there I remained. An animal. Until she found me."

Chewgar and the others had disappeared around a bend in the trail. Feyn's eyes shifted from one empty space between the trees to another, as if he could see the scenes playing out in them, lost in that memory of the chase. Maxan watched him, his own mind recreating the grisly scene. He imagined Feyn crouched on all fours—his snow-white fur stained with the blood of his fresh scar and that of his victims—darting between the trunks, leaping at the raiders' backs, and tearing scraps of their clothing. He imagined red sinews caught between the wolf's fangs as he ripped them out.

But he didn't judge him. Instead, Maxan tried to feel what Feyn had felt. *In the final moment, as he said, with his mate.* And he found it wasn't so difficult. He imagined himself holding her, looking into her lifeless eyes, and the hollowness that flooded his heart nearly made the fox stagger. From that imaginary vision, he suddenly revisited a very real one, another final moment, and the pain that had felt so similar, when the slender black-clad assassins had struck his mother down with their thin swords. There had been a voice then, inside his head, demanding he charge them, begging him to give in to the rage as Feyn had.

He remembered that voice. It belonged to a stupid little fox boy.

And there had been another voice. The voice of reason.

Run, it had said.

Maxan shook his head, bringing his mind back to the present.

"Folgian," he said simply, hoping to hear the rest of Feyn's story, eager to fill that hollow agony in his chest with anything else. "She found you."

The wolf drew his gaze away from the trees, nodded at the fox.

"I had been astray. I know not how long." Feyn resumed his stroll along the trail, and Maxan fell in step beside him. "I had no recollection of anything. She told me, much later, that I had stalked her through the woods for an entire day and approached her in the dead of night. While it's true the animal in us is not entirely bereft of intelligence, so powerful is its hunger that it foregoes all strategy when it catches sight of its prey."

"You're trying to say you fell into her trap."

Feyn turned to Maxan, his ruined lip lifting into a smile. "She told me later that my thrashing at the makeshift bonds she'd made kept her awake all night, and even as she rose the next morning, still was I restless."

"Why didn't she just…"

"I asked her once. Folgian said that in my eyes, she saw beyond the beast. We had never met, but she knew who I was, who I had been. I do not mean that in a literal sense. She had never known the wealthy knight-commander Feyn and his record of service. I mean… she saw that I was more than an animal. And when she found me..." Feyn trailed off again and drew in a deep breath. "She needed me. She needed ... anyone."

As he listened, Maxan tried to imagine the bear over-powering a savage wolf, but the vision fell apart every time. Withered and frail as Folgian was now—as he recalled her rocking before her library's hearth or reclining in the king's court—he couldn't picture her any differently. He couldn't pic-ture her getting the best of Feyn.

Then suddenly, the puzzle came together. "Bane," he said.

It turned out Maxan's intuition was correct. "Indeed," the wolf said. "Folgian was on the run."

"Rinnia said her master did it. Poisoned her."

"Salastragore. Folgian never spoke his name. She only once told me that the creature that had done that to her was—*is*—the world's greatest adversary. And I believed her." Feyn laid a paw on Maxan's shoulder, bringing them both to a halt. He met the fox's eyes. "Until that night in the library. When she said his name. To you. To Rinnia. That's when I knew. The Mind, the campus, the tower. My training. The king's war. All of Folgian's lessons and secrets and strategies were designed to seize more and more power. All those years that I learned from her, I bled for her, I gave to her... I have killed so many in her name—or worse, torn their minds apart like paper. Species of every nation, young and old, those she said were spies and assassins *he* had sent to finish what the bane started. Was any of it true?"

The wolf's lip curled into a snarl. "It was a lie. All of it. It was all just Folgian's personal vendetta. She kept the truth hidden from me. This," Feyn said, tapping the satchel at his side that Maxan knew concealed the glowing relay, "is not some-thing to be feared. It is the very object that could save us from the Stray."

They had stopped on a stretch of the trail between two hills that fell away in a sharp decline just a few steps farther. Feyn's piercing eyes fixed on Maxan, searching. *For what?* Maxan knew Feyn wasn't just telling Maxan his deepest secrets.

For an answer. He's asking me a question.

He wants to know if he's doing the right thing.

How should I know?

The right thing hadn't always been what Maxan himself wanted.

Run away. Start a new guild of thieves. Steal. Carouse. Escape. Revel. Destroy. Let the world eat itself until nothing's left. Then the world'll get you too.

Yes. I wanted that. More than anything. But I changed.

When?

Chewgar. And the snake. And Bane.

Now Maxan understood. Feyn served at Folgian's side because he wanted his master to realize her vision, to save the world from itself before she died. But Feyn was exactly who Rinnia warned him about. A fool who had convinced himself he was doing good. A fool ready to die thinking he had.

"How are you so sure the relay will even work?"

The wolf winced. His paw fell away from Maxan's shoulder.

"If you can even get it all the way up there in the first place?"

"I believed in Folgian. She ... spoke to me. She brought me back. And I gave her my life. My service. All my hope. I was the arm that held her up. And together we built the Mind. I believed her teaching could lead me back, that someday I would wake up and find the beast inside would finally be silent.

"Although she betrayed my belief in her, I still believe in the Aigaion. I believe that this will work. What I saw in that pit when I died... it's real. I believe it is where I am meant to go. When the time comes for the limits of our belief to be tested... if they break... we either believe again after the betrayal, or we let the betrayal consume us and change us into someone we don't want to be."

Faith in the Mind. Or faith in the Monitors. Folgian. Or Salastragore.

I don't understand either, Max.

Something just wasn't right. Whatever kind of complete picture Maxan had been trying to fit together, Feyn had just overturned the table, set all the scraps of this puzzle on fire. To go from believing one thing, trusting one master, to another, so fast, so...

Desperately.

Maxan looked away from the wolf's gaze, which was still imploring him to say he was right. He saw that the trail came to an end at a break in the trees a hundred paces away. The rays of Yinna broke through the puffy clouds and hung diagonally like long white sheets in the sky.

Saghan stood there between the pillars of dark trees with his arms folded, framed by the light, as though he stood at the exit of a deep cave. His tongue flicked the air, and his whiplike tail thrashed lazily against the tall grass that grew on either side of the path. The texture of his ornate leather armor blended well with the shadows of the Denlands. The green of the snake's scales matched the colors of the leaves. But his slit orange eyes were completely foreign in this place.

Maxan recalled the night he had first seen those eyes. They had glowed brighter than the fires that later consumed the inn. Back then, those had been two points of pure hatred and rage. Right now, their light was dull. They were just impatient, irritated, perhaps exhausted from waiting for the wolf and the fox to catch up.

"We're almossst there," Saghan hissed at them. He turned about and slithered along toward the light.

A wide expanse opened ahead. An enormous, perfectly circular valley yawned before them, covered in green as far as Maxan's mismatched eyes could see. He reckoned the whole of

Crosswall could fit inside the deep bowl of land. The sight of it took his breath away. Yinna had passed beyond the canopy directly above them, marking the time as long after noon. The day-star's rays painted the sky a shade of gold that seemed to fade into a richer orange with each passing moment. The air was so clear that Maxan could see where the land sloped upward at the other end of the valley, miles away. At its far edge, it was crowned with a flat green canopy, and beyond that, he could just make out the veiled, purple ghosts of the Corvidian mountains, dusted with lavender caps of snow.

Maxan couldn't help but take in the majesty of the scene. From below and to the right, a flock of innumerable wild fowl were taking flight. He swore their collective shadow tracing along the leafy canopy below was more than enough to shroud Crosswall's western district.

Above and beyond it all, however, the horizon was a jagged line of gray clouds that not even Yinna's warm light could color. And at its center was a black triangular form, like the jewel of an ashen crown, set uncannily straight against the natural frame: the Aigaion, ushering in a storm.

Of the companions' species—snake, wolf, fox, and even the rhino and squirrels loitering ahead on the path leading into the wide valley below—none of them had been blessed with particularly keen eyesight. But Maxan raised a paw above his brow and peered over the bowl-shaped valley as the flock of fowl fluttered away north. He saw something they left behind, one particularly large bird, a straggler.

"Is that Sarovek?" he said.

Saghan craned his long neck, as if it would give him a better vantage. It didn't, of course. "Must be," he said anyway, the brilles refreshing his slit eyes to sharpen his poor vision as best they could. "She's marking our destination. Good, because it would take me all day to find it by myself beneath that sea of green. Let's go."

While the idea of the journey's end seemed to renew everyone's energy, Feyn lagged behind, his gaze fixated on the distant Corvidian's lazy circles above the canopy at the valley's center.

"What is it?" Maxan said. The others stopped again and turned.

Only Pryth and Pram seemed to see their master's snarling expression for what it really was. They exchanged a worried look and hopped from Chewgar's shoulders, their eyes following Feyn's line of sight to the circling figure.

"What's wrong," Saghan said.

"Your friend," the wolf said at last, his fierce gaze never straying from the valley, "is likely dead."

THE PILLARS OF LIGHT

"**S**he's here," Principal Harmony assured them. All but her gray-feathered wings and head were obscured by her black robes. The only things blacker were the owl's enormous pupils. Even with the winds sweeping through the bottom of the valley here, whipping the trees and bushes into a frenzy all around, she never blinked those abyssal black eyes.

Harmony stood at the edge of a jagged cliff, like a giant's spear point thrust through the green flesh of the world, towering at least a hundred feet over the companions' heads. Saghan had whispered that this place was the very landmark they needed. "The station under the spear."

Maxan recalled the heated conversation that the snake had had with the wolf on the trail when the extraordinarily tall rock came into their view through the trees, how Saghan refused to leave his Corvidian sister behind, how he insisted he could handle anything the Mind had in store for them, his hissing voice dropping ominously. But Feyn knew better. The wolf had reasoned that turning around and proceeding another way would only expose their back to the knife, that Harmony had found them here, that she could find them anywhere.

The trap could not have been avoided. They were already in it.

"Show her to me," Saghan shouted up at Harmony.

The owl was as still as a statue for several seconds; only the black fabric of her robes moved in the wind all around her. Finally, she called down, "The artifact." A talon unfolded from the shadows of her sleeve. "If you would."

Saghan's head swung to Feyn. "The relay," he said, as if the wolf hadn't heard. The snake unfurled the long fingers of his scaly hand, holding them before Feyn expectantly.

Feyn looked at them with scorn. "What is your intention, snake?"

"A trade."

"You would defy your master and doom us all to live as Stray?"

"Not all," Saghan said venomously. "Just you." He jerked his open hand at the wolf. His other hand wrapped around the hilt of the thin sword strapped to his side.

Feyn's lips curled into a snarl. He shifted the satchel from his hip to his back, away from Saghan.

"Don't think I intend to let her keep it," the snake hissed.

Maxan saw every muscle in Chewgar's arms tense, ready to heave the great sword off his shoulders. Pryth and Pram stood behind him, their eyes darting between the gray owl caller high above them to the snake just a few feet away, both of them probably trying to determine which posed the more significant danger.

And Maxan, arguably the least threatening of them all— *Just a little fox, a guard of Crosswall so very far from home, a rooftop shadow very far away from any rooftops where he could be of use*—stood behind them all, the fur prickling on the back of his neck from the building tension as though lightning were about to strike. He didn't know what to do. His eyes darted about, sweeping over the shallow creek gurgling ahead of them against the jutting cliff's edge, then up to the gray owl looking down on them all, and to the foliage to either side of the towering rock. There, he saw something stir in the leaves, more than just the gentle rocking motion of the winds. Something metal. His ears perked up at a clicking sound. Then came another, just to its left. His ears fanned to the left side of Harmony's high rock, where the creek disappeared among the trees, where another series of clicks sounded just loud enough for those species gifted with heightened hearing.

Crossbows.

And something else.

No…

Chuckling.

On either side of Principal Harmony, three of the Mind's sentries materialized, two of them—a rainbow-scaled lizard and a wolf with fur as black as midnight—leveling crossbows down at the Monitors. The third was a familiar, murderous hyena. Yacub had traded his tattered leather armor for plates of steel belted to his arms, chest, and shoulders, all of it emblazoned with the triangular sigil of the Mind. The hyena wore a scholar's red robe around his waist like a sash. The only things he hadn't given up were his vicious ripper sword and his horrible cackling laughter.

Yacub pulled hard on a chain, dragging a weight behind him, scraping it audibly across the rock. He kicked Sarovek's side, rolling her nearly over the edge, and laughed wildly. From so far below, it was impossible to tell if the hawk was alive or dead.

"Feyn, the hour is late," Harmony called. Behind her, the first wispy edges of the dark gray clouds crept into view, swallowing whatever shred of twilit sky they could see. Seconds later, the first few drops of rain pattered down gently on everyone beneath. Within minutes, the storm would be upon them.

The gray owl's voice was never shrill, never loud, always calm and soft. Yet it seemed to carry powerfully in the open space all around them, more intense than the wind. "Your apprentices return with me. The Monitors can leave with their lives. Even this one here. But you…"

Without flinching, Harmony issued the order. "Kill the wolf."

A hail of bolts came at them from multiple angles, but Feyn had recognized her intention long ago. His claws surged outward, an air-rending bark erupted from between his twisted maw, and a bubble of force blasted every one of the deadly projectiles harmlessly away. The trees on either side of the tall stone rocked violently back and snapped straight again. Water flowing in the creek became a wave folding over itself, slapping against the rocky base. A breath later, the world grew still again.

Maxan and the others felt the rush of wind but were unmoved. The fox patted himself down, his mind trying to catch up with the idea that, no, in fact, he had not been skewered by a crossbow bolt. The only things pelting him now were raindrops.

Harmony appeared not to care that her sentries' volley had failed; perhaps, she'd even anticipated it would. It was impossible to tell, so unnervingly vacant was her stare.

What happens now? What do we—
Do we just stand here and—
Shit on this!

"Principal!" Maxan cried out impetuously. "Do you even know what the *artifact* is? What it can do? What it means? We can't just lock it away and hope everyone just … *learns* to live with each other. We have to *use* it. Before it's too late."

Everyone was looking at him, but there was a mix of reactions. Pryth and Pram, most of all, seemed relieved that someone was voicing this appeal. Chewgar stepped in front of the twins, shielding them from the unseen enemies in the trees. Saghan seemed gratified only because Maxan's outburst had bought them a few more seconds to plan their next moves. Maxan saw his slender fingers slithering into the satchel at his hip.

Maxan's eyes settled on Feyn, whose head dipped ever so slightly in a nod of thanks.

The fox arched his back to shout up once more at Principal Harmony. "An end to the Stray! A *real* end. It's what Folgian wants!"

The gray owl cocked her head. For the first time, she blinked, her eyelids snapping over her black pupils. Those dark points were focused entirely on Maxan now: scrutinizing, measuring, judging.

He felt the fur bristling beyond just his neck now, rising in a wave all down his spine.

Harmony spoke in her most honeyed tone yet, her voice eerily amplified in this place. "Folgian is dead." The proclamation thrummed in the empty space before the swelling patter of raindrops all around drowned it out.

The clouds overhead seemed to suddenly pick up speed, morphing from gray shadows to rolling waves of oily black. Crackling lines of white spread through them like veins, and thunder rattled the world below them an instant later.

Even from this distance, even in this fading light, Harmony could read the bewilderment on Maxan's face easily enough. But she was more interested in the shock and horror written on Pryth's and Pram's. The gray owl cocked her head to the other side now, regarding the twins, her emotionless eyes warming with something that might pass for pity. "Ohhhh," she cooed, a whisper that carried in volume far below. "Children, I was certain you had helped him. But I see now your faces. So innocent."

Harmony blinked again. "Your master did not tell you ... what he has done."

The squirrels' bushy tails jerked nervously in the rain. They took a step away from Feyn. Pryth's eyes were drawn to his sister's. Some meaning was passed there. He nodded, swallowed a nervous lump, then turned back to his master.

The rain fell heavier now, soaking the wolf's snow-white fur until it stood up in spiky tufts, but the downpour did nothing to conceal the shadow of fury that crossed his face. He shook his head fiercely, scattering drops of water all around, and looked again up at Principal Harmony, snarling so deeply it seemed his wicked scar would split open.

"YOU LIE!!!" Feyn suddenly lurched forward, coughing, rasping for breath, and he fell to his knees. His arms wrapped about himself, as though he were catching the phantom tail of a wild beast escaping from his chest. "*You* killed her. And you told all of Leora it was me?"

Saghan slinked away to the right, and Chewgar stepped to the left, shuffling Pryth and Pram to safety behind his thick legs.

Harmony raised her taloned hand, and Maxan barely heard the clicks of reloading crossbows. Even Yacub had taken up one in his paws. Maxan shook the rain from his brow, squinted up at the hyena and the sentries, calculated the angles of their weapons, and determined that they were not all aiming at the wolf this time.

"Your fox friend is right, Feyn," Harmony called, holding her talons out toward the wolf. Her false accusation had disarmed whatever kind of mental barrier he held against her. Her words had ripped the invisible strings of the Aigaion from his grasp, and she had gladly, easily taken them up. "The artifact must be *used*. But *by* who? *For* who? It is only natural that the superior species of this world should rule. The artifact is power,

Feyn. And power by its very nature is wielded by those who soar above all others."

The white wolf only writhed in response, helpless, fighting against whatever invisible force was wracking his body in anguish.

High above, the roiling black clouds grew blacker still. Something dark stirred within them, parting them like curtains as it moved overhead. Whatever shred of daylight there died. The leaves, grass, stones, and everything else below the great triangular leviathan's shadow were drained of color.

"Power," Harmony continued, her voice humming, reverberant, electrified. "The only truth is power."

Her talons stretched skyward, and Maxan instinctively lowered into a crouch, ready to spring, assuming the owl's gesture called for the next volley of crossbow bolts.

But no bolts fell. Only rain. Then something else entirely unexpected fell upon them.

The black edge of the Aigaion slowed. The sound of groaning metal tore through the sky, like armies clashing in rusted armor. Maxan's stomach lurched, as though the world of Herbridia itself were grinding to a halt beneath his feet. He was entranced by the Aigaion as it finally came to a halt, the dark, wispy clouds flowing over it like the tide rushing onto the shore.

High above him, the caller—Harmony, principal of the Mind—perched on the rock. Her robes whipped about her in the violent storm. She held her taloned hands to the sky. They were trembling. But her unflinching, abyssal black eyes were locked on the fox, the wolf, and their companions below.

Jagged lines of white ripped through the clouds overhead, flickering and pulsing as lightning did, but not fading. The energy swirled and gathered at two points on the Aigaion's belly. The two points drew the lightning in from every angle, forming two perfect discs of glowing white light, as though the Aigaion itself were opening its eyes. The world below it burst into glorious incandescence as the discs intensified. For an instant, every leaf, branch, and stone, every creature and every raindrop, everything, was illuminated in pure white light, brighter than that of the day-star herself.

Maxan's eyes burned, but he could not look away.

So it was that something else—some impulse deep in the fox's consciousness—had to take action for him, as it so often had lately. Maxan found himself diving toward Feyn, tumbling over the prone wolf. He found his paws clutching at Feyn's clothes, then dragging the wolf over with all his might, carrying him along into the roll.

The pillar of light struck a heartbeat later, atomizing the very spot where the wolf had been, driving a mile or more into the ground, a sword of superheated light as wide around as an ancient Denland tree. The beam strafed the ground, carving a perfectly straight line ten feet long before fading to nothingness.

The second pillar descended where Saghan had stood. Like she had with the fox, Harmony had severely underestimated the snake's survival instincts, those enhanced genetic codes his father had designed, written deep inside his brain, alerting him to danger before it struck. Saghan dived away as the beam of pure light pierced the ground, kicking up dust and smoke as it vaporized all trace of matter. It cut away at the ground, moving quicker than its bright twin, curving in a half circle to join its origin with the endpoint of the straight line left behind by the first beam.

And then it, too, faded. Harmony's display of power had left an enormous letter D at the bottom of the valley, and Maxan huddled over Feyn at its center.

Maxan lifted his head from the folds of the wolf's soaked clothes and peered about with one eye closed. The pouring rain hissed as it fell on the glowing red edges where the Aigaion's light had scorched the ground. Steam rose from those newly carved vents as the angry color cooled. Through the rising screen of steam, he witnessed the gray owl sagging over, gasping for air, and the Aigaion—above them all—steadily moving once more. Maxan turned about frantically, but was relieved to see that Chewgar had escaped the pillars of light unscathed. The rhino stood clutching the golden great sword with both meaty hands on the other side of the chasm, his knuckles pressed so hard against his gray skin that they looked likely to burst through. Both squirrel twins clutched at his legs, the fright quivering in their faces as much as it did in his as they tried to peer through the steam and the rain for a glimpse of their friends.

Several feet away, Saghan came up in a crouch, his tongue flicking at the air, his orange eyes peering into the foliage to the right of the jutting cliff.

From that side, Maxan heard the twang of one crossbow, then another. Through the layer of steam, he saw the snake's long neck coil like a cracked whip as the first bolt sang toward it and came away hitting nothing but air. The second, however, sank into Saghan's green flesh just above his collarbone.

One scaled hand shot to his neck. Dark red blood gurgled between his fingers as he clutched the bolt. The other hand came up and flung a black orb away into the trees.

The cluster of trees ignited in a burst of orange fire. The explosive power packed into Saghan's device had once been enough to gut an entire inn from the inside out. Here, outside, even in the rain, the flames surged outward and stuck to everything they touched. However many of the Mind's sentries Harmony had positioned there, none of them escaped. One of them stumbled from the woods—his species made indistinguishable by the hissing wreath of fire melting his head and torso—howling in agony. He pitched forward into the creek, dousing every flame except those crawling up his hind legs, but he did not rise again.

Maxan's thoughts were screaming at him, but there was no time to decipher what they wanted. The twanging release of three more crossbow bolts pulled his attention to the left, where he saw them sink into his friend's chest all at once. Chewgar went down on one knee, but Maxan didn't have the time to process what that movement meant before he heard three more bolts fired from above. His head whipped around, ready to carry the rest of himself over in a dodge, but he realized somehow in all the confusion that it would not be necessary. Somehow, a wall of fire hung in the air several feet above his head, burning incomprehensibly. The three projectiles entered on one side, but only three puffs of ash emerged on the other.

Pryth dropped his outstretched paws, and the firewall fizzled to nothing.

The fox knew only three things for certain in his next two heartbeats. The angry rhino had risen to his feet, snorted, and crashed horn first into the trees on the left, snapping several saplings and swinging the length of his steel against something. And the squirrel, Pram, was rushing to him—no, not to him, to her master, the white wolf—hopping delicately on all fours over the sizzling earth and across the razor-straight edge of the chasm. And just as these things were beginning to make sense, the last certainty Maxan knew was that the ground upon which he crouched was vibrating. Rumbling, cracking, and then—

Rising?

The carved slab of rock levitated gently into the air as the gray owl caller gently lifted her talon. Harmony's mind felt the slab's presence in space separate from the rest of the ground below. She reached for it, the Aigaion bringing it to her grasp as surely as her lungs brought her air. She could hear the rain pattering sharply upon it and washing down its freshly hewn sides. The platform of rock rose vertically through the wafting screen of mist where the raindrops had met with the apprentice's fire a moment before. Even with the rivulets of water running down Harmony's wide-open eyes, they never blinked for an instant, so intent were they upon the fox and the wolf and the squirrel clutching her master.

"Go," Harmony ordered the three animals at her side. Yacub freed his ripper with a gleeful peal of laughter, his tongue lolling and lapping wildly at the drenching rain. He followed the lizard and the wolf as they drew their own swords and leapt across the empty space toward the rising platform.

The Aigaion told her something else then, so quietly that no one else could hear. Had she been only an apprentice caller, she would not have heard its whisper. But she was a principal, a master, and so she heard the object of unknown power sailing through the air from below, poised to strike her soldiers. Her mind felt it coming. With the Aigaion's blessing, time seemed to slow. She knew where it came from, where it was, and exactly where it would be. With one talon busy lifting the stone table skyward, the other came up, as quick as the cobalt-blue lightning bolt she called from the sky, and she guided its energy to that precise point in space.

Saghan's web of razor wire would have exploded at the right moment, would have snagged all three of the leaping animals, except for the lightning bolt that flashed through the sky just before it reached its proximity sensor. The energy surged through it, fried its circuitry, melted its shell, and sent its deadly contents sputtering out into the air like a burning cobweb.

But the web did catch one. Its white-hot filaments entangled the lizard from the waist down. The surprise, the impossibly painful sensation all along his lower body, sent him off balance in midair. The lizard slammed hard against the side of the floating rock; his hard black nails scratched uselessly against it, even as his tail and legs were burned off by the superheated wires. The lizard fell away in pieces and landed thirty feet below on his neck, snapping the vertebrae there instantly, then disappeared into the chasm the Aigaion's light had cut.

The snake's wide mouth curved into something like a smile, and he slumped over in the grass, still fumbling with the crossbow bolt half-buried at the bottom of his neck, his cold blood soaking his armor with the rain.

Yacub and the black wolf glided easily enough onto the rising rock and rushed at the fox they found there.

Maxan realized then that his short sword had already found its way to his paw.

Wh—? How did I—?!

Without thinking, he punched it sideways and straight into the air above him with all his strength, knocking back the wolf sentry's strike with a resounding clang.

He then brought the blade back down fluidly to lock with the teeth of Yacub's ripper. Steel slid against steel until the hyena and fox were face-to-face.

"Haa-haaaah!" The hyena blew a puff of noxious laughter at Maxan. Yacub's crooked fangs hung mere inches away from Maxan's snout. "You're a long way from home, lad! Gonna flash your Crosswall badge at me again? Haaahh!"

Yacub snapped his maw at Maxan's snout.

Maxan jerked away, off balance, and felt the hyena's knee sink into his gut. He rolled back with the force of the kick.

Dammit, Max! YOU should've kicked HIM!

"Huh?" he said aloud, looking up from the ground at the cackling hyena standing over him.

Yacub, he realized then, wasn't much with a sword either. The hyena might have been given new armor, a new purpose, but the way he stooped, the way his tongue raked hungrily back and forth over his fangs, it was clear he fought only with savagery. A wild lust to see things destroyed.

And yet, strangely, Yacub's attack suddenly ceased.

The wolf sentry—similarly armored but armed with a long sword—had recovered by now from the ringing blow the non-fencing fox had somehow sent him away with. He rushed back in at Maxan, ignoring the helpless white wolf at the edge of the platform and the little squirrel girl who cried over him, focusing instead on the only armed combatant he could see.

Yacub's ripper came across in the same instant, biting deep into the black wolf's throat, stopping his comrade dead. The wolf looked into the hyena's eyes, his face a picture of shock and confusion, not pain. But the hyena's expression was vacant. Yacub jerked his arm savagely and ripped a chunk of the wolf's throat from his body, then shoved the dead weight over the side of the platform to fall with the rain.

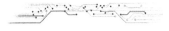

Pram's paw wavered. She had never felt the Aigaion like this before. So heavy. Heavier than she could have ever imagined. It had told her where she could find the hyena's mind when she had asked it—when she had heard him laugh, then make ready to fall upon the fox, Maxan, her friend. Before, when she had called on it to show her other minds, it had always been slow and gentle and lightweight, and following its lead felt like plucking a tuft of pollen stuck lazily on a petal. But when she saw the hyena's cruel weapon and felt its owner's intention, she knew there was no time to reach gently. She needed control, and she needed it now.

And the price Pram paid for wrenching control of Yacub's mind was heavy. Taking him by force leeched all her will, all her strength. Her head dipped forward. The intense, weakening ache crept up her spine, neck, and skull. Her eyes fluttered. Blood ran from her nostrils. Pram crumpled against her master's back.

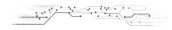

Maxan sprang up into a guarded stance, waiting for some idea to come to him, force him into his next move. He saw Feyn's eyes snap open as his apprentice fell against him. He saw Yacub examine his weapon and chuckle, baffled by the chunk of flesh on its teeth. Maxan recognized the wild hyena's intention in the way Yacub shifted his weight. Toward Pram.

So Maxan moved. All on his own. With no need of the inner voice to guide him.

Yacub reared back, his ripper raised high over Pram, slobber flying wildly from his maw, laughing hysterically.

Maxan slammed his shoulder against Yacub's waist and shoved the mad hyena away from his friends with all his might—even though it meant shoving the hyena over the edge into empty air. Yacub disappeared into the rain and the dark below. His laughter faded into the storm.

It was him, Maxan tried to tell himself, shuddering, *or it was them.*

No, I could've—

There was nowhere else to throw him.

To the other side, maybe! Or just—

Max! SHUT UP!

What have I done?

Horrified, he fell to his knees and peered over the edge of the platform to look down on the rain as it swirled into oblivion. On the chasm, the light had cut. On the ripper sword that had landed on the other side of it.

Rinnia's words rang loudly in his mind.

We're all killers when we find something we love threatened.

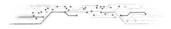

The beast in Feyn had almost gotten the better of him. Harmony's lie had thrown open its cage. Feyn did not kill Folgian, but Harmony must have known that, for years, he had dreamed of it. The wolf often imagined the feel of Folgian's bane-rotted skull squishing between his paws, the tips of his claws pressing into her eye sockets, the rush of hot pus and blood that frothed from there, green and red swirling on the white of his fur. But that daydream always shifted, and his master's head always became his mate's. The anger had nearly overwhelmed him, the beast within him had wanted nothing more than to strip away control and destroy everything and everyone in sight. He had nearly let it.

But when Pram fell against him—Pram, his little apprentice—he had clutched her tightly, his paws remembering the familiar lightness of her shoulders, the coarseness of her fur. He stroked her tiny muzzle with the back of his paw, fighting to keep her conscious. For her, because of her, Feyn remembered who he really was, and the call of the beast died away to nothing.

Pram's eyes closed despite his efforts. Feyn let the girl down gently and moved to the edge of the floating slab, his face contorted in a hideous snarl, his icy eyes fixated on Harmony. The world was engulfed in almost pure darkness as the center of the Aigaion passed over them. The white wolf's eyes reflected what little light remained from the far western horizon beyond the storm, becoming two bright beads that flashed in the dark. He saw the gray owl slumped over, the feathers at the tips of her wings brushing against the slick ground of the jutting spear of rock where she perched, now nearly level with the rising platform.

"You called too much of its *power*." The word tasted delicious as he spat it back at her. "Your Corvidian arrogance will destroy you, Harmony." Feyn snorted. He worked the tips of his claws at his side, felt the strings of the invisible Aigaion dangling in the void.

Feyn howled and lashed at the air like a whip, propelling a crushing wave of kinetic force at Harmony. The owl's wings came together at the last possible second, buffering the force. Several feathers were ripped from them and tossed aside like the gravel she stood on. Sarovek's limp body rolled away toward the corpse of trees crowning the high rock. Harmony planted her lower talons and slid back several feet, leaving scratches in the stone surface, but she withstood the blast of wind Feyn called.

She may not have been blown away, but the wolf's assault had sapped even more of her strength. When her wings unfolded, Harmony fell to her knees, gasping for breath.

Feyn had said enough. Now he would end this. He lifted his right paw, reaching for the thick trunk of an ancient Denland tree that had rooted for centuries in the side of the jutting rock. He could feel those roots; his senses merged with the rock they penetrated, raced across every inch of them. Through the insight of the Aigaion, he knew their span of time and existence. His mind held mastery of that beautiful, ancient thing. And he didn't care about any of it. His paw closed, and he felt the grip of the Aigaion closing with it around the trunk. His arm lifted, and he felt every fiber of the ancient tree tearing itself away from the rock.

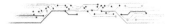

Maxan was behind Feyn when the wolf's blast of energy disabled Harmony. He rushed to Pram's side and cradled the girl. When he laid a palm on her chest, he felt the faintest flutter of her heartbeat. The sky still flashed with lightning above, and the ground quaked with thunder below. He swore he heard the clang of steel and the crashing of trees down there. But his eyes and ears were ever on the spectacle before him, on the towering tree ripping itself away from the ground at Feyn's bidding.

Now they flitted across to the gray owl, hunched over, breathing heavily, as the great tree rose menacingly behind her.

There was something wrong about the way Principal Harmony knelt on the rock. Her unnerving black eyes... The hollowness there did not match the desperation of her breaths.

She's just ... waiting for Feyn to finish her?

Or she just ... wants him to believe it.

I know a con when I see one.

Maxan cried out to Feyn, but the wolf was already swinging his arm downward, the tree matching the motion precisely, bending at its base. The snapping of wood hundreds of years old was deafening; the shock wave of sound radiated for miles all around. Maxan's ears popped and filled with needlepoints of pain. The great tree itself, that massive pillar of wood and tangled branches, exploded against the rock, right on top of the kneeling owl, splitting into a thousand splinters as tall and sharp as spears, some of which launched into the distance.

Maxan shielded Pram's body with his own, but he didn't need to.

Feyn stood and watched the chaos he'd made, the incoming spears of wood ramming into the invisible barrier he'd called before him and rebounding harmlessly away. Chunks of the shattered tree tumbled over the edge of the high rock, or rolled away down the sloping sides, carrying tangled branches with them. Feyn's eyes narrowed, searching the wreckage for any sign of the Mind's other principal.

Flashes of white drew his attention skyward, to the silhouette of a winged figure limned by the lightning. Before Feyn realized that Harmony had survived, that her wings had carried her above them all in one powerful flap, it was already too late.

The lightning bolt pierced the wolf's chest, entangled every limb of his body in crackling energy, and shot through the other side, straight into the pillar he stood on. His clothing and patches of his white fur ignited in sputtering purple fire and flaked away in orange embers. A hoarse gasp escaped Feyn's scarred lips as he crumpled over. His eyes rolled in his head, and his tongue lolled from between his clenched fangs. Every muscle in his body twitched, locked, and twitched again.

In an instant, it was over. But in that instant, Harmony had struck her enemy with an eternity of pain. She spread her wings wide and rode the softening winds downward to perch on what was left of the tree, just as Feyn twitched a final time and went rigid once and for all.

"Ahhhh," she sighed sweetly. "There now." Her abyssal eyes came to rest on the fox, the lone survivor atop the towering stone pillar across from her. Then her gaze darted to something at Feyn's side, a guttering flame there. The wolf's satchel, smoldering in the dying remnants of the rain. The lightning bolt had turned the rough fabric to embers, and something metallic, impossibly unscathed and brilliantly chrome, peeked through.

"Bring me the artifact, if you please," the owl said flatly. "I am a little tired."

Maxan tried to swallow his fear but found his throat was dry despite the rest of him being soaked in rain. Both paws were trembling at his sides. It took all his strength to maintain the grip on his short sword.

What's your plan here, Max?

You mean you're not going to make me do something spectacular before I think it?

He wanted to scan the area, search for grips along the rocky walls, spot overhanging branches to leap to, anything. He wanted to calculate his chances for survival, his chances at outrunning a lightning bolt. But he was frozen, unable to look away from Harmony's black eyes.

For the second time, she blinked. "Hold the artifact over your head please," she said, miming the action she expected with her talons. "Like this. Now."

Wait ... that's it.

What's it?

She can't command you, Max! She can't control you!

I'm not a puppet.

Just say—

"No!"

The sound of his own voice gave his arms the steel they needed to stop shaking. He didn't just think he could dodge Harmony's lightning, if it came to that. He *knew* he could. "No," he called again, louder. "You can't have it."

The owl cocked her head to the side. The points of her talons spread wide in the air, and they rolled up and down. Maxan knew what Harmony was reaching for. He had seen her do it to a hyena, forcing him to slit his own throat.

He gave her his most mocking smile and hopped forward a few purposefully awkward steps, playing along as though he were her puppet, then bent forward and scooped up the relay. The metal was surprisingly cool despite the embers cradling it.

For the first time, Principal Harmony's face displayed a discernible emotion. The thickly feathered brows ruffled, the lids of her enormous eyes veiled her gaze in fury.

So that's what an angry Corvidian looks like.

"This what you want," he said, holding the relay out to her, "master?"

Maxan's thumb caught one of the racing beads of golden light. He made to drag it through the channel, to drown the world in red, to rip Harmony's rational mind from her, to disconnect the master caller from the Aigaion. A killer owl wouldn't be easier to manage necessarily, but at least it would be predictable.

But the relay slipped from his grasp, sailed across the gap, and came to rest in the owl's talons.

"Shit," Maxan said quietly to himself. He felt his steely resolve melting away, the fear creeping back into his limbs.

"Wait!" he called to Harmony, though she didn't appear to be going anywhere. He let his short sword clatter to the ground, held up both his paws to her, pleading. "If you take it away, then the Stray will consume us all."

Harmony shook her head. "Not all. Just Leorans. You despicable creatures. No other nation fights itself more than you. You crawl through your own squalor. You raise monuments to commemorate your violent lusts. I will not allow a weapon like the Aigaion to fall into Leorans' bloody paws. This power belongs to Corvidia alone."

"What gave Corvidians the right to choose?"

"Dear boy, still you do not understand?" The owl spread her gray-feathered wings wide; they spanned nearly the entire edge of the jutting spear of rock she stood upon. In that moment, the violence of the storm subsided. The sky lightened from solid black to overcast gray. Impossibly high above them, the opposite edge of the Aigaion was creeping away within its veil of clouds.

Harmony admired her own beautiful form in the misty light. "Nature gave it to us."

Talking's getting us nowhere, Max.

She's not going to giving it up.

She's not going to let you live either.

Maxan burst into a sprint.

The sudden motion startled the owl. She lifted an arm haphazardly, calling half-formed bolts of lightning from the weakening storm. They struck the fox's tracks one after another as he raced for the edge, missing him by inches. Harmony's deep black eyes narrowed and twitched in frustration. Her talons shot out wildly, carelessly.

She can't feel my mind.

Harmony screeched in outrage as Maxan took his final stride.

The Aigaion, Max… You're beyond its power.

As his legs launched him across the gap, he felt the final misdirected burst of white-hot energy strike into the chasm between the walls of stone.

Maxan thought only of closing the gap, thought only of speed and distance. He should have spared a thought to the angle. His waist slammed against the sharp edge of the high rock, knocking the air from his lungs. He slid backward, claws scraping uselessly at the stone, until gravity had him completely in its clutches.

His right paw shot out and nestled into a crack of the cliff face, and his claws dug in as deep as they could. He sensed the dull, numb snapping of his bones, but he felt no pain in that nerve-dead limb. Miraculously, his grip caught all of his weight. He swung his body around and crashed against the sheer stone wall just a few feet below the edge.

He let himself release a groan of frustration, but never stopped reaching above and feeling for the next hold in the stone or for the dangling branches that could carry him up. Adrenaline flooded his body and fueled his scramble the rest of the way up and over.

Did I just—

—dodge a lightning bolt?!

The fox clambered up through the bed of fallen branches and leaves and rolled away from the tree's wreckage onto the solid stone of the ledge. He sprang up into a crouch, ready to dodge the next attack, his eyes locked on the spot where Harmony stood.

The owl wasn't there. She was rising away.

Shit!

What can you do, throw a stick at her?!

Ah! I've got something better!

The gray owl's wingspan was somewhat average, as Corvidian species go. Had Harmony been an eagle, a hawk, or even a crow or a raven, she would have already put enough air behind her for Maxan's plan to no longer matter. She rose higher with every wingbeat, convinced that the fox had fallen to his death, that she could put him and all the other loathsome Leoran wretches behind and beneath her.

So the thin cord that wrapped about both of her low talons and tugged her down came as quite a shock. Harmony dropped several feet before beating her wings and regaining her height. Below, she saw the fox plant his lower paws in the nooks of the tree's fallen branches and strain to haul her back.

It's working!

His fangs clenched with exertion, Maxan pulled the thin rope and fed it inch by inch into the device Rinnia had given him at the Pinnacle Tower.

The joints where her wings fused with her back were growing raw and sore with every futile beat. Harmony harnessed what little strength her body could spare to flip about midair and face the fox, one talon clutching the relay, the other rising furiously to call again upon the gray sky.

The lightning, Maxan thought, had all but gone out after the Aigaion's passing, but now a few weak lines of white streaked across the skies overhead.

You have to let go, Max!

I have to hold on! I can't let—

LET GO!

—her get away!

He was in full control of his own body and mind, blocking out the voice screaming at him—the voice of reason, the instinct for survival. Maxan was simply too tired. If he let go, if Harmony got away, if the relay went to Corvidia, he would never see it again. If he even lived past this failure, what would he do? *Be a shadow again? A useless observer? A noncombatant in the only battle that mattered?* He was tired of it all.

So he chose to hold on, even if it meant being struck by lightning.

The white light flashed. Maxan looked up expecting to see the bolt that would burn through his chest. Instead, he squinted at something above Harmony. Something long. A shadowy outline against the gray mist. Something moving impossibly fast.

Harmony's heart exploded from her chest as the splintered spear pierced her between her wings and drove clean through her body. The slick red shaft of wood thudded deep into the ground below, strong enough to part the stone, staking her to the spot. She hung there, stunned, her abyssal eyes widened with incomprehension, the unknown sensation of pain, the sudden inability to draw breath. Or was it numbness?

Or resignation? The gathering lightning above her dispersed. Harmony's talons fell lifeless to her sides. The shining relay slipped from her grasp.

The thin cord went slack in Maxan's grip.

What just happened?

But he knew well enough what happened.

Behind him, Feyn—his snow-white fur singed ashen black, the skin beneath seared and blistered—let his outstretched paw drop. The wolf's icy blue eyes rolled back into his skull as he let out a final, raspy breath from the scar at the edge of his snarl—a sound that could have been a laugh—and collapsed a final time.

THE LIVING COWARD

MAXAN SET ASIDE HIS TROUBLED HISTORY with fire to warm himself beside it.

Not really history anymore, Max. Given all our recent events.

Roughly one hundred feet past the edge of the high rock where Feyn had slammed the gigantic tree, Maxan had found and freed Sarovek from the chain binding her. The hawk knight was severely injured. Her armor and weapons were taken, and the flesh beneath her feathers was battered and bruised. But otherwise, none of her delicate bones had been broken. Once Maxan managed to rouse her (with a few loud, desperate shouts right into her earholes), Sarovek made her way back down the sloping sides of the spear-like cliff, looking for Saghan, while he ran back to the platform of rock Harmony had raised.

He met Pryth and Chewgar at the cliff's top, worrying over how they could reach Feyn and Pram—both still motionless, possibly dead—across the gap. Chewgar started to heave the fallen tree before Pryth screamed at him to stop, claiming that his rank as scholar qualified him as the lead engineer here. The squirrel approved of the work a breath later anyway, and the hulking rhino laid the makeshift bridge over the chasm. Maxan crossed to the wolf and squirrel girl.

They were alive. At least, Pram was; *alive* didn't apply to Feyn quite the same way. He looked as though he had been stricken with a grotesque plague. Most of his fur had been burned away, and he had several weeping patches of flesh along the left side of his body where Harmony's lightning had struck him hardest. Maxan knew all too well how burns like that felt. Even after the pain went away, he had concealed the marks they left behind under the leather sleeve for years. But this was far different. Far worse. He doubted Feyn would ever look the same again.

If he lives.

With Pryth's help, he lugged the two survivors to the other side. They made their way down the hill and found a cave. Not far inside was a high-ceilinged chamber with a dry floor, a welcome reprieve from the rain-soaked world of the valley outside. Without any of the Monitors to show them the way, Maxan, Chewgar, and the three callers had nowhere else to go, and nothing else to do but make a fire and wait for Sarovek and Saghan.

And Rinnia.

So they waited.

Perhaps they waited for Feyn to die.

Maxan glanced away from the flickering firelight to where the wolf lay on the cavern floor. Feyn's every breath was labored, as though the lightning had seared right into his chest and scorched the chambers of his lungs shut. He flailed about weakly, perhaps reliving the battle, or worse memories from long ago.

Pram had awoken some time ago while they were still outside. The girl was shaken, but cognizant. And now she dabbed a swath of her tunic, soaked in the cool water of the creek, against her master's agonizing burns. Her brother had quipped incessantly until Pram silently ordered him to gather kindling—who better qualified than the kid who calls on fire?—and Pryth took his mumbling away into the forest.

Outside, night had fallen quickly. After Pryth had their fire going, he was the first to break the somber silence, recounting the scuffle (his word for it) in the woods to the side of the high rock, where he had followed Chewgar's charge. The rhino had swung Locain's great sword around wildly, felling trees and foes alike, but he was overcome by the Mind's hidden sentries soon enough. Battling a massive rhinoceros took all their attention, so none of them paid the little squirrel any mind.

"But they should've!" Pryth cried rather excitedly, tapping the side of his little snout.

He described the wave of popping explosions he had unleashed, with dramatic sound effects. "*Boom! Skrish!* Torched 'em to a crisp!" Of course, Chewgar had been spared because he was already on his back by then. "I wouldn't've hurt ya, big guy! I mean, I didn't think I would."

The rhino hardly listened. Chewgar slumped against an incline of the cave wall a few feet away, brooding, working his jaw contemplatively, contributing nothing extra to the boy's story.

Pryth explained how he narrowed his command of fire to the three wounds on Chewgar's chest where the crossbow bolts had struck, and which Pryth had torn out in quick succession. Chewgar winced as he listened. Through no small amount of the rhinoceros's agony, the intense heat Pryth called cauterized the wounds. "And saved your damn life, pal!"

Chewgar's guard uniform was no better than a rag by now, the armor beneath it an irreparable wreck. All trace of white had been stained red with blood, not all of it his own, and the spots of black were due now more to burns than to the original dye. But he lived. He stared blankly into the fire, chewing on whatever foodstuff they still had in their packs, more tired than Maxan had ever seen him before.

Maxan wanted to say something, anything, to his somber friend.

But what can I say?

Say whatever will send him back home. Back to Crosswall. He doesn't need to be here.

Yeah. Sure. I'm sure he'd take the suggestion really well.

The city needs him. Leora needs him.

But he's a tribal species. No way he'd survive the road back through the Denlands without a guide. And even then…

Maxan picked at the fringes of the now-tattered cloak the Monitors had given him what felt like a year ago. He realized it had been less than a week. He tossed bits of thread into the fire absentmindedly, frustrated, thinking. Debating with himself, as always.

The fate of Crosswall without its king, his inner voice of reason pointed out, *is really rather important.*

He doesn't need me or anyone to remind him. All I need to tell him is … just … I'm glad he's here. With me. Glad he always has been.

Pryth finally finished his tale.

Chewgar's gaze was more lost in the flames than anyone else's. The dim firelight was reflected in his eyes. He was a different Chewgar now. Whatever bond the two of them had formed in their years as guardsmen—perhaps even before that, on the bridge spanning the creek, with Yovan—seemed to have diminished the moment they stepped beyond Crosswall's gate, faster than the light of their small fire in this cave faded now. Out here, Chewgar wasn't a guard, wasn't a tribal prince, or even a Leoran king. He had become a warrior, fighting and killing whoever threatened the lives of those he strived to protect.

Just like you, huh, Max?

Maxan swallowed the bitterness rising in his throat. He fed the dying flames more wood to keep himself busy, hoping the guilt would go away. But it didn't. The voice persisted.

Admit it. It's all right. You had no choice.

He snarled silently at the fire, tossing a long strip of his torn glove into it, seeing again the look on Yacub's face as he tumbled off the pillar and was swallowed by the rain and mist.

No. I had a choice.

It was either you or Pram.

It was either me or Pram.

And Rinnia was right about us.

I'm a killer.

Maxan held up his right paw, examining the furless, scarred pink flesh of his wrist and paw. Maybe he no longer shared a bond with Chewgar. Maybe now he shared one with Feyn.

I'm a monster now too.

It almost made him laugh.

He knew she could not read his mind—no one could, apparently—but he caught Pram staring at him. Maxan didn't have to be a mind reader himself to know exactly what her eyes were saying.

"It's not your fault, Pram," he said. "Without what you did, I'd be dead."

She looked away, her expression telling him she didn't completely believe him. She made something like a nod anyway, and lay down at her master's side. Her twin brother was already snoozing on the other.

"Stop it! I said no, Pram! Okay, see, now... *now* you're just making that up!"

Pryth's high-pitched tirade brought Maxan out of his deep, dreamless sleep. He opened his green eye (the gold one seemed glued shut with sleepiness) and rolled over for a better look.

"Huh, see what you did? You woke up the fox!" Pryth wagged a claw at Pram, said "Not another word outta you," then wheeled about to Maxan. "Mornin', fox!"

Feyn had not moved an inch. Only by his shallow breaths could Maxan tell the wolf was still alive. Pram knelt beside him. She flashed her twin a look so chilled it could freeze the creek outside.

"Not this time, sis! Nuh-uh! I will *not* be quiet! *He'll* tell ya," Pryth went on, gesticulating at Maxan, "how wrong you are. *Wrong*, I says! We're *not* leaving. *I'm* not! *You're* not. Right, Maxan? Maxan! Where ya think you're going, pal?"

Maxan had forced his eyes fully open and compelled his aching legs to carry him to the wall where Chewgar sat observing the two squirrels' one-sided (by all appearances) discussion. The fox gestured at the twins behind him and asked, failing to suppress a yawn, "What's going on with them?"

"Been arguing all morning. Well, sort of," Chewgar corrected himself with an exasperated huff. "Besides the obvious mind tricks and silence and all that, the boy's been talking to himself, you know. Didn't get loud until now. I couldn't hear what it's all—"

"Pram says Master Feyn says—says in his *mind*, she says, like he's *thinking* it, y'know—that we gotta go back!" Pryth almost shrieked, a sound that ricocheted sharply from the cavern walls and cut deep into Maxan's eardrums. "Oh, *we* as in *me* and…" Pryth frowned at his sister. "Her," he said, with exaggerated annoyance. He jittered his bushy tail agitatedly and cocked his head at the fox and the rhino, finally out of words and apparently ready for their opinions.

Maxan drew closer to the wolf and saw his eyelids were fluttering, trying to open. The scar that marred the wolf's face had all but melded into the weeping, burned tissue that now covered half of it. The pointed ear at the top of that side had burned to a crisp and was as brittle as a dried leaf. Feyn's breathing intensified as he tried to shift. The sound of it rushed through his clenched fangs and the hole at the corner of his maw, the one defining feature of Feyn's scar that had not changed.

Pram ran her claw tips gently through what fur remained on her master's forehead. She blinked sharply, then winced, as though someone had told her the unexpected, gruesome end of a tale. The girl shook her head somberly, then flashed another freezing look at her brother.

Pryth held his hands up in surrender, as though his sister had poked the tip of a dagger in his sternum, then he turned again to the fox. "Maxan, we should stay, right? She's making it up, right? Master Feyn wouldn't send us home? He *wouldn't*… would he?"

"Where's…" Maxan peered about the cavern.

Chewgar shook his head.

"So we're alone, then."

"We don't *need* the Monitors!" Pryth spat. "They'd just—"

"Pryth…"

The imperceptible flow of stale cavern air could have been said to be louder than the raspy breath escaping from Feyn's lips just then, but his quiet words nevertheless stopped the boy's latest tirade before it could gain power.

"Go … back…" Feyn's jaws snapped tight. The searing pain all over his body strangled what little remained of his capacity to speak, sending him into spasms of agony.

A week ago, Maxan knew absolutely nothing about the Aigaion. And even now, after witnessing a handful of callers manipulating its power to reshape the realm of possibility, he almost felt like he knew even less. But when Pram closed her eyes and rested her palm on her master's chest, Maxan knew from the serenity crossing the girl's face that she was focusing on something only she could feel. She was reaching for something beyond the layers of stone that surrounded them, some essential fabric of reality, and he knew that she found it when Feyn's sudden seizure eased before it could rattle him to pieces.

"Pryth," said a voice softer and sweeter than any the fox had ever heard.

Then it said "Brother," and Maxan could hardly believe it was hers.

"Locain is dead. Folgian is dead. Harmony is dead. Our master … will soon be dead. We can't prevent that." Pram's eyes swept from her brother to Maxan to Chewgar as she went on, not because she was seeking any kind of approval but because she was proclaiming exactly how things would be. "The Mind is leaderless without him. And the campus, the city, the kingdom, all of it will fall without the Pinnacle's guidance. We have to go back. We have to hold everything together. Because we are the only ones left who can."

Pryth bowed his head. "I guess," he said finally after a long silence.

"But what about the relay?" he added sharply an instant later, his somber tone reversing entirely. "We gotta see this through."

Pram's large eyes bore into Maxan's, then she turned to Chewgar. "Our friends will see it returned. Home. To the Aigaion. The Monitors will take it there, as Master Feyn said they would."

Chewgar rubbed his chin thoughtfully. "Except we seem to have run out of Monitors."

"They'll be back," Maxan said. "And if not. Well, we're the Monitors now." He gestured at the satchel near the wolf's side.

Pryth nodded solemnly, then turned back to his master. "If you can," the boy started but then choked on the rising tears.

"Don't let Feyn... ," Pram finished for her brother. "Don't let him go ... alone."

The white wolf coughed raggedly. His paw jolted up, contorted in pain. Maxan thought that Feyn would speak, that he would tear his way through his suffering to say something, but only a snarl escaped from his clenched jaw. He appeared to be unconscious, fighting something only he could see in a dream.

He's slipping. Losing control... going astray. We can't let them stay and see him like this.

So what if they do? It's not like—

Shut up.

Maxan no longer had to argue with his sarcastic other voice. He had always thought of it as a voice of reason, but sometimes his own thoughts were just as reasonable.

I didn't let go of Harmony.

The other side of his mind had nothing to counter with. Maxan had learned how to beat it back.

"We won't leave him," he said, answering Pram's unspoken question. "But you have to take whatever food we have left and go. Right now."

Pram nodded.

Pryth's brow knit in confusion. He said under his breath, "You call that *food*?" Then his eyes darted between the fox and his twin. "Wait, you mean like *right now* right now?"

"Before the hawk or the snake gets back and says no," the fox said. The squirrel still seemed confused. "Yes, *right now* right now."

"But what about the other one? The other fox."

Rinnia.

"What if she's out there?"

Maxan swallowed. "Then burn her," he said. "If it comes to that. She…"

She what?

"She made her choice," he finished.

Feyn's rigid claw eased back down, settling on his chest. His clamped fangs parted, and he shuddered with his next breath.

Maxan tried not to look, keeping his gaze stern and fixed on Pryth. "But there's no time to wait and see if the Monitors agree with this. You have to go." Maxan held out his paw to the rhino. "Give it up, Chewgar."

The rhino smacked his lips and snorted but handed over a bundle of the remaining bark-flavored ration the Monitors had given him days ago. Being little more than a snack to a massive rhinoceros, it would probably last a pair of diminutive squirrels for days, but Maxan didn't envy them having to endure its taste. He reached into his own pocket to contribute his own ration, and his paw knocked against something metal inside. He brought the relay out slowly, its glowing yellow beads running steadily in their chrome channels, casting shifting points of light onto the cavern walls.

He realized then he wouldn't need fire to light his way through what Saghan had called "the station under the spear," as long as he had this thing, this piece of the Aigaion, the golden-lighted artifact that could stop all the animals' minds from going astray.

The twin squirrels stuffed the pieces of so-called food into their own pockets as Maxan tucked the relay back into his, shrouding them again in the weakening firelight.

"When it's done," Pram said, smiling warmly at the fox and the rhinoceros.

"Come home," Pryth finished.

EPILOGUE

THE FADING TWILIGHT FELL UPON THE SNAKE'S slit orange eyes. His body lay inert, faceup in a field. If the snake had been able to see, he might think the tall grass swaying on the periphery of his vision was beautiful. If he had been able to feel, he might have enjoyed the soft touch of the grass against his scales, bunches of it cradling his back, his legs, his long neck.

But Saghan saw nothing, felt nothing. Thought nothing. The dead do not see, or feel, and Saghan had been dead for a while.

The dead have no mind.

His body, however, had been busy. The cells and tissues of his corpse responded to the change by executing their genetic programming perfectly. They did every time, followed every command transmitted by the Aigaion, returning the snake's soul—if he, if anyone, truly had one—back to its reptilian vessel via the signal.

The final bit of molecular matter recalibrated and reformed, sealing up the hole in his neck just above the collarbone, concealing all the internal damage that was healed also, and Saghan's body was perfect once again.

He didn't know how long he had lain there, faceup, orange eyes watching the night chase the day away, the wind stirring the leaves of the trees. He didn't know how long he had been back. He never did. But consciousness always crept in the same way. His newly reformed body told him to blink, and it was as though a door opened, allowing his mind to come back inside, away from the dark and the cold, away from the oblivion that awaited everyone after life.

His eyes blinked, finally, and his mind remembered, "Sky." His fingers twitched, and it told his soul, "Grass." It reminded him what air felt like when he drew in that first lungful of breath. He lay still for several more minutes, remembering all the sights and feelings of his life, reliving every memory of every cruelty and atrocity he had ever committed. His flesh twitched as loathsome scenes played out in his memory. Things this body had done, under the command of another's mind, without his soul's permission.

The visions brought the hate, rushing in like a tide. A heat swirling in his cold blood. If only he could forget it this time, just this one time—just forget himself—he could awaken and not remember all the terrible things Salastragore had made him do. All the fires, the poisons, the sensation of breaking bones between his fingers.

Saghan had once thought he hated him, Salastragore. His creator. His father. But hatred as a concept was simply no longer strong enough a description. Whatever feeling it was that had reanimated him in the past, breathing the life back in, if he could just find the right word to describe the heat of it, it would have been enough to burn the world.

But this time it felt different, somehow. The hatred was there, yes, but there was no heat to it. Instead, Saghan simply felt cold. Icy. He pondered what this meant, wondering if perhaps this time he had finally lost enough of himself on the other side of death, while he watched the last wisp of a cloud's indigo edge float away overhead, revealing a diamond-studded field of black and Yerda the crown jewel at its center.

"Saghan."

A voice. Familiar. Somewhere. Close. It broke his hold on the thought. It skittered away like the last cloud.

He knew whose voice it was. He lay in the wet grass and did not look away from the sky.

"Sissster."

"We need you."

Sarovek stood a few feet away, clutching her arm, broken and sagging at the shoulder. Her armor was gone; only a tattered and bloody shirt and stained leggings covered her. Her wings were ruins. They hung limp and lifeless behind her, many fragile white bones protruding from the brown feathers. It was a miracle they were still attached after all she had endured from the hyena. Yacub had not forgotten how she had bested him without the principal's aid. The hawk's voice was hoarse yet somehow had lost none of its gravity. "Are you going to lie there all night?"

He remembered her now. Part of the brotherhood. A Monitor. Like him. No, not like him. She had joined their order only recently. An emissary. Sent from Corvidia. His father's ally was her brother. Her true brother. Sent to keep an eye on his investment. A ship, which could sail through the sky. To another ship, which could sail through the dark beyond.

And then...

Saghan chuckled. He suddenly recalled his own place among all his father's schemes.

"Who am I?"

He almost expected to hear Sarovek's beak click in annoyance, as it usually did. But only a silence followed. She said at last, "You're my brother."

He fixated on Yerda's Wound, illuminated more brightly than he had ever seen before. Salastragore had once told him what force had split the asteroids that comprised her belt and carved that pit of deep shadow with the pinprick of fire at its center, which was the smoldering remnant of the planet's core. It was a bomb. Like the devices clipped to his belt. Yet infinitely more powerful.

And Salastragore had told him who had done it.

Then he understood. All the violence in his heart. All the atrocity he'd ever done. He was no different than the creature who killed the Earth.

Saghan whispered its name.

"Man."

End of Book I

The Animal in Man
continues in Book II:

Preview to
Ferocious Heart

FACEDOWN ON THE SMOOTH PEBBLES, MAXAN choked for breath. He coughed until his lungs and throat were raw, forcing spurts of putrid lake water out of his system.

Only moments before, as soon as his head sank below the surface, he had struggled against the current, fighting desperately against the flow to reach his ankle and pry off whatever had a hold on him. But the current was too strong, the thing was dragging him too fast, and he had no choice but to give up on that idea. For one agonizing minute more, Maxan focused solely on keeping his breath.

And then it was over.

Maxan's eyelids fluttered open. Before him, a curtain of white afternoon light shimmered on the water's surface, framed on all sides by total darkness.

Cave, he realized, his oxygen-deprived mind clinging to simple thoughts as it struggled to recover its awareness. *Rocks. Everywhere. Sharp. I can see the station, out there. Across the lake. Was there a rope on my leg?*

He moaned, the sound escaping from his waterlogged lungs in a rattle. The pebbles crunched under his body as he twisted around and felt at his ankle. Beyond the shore, it seemed there was nothing but deep shadows, which not even the light from the cave's mouth could pierce. Maxan didn't need to see to know that something was there. The thing that had brought him here.

A darker shadow shifted above him. It slipped silently across the ground, closer, but far enough into the light to form the slightest outline around it. Maxan recognized the shape of its oiled cloak immediately, from when it had repelled the downpour of rain in Crosswall, when he had first seen the octopus wearing it. Those reflective silvery eyes leveled on him now seemed impossibly familiar to him, though he had never seen them up close before.

Him.

His name. Say his name.

What're you—? I don't know his name!

One of the thicker tentacles that served as the octopus's lower legs slid a step forward. Another, an arm, writhed beneath the front of his cloak, pushed a side of it up over his shoulder, revealing the handles of two of his four elegant curved swords. The tentacle arm wrapped around the grip of one.

"The relay," the old octopus said simply, drawing the fine blade slowly with a pleasant scrape of metal that echoed within the confined cave.

You do know his name, Max! Say it!

Maxan's speech fumbled. Disoriented, his body still reacquainting itself with breathing, he managed to rise onto his knees. He held up a paw as the octopus brandished the full length of his weapon. "Wait, wait, wait," Maxan stammered, encouraged by the sight of the blade, thinner and sharper than a paper's edge.

"I-I-I know you…"

"The relay. Or your life."

"Wait! It's not about the relay anymore!"

"You have one chance." The tip of the tentacle holding the sword flicked a kind of switch on the weapon's handle. A small bead of light, similar to those on the relay, lit up green, and the cave was filled with a low, vibrating hum.

Think, Maxan! Remember!

I don't know who he is!

YOU don't. But I do.

Maxan looked away from the approaching length of shimmering steel and shook his head, trying to loosen the searing spear of pain splitting his thoughts in two. Half of his mind struggled to find the words to con the Peskoran into sparing his life, while the other tried to remember how he knew him.

"I know you," he said through gritted teeth. "From before. Twenty years..."

The third and final bead of light flashed on the sword's handle, red. The thrumming vibration peaked, and the blade almost appeared to be in several thousand places at once in the compact space above its handle.

"The war... the Monitors... *We* were Monitors..."

The octopus stopped, the blade just inches above Maxan's neck.

Suddenly, the pain dispersed. Maxan's mismatched eyes opened. He raised them to stare at his own reflection in the Peskoran's eyes.

"Zariel," he said. "Your name is Zariel."

The old octopus's silver eyes narrowed, then they looked beyond the fox's shoulder. A second tentacle arm emerged from beneath his cloak and gripped Maxan's shoulder hard. He pulled the fox up onto his feet and moved him around to his back. "Stand aside," he said, staring out over the water.

Maxan followed the Peskoran's line of sight and saw several dark things floating lazily in the water like pieces of driftwood, washing into the cave, inching their way toward the shore.

Odd how so much wood arrived all at once.
Odd how it all has eyes.
Oh.

Seven crocodiles rose in unison from the shallow water. They bent low at the waist, each holding a long, jagged spear level with their knees, readying for a fight.

Maxan's paw went to his side instinctively.

Before Maxan could recall how he'd lost it this time, before he could even finish thinking *Shit*, before the Drakoran crocodiles could land the first step of their frenzied charge, Zariel flicked his tentacle arm out in a swift, fluid motion, whipping the shimmering sword up and across in a half circle that cut through the air over the crocodile's heads.

The blade glowed like a rising sun on a distant horizon.

Zariel flipped the blade over and sank it almost fully into its empty scabbard at his side, leaving only an inch of it still drawn. The three lights on its hilt had winked out. The thrumming in the cave was gone.

The crocodiles had stopped. The movement seemed to have frozen them in the shallows, catching them in a state of panic. For a moment, Maxan wondered if the crocodiles who were there to kill him were thinking what he was thinking.

Ah… you missed.

A few of the crocodiles exchanged a nervous glance. One of them even chuckled. In some sort of voiceless battle cry, they sloshed their thick armored tails, churning the still water. The closest one took his first full step onto the pebbled shore.

Zariel slammed the handle home.

There was a stone-splitting crack loud enough to drown out all other sound, and the ceiling over the octopus's enemies became a boulder. It slammed on their heads, crushing them all with a force that could dent a mountainside. All light was snuffed out in an instant. The impact sent a shock wave of displaced air and energy that swept Maxan off his legs and flung him deep into the shadows of the cave.

BOOK DISCUSSION QUESTIONS

1. Is it mankind's destiny to destroy itself? Why or why not?

2. What will it take to ensure mankind's survival in the long run, for the next ten thousand or more years? (Not just solving current existential threats like Climate Change or ending the latest incarnation of The War.)

3. At what point does someone stop being 'human'?

4. Are technologies that enable mankind to alter its natural course—such as no longer dying from old age, being able to transmit our minds over vast distances of space, etc.—a good or a bad thing? Why or why not?

5. If you could roleplay any animal in the world of Herbridia, which species would you choose? What role would you play? What adventures would you hope to go on? What trouble would you stir up?

6. Thinking about your answers to number 5, would you be willing to do any of those things knowing that your actions could affect other animals' lives, whether for better or worse? Why or why not?

7. Do the characters we create in games or stories have true 'lives' and 'souls'? Should we feel guilty when we have them jump off literal cliffs because we are exploring and experimenting?

8. Is there such a thing as expendable life? If so, where is the line drawn between a life that can be spent for another's gain and a life that should not be touched?

9. What is it about violence that some members of mankind enjoy so much?

ACKNOWLEDGMENTS

FOREMOST AMONG ALL THOSE TO WHOM I OWE my thanks: my parents. Mom, you instilled in me a love of reading and an appreciation for the quiet moments of life. Dad, I don't think I could've made all this if you hadn't shown me what true dedication and hard work looked like.

Perhaps tied for the top spot is my wife. Without your belief in me, your assurance that it was okay for me to disappear for an hour or two, I never would have gotten any of this done. Even now as I type this, you're at home wrangling the little punks. Thank you for that. Forever.

And where did I go all those nights to rid myself of distraction and write? Thanks are owed to my local library, especially to its staff. No, my feet weren't on the furniture, and yes, this lid was on the coffee the whole time.

To all of my students—and to those from Gage Park especially—thank you. Little do you know I tricked you into teaching me more than I ever taught you. Who cares about conjunctions and compound-complex sentences when there's so much to learn about life? (Heads or tails? Call it.)

To my old friends Ben, Dale, Wes, and Randy: if it wasn't for all the goddamned D&D we played in high school, I'd never have learned how to dream up worlds worthy of being lost in.

Of course, I've had many teachers throughout the years that saw in me some creative spark and helped me kindle it into flame. I speak of course of Bill Myers, Harry Adrian, Rob Prescott, Thomas Palakeel, Seth Katz, Tof Eklund, Michael Tabb, and a few others. (You know who you are!)

Thank you, Rick Heinz, the friend here who certainly deserves the most thanks of all. Without you, Rick, I'd have lost my mind. Thanks for forging this path for me, for your encouragement, your patience when I'd call you in a panic. Thanks for "talking me off the ledge."

To all the members of the Authors' Guild, vets and the newcomers alike, thank you! Chief among them are Craig A. Munro and Matthew Isaac Sobin. We started this journey as rivals and wound up as friends. I love your stories, guys.

This book has gone astray and wandered to new places over the years, but I think it's found its forever-home with 4 Horsemen. Big thanks to Beau, Laura, Jen, Erika, and Val for taking this beast of a story in and giving it the love and treatment it deserves.

One more... Thanks to you, my dear readers, my dear animals. You alone are the master of your own destiny. You, and no other, choose what you are and what you will be. I hope you will be human, whatever that means.

ABOUT THE AUTHOR

JOSEPH ASPHAHANI IS AN AVID VIDEO GAMER, effective high school teacher, and enthusiastic candidate for whatever sort of cybernetic limb enhancement your megacorp is planning for the inexorable dystopian future. When he's not getting hopelessly lost in simulated worlds, he's often dreaming up worlds of his own. The world of The Animal in Man is his first and favorite, and *Violent Mind* is his first novel. He resides in Chicago with his wife and two children.

More books from
4 Horsemen Publications

Fantasy

D. Lambert
To Walk into the Sands
Rydan
Celebrant
Northlander
Esparan
King
Traitor
His Last Name

Danielle Orsino
Locked Out of Heaven
Thine Eyes of Mercy
From the Ashes
Kingdom Come
Fire, Ice, Acid, & Heart
A Fae is Done

J.M. Paquette
Klauden's Ring
Solyn's Body
The Inbetween
Hannah's Heart

Lou Kemp
The Violins Played
Before Junstan
Music Shall Untune the Sky

R.J. Young
Challenges of Tawa

Sydney Wilder
Daughter of Serpents

Valerie Willis
Cedric: The Demonic Knight
Romasanta: Father of Werewolves
The Oracle: Keeper of the
Gaea's Gate
Artemis: Eye of Gaea
King Incubus: A New Reign

Kyle Sorrell
Munderworld
Potarium

SciFi

**Brandon Hill &
Terence Pegasus**
Between the Devil and the Dark
Wrath & Redemption

C.K. Westbrook
The Shooting
The Collision
The Judgment